SUBSEQUENT THOUGHTS

A NOVEL BY
CHARLIE BURNETTE

This novel is a work of fiction. Any references to real events, businesses, organizations, or any locations are intended to give the fiction a sense of reality and authenticity. All names, characters, places and incidents either are the product of the author's imagination or are used fictitiously. Any resemblance to actual persons, living or dead, is entirely coincidental. In regards to Broad Hands Group, the scene is completely fictional and satirical. No such company exists. No adjuster, agent, policy, or procedures are true. No claim happened.

ISBN: 978-0-9839331-3-7

Library of Congress Control Number: 2015912783

Printed in the United States by Morris Publishing®
3212 East Highway 30
Kearney, NE 68847
1-800-650-7888

To my sister, Mary Ann,

whose insight and support brought light to this story.

My deepest gratitude to these folks who contributed to this work:

Maureen Angell, Lynn Barnes, Mary Ann Brookshire, Aylie Burnette, Bax Burnette, Hagan Burnette, Marcia Burnette, Taylor Burnette, Caroline Grace Christenbury, Lillian Cunningham, Andy Fanning, Craig Faris, Beth Gault, Brian Hamel, Gwen Hunter, Harry Johnson, Jimmy Jones, George Ligon, T. F. McDow, Jennifer Marquis, Connie Payne, Miller Pitts, Terry Plumb, Scott Punton, Terry Roueche, S.C.W.W. Rock Hill Chapter, Julie Spell, Nancy Templeton, Earl Wilcox, Jenny Lynn Williams.

Chapter One

Monday, June 10, 2013
6:45 p.m.

Abel Wood pulled out his collection of kitchen powders and liquids stashed under his mattress and slowly stirred the contents. The concoction rendered a mild poison, yet produced a pleasant, flowery smell in the empty ice cream cup he'd dug out of the trash. He added some medicine he'd found in the back of an upper cabinet in the kitchen.

Abel hated the last feeding of the day. "Suppertime," the leaders shouted like a command. He longed for the forest, never a meal scheduled, never a meal missed. His forest was no dream; he only wished his trees and animals back. His mother's soft, stable voice in his head comforted him, her approval of his plan.

He eased his lean, muscular frame into his assigned seat by Jacob, and the lengthy prayer began. Abel quickly panned the tightly closed-eyed faces around the table and poured the contents of the ice cream cup into Jacob's bowl of soup. With bedtime three hours away, Abel figured by morning his plan to poison Jacob would succeed. He stirred his own soup as carrots, green beans, and celery floated around the plastic bowl like a kaleidoscope. A wilted piece of celery resembled a sinister smile, and he thought of the new cancer of his mind...Paul Riordan.

***

The new day brought a warm summer morning. A field trip scheduled for the petting zoo in downtown Chafenville stood in limbo, and Abel relished the chaos. The teenaged residents, of which he was one, reacted consistently with the mentally challenged labels that figuratively hung around their necks, like signs. They clamored as ants around a sealed peanut butter sandwich, chomping to board the bus. But Jacob's nausea and screams of stomach pain interrupted the positive vibrations of a great day.

Abel watched as Joe Inman, Paul Riordan's supervisor, stepped forward. "Stay here with Jacob, and see if this gut thing passes, maybe a cramp from the breakfast we just chugged down. These kids are too excited. If we call it off, hell's going to break loose. Let me head to the zoo with the rest."

Paul violently shook his head. "Can't do it...you know the rule, two leaders."

Abel smiled as the other kids, mostly younger than he, broke out into uncontrollable chants, jumping up and down at the thought of missing the promised adventure. None cared for Jacob; all cared for the blue sky, the promised adventure, and most importantly, lunch at McDonald's. Freedom.

Joe extended his arms and smiled. "Not a big deal. The zoo's not eight miles from here ...it'll be cool."

Paul rolled his eyes at Joe's decades-old way of saying things. "I don't care if it's cool. It's a rule, and we've got no discretion." Paul cut his eyes sharply toward Abel.

Abel didn't blink and turned his attention to a more manageable target, a likeable teddy bear sort of guy. "Mr. Joe, you promised us this trip. Remember, watching the owls' heads turn all the way around, then we get to hug the llama, the one with the big smile, then Happy Meals, bringing back the toys, racing them on the concrete pad out back? You mean we *can't* go?"

An outcry of injustice emerged from the mouths of the denied like a half-empty formula bottle pulled from an infant's sucking lips.

Abel admired his handiwork of acting like someone who really belonged there and waited for the next wrinkle. When the chaotic chanting finally died down, Joe exercised his seniority. Joe always meant to please. "Rules, rules. These kids need some time away from this place. We'll figure it out."

Paul, Jacob turning green in his arms, yelled. "Figure *it* out? You really mean breaking rules established by the board who hired us."

"We're out of here. Paul, you're a lawyer, think up some exception to the rule."

Joe hurried the others out the door. Abel shuffled his feet forward like an obedient sheep, smiling as Paul's unheeded orders were stomped upon, and the defiant paraded out the front door toward the bus. He glanced back at Paul and noticed a blank, cold stare beaming in his direction. Paul's eyes dissected him, the penetration cutting to his soul, bringing Abel to this moment. He shook off the distraction and looked inward toward his mother. *Work to be done.*

He boarded the bus, and they were gone. Once again, Abel turned his green eyes back to Riordan, looking helpless with Jacob almost lifeless in his arms. He comforted himself. *Jacob should be alright.*

But a nagging urge to kill consumed his mind. He wasn't sure why. He reached for his mother's guidance, but she'd left him for the moment. Looking around at the excited residents of House of Hope, he pondered whether his garbled bunch of idiot housemates would understand. Then he considered Joe Inman, an innocent life, considerate of justice.   Yet he had an unexplained need to hurt Joe.

***

At 11:00 a.m., the phone rang at House of Hope.   The voice sounded arrogant, controlling, without restraint. "Sergeant Moore, Chafenville Police Department.   Listen up and listen good. We've got a major problem with *your* bus."

Paul took a deep breath, exhaled, and grabbed his knees. "Where's Joe Inman?"

"Dead."

"What?"

"Yeah, we pulled the license from his wallet. His throat was slit, and your so-called patients, or whatever the hell you call them, are now at large. Witnesses report they're running around like lunatics, with blood splattered all over their clothes. I'm calling you, Sir, to get some direction. *Are* they lunatics? *Will* they kill again? Should we take them down…and maybe save our innocent citizens from this stupidity?"

Paul became numb, silent, and meditative. The vision of Chafenville Police gunning down those he'd counseled pierced his heart.

"Sir, are you still on the line? Maybe you've got an idea?"

Finally Paul answered. "You don't have a clue of the gravity of this problem. I suggest you find the one named Abel. Forget about the others; they're harmless, absolutely harmless. Hurt a single one of them, and I'll sue your ass off."

Paul hung up the phone, gathered Jacob, put him in a dilapidated car donated to House of Hope by a supporter looking for a nice tax deduction and sped to the emergency room at Chafenville General Hospital. His own BMW 700 series sat four blocks away being detailed by a "hands only" car wash.

He carried Jacob to the door and placed him in the arms of some white-uniformed lady he hoped to be a nurse. "You need to treat this child. Don't release him under any circumstances. He's not violent, but he's got to stay here with you. I've got my own emergency, bigger than anything you'll see here today."

The lady in charge stepped quickly toward Paul, raising her voice. He ignored her, pivoted and ran back to the car, her words not factoring into his thought process.

"Sir, we can't. We don't know who this child is or what the circumstances are. Sir, you gotta stay here."

He jumped into the car and cranked it again. The vehicle shook as if begging for a tune-up, and he headed for the home of Les Randall, the chairman of Chafenville Board for Mental Disabilities, in Paul's own neighborhood, the best one in town. He drove the car into the driveway, slammed it into Park, and exited the vehicle, barely remembering to turn off the ignition. He ran to the back door of the chairman's home and knocked frantically.

"Whoa, whoa...what's going on here, Paul?"

"Murder."

"What murder?"

Paul followed Les' slow stride into the living room at the front of the house. Les took a seat, and Paul paced back and forth.

"Ok, Paul, calm down and explain yourself."

"Joe Inman, you know him?"

"You know I do, great guy, doing a jam-up job at House of Hope."

"Well, Mr. Chairman, his throat got slit open in the home's bus."

"What? Joe? When did this happen?"

"Less than an hour ago."

"How *could* it happen?"

"Abel Wood. Remember, the kid we accepted into our program last month?"

"Right."

"Has Joe's family been contacted?"

"Forget about Joe...he's dead...let's worry about Abel."

"How do you know it's Abel? Were you there?"

Paul sensed the professional approach Les was taking. He needed to catch his breath and focus.

"No, I wasn't there, but you're going to have to trust me on this. Abel caused this stinking mess." Paul stepped toward the large window facing the street and suddenly stopped, tripping over his own feet, his face pressing against the glass, spotting a tan Dodge Caravan, soccer ball magnet on the side. This car, Helen's car, the family carpool vehicle, idled in front of him like a nervous animal. Paul, the last time he focused on his own home situation, made a mental note to wash the car. It still screamed for attention. The driver rolled down the window. He could see Abel's grin, a smirk, defiant of authority, a "stick this up your ass" look. And as he drove off, moving shadows appeared in the seats behind. The reflections could be others or simply sunlight shining though the swaying branches of the neighborhood trees.

Somehow Abel predicted Paul's visit to the Chairman's house. Questions jumped around in his head. *How? Why? Control?* He thought again of his wife's van, his home, his private driveway, not two blocks away. He pushed his fingers through his thinning, black hair and made a fast decision.

"Les, call the cops, Abel's got my van. I've got to get home, check on my family." Without waiting for a reply from the Chairman, he sprinted out the front door, cutting through neighbors' yards more quickly than driving the wretched heap of junk that brought him there. Thoughts of his wife and two children...and Abel...powered his legs. Manicured lawns, the smell of rosemary plants in organic gardens, sounds of equipment of hired landscapers disturbing wildlife feasting on what fifty-year-old oak trees offered, and neatly trimmed concrete curbs rounding into brick-laid driveways passed through his senses as he sprinted stride after stride to his own home.

Thoughts flashed in his mind: Jason, his youngest child, ill that morning. Helen's habit of leaving the keys in the car's ignition so she'd know where to find them. Abel, sick, disturbed Abel.

After crossing the creek behind the house, he blasted into his back door and screamed at the top of his lungs, "Helen!" She calmly answered, and he took the steps to the second level by threes.

Helen popped up in bed, Jason in her arms. "What in the world's wrong?"

"Didn't you hear the car crank...leave?" He gasped for air.

"Well, no, I've been up here with Jason watching television. Why, is the car gone?"

Paul reflected through the panic taking over his mind. Jason, his youngest child, a kindergarten student at their church, lay safely in his mother's arms. His oldest, Parker, a second grader at Cumberland Elementary, had once been a topic of discussion. A harmless discussion with Abel Wood, a conversation his brief training suggested might create a bond, a concept necessary to help the patient. *Not a patient, a resident*, he reminded himself.

He recalled a direct question from Abel. "So, why does Parker like his teacher?"

A sharp fear jabbed through his gut. "Lock the doors and call the police." He hurriedly retraced his steps out the back door and toward the Board Chairman's house to retrieve the donated car.

Speeding at sixty miles per hour, he traveled to Cumberland Elementary, trying to dismiss his fear as paranoia, a trick he used to settle his mind in ballistic litigation.

Then he questioned himself simply for not calling the school, asking about Parker. Yet he had to take control, the lead. He pulled up to the front door, squealing his worn tires as he came to an abrupt stop.

He slipped on a wet floor and nearly took out the janitor mopping the hall outside the principal's office. Gathering his six-foot body out of the sloppy mess, he confronted the receptionist inside the door. "Where's Parker Riordan?"

The secretary said matter-of-factly, "Well, sir, I'm told he just left."

Taking a deep breath he asked his next question. "And the source of your information?"

The secretary looked at the ceiling. "Say that again."

Patience evaporated. "Who, for God's sake, told you?"

Her business tone went away, she seemed neutral. "His teacher, a while ago…I think he must have just left."

He shouted angrily, "What do you mean just left? The teacher? My son? Who just left?"

"Uh, uh, your son...at least I'm told...aren't we okay here?"

Paul abruptly leaned on the edge of the desk, opened his dark brown eyes as wide as they went. "No ma'am, not okay. Parker's second grade. Are you telling me you let him leave? And with whooom?"

The secretary hesitated, looked down at some papers, then the computer, and then raised her eyes toward Paul. "Sir, you e-mailed us yesterday, said Parker's uncle planned to visit. It's field day, we've got a hundred family members who drop by, watch the field games and take kids home...school ends early. Everybody's on the activities field. Parker's teacher told us through her pager that Parker saw his mother's van, and the family dog, and took off running toward his family. How do you stop that?"

Fear remained in her eyes. "I explained your e-mail to Parker's teacher, want to see it?" Paul snatched the monitor around. His own hands trembled as he began to read.

Abel Wood, Parker's uncle, has my permission to
participate in field day tomorrow and take Parker home.
Thank you for your understanding.
Sincerely,   Paul Riordan

Paul lifted his blazing eyes from the screen and whirled around, facing the secretary again. "This e-mail is *not* mine. You mean to tell me that anybody who walks into this school, after sending you an e-mail, can walk out with any child he pleases?"

"No, sir, they can't. Here's your wife's handwritten note to us, received by regular mail two days ago, saying the same thing. That's the rule, or so I'm told, and we followed it. And he showed me some I.D., had Abel Wood typed right on it." The secretary stood, still visibly shaken. "I'm just a substitute."

***

The principal threw open the door of his private office and looked at Paul. "May I help you, sir? I'm covered up here with teacher evaluations and your loud voice interrupted me. Is there a problem?"

Paul looked at the secretary, and she started to explain herself. "Mr. Blank, this e-mail and handwritten note said Parker's parents wanted his uncle to visit. The uncle arrived, came into this office, and introduced himself...a very polite young gentleman. He said he'd park by the activities field...where all the family visitors are. When Parker's teacher paged us, told me about the Riordans' car, the Riordans' dog, that Parker ran over to greet them, I said all is fine. But the teacher paged me back after a few minutes and said Parker did not return. Sir, you said for me not to bother you. Did I mess up?"

Principal Blank put his hands on his hips. "Jesus Christ! Sir..."

Paul interrupted. "I've got no time to argue, call the police. Tell them your incompetent story and find my son." He bolted his 180-pound frame back out the door. His dark hair, flowing at the back, thinning in the front, blew in the breeze as he sprinted. Hurriedly, he jerked the car door open, fell into the seat, and thought deeply of Parker and the dog Parker loved.

Shaking with both anger and fear, Paul repeatedly struck his head on the cracked vinyl padded steering wheel.

***

House of Hope inherited a big building in what was once a nice residential area. Constructed in the 1970s, the home looked large by neighborhood standards, a neighborhood now declining in property value. A benevolent gift to the cause, a $200,000 tax deduction. But the oversized brick ranch, split into three levels, was chopped up into a fortress of tiny prisons. The home's motto, proudly blazed across the nonprofit organization's brochure, read: Redeeming Our Youth From Crime. The concept of the home, reduced to the second sentence on the front page of its brochure, claimed "Admitting troubled teenage boys, under the age of eighteen, who are diagnosed with mental challenges and deemed intellectually disadvantaged to appreciate the nature of their wrong."

The typical profile for a resident consisted of a male youth with an IQ below 75, expelled from school for exhibiting behavior contrary to social norms. Usually unsupervised at home, they turned to shoplifting and vandalism. Often loners, without the social skills to develop friendships, they were left to an untaught sense of survival. Referred by the juvenile justice system, most of the perpetrators simply did not understand that taking property attractively set up on retail shelves, beckoning to be picked up, required a payment in trade.

House of Hope, a beacon of rehabilitation for Chafenville, offered therapeutic, individualized educational plans based on the resident's ability to learn. The now antiquated glossy tri-fold, handed to wealthy couples feasting on chilled half-shelled oysters, caviar covering small quail eggs, and enough top-shelf alcohol to bring a wallet to a sense of dignity, boldly proclaimed: "You, our valued and much loved benefactor, grant a **precious** second chance to give new hope for our residents to live productive and law-abiding lives."

Most attendants, dressed in formal attire, strolled around silent auction tables like sharks, protecting their bids on an item threatened to being jerked out from under them by a $50 raise from a competitor…usually a close neighbor. Every wife wanted a trophy to take home, and local artwork took on a new meaning with a glance, then a second glance, fueled by chardonnay. Women ruled the silent auction, which was anything but silent. *Social swordsmanship*, Paul often thought.

The men, on the other hand, clamored around the live auctioneer to pay thousands for fishing trips. And when the silent auction closed, the wives, unhappy with the results, pushed their husbands forward, raising their hands at the auctioneer, for an elegant dinner at a notable's home, for a more than elegant price.

Truly, alcohol, a good cause, and fat wallets made the budget for the House of Hope. Paul Riordan attended many, consumed much, and donated generously. But his involvement had shifted, now merely a mid-level employee.

At age seventeen, Abel met the technical definition for admission, found deeper in the "please donate" handbook. He stood charged, but not convicted, with two brutal murders occurring in the same time frame. The State's case contained few witnesses, all questionable. The prosecutor lacked meaningful direct evidence, and the file malingered in the dungeons of unlikeable cases. Whatever zeal remained for the case weakened when Abel's appointed-for-free attorney raised the issue of a mentally incompetent teenager, a defense he strongly intended to pursue.

The only documentation preceding the murders was reported by a psychiatrist who'd conducted a battery of psychological assessments, physical examinations, and brain-imaging. He concluded that Abel must have suffered a rare and traumatic head injury as a child, and this most likely caused severe brain damage. The doctor recorded an extensive commentary, the kind usually rendered only when the patient had money and insurance. *My patient shows signs of selected mutism, going days without speaking. Then his mind gets into a state never documented before in current psychological literature.*

At times the report sounded like a ground-breaking case study, a psychological event exploding far beyond the importance of the patient, new knowledge of a global significance. The doctor documented: *I sometimes think Abel vacillates between brilliance and a severe mental disability. One moment he readily grasps complex issues and the next doesn't understand or appreciate the nature of his behavior.*

The prosecutor, frustrated, sat at his desk, piled with stacks of papers relating to other cases needing desperate attention, and read through the in-depth psychological notes. The patient apparently, without any warning or reason, happened to stumble into a brilliant mind-set of clarity and truth. And just as quickly, stumbled out of the same brilliance into severe retardation. He slapped himself across the head, pondering the strange diagnosis, giving compelling excuses to question the strength of the case of *The State of Georgia versus Abel Wood.*

***

The irony of the diagnosis: the psychiatrist was one of Abel's murder victims, a fact Abel figured overlooked by the overworked Georgia prosecutor assigned to the case.

But as the seeds planted by Abel grew, the doctor proclaimed absolute brilliance. "This child suffers from SSS. SSS became the doctor's new wonder to the world, a selected form of the Savant Syndrome or, perhaps, a new way to categorize Abel's condition where medical science had failed before.

The murders took place one day before his seventeenth birthday, or so authorities thought. A birth date claimed by Abel could not be contradicted by a Social Security card or other form of identification. None existed. The authorities had no history on their strange, mysterious suspect. His only recorded crime was a bizarre, isolated incident in the Chafenville library, a charge which, for lack of clarity, sounded like disorderly conduct. The least of misdemeanors around this struggling town, not something the authorities even cared about.

But dead people tend to catch more attention, and murder charges prompted Abel to bring forth the very defense that came from the psychiatrist's own lips: *a criminal who can't appreciate the nature of his wrong can't be convicted.* He remembered the doctor calling this concept the M'Naghten rule.

Abel had to bring the matter up to his free defense counsel and laughed to himself when his lawyer acted like the defense had never crossed his mind. "So, my client, you know the M'Naghten rule? I guess I'll run that one up the flag pole…might fly." The lawyer never seemed to notice that the severe mentally challenged client he represented just offered a technical, constitutional argument for acquittal.

The attorney appointed to defend Abel suddenly advocated mental disabilities prevented the accused from offering any meaningful assistance in his own defense. He argued the State's circumstantial evidence lent itself to a plea bargain that did not involve traditional incarceration.

The prosecutor countered. "The defendant may very well be disturbed, simply another criminal with an antisocial personality disorder. But even the disturbed have no right to ignore the law."

Many months of wrangling between the prosecution and Abel's attorney, who often quoted the psychiatrist's report, produced a compromise: Abel would become a resident at House of Hope, not to be released until fully documented by professionals to be no longer a threat of danger to society. Abel relished his luck in manipulating his own attorney. The lack of evidence in the murders he committed was no accident. Covering his involvement gave him nearly as much joy as the killings or at least one of them. *An early birthday present.*

In the year 2013, seventeen-year-old Abel began his new life as a resident in the House of Hope, breaking the mold of its purpose. More importantly, after months of virtual silence, a voice in Abel's head talked him into a different direction. Beth. She encouraged him to be a vocal person, a socially engaged person. But tight places and piercing eyes threatened him. The voices of two women meshed within the fabric of his life. He trusted them both, probably too much, and pleasing them both sometimes felt like a juggling act. But clearly, though they never seemed to talk to one another, neither liked Paul Riordan.

***

Paul Riordan squirmed in the driver's seat in front of Parker's school, re-thinking the last hour, re-thinking his recent life choices.   Success dominated his life as a lawyer, fifteen years in a high-stress litigation practice.   Making considerable sums of money over those years, he began to question the quality of his life and of his morals.

My money comes from being smart, not being right.
People lie in graves, allegedly at the hands of my clients,
clients I can't vouch for…but a jury did.
How do I give back, repay my own achievements?

His fortune made, priorities changed, and he abruptly announced to his wife one evening his retirement from the practice of law. "I want a line of work befitting of humanity."

Helen, now the mother of two young children, didn't disagree with Paul's decision, which took place after ten years of marriage. He'd made plenty. Particularly the tire case. A career change he could afford, well earned.

He breezed through Chafenville Tech, a community college, and its abbreviated curriculum in psychology, sociology, and treatment of the mentally ill. All As under what Paul felt to be an overqualified teacher, now deceased, who rendered him well prepared for his first job: House of Hope. The idea was for Paul to learn the duties and responsibilities of every position within the home while serving under the direction of the lead supervisor, Joe Inman. Joe's senseless death beat Paul to the core.

He thought back to the beginning, entering House of Hope with an excellent attitude, one of compassion, a desire to help those entrusted to his care. But he looked at the tri-level house as a maze, a series of cages. Three staircases, thirteen rooms, and a dozen closets proved too much for two, and at times one, to control. The layout concerned him. And not a month after Paul's first assignment, Abel Wood arrived.

Eyes distant, then attractive, immediately drew everyone to the newest resident of Hope. Paul's deep instincts and shallow psychological training left him with a formulated evaluation of Abel that did not match his psychological profile, but he kept it to himself. His gut reaction burned like a raging fire, but what could he know for sure in the infancy of his new career?

To Paul, Abel had the physical strength of a mature man and the heart of the Devil. When he slept, he appeared as an innocent teen, harmless. But awake, his green eyes moved in a calculating way that gave Paul chills. He observed Abel asking questions calmly and softly. But the questions effectively stripped the listener down to the core of truth and removed all defense mechanisms. A skill any trial lawyer begged to possess.

For several weeks, he watched with amazement as Abel developed a gradual control over everyone in the home, both residents and staff.

"How do you like the salmon patties, Mr. Inman?"

"Oh, they're not bad, Abel."

"Does Mrs. Inman fix them for you much?"

"Not really...I sorta like beef myself...but mind ya, this patty's not bad...we're lucky to have it here."

"So, what cut of beef do you like?"

"Probably ribeyes."

"How much does that cost?"

Joe laughed, "Too much...ten bucks a pound, on sale."

"How often do the Inmans eat ribeye?"

"Why are ya askin' all those questions?"

"I'll stop if it bothers you."

"No, no, every Saturday for sure and usually Tuesday when the money's there."

By the time the salmon patties had been consumed, Abel had extracted enough information to size up the Inman's household financially and socially.

This guy's going to be a problem. He's playing the home like a puppet. Paul considered going to the director, demanding Abel's files, questioning the decision to place him in their facility. He would when he got time. *But for now,* I've got to be careful. If I'm wrong, and I step on my superior's toes, I'll be back in the rat race of practicing law. That's not why I came here...help, not hurt. Paul's ingrained thought processes fought against his new approach to life, so he watched Abel with intensity.

Abel, when missing, usually could be found in the back yard, feeding squirrels, mice, or stray dogs. He seemed peaceful, communal-like, almost in solidarity with the animals. Within the halls of the home, manipulation controlled his time. Although the circus bothered Paul's sense of fairness with the residents, Abel's sleight of hand had the staff unknowingly doing a balancing act. Abel's orchestrated confusion caused unneeded focus on the others, leaving insufficient manpower to properly monitor Abel.

Feeling overwhelmed with obligation for the home, Paul mentioned his concerns to Joe.

"Paul, my man, you've got to lighten up. Whenever I see the boy, he's usually in the back yard, feeding rats, squirrels, and strays. Not a care in the world, hardly a threat."

"Joe, I don't think you understand the level of control Abel has over the others. I've watched him closely...and think he could be a threat."

"Tell you what. If you are that hot around the collar, I'll double his dose of Trazodone. At least we can be sure he will be out like a light for at least ten hours every night.

"What? I seriously doubt that's even legal. You can't decide who gets what prescribed meds, hoping to control a condition you don't even understand."

"Trazodone's magic. Seems to calm down even those we can't figure out."

"Too simplistic, Joe. Everyone has a different chemistry."

"We've been doing it for years. Some kids get new scripts for it every month and don't really need it, so there's always plenty to go around."

Sorry he even said anything, Paul tucked that unwanted information in the back of his mind to deal with at a later time.

***

Paul remembered his first really private conversation with Abel. Alone in the large living area on the second level, Paul gently confronted him. "Are you happy with your life?"

Abel leaned back into his chair, rubbed his hands over his light-brown hair, and shifted his eyes in many directions, never looking straight at Paul. "How do you mean, Mr. Riordan?"

"What is it you want in life?"

"The same as you."

"I'm confused, I'm an old guy. Why would you want what an old-fart wants? You're young and, if we turn you around here, you've got a promising life before you."

"You inspire me, Mr. Riordan. Tell me about your family, show me what lies ahead if I could do as good as you."

Paul felt guilty, ashamed to have misjudged Abel. He shared his career, his family, all to a set of eyes so sincere he'd trust his life, although Abel's eyes roamed the room.

"How important is your life to you, Mr. Riordan?"

Paul thought the question strange, but answered it anyway. "My life means nothing compared to my family. If I died next week, not a problem as long as my wife and kids are content, happy."

After a good cleansing of his soul, Paul asked the question again. "Abel, what is it you want in life?" Abel's answer came quick, abruptly, nearly rude.

"My way."

Paul paused, reflected, wondered why a productive conversation suddenly deteriorated. "And what way is that?"

"It is the opposite of your way."

"Well, how do you know my way would not be better?"

"It is not about what's better or more fun, it's about who controls."

"Controls what?"

Abel looked as if he wouldn't answer the question, as if his questioner was getting too close. Paul regrouped his thoughts, but stumbled over his words to the point he sounded deceptive, even to himself. "So, something in your life makes you do things, think things. Like what?"

"Like helps me make decisions."

"Like your counselors? Like me?"

Abel howled at the ceiling. "No. Certainly not like you."

"Okay, Abel, okay, so where *are* these people who make decisions for you?"

"In my head."

"They help you?"

"More than that."

Paul looked deeply, with the dark brown eyes people around the courthouse claimed could back down a shark in bloody water. But he tried to show some sincere concern. "Abel, who's in charge of your head and your thoughts? Is it you or is it this thing you speak of?"

"Depends on the day."

"What does it usually want?"

"Why do you like the word *it*? If you insist on calling her "it," *it* wants you to leave her alone. You make *it* very uncomfortable."

"Why do I make, whomever we're talking about, uncomfortable?"

Abel stood, his five-and-a-half-foot frame barely cast a shadow over Paul. "I watch you watching me, Mr. Riordan. Why do you have to watch me?"

"I watch all our residents."

"No, you don't. Over the past three days you've worked, you watched me seventy-eight percent of the time and everybody else twenty-two percent of the time."

"Abel, that sounds a bit far-fetched...but even if it were true, how could you have monitored my actions so carefully?"

"*It*, as you like to call them, knows."

Paul wrestled with the plurality of the controlling voices, but had no opportunity to reflect on basic behavioral science, because Abel started again.

"Since I met you, you've done nothing but stir things up for all three of us. When you watch it, it watches you."

"Abel, it's you, not it."

"What's that supposed to mean?"

Paul took a deep breath, realized this situation required careful reflection on what he'd learned at the tech school. He was the so-called professional and shouldn't argue with the patient. He recalled his professor, John Winthrop, a man with significant educational qualities, talk about how a counselor's job was to offer support and guidance, not controversy. Abel very well could be showing signs of schizophrenia or even multiple personalities.

"Abel, do these people talk to you, do they tell you to do things and say things you may not want to say and do?"

"My, my, Mr. Riordan, did they teach you about schizophrenia at the community college?"

The question disturbed Paul. He thought through his detailed confessional of family and law career to Abel during the preceding minutes, but never mentioned the recent education. How could Abel have known? Why would he throw out such a question? What was the objective? Paul's legal analysis kicked in as he contemplated an answer. The adversarial nature of Paul's training took over without considering its impact on anyone but the absent jury.

"Abel, not only are you smart, but I think you're dangerous. I'm not so sure I've been educated enough by a community college to even make a diagnosis. Maybe you can fill me in."

Abel leaned forward, way forward. Paul felt vulnerable as the resident answered his question. "If schizo is too heavy, just go with oppositional defiance...nice big words you people use when you can't figure out who we are. Most of the counselors I meet haven't learned r-e-a-l good and don't try r-e-a-l hard. So, stick with oppositional defiance. Most of your professors at the...what's it called...oh, community college, will think A+."

Paul, mystified at the conversation, hesitated to speak. Abel seemed pleased. "Mr. Riordan, from some of the reports, I can't even finish second grade. But guess what, my *it* can think, and be rest assured *it* is a she…"

Paul interrupted. "What it?"

"The ones in my head, the ones you seem to hate, the ones who can't stand you and are pissed off at me for having…what did you say…a chance to exchange ideas?"

Paul, about to explode, grabbed the arms of the worn chair, and rose from his seat, towering over Abel by half a foot. "Are you back to talking about the demons you claim bounce around your head?"

Abel's voice became calmer, quizzical. "What just made your face turn red, like a beet? The demon? Think you're making friends?"

"So, who am I talking to, it or you?"

"Let's take our seats, and I'll tell you."

Abel burst out laughing, like it was all a joke, like the personhood in his head took a break, and Abel spoke for himself. "Mr. Riordan, Mr. Riordan you are killing me; I can't take it anymore. I'm just yanking your chain. Nobody's in my head but me and my low IQ. But I sure had you going."

Paul pushed the chair away, falling on his butt, looking up at Abel. "My young friend, either I'm nuts or this stupidity in your head ought to make me pack up and go home. I don't know what to call you."

Abel lowered his voice, condescendingly. "Why not call me 'special,' just like all the other residents? You people think you must fit us into some cozy head-sick compartment, like a drawer."

"Please, Abel, we're here to help you."

"You assume I need help. I don't. Why don't you assume you need help from me to figure out what your college forgot to teach you? That's why I'm about to save you some time...listen closely, Reactive Attachment Disorder. The RAD kid is neglected, abused, and usually abandoned at a young age; how is that for a fine start in life, Mr. Riordan?"

He reacted impulsively. "Abandoned?"

Abel failed to answer the question. Paul tried a different approach. "Did you go into foster care, or were you adopted? I don't recall anyone saying abandoned. I'm told your history is as mysterious as what lies in your head. So, I have no knowledge that you've been abused or neglected. I'm left with only me and you in this lonely room."

Silence again. Losing patience, Paul made a poor choice of words. "This nonsense about people in your head, that my training tells me to rid you of, causes complete confusion."

Abel stood, almost at attention. His short frame seemed chiseled out of a medieval stone, hard, strong, impenetrable. "Mr. Riordan, that's the way we like it."

Paul regrouped, sorry for losing focus. He thought of law, often making decisions on instinct. As he formulated his next question, he relied on a gut feeling, not sure of the consequences. "Who do you intend to hurt?"

A slow reaction came over Abel's face. Paul couldn't distinguish it, but it appeared something between a slight smile and a smirk.

Paul, in an adversarial mood, spoke again. "I guess I'm going to have to stop it." The blur between his careers defined the uneasiness of his own words.

Abel said one last thing as Paul watched his eyes, conveying a message. "*It* is my mother, and she has company, even though they never talk to each other."

Psychosis beyond my understanding. An unexplained chill ran up Paul's spine. *I may have made a mistake.*

***

"I hate myself," Paul shouted while still sitting helplessly behind the car's steering wheel. Never in his years of aggressively practicing law had he encountered such a horrible dilemma. He thought of the half-million dollar fee, paid in cash, for defending some leader of a motorcycle gang charged with murder. The gang, claiming self-endowed ownership of areas between heaven and hell, demanded one thing from Paul - delay. After filing motion after motion seeking court orders making the prosecution jump through legal hoops, the delays amounted to two years. When the prosecution finally called the case, witnesses had vanished, testimony had changed, and the case was dismissed. "Not my doing," Lawyer Riordan justified.

With guilt in his heart, he pulled the shifter down, placing the dilapidated car in Drive without a clear destination. He finally eased off the brake, resolving he must tell his wife. As the blocks passed toward his destination, he thought of the absolutely perfect face on the luscious woman who shared his two children, and choked back tears.

He parked the car in the same space where, less than an hour earlier, Helen's car rested peacefully. Exiting, making sure this time the keys were removed from the ignition, he placed them soundly in his pocket. After unlocking the house, he slowly ascended the steps toward his wife and son, but stopped. He retraced his steps to the driveway, rounded the house, and stared at the dog pen, door ajar, empty. He hurried upstairs and found Helen holding Jason.

Helen, the tall, beautiful woman he'd married, jumped him with a mixed look of inconvenience, anxiety, and fear. "Mind telling me what's going on?"

She'd endured years of cases of rape, kidnapping, and murder, all in support of her husband, a highly sought-after criminal defense lawyer. She bathed him with lavish praise for his dedication to his calling in the American system of justice. But Helen's defense of his career never took on a personal stake. What he was about to tell her would. He shivered at what this life and death situation might cause her to do.

He began with a simple question. "Did you call the police?"

"Well...I called 911...some lady claimed a city-wide emergency...nobody to help. So, I hung up."

Feeling gravely depressed, he motioned to Helen. "Let's go to our bedroom." He saw the concern in Helen's soft, brown eyes as she pulled the bedspread to the mid chest of Jason and kissed him on the forehead. "I'll be back in a few minutes, baby-boy."

Paul closed their bedroom door, grabbed her hand, and led her to the bed. She sat, and Paul fell to his knees, at her feet, crying. Helen looked stunned, her beautiful long, gracefully highlighted, blond hair looking disheveled from a morning of taking care of their son. During their years of marriage, tears never fell uncontrollably from his eyes. Brief tears of joy and relief and sadness fell during the birth of their children, his father's funeral. All seemed unimportant at this moment. These waters were unchartered.

He took deep breaths, relieved she asked no questions and patiently waited for him to regain the strength and stability she'd always admired in him. But when he looked up, his own fear reflected off her face, more directed than a mirror. Circumstances dictated Helen know the unedited truth.

"Parker's gone," he said resoundingly.

Her voice bounced from calm to panic. "No, no, Parker's at school."

"Parker's been taken from us...away from his school."

"I don't understand. Tell me what this is. Tell me now. Now. Now!"

"Kidnapped." He picked up the phone by the bed. The receiver dangled in his hand.

Helen stood and started shaking like a drug addict in withdrawal. "Put the damned phone down, where's my baby...who's got him?"

"Understood. I do need to explain, and you need to hear the whole thing. But right now time is on the kidnapper's side, which will work against Parker. Can I call the authorities, get things moving, then try to explain?"

Helen, sobbing, pulled up a chair, her ear close to the phone. She grabbed his leg, squeezed hard.

Paul, regaining most of his composure, dialed a number memorized from years back...the local police department. The call was answered by a female clearly stressed and obviously untrained. "All our officers are tied up. You want to leave a message or somethin'?"

He attempted to lay out the details of the bizarre story which began unfolding only a couple of hours earlier. But the dispatcher seemed to have no patience for him.

"Sir, sounds like your situation might be a 'mergency, but our whole shift is out and about trying to unravel some horrible murder in some school bus or van or somethin' or nother."

"Listen, it's all related."

"What do you mean?"

"Get your head out of your ass...I'm telling you the murderer is the same as the kidnapper of my son."

"Look, I'm nothin' but minimum wage, a desk clerk, and things are going crazy 'round here. I'll have to get somebody that actually knows somethin' to call you as soon as we possibly can."

Paul started to hang up the phone, shaking his head from side to side. But he asked one last question. "Ma'am, you mentioned murder. How many are murdered, and where are those who weren't murdered, can you answer this?"

The dispatcher breathed deep, long, sounding as if she wanted to go home. "Sir, don't know how much I'm supposed to say, even allowed to talk about. But since you seem to know something, the stuff I've heard is one is dead, they call him Joe. And a bunch of delinquents, all covered with blood, were dumped, not on the street, but at that petting zoo. Bloody kids all standing 'round looking at caged owls."

Paul sighed, knowing no mass murder complicated the already complicated. Along with the other multitude of thoughts flowing through his mind, he couldn't suppress the fact that the incompetence of the local police had lent itself to Paul's impressive record of not guilty verdicts in his criminal defense cases. But the turning tide placed him among the victims of the same system. *Justice reversed.*

Paul looked at Helen lying on their bed, curled into a position resembling a beaten puppy, tears streaming down her face. A robe covered the tightly fitted Victoria Secret he'd bought her, not six months ago, for Christmas. And less than a week before this nightmare happened, her die-for nipples looked lovelier than ever, shimmering in the pale light of their bedroom through the sheer glory of the Christmas present finally being worn. He mentally slapped himself for reminiscing, and snapped into gear, jerking the phone book from the drawer, rapidly turning the pages until he found the number of Tim Myers.

"Tim, Paul Riordan here. I need help." Paul's words shook as they tumbled from his mouth.

Tim, an excellent police officer, had met him many times in the courtroom. Paul dreaded having Tim as the testifying investigator as much as Tim abhorred Paul representing the defendant. A mutual admiration among adversaries.

"You don't sound like yourself, Paul. A problem?"

"I'm not myself. You don't know what I've been doing for the last few months but..."

Tim interrupted. "Look, you've kicked my ass in court more than anybody. Your career change has been a breath of fresh air. Trust me, I know damned well what you've been up to."

"I assume you're off today?"

"Yep."

"And you've learned to turn your police scanner off when you're off."

"Better, I threw the one in my house away years ago... more to life than the next ass- busting emergency."

"Okay, let me tell you about the last few hours in our fair city."

When Paul finished, he was uncharacteristically out of breath.

A brief pause occurred before Tim spoke. "Crap, I don't know what to say."

"Say you'll help. I'm not turning to the Chafenville P.D. I'm turning to you. And you and I both know why."

Paul waited until Tim's grunt broke the silence. "Yeah, I guess we both know why. What kind of help?"

"My boy's only in the second grade. Don't screw this up."

"Careful, my man. I'm a cop. You're a victim this time, emotional, unpredictable."

"Don't screw this up."

"I'm one man, can't make promises."

"You're the best man, my son's best hope."

Paul waited impatiently for Tim to answer.

"I'm coming over."

Chapter Two

Tuesday, June 11, 2013
5:30 p.m.

"Look, Paul, we're talking about a seventeen-year-old kid. Maybe he's got some heavy allegations of blood shedding on his record, but he's still a punk. Hardly a sophisticated kidnapping. Best I can tell..."

Paul raised his hand, not wanting Helen to hear all this, and Tim Myers, a detective who stood several inches taller, stopped talking. Paul rotated his head toward Helen, focused his brown eyes, and rubbed his hand over hers. She had a mixed look of sadness, anger, and distrust of systems she never understood. Paul turned back to Tim. "Let's give Helen some space."

She stood, offended, tearful. "Let's *not* give Helen some space. Let's give Helen some answers." She dropped back into her chair.

Paul patted her gently on the shoulder. "These are mere details, let me get with Tim and I'll fill you in later. Our child needs you."

"You got that right, one in particular."

Paul watched Tim rise from his seat at the kitchen table as the sun set in the direction of House of Hope. His wavy, sandy hair fell neatly around his neck line as he surveyed the hordes of equipment and operators set up like bad interior decorating. Tech people adjusted monitoring equipment hooked to the land line going into the Riordans' home, a line that was beginning to be used less and less, since everyone in the Riordan household, except the kids, had a smart phone.

Tim, after Helen seemed to recover from her outburst, spoke. "Ms. Riordan, your cell phone is off, correct?"

"Actually I can't find it, maybe left it in the car."

"Not a problem. I want Paul's to stay on. If we get a call it should come to either the house phone or Paul's cell. And I agree with Paul, I shouldn't bother you with police talk."

"Bother me? Parker's life means more than my own."

"Bad choice of words. Paul and I go way back. What I mean is…hell…I don't know what I mean other than your husband seems to think we should meet in private." He gestured toward another room. "Paul, maybe we could chat in there?"

"Yes, yes. Helen, we'll be back in a minute."

Helen looked frustrated, and Paul felt like he needed to throw up. He followed Tim, his muscular frame nearly filling the door opening as they walked into the study. He motioned to two chairs in the corner and Tim fell into one, continuing the conversation, like Paul was a fellow officer, not a victim.

"This kid's got no experience, won't know the ways of a seasoned criminal seeking a ransom. He won't get his way. But that doesn't translate into getting our way, capisce?"

Paul, fragile, and in no mood to joke, tried to stay balanced. "Tim, you're too old. Kojack's been off the telly since …when… the first Bush President?"

Tim laughed. "Old sayings are hard to break. So, tell me what I'm missing. What, to your mind, is this kid's game?"

Paul, wanting methodically to explain Tim's misjudgment of the kidnapper, reacted emotionally instead. "This isn't a game. God dammit, it's my son. I want him back. I'm going to repeat it slowly, Tim. I want Parker back." Paul's strong facade broke, shattered, in fact. He thought of Helen suffering beyond the door and cried, loud, hard.

Embarrassed for Tim to see such a vulnerable side, he gathered himself together, then threw up his hands, only for himself. *What's my pride have to do with this? Parker...only Parker matters.*

Tim waited, then turned to business. "Ok, Paul. Put your mind in neutral, hold your emotions...like the courtroom...where you never cracked."

Paul realized Tim was right, and he tensed as Tim grabbed him firmly by both arms. He wiped away his tears. "I'm being stupid, sorry for being weak."

"Not at all, my bad, my insensitivity, you're as tough as they come...I'd probably fall apart if I stood in your shoes."

"Stop your gibberish, trying to make me feel better. Can we focus on Abel Wood?"

They both nodded their heads at one another in a convincing manner, the objective understood.

Paul watched a smile grow on Tim's face. "What?"

Tim gestured to the window. "Looks like the basset hound you described...care to put her back in the pen?"

Paul bolted out the room, gathered Helen and sprinted outside, hoping for Parker to be by his side. Helen hugged the dog while Paul looked frantically around the yard. Tim, not far behind, caught up.

"Don't expect to see Parker with the dog. I suspect once she lured Parker to the car, she was in our kidnapper's way, he kicked her out, and she used that great sense of smell and direction to get home. Let's go back inside where we can monitor your phones."

***

Paul meditated in his big leather chair in the study as Tim rose, organizing the technical staff. Unanswered questions pulled against one another in his mind. *Where did Abel get my home address?* Not a difficult question, the phone book. *I've listed my home phone and address since the day I hung out my law shingle.*

So, how would Abel know the street? He grew up…where? I guess a remote place from here, hell, who knows where he grew up? Still easy…there's a map of Chafenville inside the phone book. Maybe Abel had a smart phone. But who would be paying the charges?

How would he know the keys would be left in the car? Just a lucky coincidence for Abel? It can't be a coincidence that he knew specific details of where my kid attended school or the name of Parker's teacher. Something's way wrong here. We talked, but not enough for him to know all that. I'm missing something obvious.

Suddenly a wave of fear rushed over Paul. He rose from his chair and shouted out loud. "The laptop. It's the damned laptop."

Tim ran into the study as if the kidnapper had Paul by the throat. "What?"

In control, Paul slowed both his speech and his thoughts. "Tim, a piece of the puzzle."

Paul recalled the event, happening just a day or two before his private conversation with Abel. That day Paul was scheduled to work from 10:00 a.m. to 7:00 p.m. His car had a battery problem and wouldn't crank after he exited the dry cleaners, intending to report for work. He recalled walking the half mile between the dry cleaners and House of Hope. He ran his security card through the scanner beside the front door, entered, and yelled at Joe Inman. "Sorry I'm late...got a dead battery over at Sixty Minute Cleaners and had to walk over."

During the day, Paul, extremely busy with administrative details, lost track of time, and failed to deal with the car. He caught a ride home with a fellow staff member and called his mechanic the next morning.

Paul's trusted garage guy dropped by his house early, picked up the key and told Paul he'd have his car back to him within the hour. Ten minutes later the mechanic called the house.

"Bad news, Paul. Someone's busted out your driver's side window. You want me to wait 'til you can call the cops to get a report for your insurance?"

"Yeah, I'll call them right now. Go ahead and replace the battery or whatever you need to do. I'll be there in a few minutes."

Then Paul remembered the laptop, lying underneath fresh hangers of dry cleaning across the back seat. Before retiring from the practice of law and closing his office, he had years of data on this computer he lugged between office and home, both business and personal. He kept back-up files at the house.

His fresh dry cleaning seemed untouched. The laptop gone, he merely bought another, downloaded off the backups, and forgot about it. He *was* retired.

***

Tim settled back into the chair in the study, his blue eyes facing the frustrated lawyer. Paul finished telling the story. "Abel's got my life from cover to cover."

Tim looked doubtful while soaking in the new information. "Kidnapping is a complicated crime, rarely working unless it's a family thing, you know, like father kidnapping from estranged mother…the kid goes with Dad as the kid's told…no ransom, no phone calls, they disappear and the trail goes cold. Other kidnappers usually fall in the real dumb or the real smart category. I suspect your boy here ain't the sharpest tool in the criminal shed."

Paul contemplated Tim's comments and thought back to the last kidnapping case he'd handled. The case came to him by court appointment, and his indigent client went by the name of Billy Cassel. Tim Myers had looked him in the eyes, "Your boy's going down."

***

Billy was a co-defendant with Ricky Curtin, both living in a rural community outside Chafenville. Not up the rocky cliffs above the river, but the flat farm land going in the other direction. They first saw Rebecca Finch standing in a corn field through the trees when they were making homemade liquor in a still in the woods nearby.

Neither had a job and both cared little for anything resembling success. They stayed high drinking corn liquor most days, the ingredients for the whiskey stolen from nearby fields. They frequently watched the elderly Mrs. Finch toil over her crop, while they enjoyed the fruits of her labor.

Paul recalled the case well, and it was clear that Ricky was in charge, and Billy would do most anything he said.

"Look at the way she dresses. That ain't no po farm lady. Them threads cost some...probably bought in that big-price-tag store downtown. We take her, and somebody'll pay plenty to get her back. Easy pickins the way she wades out in the field all by her lonesome."

"Yeh, Ricky, sounds like some big money."

Ricky had enough street smarts to fill a thimble, but Billy viewed him as a puppy would view his master. He had controlled Billy since they were kids. After twenty-three years, Ricky's leadership had gotten them only as far as making decent corn liquor.

Day after day, Ricky talked about the fortunes that would come from kidnapping their predictable visitor to the field.

"We won't hurt her, will we, Ricky?"

"No, Billy Boy, no hurtin', just gettin' rich."

Ricky laid out the plan. They would hide behind the seventh row of corn. They would grab her at the fourth. From there they would walk four miles through some back woods to an old campsite.

The plan came apart when she came up behind them from the other direction and asked "how may I help you." Ricky stumbled through rows of corn, landing at her feet. She reached down to help but he angrily snatched her from behind, demanding she come with him.

"Don't hurt her," Billy pleaded. As they walked through the woods, Billy had not been prepared for the lady's tears.

"Maybe we should take her back, Ricky."

The lady nodded with approval. "I won't tell anybody. Just let me go. I'll find my way home."

"You just shut the hell up, old lady, and Billy, you better quit talking like you got no balls for this sorta thing. Remember, we goin' be rich."

Ricky made the call from a pay phone a mile from the campsite. He had persuaded her to give him the phone number to her house by threatening to kill her pet dog.

"Put a hundred thousand in a blue suitcase and leave it by trash dump on Highway 324 where it crosses the old loggin' road. As soon as we get the money, we'll get her home." He hung up the phone before the trained police officer could get any information.

"Bush league," the officer said in frustration.

After a discussion about using an empty suitcase versus one containing the ransom, Mrs. Finch's family came up with the cash, unwilling to take any chances.

***

Paul reflected, they bet the farm, so to speak. Technology since that time made considerable advances. Put a GPS on the suitcase and nail the perp before he gets back to the victim. But then Paul laughed at himself remembering a GPS couldn't have helped considering what happened next.

The blue suitcase, filled with hard cash, rested by the side of the highway. A man and his family, seeing the suitcase, pulled over and loaded it in his car before Ricky arrived. Within ten minutes after the pickup, the team of officers surrounded the vehicle at the country store where the man exited with a two-pound roll of bologna. Interestingly, the bologna was purchased at the same country market where Ricky made the phone call.

"Get your hands up," the deputy said as fifteen blue steel barrels of various sizes were aimed at the unfortunate finder of the suitcase, a twenty dollar bill short of the original 100 grand.

After a lengthy interrogation of the man and his passengers, frustrated officers threw up their hands, knowing they blew the case, and the victim's chances had become greatly diminished.

Fortunately, Tim Myers had the police savvy to know this car with a man, woman, and child didn't fit the profile. Since the suspected vehicle was well covered by the other officers, Tim held back.

He witnessed first-hand the frustration of Ricky when the suitcase wasn't in place. Ricky ran around in circles venting his anger. As he retraced his steps back along the path he took from the campsite, Tim followed at a distance.

He watched cautiously as he heard the discussion between the kidnappers.

"The old bitch is dead. They didn't leave the money," Ricky said.

"Let's let her go. She ain't give us no trouble. She seems nice enough. We could leave town for a while."

The lady picked up on Billy's momentum. "He's right, you know. There won't be any trouble from me. As far as I am concerned, none of this happened. In fact, if you want some money, I'll give you some...leave it wherever you want."

"Shut your face," Ricky shouted as he shook the lady violently while holding both her shoulders. "Make no mistake, lady, your people screwed us, and now it's your turn."

Ricky backed up four steps and eyed his victim ruthlessly. As he walked aggressively toward her, pulling his belt from the loops of his pants, he rocked violently backwards.

The 357 magnum projectile hit the exact point of target, a shoulder shot, not life threatening. Ricky hit the ground.

As Tim stepped forward, he observed Billy and Mrs. Finch holding each other in a protective embrace, a strange sight.

They both expressed a deep felt emotion that they were allies against Ricky.

As Billy, escorted in chains, walked from the police vehicle to the station, a TV reporter from Channel 4, cameras rolling, stuck her microphone toward Billy.

"How's that lady?" Billy asked.

The astute reporter replied, "What lady?"

"The one we took."

***

Months later, Paul and Tim jousted over Billy's sentence.

"The bottom line, Paul, like I said, Billy's going down, gets life. He was part of the plan all along. Just because he turned into a nice guy and may have saved her life doesn't change anything. Besides, he's getting a better deal than his co-defendant."

"What do you mean a better deal...Ricky gets life, too."

"Yeah, but Billy doesn't get a hole in his shoulder."

Paul couldn't help but laugh. "Well, I guess I'll have to tee this one up and see what happens...got nothing to lose if you can't recommend a better deal to the D.A."

Paul knew Tim's case was too solid to overcome, but felt obligated to try. "Maybe my defense is not so technical. Perhaps this is one situation where jury nullification will prevail."

"How so?"

"The jury's vote is up or down, guilty or not guilty. They don't have to give reasons, and I plan to plant reasons in their mind that no one outside that jury room can question…whether they follow the law or not."

"So, Lawyer Riordan, I've been in court enough. The judge won't let you tell the jury to go against the law, am I wrong?"

"No, you're right."

"Then how do you plan to make a closing argument? Your client's guilty, but since he's such a decent guy… cut him loose?"

"Don't plan to make that argument. My evidence will do the talking for me."

Tim laughed. "You're calling Billy to the stand to explain how he and his buddy watched, planned, abducted an elderly woman…grandmother of many, and demanded ransom? I can't wait. Your boy's going down."

"You'll be waiting a long time."

"Why's that?"

"I'm not calling Billy, I'm calling you."

"What?"

"Actually, I'll be cross-examining you. May I assume, since you witnessed the outcome, you'll be the prosecution's top witness?"

Paul recalled Tim's long pause before the next words were spoken. "What questions do you plan to ask me?"

"Officer Myers, over the hour or so you spent observing Mr. Curtin, Mrs. Finch, and Billy, did Billy ever say one unkind word?"

"Is it true that Mr. Curtin committed every threat and every physical act toward Rebecca?"

"Billy, none?"

"And after Mr. Curtin, by himself, departed the scene when the money had been left, you followed him and arrived at the campsite only to find Billy and Rebecca mutually intimidated by the arrival of one Ricky Curtin?"

"And when you heroically shot Mr. Curtin, perhaps saving Rebecca's life, what did she do?"

Paul looked over at Tim. "You can actually answer that one."

Tim spewed out a loud breath. "She hugged Billy."

"You saved her life, and she hugged Billy?"

"Hugged Billy instead of you?"

"Right."

"Okay, Tim, my investigator talked to Rebecca and her family. They think Billy, as they put it, is a bit slow.... and you and I know that borders on mental defenses. I doubt I can prove Billy's insane or, in the eyes of the law, mentally unable to know right from wrong. But I think the jury might show Billy some compassion anyway."

"Okay, you've got my attention, but the victim needs to weigh in on any plea bargain, say twenty-five years."

"Say ten, local incarceration."

"Doubt the victim would feel too good about ten or the scumbag even staying in her community."

"Go ask her." Paul already knew the victim's answer.

Billy came by Paul's office five years later, out on parole, to thank him.

***

Paul jolted out of his flashback and met Tim's eyes, remembering the "not the sharpest tool in the shed" comment. "Tim, Abel Wood is not Billy Cassel."

Tim stood and scratched his head. "I remember that. And the SOB who picked up the suitcase… a hundred grand inside… bought a damned roll of ba-looon-ie?"

"Right."

"I believe I'd have splurged for at least a T-bone!"

Paul thought it funny what stuck in his mind, compared to Tim's mind, over the Billy Cassel case. But his reflection and Tim's humor quickly faded as they refocused on the problem at hand.

***

The phone rang. A familiar adrenaline rush and increased heart rate overcame Paul as it continued to ring, a feeling between the time a jury would walk in, and the foreman would announce the verdict. But something was slightly different about this sensation. A burning deep in the pit of his stomach let him know it wasn't pride or money at stake. Rather, his son.

Per his discussions with Tim, he picked up the phone and spoke calmly. "Hello." He recognized Abel's voice.

"Twenty seconds."

"What?" Paul replied, well aware of the technical significance.

"That leaves us with ten. Keep me on the phone, and you'll have me...right?"

"So, how is Parker?" Paul said as he flashed his eyes toward Helen and then Tim. Why would Abel bring up the fact that he knew the time needed for authorities to figure out his location?

"Parker's fine."

"What do you want, Abel?"

"I don't know, but we'll be talking."

The conversation ended after forty-five seconds. Paul watched the technicians walk in, shaking their heads. "Cell phone."

"Helen's cell phone, right?" Tim interjected.

"The tech nodded his head."

"We already checked, a smart phone...unfortunately not activated for location."

Tim turned to Paul. "Guess we know Helen left her phone in the van, just like her keys?"

Paul remembered. The iPhone, the option of global location of the user. He'd made a knee-jerk decision, and hit the "decline" button. Somehow Helen's privacy seemed more important. Feeling guilty for his impulsive choice, Paul looked at Tim. "Yes, no locator, my decision. So, feel free to kick my ass. Well deserved." He threw up his hands. "So, where does that leave us?"

"Nowhere. We don't have an answer to our first question...motive...what does he want? We wait for him to call back. Good news is we know he will call your land line, gives us a bit more predictability."

Paul's eyes panned around the room. He saw a half dozen set of eyes, each with a different thought process behind them. He glanced at the battery-operated clock above the sink, 9:34 p.m. A thousand questions flooded his mind. He chose, like he had a choice, to wait for the next call, which came thirty minutes later.

"So, who's running House of Hope?"

"Quite frankly, Abel, that's the last of my worries right now. Why do you ask?"

"Well, Paul...I mean Mr. Riordan, before Parker, it was the only thing you and I had in common. Have you forgotten about the way you looked at me all the time? Do you know how that felt?"

"What's that got to do with Parker?"

"Now, now, Mr. Riordan, you seem to be a little excited, the cops told you to be calm, right?"

"You killed Mr. Joe, then kidnapped my son, and wonder if I'm excited?"

Paul's face flushed, as he watched Tim sternly shaking his head indicating for Paul to get some control.

Paul took a deep breath. "Listen, Abel, I want to work this out with you. You want something from me. What is it?"

"The funny thing is, Mr. Riordan, you have the answer to that question...not me. You be thinking because you'll have to let me know."

Paul stood as Abel hung up the phone, even knowing the conversation was digitally recorded. The momentum seemed all in Abel's favor.

Tim, already starting the process of replay, began barking orders. "Paul, sit. Not bad, you did good." Tim turned to his tech people. "Download...I want a shrink to evaluate...damnedest conversation I ever heard."

Paul cautiously hugged Helen as he watched the tech people moving about. After a dozen replays, Paul stepped toward Tim.

"So, does this fit your kidnap mold as a smart one or a stupid one?"

Paul noticed Tim looking away as he answered. "I'm starting to rethink those categories. Abel makes no sense, scares the hell out of me."

"I thought the cop was supposed to be calm and reassuring to the victims," Paul said, trying to inflect a slight degree of humor.

"Yeh, that's what they teach us. You got some coffee around this place?"

Paul pointed to the Keurig, but Tim seemed consumed with thoughts of Abel. Paul found Helen huddled with Jason in Parker's bedroom, as if she was protecting both children from the outside world. That cruel world included Abel, the police, and probably Paul himself. He knew Helen reflected on his bizarre career change and the present consequences.

Rather than offering half-thought-out comments of comfort and optimism to Helen, Paul returned to the coffee maker and made two cups.

"Ok, Paul, we don't know much except the two calls came thirty minutes apart. Could be the start of a pattern, so we see what happens. We'll know in fourteen minutes. When you answer the phone this time, ask early on to speak to Parker. My guess is this won't happen."

Paul put down his cup. "Why? Why is that your guess?"

Tim failed to answer the question. "If he puts him on, don't fall apart...calm and soothing...that's all. Mainly listen, Parker might say something valuable. If he refuses to put him on, ask Abel why you should believe he is keeping Parker safe?"

Paul looked at his watch. "Know what time it is?"

Tim looked at his own. "Late."

"Think about this, Tim, Parker is way past his bedtime. Abel is usually down by 10:30. We are in a time frame which will be testy for both."

"Damned right, excellent point, Paul. But how does that change what we're doing, waiting for the next call?"

"No change, only a reminder that it is late and we're dealing with kids…assuming you could call Abel a kid."

"Point well taken, let's wait."

The house fell silent as Tim's instructions ended, and the brigade of players waited for the call. During the next hour and fifteen minutes, calls only came from the curious and concerned. They all got the "don't call back…need to keep the line free" routine.

Paul hated the Chafenville rumor mill. Dealing with the irrelevancy of those who were so concerned to call, but wouldn't bother to drive or walk over, became a necessary evil. And when the conversation ended with "please let me know if there is *anything* I can do," he almost wanted to scream "okay, quit your nosey-ass meddling and find my son."

The anticipated call finally came. The initial silence was the only consistency among Abel's calls. Paul, back into the loop of his son's destiny, began.

"Abel, may I speak to Parker?"

"Not right now."

"You know, if I thought Parker was hurt, or not around anymore, I would have nothing to talk to you about."

"I knew that's what you'd say. Did the police tell you to say that, or did you think it up all by yourself?"

"Abel, this is no game. I can be real easy and give you what you want without any problem. On the other hand, if I sense you're about to cross me, that Parker's not safe, this whole thing will backfire on you."

"Now what does this remind me of, Mr. Riordan? Oh yeah, that was the same spiel you gave to that corporate lawyer in that tire case. But you know what? You don't know if Parker is fine, hurt, or dead. Until you do know, you won't take chances with me. I know it, and you know it."

The conversation ended with Paul holding the receiver, too stunned to put it down. Abel had hit the nail on the head. Paul had bluffed his way with the in-house counsel of the Mira-Mile Tire Corporation to a multi-million dollar settlement.

Mira-Mile was self-insured. Paul represented a teenager who lost a leg in a car accident. The boy, his client, drinking and driving recklessly in the Chafenville High School parking lot one Saturday night, launched into a high-speed "donut," and one of the tires failed, causing the car to roll.

Was it abuse or a defective tire? Paul skillfully had developed a rapport with corporate counsel. Paul wanted a large settlement, and Mira-Mile Tire wanted to blame the tire's failure on driver abuse and quietly make the legal problem go away.

Paul had said in a one-on-one meeting with corporate counsel, "You need my help. I need yours. I think you can get me two million and a half under the right circumstances."

The corporate counsel scratched his head. "Right circumstances? I'm not following your reason."

"I'll put in your hands an affidavit from my injured client that will assure your engineers that these tires were put into such an extreme speed and turn that no reasonable commercial-grade tire could have withstood it. I'll also guarantee that this settlement will remain confidential, and the claim will merely vanish after payment. You're protected two ways."

"But if you cross me, you could use this affidavit to beat my brains out at trial. So, you don't get it until the check comes in. If at any time during the process I get the feeling I can't trust you, all bets are off. I'll march into Court with two quite articulate young people, parking at the back of the school, watching my client. They'll testify they were horrified when the tire disintegrated in front of their very eyes as my client merely took a joy ride in his car. The trial will become very public, and your tire will become a national issue."

The bluff worked. Paul got forty percent of the settlement in fee, largely responsible for the luxury of Paul's career change.

"The laptop," Paul screamed. "All of my memos in the tire case, right at Abel's fingertips."

Seven minutes, the phone rang again. "Probably another nosey neighbor," Paul said as he reached for the receiver.

"Hello."

"I'll trade Parker for Mrs. Riordan."

Paul couldn't think of a response. He looked at Tim for guidance, and Tim merely shook his head, no."

"Listen, Mr. Riordan, why don't you put the head police guy on the phone. We both know you got plenty of them at the house there with you. They're going to tell you what to say, so you might as well put them on."

"He's right," Tim said as he took the receiver from Paul's hand.

"Abel, we don't trade people. You need to figure out what will make you happy...a lot of money...a sports car...maybe a plane. If you can't fly, we'll get you your own pilot. Get the boy back to us and name your price, simple as that."

"I just did. It's Mrs. Riordan."

"Mrs. Riordan is not for trade."

Helen heard her name echoing off the walls. She made her way to the kitchen. Paul caught her by the arm as she walked in. He spoke to her softly.

"This maniac wants to trade Parker for you. Tim's talking to him now."

"Mrs. Riordan's not part of the deal, Abel."

Helen stepped toward the phone and spoke clearly. "Mrs. Riordan is the deal. You tell him that right now. You get Parker back right now, now! Do the swap."

Tim rolled his eyes at his fellow officers, collected his thoughts, and said to Abel, who started to chuckle, "Would you mind calling us back in a few minutes so we can discuss your offer?"

"You're very predictable, officer." The call ended.

Tim hung up the phone and shouted, "Get her out, this victim does not need to be in this room."

Paul gently turned Helen until his eyes met hers. "No, Sweetheart. This is not a good way." But Paul could see the resolve in her eyes and knew he had to give her a better reason.

Tim interrupted their nonverbal communication. "Mrs. Riordan, Helen, we can't...not a question of your willingness, not a question of one life being compared to another. I don't know what the exchange terms are. He could end up with both of you, a chance I'm unwilling to take."

"Well, detective, I suggest you find out what the exchange terms are."

Tim pulled out his own cell phone. "I need to consult on this," he said as Paul soaked up the dilemma and began watching the unfamiliar side of the system of justice.

***

Tim called Boston P.D. and asked for Captain Holcomb. He glanced at his watch: 11:33 p.m. Roger Holcomb and Tim roomed together at the FBI Academy. Roger could grab bizarre criminal activity by the throat, and dissect the criminals with the precision of a surgeon. He remembered Roger's words in a group discussion at the Academy when a fellow officer kept referring to crimes with no motive. "Just because you can't see the motive doesn't mean it doesn't exist. A motive you don't understand only means that your head doesn't tick the same way as the one that does understand the motive."

Even at the late hour, Roger picked up the phone and Tim related the story.

Roger lowered his voice to a sober level. "I think Parker's dead."

"Why do you say that?"

"He's on a roll...already killed one...cut his throat? Then you say he calmly walked into a grammar school, chatted with the staff, and ends up with the boy? Don't chance the mother. If he can't produce the boy, get his demand and take him out at the contact point, plain and simple."

"Thanks, Roger. I knew you'd see it with clarity."

Tim cleared his cell phone, huddled with his officers, lowered his voice, and whispered the reasons why Roger considered Parker dead. Then he gathered Paul and Helen around the island in the middle of the kitchen. "We don't do the swap. I don't think Abel's going to let us talk with Parker. Without confirmation that Parker is ok, we can't chance involving you."

The phone rang. Before Tim could pick it up, Helen grabbed it. "You let me speak to Parker if you want me." Tim, infuriated with himself for failing to control the unfolding action, waited for the worse.

As Helen spoke, Tim saw tears forming in the eyes of even the most veteran officers.

"Hi, baby. How are you feeling? Are you sure you're not hurt or anything? Yes, I'm coming to get you just real, real soon."

With Abel back on the line, Tim, frustrated as hell, took the phone from Helen, but spoke slowly and in control. "You are speaking to Detective Tim Myers." He paused, then continued. "Well, it sounds like you're going to consider your offer, Abel. What do you have in mind?"

"Look at your watch, after midnight. A new day. But I'm tired, bet you are, too."

"What's your point, Abel?"

"I'll call back tomorrow; Parker's safe, and, by the way, did you put the dog up?"

The postponement did Tim little good. The monitors discussed coming back in the morning, sleeping in their own beds. *This punk obviously knew more than I'd given him credit for...could very well call ten minutes after my team left.* No, Tim and his men would stay put.

Chapter Three

Wednesday, June 12, 2013
9:30 a.m.

The phone rang. Abel, calm and collectively, outlined his plan which he emphasized *would* unfold in three days at Confederate Park in downtown Chafenville. Tim thought, why three days? But before asking the question, he quickly figured his advantage. This highly populated area, on Saturday morning, would give authorities unlimited opportunities to cover the area like a blanket when the exchange would take place. But innocent bystanders, picnickers, joggers, moms with baby strollers, would be at risk if gunfire became necessary.

After learning the exact location where Abel could be found on Saturday morning, along with exact times and other specifics, Tim asked, "So, how will you get Mrs. Riordan and we get Parker?"

Abel cleared his voice, "Easy. I'll be driving a tan Dodge Caravan, license plate number HELEN 1. I'll park beside the statue of that Civil War guy in bronze, walk straight to Mrs. Riordan, and walk her back to the car. You can have a hundred cars, planes, ready to follow us, and I will take you to the place where you get Parker. All you need to do is follow me, and I don't expect you to let me go until I give you Parker."

"But who will have Parker while you're coming to the park?" Tim asked.

Abel hung up the phone without answering.

Tim spoke first. "If everybody stays healthy, we get both Parker and Helen back. He gets a free ride into the park, no interference. The minute Abel shows up, I'll have him covered up with my men. I'll personally escort Abel and Helen back to his car. He'll never get more than fifty feet from my officers. We'll have a squad car in front and behind. I'll have two choppers above and an army of officers trailing behind. When he finally stops, I'll have a virtual net around him. Until we get Parker, he won't be able to get out of the car. If he does, we'll have two armed officers to escort him to wherever he wants to walk." Tim chuckled lightly, "Abel didn't think this one through," he shouted to his men. "And you don't need to run that license plate."

Tim glanced over at Paul, who looked a bit unsettled.

***

Saturday, June 15, 2013
7:45 a.m.

Tim orchestrated the set-up more than two hours before the proposed arrival. True to his exact promise, 10:00 a.m., Abel drove Helen's car to a vacant parking space beside the figure of Jefferson Davis, perched high upon a concrete base. He jerked the car door opened, threw his legs out, and walked to the middle of the garden filled with visitors and plain clothes policemen alike. To Tim, an exposed, vulnerable target. He liked his chances. Abel asked, "Are you Detective Tim Myers?"

Tim nodded his head, then Abel spoke clearly, but politely. "Detective, please escort Mrs. Riordan back to the Caravan. I'll walk beside you."

As Tim walked, he felt strange that Abel, entirely a naked target to arrest, would take this chance. Circumstances reinforced Tim's suspicions this kid had no talent for this sort of crime. Basic police work dictated arresting Abel then and there. After all, he had murdered one other. But Tim lived up to his promise to Helen Riordan to hold off his men until Parker was safely returned.

Tim started to open the driver's side door when Abel spoke again. "Open the back." Tim eyed him suspiciously, but complied with the request as he watched Abel enter the car and slide over, allowing room for Helen to join him.

From the corner of Tim's eye, a poorly dressed man suddenly arose from a park bench across the street, began walking toward the car, and attempted to enter the driver's side door. Tim grabbed him by the arm. "Who the hell are you?"

Abel leaned forward. "Let him drive."

Tim jerked his head back in Abel's direction. "What the hell's this?" Tim said with a fiery inflection.

"I don't have a license, don't want you to arrest me before I get Parker back to you. Did we not make a deal?"

Tim watched Helen, slightly shaking. Fundamentals. Tim smiled, sticking with the plan. He would not be derailed, his multitude of officers stood ready to pursue. "Abel, you got your way, whatever you want."

Abel handed the driver the ignition keys. As the car pulled off slowly, Abel spoke to Tim through the opened window. "Be seeing you shortly."

Tim nodded his head, confident.

Thirty-five officers, divided among fourteen vehicles and two helicopters, snapped into a formation Tim personally designed as a spider might a web. The Caravan rambled slowly down Robert E. Lee Boulevard with the observation team easing along at the same pace. Without any warning, Tim watched as the driver of the Caravan turned right over the curb and picked up speed, heading toward a grove of large hemlock trees where an activities tent had been pitched by the park staff.

"Stay with it," Tim shouted over the universal communication system.

"We got 'em, lieutenant," replied the first car to the rear. "He's driving under the tent, and eye contact is lost," relayed the first helicopter overhead.

"The car stopped. I can barely see it for the trees. No, no, it's moving again. I got it from behind. I'm going under the same tent."

Tim got visual confirmation from every vehicle that circled the Caravan as it turned left on Maple Street.

He continued with confidence until the driver of the helicopter, hovering twenty-five feet over the rear windshield, reported. "I can't see either one, the suspect or the woman." Tim pounded his accelerator to the floor, covering the same path as the Caravan, barking orders. "Stop the damned car."

As Tim slammed on brakes, nearly striking the back of the Caravan, officers had the driver spread eagle on the hood of the car.

"You're headed to jail." Tim screamed at the man, shaking like an alcoholic rehab patient. "Better start talking, and fast."

"The kid gave me a hundred bucks. Said the woman was his mother...her birthday...he wanted to surprise her at the park with a...you know...like a nice chauffeured ride. Things happened just like he said it would. You opened the back door and put the kid and his mother in, and then I walked across the street and just got in without..."

Tim rudely interjected, "Shut up, where are they?"

"I don't know. When he told me to stop under the tent, I thought it was part of the birthday present. Then the kid shouted not to turn around, just start driving again.

"And?"

"So, I did. What did I care, he done give me the hundred."

Tim furiously thought as he rubbed the back of his head with his right hand while turning around in a full circle. Within a second, he instructed his men. "Tear the car apart, but don't leave it, I'm heading back to the tent."

What Tim found was a large storm water drain in the low spot under the tent. The grate had been removed and a five-foot pipe ran in two different directions. "How did I miss the damned hole?"

He pulled out all his communication devices. "Get city utilities on the phone, now, now, and give me two lean officers under this stupid ass tent and find out who put this tent up and why. Move it."

Tim sent two officers scrambling in each direction of the storm drain, while listening to a third officer describe the alterations they found in the back of the Caravan.

"It's cut out...like a trap door. The van's front wheel drive. Somebody rerouted the exhaust system. They eased out...merely dropped straight down from the back seat into the drain. Gone in a matter of seconds."

"Look at the grate, a heavy grill, how could they pull it up?"

"Got your answer right here, Lieutenant. There's a hydraulic jack and steel cable to the side of the floorboard, not a problem with this kind of equipment."

Tim fumed, his head about to explode, as he was handed the storm water plans of the park. Time burned away as he studied, contemplated, and made a guess. He grabbed his monitor. "I think they would have taken the route going straight under the park, toward the river bending around the north side. He figured Abel got a twenty-minute jump on his men milling around the pipes, waiting for direction.

"Officer, have you made it to the river?" Tim barked into the police communicating device.

"Yeh, Lieutenant, I'm coming out right now."

"What do you see?"

"It's just the river bank and nobody's here."

"Keep looking, I'm coming over land." Then Tim changed channels. "Get both choppers covering every inch of the park, both ends, and the river's edge."

When Tim arrived at the river bank, he saw what every officer had missed...boat prints. "He's not on the banks, that little bastard's got a boat. Look at the tracks. It's a Jon boat and you see this tail-like mark in the middle? He's got a motor, and by my estimation, they left here close to half an hour ago. I want a ten-mile sweep in both directions of this river."

"But, Lieutenant, that's going to take some more men."

"So what? Get the National Guard."

"Put the word out, it's a dark green Jon boat."

"How do you know that, Lieutenant?"

"Clues, dammit, clues...remember you're a cop. The green paint on those two small rocks got there when the boat was dragged over them."

"Good eye, I missed that one."

Tim rolled his eyes. "Well, better pick up that piece of plastic between your feet before you miss something else."

"What is it, Lieutenant?"

"The high-tech GPS we put inside Helen Riordan's belt. A big help that turned out to be."

"Didn't we use two?"

"Right, I placed the other on the car frame when we turned Helen over. Still sitting in the same place at the other end of our fine and dandy tunnel...again...no damned use to us now."

***

Abel spent a lifetime on the desolate land between the banks across the Shady River, on the far side of Chafenville, and the rocky hills which climbed up from the water to a ridge that ran thirty miles in either direction. The land had little monetary value, not farmable, and the rock cost too much to excavate to have any commercial development potential. Abel spent years exploring the land, for the most part, all by himself. Cliffs, gullies, and caves became his private playground, an escape from the horrors at home. He distanced himself mentally from bleeding, painful stuff, and those responsible for thinking it forgotten the next morning. But Abel forgot nothing, forgave nothing.

Chapter Four

1995

Ed Wood and his daughter, Rachel, religiously attended the 7th Chapter of The National Fellowship of Friends, a church some fifteen miles, looking at a map, from the city limits of Chafenville. The band of members simply called the church "The Fellowship." A gravel road, winding up a hill above the river, provided passage to the mostly overlooked place of worship. The founder and leader of the eighteen Fellowship chapters was Reverend Chris Bordo of Brevard, North Carolina.

Bordo preached his dedication to restoring the balance between humans and other species on earth. There was one commandment that each member and his family swore to live by and was strongly encouraged to demand others to follow: "THOU SHALT NOT PROCREATE." He carefully monitored his eighteen flocks, scattered about the rural mountains in an area where Georgia, North Carolina, and Tennessee come together. "God's triangle," Bordo proclaimed, "where God granted no sinner the right to procreate." And when the sinner disappointed the Lord, the preferred methods of extinguishing the unwanted were suicide and abortion.

But the Creator had bestowed upon Reverend Bordo the truth of His will. A couple married in the tradition of The Fellowship, by the preacher himself, received the grace of God's permission for creation. Those couples, committed to The Fellowship, relinquished half of their possessions to be held "in trust for the Creator," thus satisfying the ten percent will of the Lord and the forty percent needs of their leader.

Rachel, age sixteen, hid her pregnancy well until about the seventh month. Ed Wood, who'd broken bread himself with

Reverend Bordo, felt the will of the Creator calling for dismissal of this bastard child. He recruited Sarah, a midwife from The Fellowship, who once claimed Rachel's mother as her best friend, before she committed suicide. Sarah agreed to perform an abortion on the unworthy Rachel Wood, ridding her of this godless creature in her womb. Rachel, refusing to kill her baby, tried to run away from her father. He took her to the basement of their home, far from any paved road, and tied her arms and legs down on an old table he used to skin catfish. Rachel screamed and yelled and thrashed around, but he heard nothing once he left and shut the basement door behind him. Ed then took a moment to pride himself for building such a sound, insulated, sturdy home and caring for his little family so well.

When Sarah arrived, he escorted her down the basement steps, opened the door and found the child crowning between his daughter's legs. By the time Sarah unpacked her bag of instruments, Rachel pushed hard and spewed the baby upon the dried fish gut-covered table. She cried out loud, "I name him Abel. Give me my son."

Sarah looked at Ed, a fish cleaning knife curled in his hand. Eyes met, and Sarah stared harder. She pushed down his inclination, his arm bouncing like an impatient child.

The mother cuddled Abel in her arms while Sarah cut the cord and cleaned the mess.

Not knowing what to do at that point, Ed asked Sarah if she was willing to help. Locking Rachel and the baby inside, with a padlock on the basement door, they walked out into the front yard, and he led her in prayer. "Creator, we have failed you. You called upon us to curse sin, and yet sin lives in our home. Your faithful servant Sarah got tripped up by the devil, who delayed her and caused your will not to be done."

Ed carefully explained how God had taken Rachel's mother, but as a blessing sent Sarah to fulfill his needs. He mumbled some scripture about a man's place as head of the household. With the baby's cries muffled by basement walls, Ed removed Sarah's clothes in the desolated front yard and had his way with the midwife. After sex, he prayed again. "Lord, thank you for Sarah's blessing. Speak to her, Father. Show her your will for her to care for the sinner Rachel…and her sinful offspring. Talk to Sarah's heart not to blame herself for the devil's delay, but rather undo the devil's doing by staying here, paying your blessings on me, your faithful servant."

Feeling no choice, Sarah became the household caregiver and holder of the secret. The shame of Rachel and Abel would not be cast upon the home of Ed Wood. To the world, neither existed. Twice a week, Ed and Sarah attended services at The Fellowship. The fabricated story of Rachel's rude departure from her father's home, casting herself in a world of sin, caused arm-lifting to the heavens by fellow church members and pacified their curiosity.

***

Rachel and Abel lived in a locked basement, though living provisions came regularly and adequately. She grew tired of begging her father, and a woman she thought to be her dead mother's friend, to be released. All pleas were met with a twisted, morbid recitation of the Bible. So, she focused on Abel, the first two years flying by, keeping him healthy and mentally alert. Every childhood book her departed mother secreted into the house was stored in a large chest under her mother's clothes in the basement.

He learned to roll over, crawl, then walk in a dampened space devoid of sunlight, only lit by a globeless light fixture. Lye soap, musty rags, and brushes were thrown in disarray upon shelves above the fish-cleaning table. A twenty-foot by twenty-foot dungeon, with a leaking toilet and a dripping sink faucet, gave her means to clean her son, dispose of his waste, and scrub the emotional scum of what existed above them, off their skin.

But with all hours of the day to devote to her son, and so many books, his development progressed rapidly. Her heart ached trying to contain the love she so badly wanted to show Abel. Yet she felt as complete as a caged animal could feel.

Her son somehow filled a bottomless void. She whispered, "The color of your hair, the color of your eyes make me feel like I'm looking in a mirror, my beautiful child."

But elation with Abel's progress gave way to heat flashes, vertigo, and disorientation. Soon nothing seemed to matter.

***

Ed often went to a market where no one knew him, buying diapers, bottles, milk, and food for Rachel. Sarah would find medicine, baby clothes, and toiletries. Ed purposely left supplies in the same place every time, never venturing beyond the doorway, always locking back the thick, metal hasp.

Life for Ed went along the same as usual, going to work at the factory in Chafenville, coming home to eat what Sarah and the good Lord prepared, usually getting some flesh of God's gift of Sarah, watching the one television station available from rabbit-ear reception, and then bed. Twice a week he helped others from The Fellowship keep the commandments of Bordo. He owed nothing to the sinful wreckage in his basement below.

Ed got comfortable in his existence between a dungeon, work, spiritual services, and one slave-like sex partner. Sarah left him after a night of his demanding nonreciprocating acts that pushed her beyond tolerance. "God did *not* promise you this," she whispered, knees bent on the wooden bedroom floor. She never returned.

Ed thought of his wife, now dead. Rachel's mother. He met her at the church, a mere thirteen year old, breasts newly budding. By fourteen, with the help of the then young Preacher Bordo, who convinced the father to let Ed have this young, soft flesh, she became Ed's. Yet Ed shared her pleasures with Bordo. When Rachel was born Ed claimed her as his own. But between Ed's demands and sharing of the fruits of her loins, Rachel's mother committed suicide, throwing herself off a tall rock ridge. She was sixteen.

He continued to leave provisions inside the basement door, but one day found them untouched. He wandered into the room finding Abel standing up in a make-shift crib, pointing to his empty bottle, and Rachel lying in an old dresser of clothes owned by her mother. He felt her head, seemingly burning like eternal damnation, too weak to move.

He left Abel with a filled bottle, took his mother to The Fellowship, and asked them to pray over her, saying she had come home sick from living in a sinful commune out West for a few years. He begged his fellow worshipers, "Too distant for me to rescue, but the Lord brought her home, to our Fellowship. What would our God, our Reverend Bordo, ask us to do to heal my child?" Faith in numbers had more power than rich doctors and man-made medicine. Men lay their hands upon her, some groping her, in the name of the Creator.

Rachel partially recovered, but her heart was greatly damaged from her high fever. She slept upstairs and cared for Abel in the basement, her father never allowing her to bring him out. She lived for three more years, reaching her son's fifth birthday. In that time, she devoted her life to him in the basement, spending every ounce of energy left in her body, teaching him, talking to him, and showing him pictures of the world outside.

But the spirit of joy and laughter left her young body. She cried more and cursed the evil men who watched and touched her, warning Abel to beware of people who watch you too closely. "Evil is in their hearts, and they will steal your peace."

During the end of her waning life, she spent every moment crawling out of the bed and down the stairs, teaching him to care for himself. She talked to him about the people upstairs and insisted he rely only on himself. "Trust no one." Without Abel ever being outside, Rachel did her best to teach him what rain and sunshine felt like, the difference between city life and country life. Abel loved the pictures of the forest best. He loved the animals and never seemed to run out of questions. Abel was her sponge, soaking up every word, faithfully remembering.

***

Abel spent two days staring at her lifeless body, speaking her lessons as fluently as he could, coaxing her to respond, begging her back to life. His mother died. He knew this not from her ceased breathing, not from her unresponsive eyes, not from her cold flesh. *She spoke to him in his head. We are together, son.*

***

He cried, standing in the sunlight for the first time, as his grandfather dumped his mother's body into a deep hole in the back yard. Abel looked around, seeing trees and animals he recognized in books his mother had read to him as long as he could remember. But quickly his grandfather, a person he had heard, but had rarely seen during his short life, dragged him back into the house, down the steps, and into the dark room he knew as home. The door shut loudly, louder than usual, and the padlock rudely snapped.

The next day, his grandfather brought in a large dog cage and shoved Abel and his bedding and books in with him. After all, Abel had cost Ed his only daughter.

Abel, between calendars and rhymes his mother taught him, believed this day to be his birthday, the day of his mother being tossed in the ground. Sadness surrounded him in his familiar, dark room, now clouded by rusted steel bars, forming a tighter impoundment around him.

Ed Wood sat in front of the cage and shouted at his grandson that his mother was dead because he was a bad boy, and he made his mother sick trying to take care of him. Every day after work Ed sat in a chair in front of the cage, and watched Abel in confinement. Ed's eyes were relentlessly piercing, like sharp blades forged of evil slicing into Abel's soul. The fingernails, yellowed from chain smoking full-length Camel unfiltered cigarettes, clinched the wire of Abel's cage. Ed, a graying, greasy-headed man who called him grandson-from-hell, watched him eat and watched him sleep. Sometimes he would jab a long stick at him, drawing blood, and yell at him saying he was full of demons, "mother-killer-demons." But most of the time, he just watched him in silence. But the look in his eyes screamed louder than his cursing voice, his ugly teeth, and depraved hands.

Torment grew inside his shrinking cage and pressed harder upon his soul. Sleep gave escape from his nightmare. Awake, the agony seemed endless, a feeling of a slow drowning. In a flood of dark, black fear at the hands of his grandfather, her voice came to him again, soft as a whisper, smooth as his mama's silk touch. *You're never alone, Abel.* And then he wasn't.

***

Ed sat in a recliner chair in front of his television, with only one good channel. When he adjusted the antennas, sometimes adding aluminum foil, two other channels faded in and out. Life seemed simple and complicated at the same time. Kind of his throne above the basement below. Anger for Abel grew more pointed since Sarah left. He recalled the Reverend Bordo ministering to other men in The Fellowship as to their entitlement to their daughters as a part of God's grace. Sacrificial lambs, obeying your father, even the Golden Rule gave support to the Reverend's message that under proper circumstances, a daughter became her father's. The sacrificial part came upon a generous gift by the father to The Fellowship to receive the blessing of the Reverend, opening the door for the father to enjoy the fruits of his own offspring.

Ed toiled in a sweat-shop, a mill down in Chafenville. When he left work, headed for home, he crossed the Shady River negotiating his self-maintained pickup truck over a dilapidated wooden bridge hardly wide enough for two cars. Across the river, the bridge dumped him onto a gravel road, and he stared upward at the most horrendous rock-laden hills in Georgia. His old truck screamed like a scalded pig as it climbed, a nerve-racking ride. But as he pulled into the narrow road leading to his house, his disposition changed. He owned the castle.

Justification came to Ed when the undeniable, all knowing Reverend Bordo said life begins again at the fruit of your daughter. And when Ed had a hard day, and gave generously to The Fellowship, entitlement was earned.

But Ed soon learned Rachel not only nurtured Abel but taught him also. The jabs, both physical and mental, elicited clear, cogent, and persuasive responses from Abel. "Are you my grandfather?" He pointed to books. "Will you show me some squirrels? I saw them up there."

Ed decided to chain him outside, like a dog. With a thirty-foot leash, Abel gained freedom unknown before. The remoteness of Ed's house and the unlikely visitor posed little risk of Abel's backyard restraints ever being discovered, rain or shine.

***

Years passed as Abel developed animal instincts, animal agility, animal strength. But every day he thought over all his mother's teachings. In due time, he rock-scraped a link of the chain through, leaving a length of ten inches dangling from his neck. He escaped, nine years of age, caring nothing for what Ed Wood might think. Freedom. But he would always remember Ed.

***

Abel more than survived on the food that people left at the campground not far from the banks of the Shady River. He thrived, growing taller and stronger as he roamed the rocky hills which climbed up from the water to the ridge spreading out into an eternity to his eyes. A hard freedom, but freedom nonetheless. Outdoors, with no chain liberated his thinking, planning. Removing the metal collar around his neck caused some scars. But an open sky and woods full of unrestrained creatures stood as miracle payback for the pain.

But the horrors of the past wouldn't leave his mind or his mother's. And they agreed the future held no peace without resolution with Ed, but tension built between the two as to how. Mental chains of the past were more powerful than steel, locks, or pointed weapons. The basement, the chain, his grandfather, never left his thoughts. He often returned to the edge of the forest to look at the house of his dreaded roots, but never at night. The squirrels slept at night and so would he. For three years, he ate what the forest offered, took shelter that the forest offered, and learned every lesson the forest offered.

***

"Strange," Abel whispered to himself. A sunny day, Ed supposed to be at work, lying instead on his bed, sleeping, snoring. The window was open at the bottom, so Abel opened it a little wider and slid in with a long stick that looked a lot like the one Ed used to probe. Quick and light as the wind, Abel jumped on the bed and stood above Ed's head with his stick. He waited for Ed to awake and perched himself above the target as would an eagle. At first movement, he precisely aimed and stabbed an eye clear through his grandfather's brain, holding it steady and hard, waiting for the body to stop movement. Then he did the same with the other eye.

His mother's will prevailed, and he started to head back into the hills. But coming in the door, he heard voices. "The factory shift foreman said, "Ed didn't call, didn't show. Let's check out our Fellowship brother. Ed, how you doing?"

Abel froze. Men stood between him and the open window. They spotted Ed, the blood, the gore of missing eyes. A caged animal once again. Three men locked onto Abel's head and legs. Unable to move, he heard their panic.

"It's that crazed animal Ed keeps talking about in tongues at church, what we could never figure out."

"Yeah, something to do with Rachel, God's curse. Remember when we all laid our hands on her?"

"Shut up about that. We've got to get the preacher, the big preacher."

They spoke of what the boy might tell the police about their demon-removing tactics with his mother years ago, when she had her fever. "I've got one bar on my cell, I'm calling

Bordo." A moment went by with the man talking excitedly in the phone, until he slapped it shut.

"Bordo said get the boy to the church, quickly, quietly. Hold him until Bordo gets there himself."

***

The limo driver chauffeured Bordo through the mountains and into Chafenville. They crossed the narrow bridge in a sparkling, black Cadillac and started to climb a gravel road that provided passage up to the church. The whole trip had taken nearly four hours. Chris pulled down a mirror. His rich, thick black hair seemed in place. He smiled. Expensive dental work reflected smooth, caring upper and lower rows of white-pearled, passionate persuasion. An investment with uncountable returns. Then the eyes. Brown, sincere. He only hated his height, less than five and one-half feet, but felt he made up for it by lifting weights, carving his body into a pleasing shape for women. He slapped the mirror closed, he met the threshold for what lay ahead. This was a man's thing, not a sermon to persuade the faith of all. Mostly this consisted of damage control of a local branch of The Fellowship who needed the head minister's guiding touch. Chris exited the limo and watched the faithful nearly bow to him. "Take me to the child."

He found Abel tied up with rope in the confessional. Chris took a careful look, smiled genuinely at him, and pulled a candy bar from his pocket. "Son, I'm here to save you." He whirled in the direction of the men. "Untie this child." He lifted the boy from captivity, placed him gently into the back of the limo, and handed Abel the unwrapped candy. He gathered his faithful, told them to return to Ed's house, and call the police. "You will say you came to check on your sick friend, Ed Wood, and found him like this. Say nothing more, nothing less."

***

Abel shook with fear half the ride back to wherever the huge, black car was taking him. He shared the back seat, an area bigger than his cage, with a mild-mannered gentleman, the one giving him the first candy bar of his life.

"Calm yourself, my young friend. Tonight you sleep in your own bedroom, have whatever you want to eat or drink, and nobody will bother you."

Abel reflected on the last few hours. His animal instincts had failed him as he tried to fight off The Fellowship men after his accomplished murder. He drew upon his mother's teachings, the books, persuasion. "Thank you, Mr...."

"Call me 'Chris.' A bunch of folks have fancy names for me, but I'd like to be your friend, if that is alright with you."

Abel sat in silence.

The car pulled into a drive with big rock columns on both sides. Rocks didn't impress Abel, he'd roamed around much larger. But these were stacked straight, like on purpose. Then lights and big bushes the same size and a castle...bigger than the one in the beanstalk book...appeared like magic. Abel turned to his first friend. "Is there another one of those candy things in there?"

The Reverend laughed. "Yes, Abel, yes!"

And at the age of twelve, Abel found himself among the finest accommodations and the finest teachers, "home school teachers" they were called. Chris talked to him kindly, lovingly, reminding him of his mother. And to Abel, his dead mother left this earth with wings, like in the angel book, flying herself to a place far away from Ed, and he was pleased, and pleased to be in Chris' presence.

And even more, Chris satisfied animal needs: food, dry, warm, hunting opportunities. Chris also layered careful thinking, like his mother taught him. She spoke of how smart animals operate, the ones who survived, even though she never got out of the basement to show him. Abel thought of the forest animals, sharing his many daily hours in their woods. He liked Wood being his last name. He remembered watching slow worms, smart robins, slow rats, smart hawks. Abel liked birds. Everything that haunted him, giving him awful dreams, could have been avoided simply by being a bird. He took comfort that if he ever became a bird, he could see his mom in heaven.

Abel's teachers consistently praised his progress in subjects. This reinforcement fueled his desire to do more, do better. And he did. Teachers would eventually throw up their hands, after he absorbed all they had to teach and begged for more. His mind layered with facts, concepts, formula, and methods. Abel, at first, wanted Chris Bordo to know of his excellence. But time and thought brought him to a point of distrusting the man who brought him here.

***

Chris Bordo loved lavish living and kept most of his expensive follies out of the view of his flock. Piles of money flowing from The Fellowship chapters, along with other loyal worshipers around the globe, fueled his life style. His self-directed investments performed better than the S&P 500. Money placed in well-diversified accounts compounded nicely, returning rates hovering higher than the cliffs above the river where Abel's grandfather's church stood.

Rev. Bordo made a point to be kind and loving toward Abel, hoping to create a bond, good will with the boy. Bordo's lofty position in The Fellowship afforded him only involvement with the pleasantries of his organizations, and he no longer got his hands dirty with botched up abortions or suicides gone haywire, and seldom did anyone question him about his own affairs.

Chris' outpouring of affection for Abel seemed necessary, a child with too much baggage not to have his trust. He taught Abel to drive, which came in handy when Chris had parties. He would provide valet parking for certain guests, and by the age of thirteen, Abel could handle most any kind of car.

Abel was invited to mingle with many of Chris' guests, men of money, religion, agendas, from around the world, and join them for dinner. Abel seemed fascinated by the intellectual conversations he was allowed to hear, and Chris encouraged him to research the doctrine of FOF and world history in general. He would beam with pride as Abel amazed guests with his ease in relating to most any subject. Chris received daily reports that Abel was challenging his teachers with a passion for psychology, science, computer technology, and an all-too-well understanding of the Fellowship of Friends. Chris knew he'd made the right decision bringing the child from the depths of the mountains into the headquarters of The Fellowship.

***

By fourteen, Abel had completed all the high school curriculum. But the final years of college courses were taught by one teacher, Beth Cunningham. Unmarried, the daughter of a farmer, both parents deceased, Beth knew she was a perfect candidate to fill the job. She considered herself an academic overachiever and double majored in Education and Psychology. She graduated with highest honors from Western Carolina University, but returned to the farm house, now her inheritance.

She taught her tireless student everything he wanted to explore. The human brain interested him most. He wanted to know stuff about neglect, abuse, abandonment. He questioned her on how the roles of alcohol, drugs, and genetics played on the mind. She shared her knowledge, but sometimes felt another student sat beside him, even though the chair was empty.

Outside of the academic world, she felt hollow, inadequate to find a mate, inadequate to conquer a place in the business community. Her farm, her simplistic life, the Bordo job, suited her fine. But one young man lit a flame in her soul, and life suddenly had a pointed meaning.

Abel became her passion, and she let the other home school teachers know she wanted charge of him. Bordo acted like he considered the idea of Beth's exclusivity compelling. The other teachers, though loyal to the word of God, had issues with family or their own biblical interpretations. Beth wanted nothing but Bordo's occasional thanks, a paycheck, and freedom to teach Abel. So, this was allowed, and the other teachers left.

Each morning, Beth rolled her short, stubby body out of bed with the rising sun and splashed water over her rosy cheeks. With no makeup and a dress below her knees, she left her farm house no later than 7:00 a.m., drove to The Fellowship and stayed until 5:00 p.m. She knew Bordo's security people watched her come and go, *but so what?* Only trips to the grocery, Wednesday prayer meetings, and Sunday worship services interrupted her routine with Abel.

Beth knew little about how Abel came to live with Bordo and felt uncomfortable asking personal questions of her student. He often asked her questions, though the words seemed designed toward an alternative purpose. Often she felt a connection, as when Abel confessed to her about a troubled past and wanted her to teach him about deep psychological abnormalities, how they came about, and what became the consequences. She saw behind Abel's eyes a controlling figure, as if someone gave him permission to ask. *Like someone gave him permission to like me!*

She learned he hated eye contact, touching. He hated sitting anywhere he felt confined. Beth gave in to all requests, taught at a distance, never staring, never touching, never probing. But she loved him, harbored him in her heart as *her* son. As long as she had access, exclusive access to her pupil, she'd follow Abel's rules. And she taught him often and well. She exhausted resources from Brevard College and brought back volumes of hard-back and e-books. Abel read, discussed, and they debated over significant issues, particularly those involving the mind and human behavior. When he raised questions she couldn't answer, she made day trips to an old psychology professor who taught her graduate courses at Western Carolina University. No level of difficulty seemed unapproachable for her student, and he amazed her daily. But lessons were awkward. When not looking at a computer screen or a book page, she usually looked at an opposite wall, fighting to lock eyes with her pupil. *My son.*

***

Abel, in time, learned the layout of Bordo's carefully organized complex. Years of careful exploration provided interesting opportunities. A security-laden computer, on the Reverend's desk, was not one of them. He discussed this with Beth.

"Why does Chris, I mean Reverend Bordo, as you have to call him, have secret places?"

"Abel, we all have secret places. Some are under lock and key, like you describe the Reverend's. Some secrets are locked away in our minds, maybe our hearts. I have secrets hidden, do you?"

"I don't want to answer your question, so I won't."

"Why not?" She caught herself stealing a glance and looked toward the ceiling.

Wanting to avoid her question, he heard his mother's voice and knew he had to tell Beth something personal to get her help. "I do have a secret locked in my mind."

Beth leaned forward, gently. "I'm here for you. Will you share this secret with me?"

Abel hesitated until his mother stood straight up in his mind, placed her hands on her hips, and said, "Tell her now."

And Abel, for the first time in his life, shared the story of his past.

Beth cried, and Abel did not like the tears. "I told you these things because I need your help, not your sympathy."

She wiped her eyes, "Yes, anything."

"I have questions about the mind, my mind. We need, I mean, I need answers about a lot of things we have yet to talk about. Will you help me?"

"You know I will."

Abel's unending questions required Beth to spend her leisure time at home researching to prepare herself for the barrage of follow-up inquiries Abel posed each day. And she felt needed, alive beyond any calling before. She loved Abel Wood.

***

Abel's mind, consumed with all his mother wanted, looked across the room at Beth. You have taught us well."

She looked puzzled. "Us?"

He backed off, changed the subject. "Will you do me a favor?"

"Yes, I think."

This was the closest he had ever been, his eyes rested upon her as he spoke, and he actually felt comfortable. The comfort came from looking through his mother's eyes.

"What, Abel?"

"There is a file, a plain manila folder, behind the secretary's desk where you pick up your paycheck. I think it has a bunch of passwords, it says 'passwords.' I see it, but the secretary's always there, can't look in it. Will you get it? She wanders in and out when you're there, not when I'm there."

"Why Abel, what's so important?" She looked in his eyes.

He turned away, speaking at the ceiling. "I think some things about me might help me understand myself. All these things you have taught me about understanding and coping…all this psychology stuff from your university is about other people. I need my own answers."

Beth looked firmly away from him. "I'll help."

***

Abel sat in his usual seat, middle of the room, unconfined, when Beth walked in. "Here's the file, want to look at this together?"

He thought, carefully, manipulatively. "Okay."

The Westminster chimes, wired to the headquarters' speaker system, struck eight at night, three hours after when Beth usually left. Her uncashed paycheck in her pocket seemed inconsequential. Her desire to help Abel burned in her heart. "I should be getting home."

He looked through the file. "My guess is Chris' password for what I'd like to see is 'gravy.' Come look if you want…or go home."

"I'll go with you."

Abel smiled a bit mischievously. "Chris is out with his men friends. He gets sloppy when they visit. His office might be open."

Awkwardly, the two entered into the office, shut the door, and Abel fell back into the Reverend's high-back leather chair. Turning on the computer, the word "gravy" opened the desk top. He quickly accessed the documents he wanted upon entering the simple password, "chosen." He wondered why Chris couldn't remember "gravy" or "chosen." *Why write them down?*

Only one electronic file contained the name he searched for, "Abel." He clicked it. Beth stood behind him, no eye contact.

***

7:00 a.m., the next morning, Beth drove her car, a '97 Taurus, inherited with the farm, into The Fellowship complex. She was greeted by the Reverend himself.

"Good morning, Beth, how are you?"

"Well, and yourself, Reverend?"

Angrily Bordo moved in closer, and spoke quietly. "I'm not here to chit chat. Appears you were here a bit late last night. We *do* have video all around this place in case you haven't noticed."

"Abel and I worked late, trying to finish up the higher learning…what you mandated I do."

Bordo stepped closer, rudely. "I mandated nothing of you snooping around my private business. Go home, you're fired."

Beth's head felt about to explode. "I am Abel's teacher."

"You were."

"I will always be."

"I'll get the guards…they'll show you out."

Beth backed away and raised her voice. "Not so fast."

"What? You want to be thrown out?"

"I want to be left alone, to do my job, you'd better not push your luck."

"I don't need luck, what in the name of Christ are you rambling about?"

"You'll need plenty of luck when I tell the authorities your story."

"My story? You have nothing."

"I have plenty, and know exactly what you've done. You committed adultery with Abel's grandmother, fathering Abel's mother. Then Abel's grandfather screwed, or should I say raped, Abel's mother, fathering Abel. You are a sick, sick man, and Abel needs to be with me…a Christian woman who can counsel him past all of your sins, your stupidity. No, I dare say I'm not fired, or I go to the police authorities. I want Abel...what's it going to be?"

Bordo shifted into a calming voice, looked around, and lowered puppy dog-looking eyes in her direction. "You are absolutely right, Beth. Abel needs you. Let's go get him together."

He lightly touched Beth's arm, leading her to the steps up to the area where she tutored Abel. She winced at his touch but felt relieved, vindicated. The only thing left in her life was Abel, and she would keep him under her own terms. She regretted using the word "screw," but anger had gotten the better of her.

They stepped upon the top step together, and Reverend Bordo stopped, pivoted around her, and moved his mouth close to her ear, whispering. "Look over this lovely landscaped wonder of nature, consider the quality of life you've had with Abel." He grabbed her firmly underneath both elbows. "Then consider your disgrace to your God and to me." He propelled her upward, outward, over the rail, and her body succumbed to gravity, forty feet of it. She struck iron, concrete, then the earth itself.

***

Abel eased out of bed and dressed. Beth should be knocking on his door soon. He heard Chris yelling to security for help. The voice seemed out of control, unusual for the man who sometimes claimed to be his savior. He stumbled out of the patio door of his room, to the balcony rail, and gazed onto the lawn below. Beth lay bleeding, crying, helpless. He descended the steps by threes, then stepped slowly, carefully moving toward her.

Their eyes met, uncomfortable for Abel, infinite for Beth. "My young prince, do you know I love you?"

He felt obligated to nod his head. He was not sure he loved this woman. He did not want to see her eyes. But she had taught him. She was the constant in his place of food and shelter, shelter much bigger than a cage.

Then he realized she was hurt, fading. Blood gushed from her mouth, choking back words she tried to speak. But he already knew and spoke the words for her. "Don't leave me." She nodded her head, confirming what he said. But she struggled to say more and took a deep breath. "Your Chris did this to me. I tried to protect you, he knows I know…about your father, grandfather, that monster. Abel, tell the authorities he killed me and protect yourself at all costs. Don't ever let Chris hurt you."

Beth died, not in his arms, but near. He didn't look in her eyes. He placed two fingers over her deathly, open eyes, and closed them. He didn't understand tears, but he felt the need to cry, as Beth had for him. But his mother shouted to him: *don't be weak, don't cry.* So, he shed none. But he wished deeply, passionately for Beth to stay with him. Then he called the police.

***

Sirens, lights, and loud policemen stormed the complex. Abel hid the file but gave the authorities a short, concise summary of why Chris Bordo killed Beth Cunningham. "He asked her for sex, she refused, he killed her, I watched the whole thing."

He returned to his room. Outside, Bordo shouted denials in chain reaction, from alibi to no motive, to his Christian commitment, to the commandment thou shalt not kill. The authorities conducting the interrogation seemed to be losing.

Then, in quieter voices, he heard protective service people talking of his fate outside the patio door.

"We know nothing about him. There's no file. He looks to be sixteen and, unless we find a relative, he'll go to a foster home, crammed into a room with a bunch of young thugs, like a cage."

Panic struck. Thoughts ran rapidly through his head. He owed Beth. Justice to her killer. His testimony would be necessary for a conviction. Without him, Bordo keeps doing what Bordo does. *But back to a cage?*

Close to staying, carrying out what he started with the police, Abel heard a voice. It came up without warning, a voice in his head never heard before…not his mother's. And the voice clearly lacked the strength of his mother, but it was clear all the same.

"Run, Abel, run."

Abel needed to hear nothing more. He grabbed a few things from his room, raided a safe in the church office, climbed a security wall on the rear of the complex, and escaped. He wanted no cage. He would walk home to the hills rising above Chafenville, a place where no one could find him. As he walked, he thought of Beth, but the last look she begged from his eyes bothered him. *She is not my mother.* He'd watched Beth die the way it appeared a buck might watch a wolf kill his doe, look momentarily and quickly leave. Nature. But contrary to where nature would have left things, Beth remained in his head. Beth yelled *run.*

His anger welled up in the truth of Beth's death and the convoluted way Bordo had fathered him. But cages and eyes and prodding with sticks bothered him the most. He would miss the free meals, miss Beth's lessons, but craved the freedom of his hills...a hundred miles away. He felt his back pocket, packed with money from The Fellowship. And more valuable than the money stuffed in his pocket was the knowledge filling his brain with the countless hours of study under Beth's direction. He owed her, but couldn't grasp a way to pay...the way a turtle, stranded in traffic, couldn't thank the one who picked it up, turned it over, and moved it to the side of the road. Another chance. And Beth, *oh Beth,* he tried to dismiss her from his mind. *Maybe she cared as much as my mother. I might still find out.*

Chapter Five

July 2012

Abel reunited with the land of his past. With no professional surveyors in the area, the understanding of the terrain was basically local knowledge. He knew the land as well as anyone, often coming across caves he believed few knew existed. Over the years, some of those places of solitude had become Abel's sanctuary.

He felt for the third time the money awkwardly bulging in his pocket and decided to hide it in the back of a cave. Recurring thoughts of Beth, his teacher, crept into his mind. Psychology, religion, candid conversations. While his mind wouldn't let Beth go, his own self-doubts channeled into anger against people as a whole.

Freedom. The woods breathed his right to exist. This wilderness held the only civilization he believed he needed. Eyes watched, but they were good eyes. His homecoming to birds, squirrels, deer, and raccoons sealed the completeness of his solitude among the hills and rocks.

Though his head exploded with teachings of Beth, he pushed them aside, made a primitive bow and arrow, and began to hunt. At first the unwanted - rats, moles, coons, possums - filled his belly. But a few deer, taken without guilt, soon became the golden-brown feast rotating above the open campfire.

A hollowed-out log, as comfortable as any lawn chair, held Abel's body at a comfortable distance to the raging fire. The realization that, perhaps, the finest of all meat sat in reach of his knife. But lustful thoughts of flesh also slithered into his list of wants. His body longed for things he once cared nothing for, and he kept these needs away from other voices in his mind.

***

Chafenville beamed its attention to Abel, standing on the far bank of the Shady River. When his mother lived, she told him of a downtown park. He intended on checking it out, but Ed's killing and Bordo's taking him away put an end to that. He hated Bordo. *The bastard is a rapist, creator, and destroyer of everything meaningful in my life...the man who took me away with a candy bar.*

The lights across the river looked better this night than the quiet hills behind him, and Abel swam across. His shirt and pants dripped going into the park. He sat with the best view, away from the most people, and watched a clown doing tricks at sunset. Fragile globes rose up from the clown's hand-cranked bubble machine, captured by the last rays of the day. Hundreds of peaceful, carefree bubbles filled the air with a gleaming beauty each to itself.

The magnetic force of the evening, the lost sun, the symmetry of streets scared him back to the river's edge. Swimming across in the fog-covered blackened water, he jumped up on the far bank and stared at the 1000 feet of elevation yet to climb. He attacked the mountain with no hesitation, *Abel's hill*. He settled back into the comfort of nature, self-fulfilling, self-controlling. He slept.

When it rained, he had his caves; clear skies brought him out under the stars. Either way, the same satisfaction, night after night.

He watched animals mate. The computer at Bordo's place, no longer available, deprived him of his nature to Google, an open invitation to hunt with words instead of bows. Thoughts of the rituals of animals he watched mating, things he felt inside, and upon his own body, weighed heavy. So, he cleaned himself, shaved with a sharp blade, and put on a clean set of clothes he'd bought at a trading post a few miles from where he slept.

Rather than swimming, arriving at the banks of Chafenville dripping wet, he found a deserted Jon boat, patched its holes, made a paddle, and crossed the river. When he landed on the other side, he pulled the boat up in the weeds to be hidden. He spotted a large pipe appearing to be coming from the direction of the park, and decided to explore. The pipe was huge, nearly six feet in diameter. He popped out of a vertical grate, and found himself near the performing clown. He walked past the bubbles, only hesitating to swat one, and left the park. He felt sexual.

Downtown Chafenville gaudily glowed with a sinful hue he remembered, feared, and now sought. *My body talks to me.* He decided to stroll around, see what the night offered. A neon light flashed "Gentlemen Welcome."

A lady approached, lipsticked up. "Want to have some fun?"

Abel hesitated. Confused, he turned away, hearing her make some comment about his tight ass and what she'd do with it. Two blocks over, the buildings got taller, all with government names, all closed, except one: the Chafenville Public Library. He stopped.

The clean glass doors gave view to a line of computers. *Oh my God*, he thought. Google, CreamyGirls.com, the website he'd scanned when all had left the Bordo offices. The technology not used in months jumped forward in his mind. *I don't know if I believe in God, and I don't think that way except when I'm Googling.*

He pushed through the doors, three computers on his left. Three girls near his age, the best he could tell, were checking him out, hard. He headed for the computer furthest away.

"Firewalls," he mumbled under his breath. He quickly reflected on his self-taught training, with some help from Beth and an I.T. person he got to know at The Fellowship headquarters. He broke through with a few key strokes and had an open view of the WWW.

He found an independence, not unlike the woods, only him and his screen. He went for porn. Lust without introductions, sex without talk, completion without any debt. Like watching the animals, only closer, and the parts were like Abel's. Air conditioning of the building cooled his rising temperature. He leaned back in his chair, relaxed, hard.

"Son, turn it off, we don't allow this sort of thing."

Abel turned, pushing the front of his pants down, and stared at a policeman, fat, grinning. "Boy, you'd better put a leash on that thing."

Abel said nothing, rose, and started walking toward the glass entrance doors.

The officer grabbed him by the arm and, without warning, slapped a pair of handcuffs around his wrists. "Not so fast. You can't dance into this place, pull up your jollies on the porn screen in a public library...especially in front of bunch of gals...especially when one of their mothers picks 'em up and spies your skin flicks." The fat policeman, holding Abel by the shirt collar, laughed hard, grabbed his belly, until he could talk again. He lowered his voice. "Look, young fellow, I'm here because that mother screamed at the librarian until she called 911...and I got the call."

He pulled Abel out through the door, down the steps, and toward the blue blazing lights on top of the patrol car. "Now that we're outside, I'm gonna tell you something. I don't give a rat's ass about you sniffin' a little pussy on the computer screen. But I got rules to follow. So, what's your name, Mr. Talkative?"

Abel continued his constant silence, trying to predict where this was headed.

"I told you to tell me your name, dumb ass." The guy Abel thought of as *fat and stupid* pulled his pants up and over the bulge of his waist and screamed, "Guess what, Can't Talk, you've pissed me off. I could have taken you home to your parents, made a little speech about causing a little disturbance in the library, and left to catch some real criminals. But noooooo! You have to be a snotty-nosed juvenile. So, that's where you go…to the station house. Got anything to say now?"

A minute passed in silence as the patrol car made its way through downtown traffic. "That's what I thought, so it's hopeless to ask your age, address, why you like naked women, right? Or were you lookin' at that really weird stuff?" The fat cop snickered, bouncing up and down in the driver's seat.

Abel kept his silence. Without a name, address, Social Security number, he couldn't be connected to his hills, the ones he longed for, or his murder. Common sense. Wait for a break, then run. No way to trace him.

A call came over the police radio. "A shooting, stabbing, melee, over on Green Street. Can you respond?"

The fat officer answered. "Call that psycho, shrink, whatever we call that broad that figures out screwed-up juvies, 'cause I sure as hell got one here. I'll drop him off in front of the station. Tell her to meet me. Then I'm gonna bust some heads over on Green Street."

***

Abel, pushed out of the car by the fat cop and still wearing his handcuffs, stumbled upon the sidewalk. A kind-looking lady laid her hands on his shoulder. "You look hungry. Let's get some supper."

He considered running with the handcuffs, but he couldn't paddle the boat, couldn't swim, and remembered the scars around his hands and neck from an earlier time. Instead, he followed her into the station house, not wanting to risk more fat cops.

She opened a door labeled "Observation" and took a seat in a room about twice the size of his cage in the basement of the home of his grandfather, now known to be his father. Abel fidgeted in his chair, not wanting to share the eyes of this woman. But her voice was soft, pleasant to his ears, not unlike his mother's, not unlike Beth's. She summoned an officer outside the door, who removed the handcuffs, gave him a plastic tray of food, and left them alone.

He figured her to be in her early thirties. Her wavy, brown hair fell neatly around her shoulders. A white lab coat covered loosely what appeared to be shapely, well-developed breasts. Tailored black slacks highlighted long, nice, well-toned legs. A pretty lady, not unlike the ones on the computer.

"My name is Marilyn Thomas, a social worker. I hope to be of help to you. May I ask your name?"

Abel stuck to his reluctance to give clues about himself. In his silence, he contemplated his stupidity of thinking he was in the woods while he sat at the computer in the library, blocking out the people around him. He questioned his impulsiveness in coming to town in the first place and thought of his boat, his hills, his bed made of wood and pine straw, his hidden money.

He glanced at the ceiling, away from Marilyn, and acted unresponsive, disengaged with his environment. Psychology

201 well digested in his mental banks from Beth's teachings, *Autism A to Z*, one of their favorite books, became his blueprint for responding to this social worker. He loved acting withdrawn. Silence became Abel's MO, and he delighted in Marilyn's not knowing whether he was deaf, defiant, or traumatized. Unfortunately, this silence forced her to take him to child services and place him in protective custody for the night. The officer appeared and slapped the cuffs back onto his wrists, again, without warning, depriving him of a meaningful chance of escape.

Tightening places: jail, the room in which Marilyn interviewed him, the threat of what people in authority kept calling "foster homes." Abel wanted none of the confinement and especially none of the piercing eyes. But as he looked around, cages of unknown dimensions surrounded him. Captivity jerked his wilderness and freedom from his life's fabric. *I've caged myself.*

He spent a night in an unknown house, locked in a bedroom. He stretched out across a musty-smelling bed and concluded, as sure as gravity, what pulled a baby bird not yet able to fly crashing to the ground, that he was headed to jail. He'd promised his mother in the basement no longer to be a baby bird. The promise now had meaning.

The next day, the officers removed him from his locked bedroom, gave him a ride back to the police station, took his finger prints, and led him to the same observation room, the same chair, and left him to wait for Marilyn. She had a relaxed way about her, almost likable. But the circumstances precluded anything to like, and Abel's mother's voice cautioned him, reminding him Marilyn held captive power over him and, he suspected, would use her eyes against him. She was likely no better than the father he murdered.

She entered the space from the other side of the room in the direction his chair was pointed. Smiling gently, she eased into the empty chair facing him. "Young man, I'm going to give you some tests. The first one doesn't require you to talk. In fact, even if you don't hear that well, you can attempt this test by looking at the words and pictures. Our little test will give me an idea of your level of intelligence.

Abel knew this test, WISC, developed by some guy named Wechsler. Beth taught its fundamentals, actually gave him the test. He remembered thinking how much he'd like to have administered it to the men who captured him after Ed's eyes could no longer gaze at him. *Idiots.* They'd have scored in the 70s. Abel scored 140, genius.

He smiled inside and nodded his head ever so slightly to give her an unconfirmable reaction. With that, she discussed the second test. "Then I'll give you another test that will measure your grade level for academic achievement. Again, you don't have to talk, merely push buttons on a computer screen, similar to the ones you used on the computer in the library. She raised her eyebrows. "Remember that?"

Woodcock-Johnson, a basic tool to measure academic achievement. He and Beth gave it to each other, a year apart. She scored higher the first time, he the second. He wished she lived outside of his mind, to appreciate what lay before him. But on second thought, Beth knew. As his mother knew.

Abel began to relish what was about to happen, knowing he would not talk and only push buttons. The games began. He deviated only once from the plan.

***

Marilyn retreated from the observation room, stunned, looking for a phone to share her miracle. She called her closest colleague, John Winthrop. "I've got my perfect case study sitting right on my lap. You're going to love this."

"Your lap? Tell me, please, my love."

"Stop it, John. Figuratively on my lap. Professionally, I've never seen anything like it. But you, your education, hours in research, maybe this is fundamental, simple for you…"

"Slow down, Marilyn. Explain your dilemma."

"He scored a 46 IQ on the WISC, no question. As a backup, I've used the Woodcock-Johnson. He took it willingly, looked like he concentrated, gave an honest try, probably K-4, no better than a 1.5 grade level. He's clearly intellectually disabled, no matter how you crunch the numbers."

"How old is the subject?"

"He won't say, my guess is seventeen or thereabouts."

"What's so compelling about mental disabilities? We deal with it all the time."

"He asked if I had a medical license."

"What?"

"After the test, I explained who I was, what I could do to help him, and mentioned my extensive training and ability to make a diagnosis. I was humoring myself, knowing this kid had no clue what I was saying, so I stretched my credentials a bit. That's when he asked me the M.D. question."

"Marilyn, I'm floored. Surely you misunderstood him."

"No, in fact those words were the only thing he said the entire interview, the entire testing, where he only pushed buttons. He wanted to know if I was a doctor."

"And since you're not, you think he challenged you? How could a severely…what we'd call imbecile a couple of decades ago…have the mindset to take a jab at your level of expertise?"

"My point exactly."

"I'm coming over. Where are you?"

"Police station."

***

Marilyn sat in the connecting alcove from the observation room, where the subject sat, still locked in from both sides. John Winthrop entered the alcove abruptly, confidently. His heavy frame filled the doorway as he authoritatively nodded his head, covered with wavy long blond hair. She stood, almost like obligated to acknowledge his omnipotent presence.

They settled into their chairs, and John requested complete details of Marilyn's encounter from the beginning. "Leave nothing out."

When Marilyn finished, he cleared his throat. "Verbatim, what words did he use to complete the only sentence you heard?"

"'Are you a medical doctor?' Best I can remember."

John slapped his hand across his knee and smiled. "Quite explainable, my love, you were wearing a white coat, looked like an M.D."

She looked at the floor, nearly embarrassed.   "I left something out."

"What? Why am I here?"

"He ended his question by adding, '…or just a doctor of drama?'"

John jumped from his seat. "Nooo, not a chance. Unless."

"Unless what?"

"Unless he's manipulating the assessment process to keep us in the dark."

"You make this sound like a game. Maybe he's nothing more than a disturbed kid who got caught with his hands down his pants in the public library."

"Don't be so simplistic, Dear. If I take you at your word, what this kid said to you, he cunningly formed the diagnosis and played it out for your professional approval."

"I don't get what you're saying."

"He may be a con artist...in a patient sort of way. Remember we *are* sitting in a police station."

Marilyn scratched her head, feeling uneasy about her evaluation. "But, John, what if my test results are correct, and he performs on the level of severe retardation? My diagnosis *is* based on standardized testing."

"Marilyn, slow down. What do you mean, *your* diagnosis? Remember, and I mean you no offense, you aren't licensed to make a diagnosis. In fact, these tests you just administered are legally and necessarily *my* tests, done under *my* supervision, leading to *my* diagnosis. Are we clear, Madame Social Worker?"

"Quite clear. Funny how I do these tests all the time, with little input and without any objection from you. Then something big pops up, and it's all about you. Remember, I was there, you were not."

"Now, now, Marilyn. Keep your professional emotions intact and consider this: "Your reliance of the standardized tests leaves us helplessly searching for an explanation for his comments which assume a knowledge of medical licensure and dramatic productions. Unfortunately, Marilyn, you are the only one who heard him, neither the WISC nor W-J can verify our suspicions."

"So, what do you propose?"

"First, I'd like to review all the test results."

***

John spent an hour shifting through the electronic data. He looked up. "Interesting."

"John, that's where I need you, your expertise, your guidance."

"Fair enough. Your tests indicate he is severely mentally challenged; his statement to you shows a degree of brilliance. One of three things must exist. One, as your standardized tests show, he is intellectually disabled and the statement you remember was a fluke, not medically significant....or, two, based on his statement to you, he is rather smart and has manipulated the tests, quite a difficult thing to do...or three, his brain has sustained a traumatic injury, rendering a psychological profile that is abnormally complicated."

Marilyn sat and moved to the edge of her chair. "Meaning what?"

"I'm not prepared to say right now." John gave a wicked smile. "But the possibilities are exciting."

"Care to share?"

"Perhaps. But take a deep breath. I'm about to tell you something which is formulating in my mind as we speak. What if he is an autistic savant?"

"You didn't teach me much about that at Chafenville Tech. Fill me in."

"Before I do, you make one great point. I've never met our new friend."

***

Abel, sitting in a room painted pastel for a calming effect, felt nothing the color intended. Instead, his ears focused on the voices in the room beyond, which rose in the excitement of discussing *him*. He heard everything.

"Marilyn, before we meet the patient, come here."

The muffled noise sounded like people having foreplay, some romantic interlude, and Abel was confused. But he had to suppress his laugh at Marilyn's next comment.

"John, after he spoke, I had to leave, get some space, digest this information. But as I left, he smiled the craziest smile, like he loved jerking my chain."

"I'm about to make some notes, my princess. Okay, we know he can hear, or how could he know to respond to your overstated credentials. We know he can verbalize; he talked to you."

"True, true. Well, the hearing part technically is an assumption, a very well-based assumption since he took the test, pushed the buttons."

Playful noises preceded John's response. "We'll know more, in a bit, about the quality of his hearing. Put that bag in the trash over by the outside of the door behind the patient. I'll massage you while you retrieve it."

"Get your hands off my boobs.   This kid, although you've never met him, scored way below anything that a court of law would allow the prosecution to convict. Bottom line is he's incompetent. Incompetent to commit a crime, incompetent to be convicted. The legal folks call it the M'Naghten Rule."

"I taught you the M'Naghten rule, remember. But for the sake of verifying my teaching ability, refresh my memory of this subject matter while I refresh myself on your boobs."

"The M'Naghten rule, still good law in these parts, says....ohh...a little easier on the nipples...that one who cannot appreciate the nature of his wrong can't be convicted."

"I'm appreciating the nature of these luscious nipples, what does that make me guilty of?"

***

Abel thought of his mother and what she said of faith. He thought of Beth and what she said of psychology and those who practiced it. He thought of Marilyn and wondered why he ever became interested in nipples. He thought of the M'Naghten rule....no appreciation of what went wrong...which justified his plan.

***

Marilyn and John entered the room. The man looked to be about forty-five, and, to Abel, the man dripped contempt from every pore in his body. His blond hair looked to be bleached.

They both smiled, hers sincere, his distrustful. Didn't matter, he viewed them the same, hurtful. He took a deep breath, leaned back in his seat, and waited for things to develop.

Knowing he would remain mute but wanting to have a little fun, Abel reflected once again on one of Beth's lessons. She had a copy of a Charles Darwin publication, *The Expression of the Emotions in Man and Animals.* He recalled the scientific research on nonverbal communication and behavior and remembered how he and Beth laughed about how animals and people differ so little in the way they related to each other nonverbally. *Even these two will be able to figure out what I mean through my head motion, posture, and facial expression. But they will get nothing through my eyes.*

***

John spoke first. "We don't know your name, but I suspect you do." He leaned closer, sharing his eyes, improving his smile. "My name is John Winthrop and I am a medical doctor." He turned to his assistant. "And, of course, you know Marilyn. We are here to help. Would it be okay to know your name?"

Abel sat. Still. Unresponsive.

Marilyn broke the silence. "Earlier, not long ago, we talked, did a test. I must say you were quite cooperative. You pushed buttons like a smart, helpful kind of person. In fact, I thought of you as a friend."

Abel, still somewhat reclined in his chair, opened his eyes a bit wider, exposing them to his interrogators. John Winthrop looked encouraged.

"Young man, and I don't mean any offense by calling you that, but I see some greatness in your eyes, think maybe you understand things." John gave a playful laugh and slapped his knee. "Maybe better than I understand things myself."

Abel hated this man. Abel loved his weakness. When Marilyn injected this man into the interview room, the space had grown even tighter. Abel almost felt sorry for her, considering she'd attached her emotions to what might be a death wish. He didn't think this on purpose, but considering what brewed in his mind, and the minds in his head, he feared John Winthrop's future. He hoped Marilyn could divorce herself from this downward spiral. But this was Marilyn's decision, and not his responsibility. He had enough on his mind.

The interview continued. He reflected once again on Beth's lessons and chose a series of nonverbal responses, beginning with pulling on his left ear every time he wanted the therapists to think the question made him uncomfortable and raising his eyebrows every time he wanted to project agreement.

Questions rotated between the two trying to dissect his mind. He found entertainment with the satisfaction beaming from their faces with perceived craftiness below the surface of each question.

"We can have you fingerprinted, throw it out into police cyberspace, know your name before the day's over. Why not tell us now?"

"We know you know computers. You broke through the firewall in the library. Where did you learn this?"

"You asked Marilyn was she an M.D.; we know you can hear, right?"

Then Abel waited for the obvious. He figured these two, as brilliant as they considered themselves, would have waited longer and approached him in a less predictable way. Marilyn rose, disappeared behind the door in front of Abel while John busily asked more questions, distracting him from any noise behind. When the paper bag, filled with air, exploded inches behind his head, he didn't flinch. He slowly raised his eyebrows as Marilyn walked around him and took her seat again.

John spoke again. "Are you deaf?"

Abel pulled his ear.

The session ended, and the therapists retreated to their room for discussions. This time their voices seemed lower, controlled, muffled.

John spoke first. "Damnedest thing I've ever encountered. I want to personally retest him, but this time, I'm hooking him up to a polygraph. Even this piss-ant police station must have one. Call the chief, get him hooked up. If he's jerking us around, I'll know."

Abel weighed his options. The door in front of him was locked; he heard the click. The one behind him, however, unlocked. Marilyn forgot about it after her failed bag pop. But police roam all over the station, and even without handcuffs, he might not escape. The M'Naghten rule made his decision. He'd overheard the plan, he knew the challenge. Funny thing was that Bordo, not Beth, taught him about the polygraph. The good reverend thought it wise to train those in his complex about avoiding deception if the test was ever administered by authorities trying to tap into what happened on the premises. The concept simple…ignore the question…think a question to justify your answer. The truth being in your own thought process.

But Abel answered no questions verbally, only pushed buttons. The concept taught by the reverend would have to cover nonverbal answers as well. *Well at least this day will not be boring. Bring it on, Doctor John Winthrop.*

A detective set up the machine and sat behind Abel. John and Marilyn entered through the opposite door. John took charge. The tests lasted two hours. And the polygraph operator, the test giver, and his assistant left the room. And Abel stayed seated, his ears tuned.

***

Marilyn collapsed in a chair in the alcove outside the observation room and confronted John. "The lie detector guy never raised his hands to indicate deception. He scored exactly, exactly what he scored when I gave him the test."

John sat in the other chair. Damnedest thing I've ever seen. You sure he said what he said...about the drama queen stuff? But for that claim, there's nothing remarkable about this severely diminished mind."

"Don't question me, John. I swear he said it."

"I trust you...only wish I'd been present. A well-trained eye might have lent some help to understanding our quandary."

Marilyn rose from her seat, crossed her arms, and glared at the superior being talking down to her. "So, Doctor Winthrop, which of your three possibilities fits?"

"Savant syndrome...I think...which is terribly exciting. I'm so glad you stumbled into this young man. A psychiatrist rarely gets this kind of opportunity."

"John, Sweetheart, this is rich, tantalizing, what we strive a lifetime to analyze. Care to be my consult?"

"Yes, yes, yes!"

"Lower your voice, this *is* the police department, though we *do* have privacy. Damn, I'm excited." He unbuckled his belt, pulled down his pants, and shifted to the front of his chair. "Anything we can do quickly?"

After the emotion died down, John took a serious look at Marilyn. He chose his words slowly, carefully, and delivered them in a near whisper. "As you know, I gave up my professorship and lost my tenure at U.T. two years ago. I claimed I needed a career change, made everybody around Chafenville think my decision to teach at Chafenville Tech, a school for buffoons, had something to do with benevolence."

"Buffoons? Remember me, your student?"

"Sorry, Babe. You broke the mold, justified my efforts. You know the others I'm talking about."

"Got it, John. So, go on."

"Truth is, Marilyn, I lied, got fired at Tennessee for a bunch of made-up crap...politics."

"John, I never knew."

"Worse day of my life. On the way out those idiots had the nerve to call me "Sigmund Fraud.""

"Horrible thing to call you...and with all you'd accomplished?"

"True, and the sad thing is I'm one hell of a researcher, teacher, have a passion for our profession. I'm a psychologist, the full Ph.D., loaded with certificates, degrees, awards. Hell, my classmates called me Sigmund, but for the right reasons...a genius. Then, after all that, I got in medical school, my damned M.D., a full psychiatrist. That all went down the toilet when some ambitious grad student claimed I...well let's not get into that. Some thought it sour grapes. I knew it to be sour grapes."

"John, why are you telling me this now?"

John lowered his eyes, locked them on Marilyn's, dropped to one knee, and held her hands. "This case will catapult me over the Tennessee River, over the arrogant

University of Tennessee, and will likely land me in Ivy League. I'm talking plush vacations at Martha's Vineyard, not camping out in the Smoky Mountains."

"Slow down, John, aren't you jumping to conclusions? Let's talk about our patient. What do you think?"

"I suspect we have a bona fide savant syndrome of super proportions."

"Say that again."

"You know, like autism accompanied by what Treffert called an 'island of genius.' The profession has gravitated to the term 'savant syndrome,' but it means the same, a defective mind with brilliance showing in a limited way."

"But you diagnosed him 'super savant syndrome.'"

"Yes I did! You have no idea how big this is...a new, expanded discovery, and I just named it...super savant syndrome...SSS....maybe my jealous colleagues will call it tri-S or triple S. This is so damned exciting."

"You act like this is all you. I seem to recall this is my patient; you are *my* consult."

John regrouped, walked around Marilyn, ran his fingers through her hair, and let his lips fall upon her ear. "Who do you think I want by my side on the shores of New England? Who do you think has kept me here in this podunk town for so long? Who have I come to love, both in heart and mind? You, my love. You'll be my partner, every step up the ladder of success."

Marilyn turned, hugged this well-educated man, one she had a crush on. And her new patient seemed just the trick to seal his affection, like her golden knight, carrying her away from a town she as well considered a dead end. Life looked promising.

She looked up into his eyes. "Let's dismiss our patient for the night. Then we've got to figure out how to keep him under our care. I suspect given liberty, he'll walk away, may never see him again."

John dropped his arms from her shoulders and lowered his voice. "Damn, you're right. Based on what you've told me, he's really committed no crime and neither of us has seen any violence."

Marilyn lowered her voice also. "He's hardly said a word, could be deaf or hard of hearing. I'm surprised the cop didn't cut him loose when he confronted him at the library."

"You're right again. That cop got you involved instead of taking him straight home or dumping him off on the curb outside the library with a 'don't jack off in public' reprimand. With no history, and the kid not talking, I'm surprised he didn't take him to the local ER, for a psych evaluation. But you know what, those moonlighting ER docs would have determined, without a whole lot of thought, he posed no threat to himself or society. They would have cut him loose, this patient would never have made it to the psych ward, the fourth floor, my floor. Marilyn, we got lucky."

"Lucky how?"

"Lucky a lazy ass cop picked him up at the library, didn't want to fill out all that paper work to get him evaluated, knew one phone call from the station house would let him dump the kid in your arms. Again, our luck. Trust me, this town, Social Services, will not hold our patient long. Our time may be limited."

"What do we do, John?"

"Tricky. Social Services, and you know those folks only want the abused ones, won't see this boy like that. I'll have to be proactive."

"Meaning what?"

"I'll talk to the director, but my guess is I'll have to go to the Probate Judge. Stay tuned, my love."

John rose and motioned Marilyn toward the door where Abel sat waiting inside. Let's excuse our patient."

***

Abel watched the two resume their seats in front of him, looking entitled, more possessive than at their earlier entrance. John spoke first. "Since we still don't know your name, or much about you at all, you'll remain a guest in the home you visited last night. Hopefully, we'll have another nice chat tomorrow. Does this suit you?"

Both looked at him hard, waiting for a response. He reached for his left ear, but, instead, wiped his hand across his nose. They looked confused, almost disappointed the ear pull had not happened. Then they disappeared through the same door. Abel waited for his ride.

***

John met Ginger Eber, the director of Social Services, on the steps of the foster home, a mere eight feet from Abel's nailed-shut window. She looked agitated and a slight sweat beaded above her upper lip.

"Doctor Winthrop, this is highly irregular. You have a juvenile who, according to police, is charged with no crime. No parent has come forward. But we need a court order to hold him further. I stuck my neck out to keep him, and I mean in quotes, "safe." This is emergency protective custody which my department has authority to implement only under emergency circumstances. Tell me, Doctor, what is the emergency?"

"In my judgment, releasing this minor into the community, not knowing where his parents are, is a risk."

"A risk to whom?"

"Can't say at this point, need time to evaluate."

"Okay, maybe a risk, one you've not decided upon, but certainly not an emergency. Doctor, you can't even verify he's a minor, you can't certify he's a threat to society." She crossed her arms tightly across her chest. "You can't verify squat…and I'm nervous."

"Ginger, you need to trust my expertise on this. I think, for deep clinical reasons, this constitutes an emergency."

Ginger rolled her eyes. "Deep clinical reasons?"

"Exactly. I'm relying on a decade of education, life in the trenches. What might you question?"

"Maybe a diagnosis? You are a medical doctor, a psychiatrist, what our local hospital continuously rams down my throat to do what you say. So, tell me again, Doctor, what are you saying about a boy who, in my ignorant world, seems not a threat?"

Winthrop cleared his throat and raised the pitch of his voice to project his authority over this social worker. "As you said…my gut feeling is this boy poses a threat to himself and society as a whole. Do you wish to buck my advice, take a chance with your career?"

She rolled her eyes, conceding her insubordination, and said, "Forty-eight hours, the legal limit of my emergency custody, ends tomorrow. The police don't want him, my authority's expired, and nothing is left but you and the Probate

Judge. You're pleading your case to the wrong person. Are we straight?"

"Yes."

"He stays tonight. With no court order, he is cut loose at noon."

***

John and Marilyn spent the night around John's kitchen table, except for twenty minutes of distracted sex, their minds half on lust, the other on the unnamed patient about to get away.

John pulled up his underwear. "Problem is we've got no cop, no counselor, no prosecutor with a burning desire to nail this kid. Everything is backwards. The authorities are always breathing down our necks for a 'danger to society' or 'flight risk' to get a judge to deny bond or issue a questionable arrest warrant. And we step up to the plate, bend a few rules, make a diagnosis to help the cause. Here, we're standing in the surf before an ocean of important science, beckoning to be discovered. Where's the quid pro quo?"

"John, what are we to do?"

"In the morning, I go see Judge Gault."

Chapter Six

August 2012

The Honorable David Dixon Gault walked into the courtroom, his robe thrown over his shoulder. John Winthrop, the only other person in the courtroom, rose.

"Sit the hell down, Doctor, it's only me and you. Want me to wrap this robe around me?"

John shook his head.

"I've read your report this morning before you arrived. You want me to do an involuntary commitment of this unnamed boy you're calling John Doe? A person not charged with a crime, but one you call a danger? A danger to whom?"

"Judge, I know this is a bit touchy. I think he is a danger to himself."

"Doc, you know what I hate about this job?"

John shifted into his therapy voice. "No, please tell me."

"These damned commitment cases. Don't get me wrong, I love this job for the most part. Hell, I grew up here, know the people, know family connections, get paid a lot. So, when a family member dies, assuming they have enough assets that anyone cares about, they come to me, their probate judge, their elected official who guides them through a difficult time. Know what I mean?"

John squirmed in his seat, not knowing where this was going. "Yes, of course, I know what you mean, Judge."

The judge looked around the courtroom, like it was full. "And I hug those poor souls, pat 'em on the back, get them through probate so the heirs can sell property and collect what I like to call the inheritance your dear mama wanted you to have. I'm a hero. They vote for me the next election, tell their friends, who also vote for me, and I win another term. Did I mention I get a lot of money?"

"You did, Judge.   You also mentioned you hated commitment cases." John suspected what was coming next, and he predicted correctly. John was ready.

"Right.   Commitment cases fall in my court for some God-forsaken reason. I hate them because I'm asked to commit, which in my book is no less than throwing them in jail. These are folks who might very well be nuts. Or they may very well be perfectly sane people with a family having an axe to grind. Are you following me, Doctor? I can't lie that there may have been occasions where a family, with a bunch of money, hires a crafty lawyer to come in here and convince me to do an involuntary commitment of a person no less nuts than me. Bugs the shit out of me."

John had to pause a moment over the "less nuts than me" comment. "Judge, I understand your judicial responsibilities and the difficulty of applying your discretion."

The judge rose, wrapping the black cloth around his shoulders, like he needed the power of the robe to apply his "discretion." "So, Doctor Winthrop, is your guy nuts or what?"

"Like my report says, the patient poses a threat primarily to himself, but I can't rule out society as a whole."

"What the hell does that mean?"

"The diagnosis is cutting-edge science. If you'll permit, I'll explain the technical ramifications."

Judge Gault interrupted. "This is no trial. I just wanted to eyeball you, get a feel for where you're coming from. You certainly must know that an extended commitment, and now you know what I think of that, requires a trial. Your nut gets a lawyer, his day in court."

"Yes, Judge, all I want is your temporary order, a temporary commitment, until the trial can be set."

"Okay, Doctor Winthrop, you win on that one. But you better prove he's nuts, and I know you psycho-types don't like that word, but I'm the judge, and I grew up knowing the difference between a nut and not a nut. So, be forewarned, if I determine he is merely slow, or likes a fight, or ain't popular, or has a family…or a doctor for that matter…with an axe to grind, he will not be permanently committed. You understand me, Doctor?"

John had won the day. The trial would not be set for weeks. "I understand perfectly, Your Honor. But one other matter. Since this commitment, temporary as it may be, is medical in nature, I'd request the commitment be at the psych ward of Chafenville General Hospital."

"Makes sense… I'll write it here in my handwritten form order. These fill-in-the-blanks save a lot of secretary time." The judge winked. "And taxpayers' money."

***

Work to be done. A tight timeframe. John's options stewed in his head. He went directly to his office at the hospital, pulled out a legal pad, and began to write random thoughts, later to be fine-tuned by his research.

1. His risks to self are having the brilliance, let's say, to break through the firewall in a public library's computer system, but the utter inability to know his own home and family. Say we release him, fully

unmonitored, he stumbles upon a government computer, taps into it, wreaks havoc on vital security. His high-level cognizant functioning is a narrow slice of his mental pie. His access to sensitive security matters is tantamount to placing a three-year-old alone in the control room of a nuclear power plant. The danger is to himself and society itself. This justifies what the Probate Judge ordered.

2. My credentials to manage this case are I'm a psychiatrist with extensive training in the clinical work of administering and evaluating psychological and intelligence tests, and providing a sound diagnosis in learning and/or cognitive disorders.

3. Marilyn brought me into this case because I'm her professor, taught her at Chafenville Tech, raised her to be a Licensed Clinical Social Worker (LCSW). She now works for County Mental Health, under my direction, and has been assigned to work with the Chafenville Police Department, when needed. Marilyn does not possess the expertise to evaluate psychological or intelligence tests, although she assists me in the administration and evaluation of my testing. Who else would she turn to?

John stopped his memo and thought best to meet again with Marilyn. He suggested in a quick phone call they get together at the bagel shop across from Chafenville Tech, a place where the professor planted seeds of passion, along with the seeds of learning to his enamored student.

They squeezed into the same side of a table booth and John spoke to the urgency of the task before them. "Chances are, the time between now and when a juvenile petition is likely to be denied, stands as my only opportunity to reach psychological stardom. Do we really want to find his family, just yet, before I explore his brain, before I document my suspicions?"

"John, shouldn't we be open to more facts?"

***

He left the bagel shop, pulling out his legal pad, and resuming his memo.

4.   "I'm joyous to have the patient in my ward at the hospital. The staff reveres my credentials, the best the hospital has ever known. The room is tight, controlled. I'll be eyeball to eyeball; he'll have no escape. I'll dissect each and every thought from his mind. Besides all my missteps, this is my calling. This juvenile is mine, my coming of age.

5.   But is this ethical?

He ran back to the parking lot, catching Marilyn before she drove off. He posed the same question.

She reacted. "Might very well be unethical."

"Disagree. Ethical indeed. Marilyn, this case, our goldmine, needs to be protected. If anybody in our business, profession, gets to the meat of our patient, we'll be footnotes, forgotten."

"But John, isn't the best interest of our patient, what you taught me at Chafenville Tech, the goal, our mission, our calling? Seems you used that word…calling…a lot. I think I fell in love with you during a lecture, one where your words touched me. I felt a calling."

John stroked the back of his neck and pushed his blondish hair behind his ear. "Me, too. Now do you understand we must protect our calling, our turf, our research…which began forty-eight hours ago?"

"Our turf?"

"Yes, our collective diagnosis of newly creative psychological science."

"John, you sound so positive, so futuristic. You sound so damned exciting."

John shifted into an authoritative voice. "Cautiously excited, I know how best intentions can blow up in your face. Our creativity, our future must be approached methodically, and above all else, protectively. Are you with me?"

"Yes."

They decided to go by the foster home to check on their prized possession and finish the conversation. After confirming the patient was in a locked room, the two sat out on the porch alone.

"John, what will happen to our unnamed patient after our testing, diagnosis, and recommendations are complete?"

"Too early to say. Maybe without much effort, we get a name, his history, how he functions in life. On the other hand, we may have a tough nut to crack, but crack it I shall. I've got an arsenal of tools."

John returned to the hospital and finished his memo.

Chapter Seven

August 2012

Abel sat by the nailed-down window, legs numb from lack of motion, mind struggling for new thoughts, ears sharp as tacks. He heard Winthrop, his interrogator, out on the steps. Beth may have taught him too much at the Fellowship Headquarters. Beth may have taught him too well. But one thing for sure, John Winthrop would not crack him.

Rachel, Abel's mother, talked to him most days and gave him compass, anchor, and purpose. Life had no meaning without his mother. Most of those who ever knew her...Abel's father, church people were dead. But Bordo, as far as he knew, lived. He wished his mother had known Beth in life and hoped they could be friends in his mind. But, they always seemed to want to stay out of each other's way. He thought it strange his mom and Beth came to him individually, avoiding discussions like the plucking of Ed's eyes. They focused on the future.

Even after hundreds of sermons from the God-Ordained Reverend Bordo on the sins of killing, there was still a debt to repay, and these people who grabbed him in Abel's father's house were easy targets. After returning to the hills, he picked them off one by one.

In the woods, he tried not to dwell on inconsequential dead people. Everything in the woods, the hills, fierce nature, animals surviving, gave a son trying to stay connected to his mother, raped in these same hills, comfort.

Abel stewed in his current surroundings, and he guessed he had left his comfort zone, chosen sin in a moment of weakness. And now he sat in a new cage, and he knew from comments on the porch he was headed to a still newer cage, a smaller cage. Abel would listen more closely to his mother. He hated cages. He hated eyes. But he loved his mother, and maybe Beth. But as he thought of it, love was the wrong word.

***

Police escorted him from the foster home headed to an unknown destination. Abel reflected on the foster home he barely knew, many hours locked in one room. Never once did he meet a fellow captive. But he could hear pleasant things, positive things, like celebrations of life. When questions came from the other children about him, quickly the staff made comments of dangerous, evil, leave him alone stuff. And he felt alone. Alone was what he knew, what he trusted. But he was not alone, he was captive to authority. He saw names on signs going in and out of the foster home, bouncing around like balloons: "welcome home"…"home for the best"…"home to get home"…"homeless no more"…"home again"…"home sweet home." These were obviously for others in the foster home, others better than Abel. He didn't care. Maybe he did.

***

As the fortified van pulled away from the foster home, Abel, having not slept in days, fell victim to the motion of the dark, tight quarters, and dreamed a nightmare, his truth. Around him a new cage, a new person, like Ed Wood, ready to poke him with a sharp stick. He awoke, and looked inward to his mother.

Rachel would talk him through...just like the first cage...just like Ed's deserved ending. She would explain things to him, like Sarah's disappearance.

And even now, where Abel had sinned in front of his own mother, she understood about the crossing of the river, of the library, of some unfulfilled lusts that Abel suffered. Rachel would call the shots, and he was damned sure John Winthrop to be Rachel's next victim. Rachel protected Abel; he owed her his life, he owed her his loyalty. And Beth.

***

The smell of disinfectant filled Abel's nose. Off-white colored walls surrounded him, not unpleasant, definitely unfamiliar. He remembered arriving, remembered niceness all around, remembered a syringe, then remembered nothing. When he gained his senses, he didn't like it, neither did his mother. He waited for the expected...Winthrop. And he appeared like an angel, white gown, fluffed-up blond hair, eyes of wisdom, eyes of whatever-it-takes.

Abel shook his head around, trying to clear his mind of whatever the angel before him had pumped into his veins. Winthrop merely stood there waiting, a therapeutically designed approach that gave Abel plenty of time for refocusing.

Finally the great therapist spoke. "You look rested, my young friend. Maybe a good night's sleep brought back your name. "I'm John; I'm sure you are...?"

Abel did not reach for John's outstretched hand. Instead he looked away from the eyes of the doctor. No further names were exchanged.

John began again. "I'm about to give you some tests. What kind depends on you. Stay silent, ignorant, and we'll give you more of the push buttons, the type you seem to like. Or, if you give us some encouragement, the kind we got when you told the Doctor Marilyn you didn't think she was a doctor, we'll change course, give you the benefit of every doubt. Wait for you to show us why we're wrong to have ever thought you're anything but absolutely, wonderfully smart, college bound."

Abel sat stone-faced. He'd never let his mother become victim to this self-righteous, psychological wonder. Winthrop could have learned lessons far better from Beth than whoever prepared him to land a job at Chafenville Technological College. The authorities who transported him from police station to foster home, to some kind of hospital, kept talking about the college, and this overqualified doctor. Abel was not as impressed.

He decided quickly, if for no other reason than his own entertainment, to give a verbal response. "Co-co-co...college?"

John took charge very quickly. "Yes, Yes. I did say college. Is that what you said?"

Abel said nothing.

John used eye contact, then body language, like the leaning on a billiard table, trying to influence the shot, an outcome, a response. "You said college, I heard it clear as day. We are making progress, we are understanding you, we are about there." John reached out, touched Abel's arm, and emulated words of success, conclusion. "Take a deep breath, my newfound friend, we'll break through these things in your mind holding you back."

Abel started to say *you'll never rid my head of my mother,* but he thought better and grabbed his ear.

The hospital room, much larger than Abel thought and more insulated than the police station interview room, had a window, solid thick glass, no handles. When the doctor left the room, Abel darted for a glance. Trees below held birds, squirrels, freedom. He breathed in deeply, trying for a scent of what he saw…useless. He thought of his mother's displeasure with Doctor Winthrop. He owed his mother too much to let some man succeed in ostracizing Abel's creator, teacher, and friend from his mind.

***

John Winthrop left his patient's room and walked the short distance to his private office to wait for Marilyn. He delighted in the hospital-assigned quarters bestowed upon him as the only psychiatrist for fifty miles in any direction. A desk, a couch, a stocked refrigerator graced the private office he could use for medical business or medicinal pleasure. After all, he represented the only prescription-writing member of the fourth ward staff. He popped a pill anticipating Marilyn's arrival from duties at the police station as the twenty-buck-an-hour police juvenile worker, and thought of his new patient.

College, the little pistol picked up on my pre-planned word…representing academic excellence.

Marilyn knocked. He took a seat at his desk, chin up, authoritatively, then quickly changed to the couch, submissively, legs slightly spread. "Come in."

"Sorry I'm late, how did your interview go?"

"Bring your vivacious body over here. We've got lots to talk about."

She sat at his feet, facing him. He reached over, pivoted her backwards, and pulled her toward him, landing the back of her head upon his abdomen. "Baby, once again our patient has bolted out of his retarded diagnosis. He brought up a new topic, 'college,' like a dream come true."

"I'm not following you, tired as hell. What gives?"

John raised his voice. "Think about it. He has said his second sentence, and both are of a higher learning plane…one, M.D., two, college! Don't you find this remarkable?"

"I'm whipped. One stupid gun-packing, marijuana-packing, rubber-packing kid after another has left me wondering if the future of society has a fighting snowball chance in hell. So, tell me what's remarkable, Professor."

"Stay focused, my sweet piece of ass."

"John, don't call me that."

"Sorry, I'm excited as hell, and horny as hell."

"Well…feeling your bulge growing on my back…hell, I'm getting horny as hell, too."

"Lock the door, Marilyn; this is our special space."

***

Abel become disinterested in the window as the sun set and lost its glow. Both the doctor and Marilyn, entering the room, staggered slightly. He saw in their glazed eyes a loss of control. He'd seen the same in Ed, the Reverend, the Reverend's friends, men at the trading post. Now Marilyn and John. Both were high. An opportunity.

Winthrop took the lead. "Young man, college bound, my new friend, remember Marilyn, Doctor Marilyn?" He snickered at his own comment.

Abel watched in amusement as Marilyn attempted to rise to the occasion, slurring her words as well. "Good to see you again. We have a real treat in store for you tomorrow, some more fun tests."

They stared at him and glanced back at one another, looking for validation. They whispered in each other's ears, like excited children, then broke apart giggling. Finally, they reached a decision to leave. As they headed to the door, Abel turned his eyes to the window. Hearing the lock click slowly behind them, like they were listening, Abel turned his voice toward the door, and said: "No professional shrink sees a patient drunk and keeps his job."

***

John and Marilyn stopped their impending step away from the patient's door. They looked carefully in each other's eyes, and acknowledged each other's condition. Drunk. Friday night would roll into Saturday morning soon. They mutually agreed to let the night pass.

***

Twelve hours later, Marilyn sipped coffee. She waited for her cell phone to ring. An hour later it did.

"It's John. Did we hear what I thought we heard last night?"

"Maybe, why don't you say it first?"

"Damned, Marilyn, you're like some board of ethics. Coy, discreet, polite, but then want me to record some confessional. Something to come back to haunt me, take me from academic stardom to…well…Chafenville Tech."

"Stop your paranoia, John. Did you hear what I heard or not?"

"Who knows with this kid? I suspect this is one more layer to the mountain of confusion. The "M.D.," to the "College," to a commentary over our Friday night ethics. He could be a disabled mute or a brilliant spy who plays well to the chairman of the disciplinary authority that controls my license to practice medicine. A broad spectrum, wouldn't you say?"

"I'd say paranoid, again."

"Okay, okay. You. Marilyn. Tell me what he said."

"I'm not sure…maybe something like we were drunk? Might not be doing the right thing? Hell…I *was* drunk. Those nice pills in your office.

"Stop it, Marilyn. We'd had a long day, a bit of a relaxation, that's all."

"What did you hear him say, John?"

"Can't say verbatim. But something like questioning our ethics. Nobody with my present diagnosis could verbally transcend that many issues. My diagnosis must change. Our loyalty, our secrecy to one another must strengthen."

Marilyn heard through the phone the sound of mattress springs, like John bouncing impatiently as his voice rose to a high pitch. "And I'm even more than excited over my new patient."

"*Now* do you believe he asked me if I was a doctor of drama?"

"Never doubted you for a minute. But since he talked down to me, too, well…proof's in the pudding."

"John, I don't know what to say. I do know you are the best thing to happen in my life. I was stuck in a place, a community college designed to keep me marginally educated to succeed, but never get out of this town. Then you show up, more qualified than this area deserves. As you say yourself, you have the ability to teach the doctors themselves with your special knowledge of psychology. Maybe U.T. didn't work out, at least for now, but you are definitely *my* salvation. You, my lover, have taught me more than this school could ever offer. I'm the best around...except for you. I love what you have done for me. You, and only you, can explain where we are with this patient. So, tell me. I don't know what to make of last night."

***

John needed to think, contemplate a complex patient, a complex hangover. He hung up the phone, not ending the conversation with Marilyn. He weighed out his fear that an involuntarily committed patient could somehow call his ethics into question. Marilyn was right...paranoia. The issue had nothing to do with his ethics. John shouted it out in the privacy of his own apartment. "The issue is not an issue, it is a discovery, a new discovery of the human mind." *This young man strikes when I'm weakest...not focused, dwelling on myself, lusting on Marilyn, or drunk.* He considered all he'd read in psychological literature before, during, and after his degrees. This patient had the makings of cutting-edge science. And John Winthrop owned the rights.

Chapter Eight

June 15, 2013
3:00 p.m.

Back at the Riordan home, Paul shook like a drug addict in detox and looked eyeball to eyeball with Tim Myers, detective in charge of the kidnapping of Parker Riordan, and now Helen Riordan. "You said earlier you thought Parker was dead, he's not. Do you think Helen is dead?"

"You know the protocol. I can't say."

Paul pulled his own thinning hair. "Suspicions, then."

"I like that word, suspicions. Noncommittal."

"Damn your time, answer the question."

"Sorry, Paul. I suspect this lunatic is capable of things good law enforcement can't predict. Care to know why?"

"You know I care."

"Abel has a background unfamiliar to mainstream criminal justice. Ultimately, motive drives people. Paul, how many times have I heard you argue to a jury, begging them for a not guilty verdict, to consider the lack of motive?"

"Often. So, what's your point?"

"You were often right. As cops, we find focusing on opportunity, fingerprints, DNA often a waste of time. When we forget motive, the reason for the crime, we lose."

"And your point about Abel is…?"

"He follows no rules of mainstream criminals. I can nail down a motive of most any criminal in Chafenville, then build evidence around the motive. But Abel's motive is elusive, senseless, unpredictable."

"Like *why* he kidnapped my son?"

"Yes, but more than that."

"Because Parker wasn't enough?"

"Right."

"And Helen came into play, not by our motives, only by Abel's?"

"Right."

"Thus your inability to nail down an understandable motive."

"Right."

"And the plan?"

"Kidnapping Parker was hard enough. The difficulty of orchestrating what happened, near impossible, or at least I thought."

"And the plan?"

"For the last few days I've pulled every string I can think of. The computer-based inquiry, as you might guess, gives us little…except some bizarre library incident."

"Bizarre, what did he do…and how do you know it was Abel?"

"Fingerprints, taken from when he was processed through our department, match what we got off Helen's car. Quite frankly, considering the day and time he was taken in, I'm surprised they took the time to roll his fingers through our inked-up, push-as-you-go, archaic way of fingerprinting noncharged juveniles. But they did, right after they lugged him from a foster home where he spent the night, back to the station, and we have a match."

"Meaning what?"

"Meaning nothing, unless we get more."

"Back up. You said something about a library incident."

"Right. For what it's worth, he, or at least who we believe to be him to be, broke through a library computer firewall, and looked at porn."

"Porn?"

"Yep, but what does that tell us? This isolated incident is the only sliver of information available in the depths of computer cyberspace. And believe me, I've called in favors from the FBI and cashed in an IOU from a buddy at Interpol. Nothing on this kid. Not a Social Security number, not a grammar school entrance, not one pearl of information. Nothing from T-ball to high school glee club, or from Cub Scouts to a grocery stock boy. He may as well be a raccoon, miles from here, up in the hills."

"Raccoons don't look at porn."

"Granted."

Chapter Nine

September 2012

Only an orderly and a CNA moved in and out of Room 402. Winthrop's instructions were clear: no discussions with the patient. Abel figured if he spoke, the staff would treat the event as a major emergency and notify the doctor immediately. Testing took place only in the presence of the unnamed patient, Winthrop, and Marilyn Thomas.

Abel sized up the rules, the players, and the limitations as quickly as scenes unfolded in his rather spacious room. Before the real action started, he actually could jog around the room, stopping every so often to gaze downward from the fourth level upon the tops of trees. The sight gave him a new perspective on the winged and four-legged foraging among the limbs.

The man with the mop smiled a lot, never talked, whistled a bit, and seemed content with life. Abel watched with pleasure the slapping back and forth of the fibers keeping the floor clean and shiny. The mop man never stared, never restricted his movement, never judged.

Mabel, engraved in her name tag above the letters CNA, got closer than Abel liked, but her eyes stayed on his arms and legs while she checked blood pressure and other vital signs. He could tolerate her in this big room for short periods of time.

But then long, uninvited interruptions began. Mabel always respectfully called his two interrogators doctors. Marilyn started calling John the "good doctor," which seemed absurd. And the good doctor always started with: "My friend, we're going to have a little chat." And the chats they had, one-sided chats, grated on Abel's and Rachel's nerves.

"You remain silent, but we know you talk, have heard you talk. Most of my patients are eager to talk. Talking is what I do best, why I'm here, why you need me to help you through your reasons for not talking. Understand?"

Then Marilyn chimed in, like the cheerful, morning robin perched upon the good doctor's shoulder. "He's right, we know you say things. In fact, you say things so smart that I, myself, find amazing. How do you know so much?"

Abel started to raise his eyes, but the uninspiring chat convinced him to pass.

"Young man," the good doctor said, "the look in your eyes tells me you want some help, some guidance, some validation of who *you* are." John leaned his eyes close to Abel's, nearly locking with them. Abel, feeling caged, ready to be poked, jumped back, a reaction he'd avoided so far, a reaction inconsistent with the his cool demeanor when the paper bag was popped behind his head. He felt ashamed, his mother felt betrayed.

He heard Rachel's voice. "Son, this man's about to cage you again."

But Abel kept his composure and lowered his eyes.

***

Back in the office, John took the big leather chair and gestured for Marilyn to take the small one. "Tight spaces make him react. I've found the needed stimulus."

"And what will you do with your new knowledge?"

"Finally get to the bottom of this kid, what makes him tick. Why this remarkable case study has fallen into my lap."

"Nice, John. Can you be more specific?"

"I would like to try some cognitive manipulation to trigger a psychotic episode. Would he speak to save himself?"

Marilyn stood and placed her hands on her hips. "Or would he emotionally implode? This is outrageous, unethical, probably unlawful…he's not a prisoner of war for God sakes."

" Yeah, but the M.R.I. is completely normal. Our issue can't be addressed with standard protocol."

"What are you talking about, mind altering drugs, torture?"

"Sweetheart, hear me out. I'm not talking about using drugs. I simply want to stimulate some of his phobias in order to expose them, strengthen them, and coerce a verbal response from him, that's all. Have you noticed anything he withdraws from or dislikes?"

"He reacts adversely to others moving into his personal space, he does not want to be touched, although a women's soft, kind voice appears to relax him."

"Which clearly means smaller spaces create anxiety."

"So, what about the soft voice?"

"We've already tried positive reinforcement…it didn't work."

Marilyn thought about this for a moment. "The foster home manager said he was drawn to the outside preferring to sit as close to the window as possible. He is pulled like a magnet toward the sun, wind, and the night sky. She said had there not been bars on the windows he looked like a bird ready to fly away."

"How would she know? The door was locked."

"Guess foster parents go outside a lot, getting away from the chaos; she probably saw him through the window."

"We're high tech here, hidden cameras from all angles, except for the bathroom. We know he likes the window. So what's your point?"

"She also said that when he walked from his bedroom into the large living room, his face became calmer. And when he walked outside, about to be transported, he'd breathe a large sigh of relief. Bigger space and bigger light seems to please him."

"Now that's some information I can work with. I'm considering some strategic modifications to his hospital room."

He leaned back into the rich leather chair, rubbed his chin, crossed his arms. "I'll talk to the building superintendent."

"What? You want him to interview our patient?"

John smugly said. "Not at all. Remember I told you space is our new tool in treating the patient. Stay tuned, darling, stay tuned."

***

Heyward Moffatt stood nervously in front of Doctor John Winthrop, a man Heyward learned from administration was to be given whatever he needed.

"Your first name, my friend?"

"Heyward, sir, I mean Doctor...sir."

"Relax, Heyward. I just need a bit of help in room 402."

"Yes, sir, is the air out, a plumbing problem? Something I didn't know about?"

"No, no, Heyward. The room's fine. Your maintenance is excellent. Impeccable, I'd say. Look around my office, spectacular, clean as a whistle, not a broken appliance in sight."

Heyward relaxed a bit. "So...why am I here?"

The doctor leaned in Heyward's direction. "I have a patient in this room who is very sick. It's not a heart attack, not cancer, but sick just as much. The sickness is in the patient's head, understand Heyward?"

He chuckled like he knew an inside joke. "I guess. After all, this *is* the fourth floor."

"In all your dealings with walls, toilets, wiring, I bet you never thought you might contribute to the healing of a patient."

"Got that right, Doc."

"So, are you with me?"

"Not sure what you're asking."

"I need you to move walls when and where I tell you in this room."

"What?"

"Heyward, one day I might tell you to make this room three-quarters its size, the next day ask you to make it half."

"Doc, you don't understand. Construction is to code. Engineers designed this building, this room we're talking about. Building permits have to be pulled, drawings have to be presented. You can't go changing a structure when you feel like it."

"Heyward, I know more than you think. I'm not asking you to change any structural aspect of the building, only to position nonstructural walls to limit living space. Do you understand?"

"Doc, I'm supposed to keep you happy. Maybe after I get a feel for what you want we can move forward, help your patient as you say."

Doctor Winthrop stood, stuck out his hand and smiled. "Excellent, Heyward, come back at ten tonight."

"I'll be in bed by then."

"Thought you were to keep me happy."

"Very true."

"This will be a strategy meeting, keep you less than an hour. The real work starts at eleven in the morning."

"See you at ten, Doctor Winthrop."

***

Abel slept soundly after the doctors left his room. The slip-up on the eye contact left his mind once he got a glimpse of the sunset and the animals retreating into the parking lot trees for the night. Left alone, this room, decent meals, and running water, were considerably less than oppressive. It reminded him in a way of The Fellowship headquarters, comfortable. Only Beth had been replaced by people trying to steal information from his mind, instead of Beth's constant drive of intelligence. Abel wrestled with how Rachel would feel about Beth. They never talked…seemed to avoid each other.

Morning came with the sound of Mabel's voice, the CNA. The absence of those who asked questions brought welcome relief. She wore a starched-white uniform, like a nurse of the past, like Catholic nurses Beth taught him about. He shifted in his bed, a bit uncomfortable with a woman in his space. He didn't mind so much. Her pleasant humming of an old gospel hymn actually gave him peace. He opened his eyes. She smiled, but as the rules dictated, didn't speak. But he was beginning to see a nicer, more sincere smile, as days passed. She left, and he slept soundly again.

Then the doctors, then questions, then insinuations about space, freedom, and his future. He remained silent.

The next day brought another plastic-covered breakfast tray, some fruit, bread, and ham. He spoke nothing and ate everything. The sun creeping in his window assured him his hills, his home breathed for him, his mother breathed for him, everything he needed, loved, though he avoided that word, waited for him. His next move would come soon. He waited patiently, because when the people pushed him into this facility, he noticed security locks and thick doors. His escape might be complicated by locks or doors or people of which he had no knowledge or control.

Abel thought of his stumble in the library. He mentally kicked himself, painfully, every night for his stupidity. He didn't want to be stupid now. His enemy was John. Rachel insisted Marilyn would be an adversary as well.

In Abel's room was a bathroom. After a long night's rest, he needed it. He shut the door behind him and relished the privacy. As he sat on the pot, he relaxed, thinking the sun would finish rising soon and his window would reveal a new day of animals. He smiled and grimaced at the same time.

Eleven o'clock flashed on the TV screen which, other than the time of day, did not function for patient...unnamed. Abel thought his circumstances to be manageable; he'd had a pleasant morning, but needed some preparation time. He knew some stuff from Beth about the law, the constitution, freedom. He hoped his patience had paid off; his freedom lingered close to the stool he sat upon. He hoped, he hoped.

The door of his room burst open like a massive war rage, something he caught in a television documentary of some holocaust at The Fellowship headquarters. Abel took a deep breath and waited.

First, a man with a tool belt, moved cautiously into the room. He moved faster as the familiar Dr. Winthrop seemed to propel him forward. Once everyone in the room settled, the doctor started shouting commands. "Take the patient to the activities room while we adjust this room."

The doctor looked Abel in the eyes, hard, and a bad sensation filled Abel's body. He was bodily handled by two muscular people with badges reading "staff."

***

Room 402 vacated. Only left were John Winthrop and
Heyward Moffatt. They both looked around, eyeballing the
walls, the floors, the ceilings, the angles. A good two minutes
passed before anyone spoke. Doctor Winthrop took charge.
"Heyward, make the necessary adjustments. This afternoon I
want the living space reduced by twenty percent. I may, day to
day, want a fifty to eighty percent reduction. Other times I
might want the entire space restored."

"Sure about this, Doc? Seems awfully strange…and
definitely in violation of county codes."

"Treatment of mentally challenged patients is strange;
they don't think like the Heyward Moffatts of the world.
Treatment has to be tailored, structured to produce healing. I'm
trained to heal, you're not. I don't expect you to fully
understand, I expect you to comply with my
requests…understand *that* concept?"

Heyward began unloading tools. "Yes, sir." Barking
orders at his hand-held monitor, he ordered a long list of
materials. "A dozen two by fours, sheetrock, plywood, no nails,
screws…we'll be pulling it all down before the weekend."

***

Abel sat in silence in the activities room. Only Marilyn
stayed. No other patient came in or out.

"This is a pleasant room, pastel colors, nice plants, cool temperature. Lot better than that cramped room of yours, think?"

He noticed her watching to see if he looked around. He didn't. He'd sized up the room the first minute he'd walked in. What he liked most was the large window, though bolted shut. After another moment of silence, he rose, walked to the window, and placed his forehead upon it. The view offered the rear setting of the hospital grounds. Thick woods grew past the parking lot. He looked hard for an ally.

Time felt absent as the big window opened its view with no interruptions from Marilyn. It may have been an hour or more when the tranquility shattered as John Winthrop paraded into the activities room. "Your room's clean...let's go back."

The enlivened pitch of Winthrop's voice disturbed Abel. Escorted by the same crew, he walked the halls and absorbed the stares of other patients. Deep-socketed eyes, frowns disapproving of his existence, smiles with unknown intentions, brightened eyes begging for help, followed him down the hall. Nobody seemed content.

He landed back in room 402 in the shadow and authority of Winthrop. Something changed, the bathroom, his private area, where he thought of Marilyn in a different way, stood separated by a dividing wall. In fact, the wall stretched across the room, cutting it almost in half. And a door gave entrance to the space containing his bed. As he passed through the door, slightly shoved by his escorts, he saw locks, deadbolts. He heard the door close from behind, followed by a loud crisp snap of locks. He turned to his window. Plywood covered it. Only the clock flashing on the TV gave any light. Only depression illuminated in his mind. The room was dark, his life was dark.

The clock being his only reference, he knew to the minute one hour had passed when the blinding light from the door jolted his eyes, followed by the grating, academic accent of Doctor John Winthrop.

"I've noticed you seem a little concerned with tight places. Don't say anything quite yet, and I feel a bit stupid to suggest you would say something. Right? The doctor paused a while. Right, of course I'm right."

Abel turned his face to the light from the hall, basked in its sunlight qualities like a mild day on a windy river's edge. Winthrop stepped toward him, cutting off the glare, and knelt, putting him eyeball to eyeball with the patient.

"We have just begun, my unnamed friend. Enjoy the darkness, enjoy your shrinking space. Once you understand I am here to help you, once you understand I control your space, once you understand I, and only I, can release you from unpleasantness, can we make progress."

Winthrop left the room, the door bolted down, and darkness overcame the smaller room. Abel went to bed. After two hours of sleep, he challenged the seams of his captivity, the door, the wall; all resisted with the strength of an oak.

The window, a mere piece of plywood. He ripped it off. He watched the parking lot below the trees, lit up with artificial lighting of silver-colored long-armed street poles.

The sun finished setting, the day faded, the pole lights strengthened, and the animals retreated to their beds. He watched until his legs ached. *9:53* by the clock. He walked from the plywood-free window, crawled into bed, and dreamed of his animals.

The daylight and a squeaking door hinge awakened Abel from a sound sleep. "Hold up everything. I'm calling Doctor Know It All."

Abel recognized Heyward Moffatt. And at least for a few hours, his cage stood out like an illuminated jewel among the wreckage of bad construction closing in upon him. He smiled, but for a moment. Winthrop couldn't be far away.

"My, my. We've shown a bit of anger, haven't we?" Winthrop smiled, like registering a win. "So, would you like to talk, give me a reason to reinstate privileges, space?"

Abel kept a straight face, showing no joy, fear, or ambivalence.

"Have it your way, then." Winthrop pulled out a hand-held radio. "Send the staff, take the patient to the activities room...and get Moffatt back."

***

Abel spent less than two hours in the pleasant surroundings, and passed most of the time in front of the window, listening to Marilyn's commentary.

"I know you don't like these tight places. We're not doing this to harm you; we're trying to get you out of this shell, let you open up like you've done several times. The words you use, the way you apply words makes us know you're smart and well versed. Maybe tell me a little about yourself and I'll personally see that Doctor Winthrop gives you the same privileges he has."

Abel wanted to say, *Like screwing you?* Instead, he focused harder on the parking lot, like he wasn't listening.

***

Room 402's window was double layered with thick plywood and held in place with lag-bolt screws. When the door locked behind Abel, he pivoted and looked at the clock, 10:14 a.m. The only difference in the blackened room was an odd-shaped light switch that glowed in the dark. He flipped it upward, and the florescent fixture beamed generous light upon his limited space. With no window, he rummaged through a hospital drawer and found a Bible. The powers of Bordo demanded strict teachings by the instructors, but only of selected verses, the ones justifying the cult, The Fellowship, Bordo's ways.

He decided to read some New Testament, the most exciting option he had at the moment. He flipped through some pages and landed on *John*, the name of his hated doctor. But an opposite character appeared in the pages, Jesus. Doctor John Winthrop wanted Abel's life. Jesus, the arm of God, was willing to sacrifice his own to save Abel's. *Strange.* He considered Ed, his grandfather-father's Bible-pounding rantings in the basement. The sin that brought about Abel, all his mother's faults. In contrast, the words pouring from the pages of *John* seemed peaceful, redeeming.

Then the light that shown on the pages went out. The tightened space, the dark, the solitude became his cage without his mother. He tired of Doctor Winthrop's games.

Sleep being his only option, he wrestled with his pillow, not knowing what tomorrow would bring. His eyelids cracked, his sleep light.

The pleasant humming of Mabel, outside the newly created door, woke Abel. No light penetrated the room. He cast his eyes to the clock, 6:45 a.m.

"Ain't right, ain't right," she mumbled between the verses. "Like a slave, a youngster. Ain't right, ain't right. That's all there be to it."

He knew there were several hours before Winthrop, who never worked early, came to extract Abel's obedience. But the stress of tight places, no light, and eyes he couldn't control, wore on his mind, even if not on his mother's mind. He decided to escape. "Mabel, I've soiled myself. It burns."

"Lawd, Child. That's the first I've heard you talk. I'm comin' in."

Then the locks, in a slow cadence, began popping, and the door opened, followed by blinding light. Abel shut his eyes, then eased his lids slowly apart, adjusting to the glare. The new entry door gave view to an empty hall...and Mabel stood to the side, looking upward like ignoring the world, no obstacle for whatever he needed to do.

Not wanting to hurt Mabel, who'd done him no harm, he eased through and past her. He bolted out the other door and stood in the hall, looking right and left, searching for an escape from the fourth floor. The only sound came from Mabel's voice, sounding like a hymn to God. "Take care of that boy, precious Jesus. He need yo' mercy."

He sprinted to his left, down the length of the hall, and jerked the door to freedom hard. The door knob was stiff, the pull gave no leverage, the strength of his entire body moved not one inch of its metal and fortified glass. The hinges almost laughed at his effort. He saw people through the glass meandering in front of the elevator that brought him up to the "nut ward," as he'd heard visitors call it. He pressed his face to the glass. The wires reinforcing the glass clouded his view, but he could make out people crowded in front of the elevator, the visitors' sitting room of the fourth floor. He knocked. Waved.

Pressed his face again to the glass, expressing an innocent, peaceful look, a matter-of-fact look for someone to open the door, like his hands were full. One totally inconsistent with how he felt at the moment.

No one came to the door. He pounded harder, louder. Knowing his time to escape was short, he began to shout the noise of a captured bird of prey. Then the people outside moved back, a crazed man who scared them. Footsteps approached from behind. He inspected the door's lock and realized they were many and all dead bolted. One would need a key from either side.

The footsteps were upon him; voices had a multitude of pitches."

"The doctor's gonna be pissed."

"Hold him, watch the syringe, I'm going to sedate him."

Then he heard, far behind a quiet sobbing…Mabel. Then the color grey filled his mind as noises slurred and things blurred, a surreal moment.

***

"My, my, Mr. Patient. You want out? Simply talk."

Abel, though very groggy, pulled his ear and looked away from Doctor Winthrop.

"Fine. Let's see what this room looks like tomorrow. Nurse, give him some more sedative."

Heyward Moffatt rubbed his neck vigorously. "Doc, you've got this room down to the size of my dog's cage. She's a Chihuahua."

"What can't you understand? A medical breakthrough is about to happen. The end justifies the means."

Heyward looked to the stars. "I don't know what the means means. I know the county inspector, and the only justification for the means will be is his mean foot up my end, as in my sorry ass. And I guess it's not for me to say that this arrangement you've got going on with this patient don't quite sit right with me. And guess what? I'm not the only one on this floor with those feelings."

"Heyward, Heyward. If you want some more authority, let's march right down to the first floor, the administrator of this hospital, clear this matter up right now."

"No, Doctor Winthrop, I'd likely lose my job. Word from the top is you are the man in this part of the state. Guess that means big bucks to the hospital. I've been told to keep you happy. Forget what I said, I'm a hammer-toting fool. You make crazy people well…well, who am I to question?"

"Heyward, thank you for your confidence. I'm helping this sick boy the way you're helping the air conditioning to keep running."

Heyward rolled his eyes. "Okay, Doc., three feet by ten feet…with a small window."

***

Abel recalled being moved around in a groggy state, but didn't remember returning to his room, a room now with walls so close, sweat secreted under his arms, his forehead, all over. He walked from the television set, to the foot of his bed, and crawled toward the headboard. Walls brushed either side of him if he varied from the path. No room, no light. A small seam of a square gleamed a tiny shadow of another color from the inside wall. He closed his eyes, slept for a while, and wanted to run. Run through the forests, run to his mother, even run back to Beth. Nowhere to run, no desire to sleep anymore, no light to help his judgment caused his body to become neutral, not knowing what's next. Breathing took an erratic cadence. The will to eat, to drink, evaporated. His cage, his grandfather, his dead mother all visited his mind. His will to live stifled.

***

Abel, curled into a fetal position on the floor of his space, smelled food, heard pleasant voices, and saw a light. He figured his time for death had come. Either creator, counter creator, or nature, had arrived to take him. Then a familiar voice, an unpleasant voice resonated on the walls along with a blaring light that earlier was the strange square on the inside wall. He adjusted his eyes to a small window about two feet by two feet.

"Good afternoon," announced Doctor Winthrop. You've been in here a while, had time to evaluate where you are, what you are. I've brought you food, sodas. More importantly, I've brought you light and I'm prepared to give you space. In fact, I'm prepared to give you freedom…cut you loose from this confining hospital."

The window opened further. A gracious amount of hot, steaming food, the kind he'd eaten regularly in the days before this last lockdown. His will to die left and survival instincts took over. He ate, he drank. He ignored the doctor watching him.

After he finished, the light from above turned on. His eyes hurt from the glare, but he adjusted. Then Winthrop spoke again.

"Enjoy your full belly, your light. I'll be back shortly."

Abel reoriented himself in the long, narrow room. *What's next?*

An hour passed and then the wall with the small window started to shake. Gently at first, then violently, a roar of thunder from both ends. The walls fell and exposed in a brilliance of light, two men holding drills, sweating from the labors of removing the wall.

Abel's original space had returned. He looked around his full, generous hospital room. A door to the hall, full access to the bathroom. He turned and looked for the outside window. The men with drills removed it in short order, and natural light shed its grace on Abel like a blessing. He stood in the middle of the glow, not aware of Winthrop in the shadows. He basked.

"Glad you're appreciating the short-lived outside world I've given to you. Staff will take care of you, but will strap you in a jacket to keep you from repeating the shenanigans you did a few days ago. And then you and I are going to have a nice chat. See you in a bit."

***

Marilyn ran her fingers through her hair as John walked into the office which bore his name. "Explain to me, medically, professionally, what we are doing. You restricted his living space to inhumane levels, regulated food, water to your satisfaction, and cut off all light."

John interrupted. "We are almost there. If he stays mute I'll look like a heel to you, if he talks, I'm a hero. Will you give me a few hours? My training tells me I've hit the right nerve, you know, with an appropriate balance, of course."

She smirked. "Right. Of course. Okay, Doctor, Professor. But understand this, I don't have to like it. This shallow young man is kind of likeable, whether he talks or not. Why treat him like an animal? No, never mind. I know your response. I hope this is over soon."

John winked. "Stay tuned, my love."

***

Winthrop's return dissected Abel's soul. The straps around his body made him feel helpless to escape, but no restriction of his mind.

The good doctor moved forward, close. "Nice try. A break. Defying my authority. I told you I control your space."

Abel looked above Winthrop's eyes, unrelenting.

"This Mabel. She made a bad mistake in your security. She'll be fired, replaced. You'll not get another chance like you had earlier."

Abel thought briefly of the injustice of firing Mabel. But actually she did mess up. Actually, she did what she did on purpose. He thought back over the seventeen years of his life, trying to recall how many times such a thing…someone who really cared about him…had happened. Only his mother…and maybe Beth.

"And furthermore, my unnamed patient…"

Abel, for the first time, interrupted. His commentary designed only to bait the doctor. He wanted to feel no obligation to Mabel. "That black woman did nothing. I busted the door while she opened it."

***

John mentally went wild. The patient spoke directly toward an accusation. He spoke on John's terms, not his own. Professionally the glass ceiling, one capped by documented patients, shattered in his mind. This new patient bore the brand of an absolutely new diagnosis.

He gathered his wits, reeled in his excitement, and carefully considered his next move. A conservative one. "Okay, the CNA, Mabel we call her. You called her 'that black woman.' What would you like to do about her...tell me?"

Abel looked like before, no interest, unresponsive, silent. John continued. "So, you busted the door, not her fault. Are you saying your fault?" Nothing.

***

Then Abel purposely rolled his eyes back into his head, creating a thoughtless appearance, one consistent with the mental concoction he was designing for Winthrop.

He watched as John regrouped, obviously weighing out his training in therapy, counseling, science. Then the doctor backed off. "Let's take a break. You can have your large open room for the moment. Enjoy your night, a long sleep. We'll talk tomorrow about this room, about your freedom." He walked out with the light on and gently closed the door.

He knew Marilyn saw the whole episode on the monitors inside his office. He balanced his ideas while he strolled back to where she waited. She met him at the door.

"Wow, John, he talked, he defended Mabel, he took a moral stand. All in response to you. How did you know?"

John smiled. "You stayed tuned, didn't you? Marilyn, sometimes, particularly with difficult cases, you must give the patient some choices. In this case, rather than speak because of his tortured space, he spoke in defense of the innocent."

"So, how does that fit your diagnosis...savant syndrome...SSS?"

"I was kidding about Super Savant Syndrome. The term doesn't exist..." He grinned. "...yet."

"John, please, I have worked with autistic people before. I know there's a large range of complex neurodevelopment disorders, characterized by social impairments, communication difficulties, and restricted, repetitive, and stereotyped patterns of behavior, but I do not see Abel fitting in the spectrum of autism at all. So, I'll ask again. What's wrong with this kid? What makes him so completely different from anyone you have ever encountered?"

"Remember that movie, *Rain Man*? Well, you might be too young for that, but it exposed millions of people to autism as well as the autistic savant phenomenon. The movie gave the impression that all autistic individuals, like this character Raymond, have these remarkable abilities. You see, Raymond had a great memory for ball player statistics, memorized parts of the telephone book, and counted cards in Las Vegas. But the truth is, savant abilities are actually extremely rare. Statistically, science has never identified this combination of characteristics we see in this patient. If you catch my drift now, we may have found the one needle in a million haystacks."

Marilyn's face turned red. "Dammit, John, quit talking about Hollywood and haystacks. Answer the question. What's wrong with this kid?"

"Great question. And here's the hard part. He continues to show brilliance on occasion, yet there's no consistency."

Marilyn pulled him into the office, pushed him into the big chair, and sat on the small chair's edge like the student she was. "So, tell me the inconsistency you speak of."

"Let's review, my dear. Comment one, the drama queen. Comment two, college. Comment three, our intoxication in his room. One through three is all about a thought generated impulsively to question our authority. Defending the CNA is a different concept."

"So?"

"So, our little island of brilliance, in the sea of retardation…savant syndrome…has a multi-faceted motivation."

Marilyn scratched her head. "So, does this multi-tasking gift make him more or less SSS?"

"Clearly special beyond special. And as excited as I am at this very moment, I need more time with him tomorrow. I need time to prepare for him."

Marilyn exposed a ripe luscious nipple. "Time for this first?"

***

For what seemed months now, Winthrop tormented Abel. But he persevered with Beth by his side. She clung closely, often silently, but always a guide through the hellish waters created by the crazed doctor who rattled his cage. And Rachel didn't seem to mind. And through the agony of tight spaces, piercing eyes, and pointed questions, he and Beth made their own evaluations, diagnosis. The name of what Abel thought Winthrop to be hanging around his neck, like a sign proclaiming a disease, wouldn't come to mind. He thought it sounded something like servant, a waiter or a slave to something. But the name didn't matter if Abel knew the meaning. You don't have to know the word opossum to know sharp teeth, a bad taste, and don't steal its food while the animal is close. And Winthrop's questions, day after day, pointed to only one thing, a condition that he and Beth had discussed one afternoon at The Fellowship headquarters. It meant stupid most of the time and smart a little of the time.

Abel laughed out loud. He knew the cameras around his room recorded the outburst, but nothing recorded his mind. Winthrop had him all wrong. His silence wasn't stupid. Brilliant, to the contrary.

He stumbled around the room in boredom and found a Bible in a bedside drawer. He knew looking at a book would drive Winthrop crazy. *Not a bad idea.* He thumbed to a familiar place, Genesis, where the character Abel, spelled just like his, is introduced. *He has my same name, was a good person, did things that pleased God, and never hurt anyone. But yet God never stopped Cain from killing his good brother. And God allowed Cain to live. Seems I'd be better off as Cain.*

Abel remembered his mother and Beth saying the Bible could teach you how to live a good life; it was truth and the truth would set you free. *Where was God when my mother died, when Beth died?*

As sleep fell upon him, he thought about Winthrop showing up the next day. He'd enjoy a long sunrise at the window. Winthrop never was early. And space, at the moment, was plentiful. He hated Winthrop for having to appreciate such degrees of captivity. He wanted out.

***

John woke up from an early celebration on his project beside a woman, young and pleasing, but out of his league professionally. An empty wine bottle sat on the night stand where they lay, all that was left from a hurried convenience store purchase. His head ached and throbbed as he arched his neck, looking for a clock. 10 a.m. He'd barely make an 11 o'clock call to the unnamed patient that should be commanding all of his attention. The woman, now making coffee, was a distraction.

Still upset with himself for wasting a perfectly good night of researching his theories, he waved his security card at the fourth floor main entrance and rubbed his aching forehead with the other hand. He started to swing by his office, but noon approached and much case development remained. Room 402 loomed up the hall like a stocking on Christmas morning...after an over- indulged Christmas Eve.

"Good morning, my young friend. Shall we share some secrets, some places in our minds that trouble us? Or maybe some places and times that brought us to this point?"

Abel lifted his eyebrow without any particular motive that John could see. He thought his patient might have understood his words and perhaps agreed, like a consensus of the minds.

"Now we have an understanding, I presume."

Abel looked disengaged, out of the conversation, and John thought a break might improve things.

"You need time," John concluded, and left hurriedly to brainstorm with Marilyn.

"John, why did you leave?"

"Can't you see, he's in his catatonic state, delved back into minimal thinking, just enough to make his body parts work?"

Marilyn pushed him into the office, raised her hands, and tightened her lips. "So?"

"So, I will now sit at my desk for a moment and figure out a way to lead this patient to the part of his mind that will shed better light on his condition. And I can assure you, my dear Marilyn, he goes to these mental crevices only when I push the right buttons, so to speak.

"Which are?"

"Marilyn, my student, my assistant, can't you guess?"

"Tight spaces, piercing eyes?"

"Precisely. Now go doll-up or something while I figure this out."

***

Heyward Moffatt followed the hurried footsteps of Doctor Winthrop down the hall, toward room 402, listening to a battery of orders. "Heyward, follow my lead, I want him to think you're about to suck the life out of his space."

As they reached the door, Winthrop jerked the handle and walked forcefully into the room. "Let's start with the window, double boarded, double sets of screws. Then push the walls closer to the window. Nothing but this bed should fit. Bring lumber in now!"

"Yes sir." Heyward quickly stacked some plywood in front of the patient.

The doctor excused the maintenance man, closed the door, and confronted the patient. "My friend, you are about to suffocate in the tightness of this room, and for a very long time." He pointed to the wood, the window, and posed his body along the proposed new wall. "Is this what you want? Before you speak again? Before I can learn anything about you...to help you?" Winthrop leaned close, eyes penetrating. "Security told me they monitored you reading the Bible. Not just looking at it, reading. Do you know how to read?"

Abel stood. Abel spoke. "I know you are Doctor Winthrop. I know that now, but I won't know it soon. You come and go in my head."

Winthrop fell off the edge of the chair he'd taken, but quickly pulled himself up. "Yes, of course. I know you come and go. Can we talk while you're lucid?" Winthrop caught himself. This near retarded knew nothing of the word "lucid." He changed his lingo. "I mean while you are here. With me."

***

Abel started to resort to his faked catatonic state. But he could not stand, even for another night, the cage. And one thing Abel knew of this hated Doctor Winthrop: he had the power to cage, and the power to release. So, Abel spoke again. "I'm still with you. I want out. I belong in the woods…by myself."

Winthrop's interest appeared peaked. "I can give you that." And as hard as it was to bear the eyes of this despised, deficient doctor, Abel hung as the good doctor came close to his face. "I promise you freedom." He seemed believable.

Winthrop began again. "I ask for only one thing…while you're still with me…simply your name and where you grew up."

Abel spoke quickly. "I'm fading away from you, but if I tell you both, you'll let me go now?"

"Yes, yes. Now, now."

"My name is Abel. I grew up across the river." He stood for his escort out of the room, the hall, the shackled door, the elevator, beyond the revolving entrance doors, the trees where birds would fly in and out, the park, the river bank. He would swim home.

But Winthrop had slammed the door, locked it from outside, before Abel could finish his thoughts. A betrayal.

***

John hurried into his office and told Marilyn of the successful visit. She gave him a high-five into the air, and he slapped her hand, fully entitled, but with a look on his face that the accolades of his success were only beginning. "Oh, John, you did it!"

With a smidgen of insincerity he replied, "Couldn't have done it without you."

"So, where will he go when you release him? Will he be alright? Should we give him money, pack a lunch, give him a ride home?"

"Abel is going nowhere."

"What?"

"Our work is barely started."

"You made him a promise."

"A cop makes a kidnapper a promise…and the cop lies. The ends justify the means."

"He's no kidnapper. He's a young man with problems trusting people. He trusted you."

"I'm a trained professional. To throw this patient from this hospital, not knowing minute by minute if he's sane or completely psychopathic, violates every oath I've ever taken as a physician. Abel stays."

Marilyn threw her hair back. "You're the kidnapper."

"I'd expect that uneducated comment from a Chafenville Technical College graduate."

Marilyn slapped him and left.

He dismissed the stinging upon his face as a consequence of the competitive world of medicine…*and some damned good sex.* Then he rethought his success. *Abel?* And he wondered why he didn't push for a last name. *Maybe tomorrow.*

***

Abel looked at the locked door, the broken promise, and his own stupidity. Tonight both Beth and Rachel would weigh on his mind. Revenge felt too simple. Betrayal, more than anything else, permanently scarred his mind. Now Winthrop,

and he feared Marilyn also, joined the company of Ed Wood.
The night would be long, filled with real thoughts and dreams he
could not distinguish between.

***

Two days later, Winthrop, armed with useless facts
bought with money paid to private detectives holding only a
name and place, confronted Abel, impatiently waiting for
answers.

"I bet you're asking yourself 'what's in it for you?' This
is the kind of question a motivated, thoughtful patient might ask.
Yet earlier testing shows us a much different subject. Even
hooked up to a polygraph, you scored unbelievably low, yet now
you speak with authority, a purpose, an intelligence. Can you
even understand what I'm saying? Have you relapsed back into
the part of your brain that renders you intellectually disabled?"

Abel avoided his eyes, gave no hints, and hated the man
claiming to know his mind. This man, diplomas hanging on his
office walls like trophies, seemed attached to some idea that the
"subject," as he referred to the patient, had swings of knowing
and not knowing, sometimes near brain dead, and at other times
a human with purpose. He definitely had a purpose, and the
multitude of diplomas and certificates hanging on the walls of
Winthrop's office, all committed to memory by Abel, seemed
ridiculous. Beth knew more than this bozo. But if Winthrop
wanted to celebrate in his ignorance, so be it. *Doctor, have your
way, then I'll have mine.*

Abel wanted the freedom to enjoy his emotional
manipulation of Winthrop to himself, but Rachel and Beth

loomed close. The penetrating eyes, the tightening of space, brought his voices closer to the vision of his mind. He would figure out a way to make everyone around him content.

***

Session after session. Eyeball to eyeball. Glorious victory after victory, spewed like proclamations from the good doctor's lips. And Abel, denied of his promise, sat face to face with Winthrop who chose to violate places in his mind the doctor knew nothing of.

"Abel, I sense in your eyes you are lucid, following me. Can we talk?"

"Abel, I know you want freedom. I may have promised you that…and it will come. But for now, I'm here to protect you from the big unknown out there. Just a little more talk from you and we'll be free as soaring eagles."

Buzzards, Abel thought. And the big unknown would belong to the good doctor.

"Can you tell me a little of your past, your mom, a pet, a best friend?"

A large, round clock on the office wall, though battery operated, clicked the seconds of agony.

"Abel, I'm about to not be nice again."

"Abel I'm about to send you to a room, your room, tighter than ever."

He cursed himself for giving Winthrop his name. It gurgled from the doctor's mouth like vomit.

"Abel, I've looked through my files. I've spent hundreds of hours with you, no kidding. Many times, I've given you kindness, compassion, and understanding. Not once have you reacted in a positive manner. In other words, your brain only functions when stressed with the exact opposite...negative reinforcement. What motivates you to react in any intelligent way are mean, rude, threatening stimulations. You are your best when faced with living in a windowless dog house."

Oh? Abel calculated the hours of fabricated kindness claimed by Winthrop, and wanted to say, *take one zero off your calculations and even ten hours is a stretch.* Bordo, a man who could exaggerate numbers, helped him with that thought. Abel said nothing.

Winthrop started in on him again. "So, my patient, my Abel, the one who cares nothing for kind words, the one who ignores those who want to cure you, want to bring you to a better life. Truly, I can heal you, rid you of the baggage that damaged you...which are usually people...can we talk about these people?"

Abel thought of nothing but the "dog house" comment. But others in his head focused on the doctor's "damaged baggage" comment. And the folds of his mind reacted unkindly.

Winthrop pulled his chair closer and closer, like setting up the final scene. "Now is the time to decide your future. Your willingness to talk can open doors for you, big places, nice food, help from me. I can bring you peace, joy, and a focus on your most amazing talents. The place in your brain that functions like a genius will open up to me, and you and I will make medical history. Or if you continue to fail to open up to me, your life will be quite unpleasant. I'll touch you in ways you won't like."

Abel clamored for one more folly at the good doctor. "Are you gay?"

***

John summoned the orderlies to return Abel to room 402. When the door closed he looked over at Marilyn.

"Dammit, John, I can't tell if you're a manipulative genius or a…who the hell knows what."

"Try to see the best in me."

"But you bullied him, threatened him, he's retar…excuse…challenged. Can't you see, and I apologize, you've simply lost control."

"Are you kidding? My student? The issue isn't what I said to him, the issue is the new discovery of a distinctive, unequivocal statement, from a patient who might go a decade without speaking. And now, once again in response to my calculated stimulation, he, this mostly imbecile, has now raised a new question. Did you hear it? 'Am I gay?'"

She laughed until she gained control. "Are you? More likely bi. Actually, you're whatever you call a person who only cares to please himself. And I'm tired of faking orgasms."

"Quit acting as stupid as this town, this university that spells its name with a 'Tech' on the end, a place nobody ever heard of."

"Stop it, John. Maybe you stumbled across a patient in our stupid town, a person whose mind bleeds confusion. He is sick! And my heart reaches out to help cure him, not display him in your trophy case."

"Marilyn, there is nothing more important to me above the patient's well-being."

She stood, staggered a bit, and slurred her words. "I'm not sure what you or even I think is important. I'm struggling to find a way out of this miserable place and you are too. Not only is it awkward, our care of this patient is bloated in our own self-interests. And you're asking me to weigh out your obligation to help a child with his mental struggles versus an overeducated man who's milking his patient for his own ends. And the scales in my mind lead me to question your values, wonder if this boy could use another doctor."

"Say what? Marilyn, are you drunk?"

"Say nothing. You've told me all before, I'm not qualified. Sure, I've had a bit of wine. But maybe you don't know this child-patient the way I do. So, maybe give me some credit."

John glanced toward his watch, trying to end the conversation.

Finally Marilyn, regardless of her intoxication, spoke the last words. "You see a way to rise above everybody who got in your way, got in your path of your success. I know I'm not what you are. I know I'm not able to dissect complications of the mind the way you can. But what are we doing to this young boy? Is the object to help him or you?"

                              ***

Abel looked at Heyward Moffatt, the man Doctor Winthrop used as a tool to suffocate him back to his understanding side. But the doctor had failed to consider the tremendous hardware Heyward carried. A large utility belt carried not only tools but also keys and pass cards to every door in the hospital. Abel took careful inventory of what Heyward had around his waist.

The time had come. Threats of more isolationism, small spaces, and more eyes. The television set, itself, became Abel's weapon. And with the determination of a wild, caged animal, Abel snatched and brought the appliance crashing upon Heyward's head. He quickly unbuckled the maintenance man's belt, dangling with an array of keys to freedom. Cameras caught the knockout punch, the stripping of the belt, the opening of the door once a gauntlet to him. But cameras are no better than the people who care to watch them. Quick and agile, he negotiated through barrier after barrier and sprinted out the front revolving door to freedom.

But Abel's plan carried too much baggage. The mostly pleasant Beth jockeyed for position in his mind, often at odds with his soul-connected Rachel, his mother who pulled him emotionally toward the bars as she perished in front of his cage. These people wanted more than his escape, the hatred for John Winthrop buried deeply in his mind. And those who shared the depths of his mind commanded revenge for themselves more than Abel. No choice.

Chapter Ten

October 2012

A deer hunter with a long-range scope watched disturbing, but vague, images as Abel dealt with his victims. The hunter, a thousand yards away, couldn't get a clear look at Abel. The hunter pulled out his cell phone, had one bar, and tipped the Chafenville police as to the location of what appeared to be multiple killings. The authorities acted swiftly, decisively, with a dozen officers.

***

Abel slept soundly in a grove of hemlock only a short distance from the trail where he had murdered his victims only moments before. Dead tired from the preparation and execution of rendering justice to Winthrop and his assistant, he needed a long rest. A crowd of gun-packing deputies stormed his space, waking him with no room for escape. Shocked at the turn of events, he wrestled with the unlikely chance he'd be caught. He remained silent, and soon became aware of the hunter with the long-distant scope.

At the station, police put together Abel's history with the victims, one a psychiatrist, the other a social worker with some psych courses under her belt. They arranged a line-up. The hunter's guesswork, looking through a one-way mirror at the police department, proved indecisive. With no other suspect, they locked him up in a small cell.

An interrogation took place. A half dozen uniformed officers lined the walls as some smart-ass detective rattled off questions. Considering the fact Miranda warnings were administered, and the accused chose to be silent, the impatient interrogator, having none of his "why were you in that grove of trees" or "who can vouch for you" repetitive questions answered, he resorted to the "talk, damn it, or you'll rot in jail" tirade.

The only humor to Abel was one of the uniformed officers in the intimidation parade happened to be the same fat officer who arrested him at the library. No recognition.

The injustice of jail without evidence weighed heavily on Abel's court-appointed attorney. The tightness of the room weighed heavier for Abel.

"My name is Ivan Douglas. I have been appointed by our local court to be your lawyer. Do you know what a lawyer is?"

Abel wanted to cut out the formalities, but this man had a code of ethics, supposedly, but so did Doctor John Winthrop. He decided to test the waters. "Tell me what is the attorney-client privilege?"

The lawyer rubbed his chin. "Means I can't tell anybody what we talk about."

"You take that oath seriously?"

"Like religion. If you can't trust my confidence, I can't be very effective as your lawyer, understand?"

Abel didn't answer the question. "So, Lawyer Douglas, have you heard of the M'Naghten rule?"

Ivan Douglas stood. "*You* know M'Naghten?"

"I'm no lawyer, why I asked you."

"Fair enough. Simply put...one charged with a crime who doesn't know right from wrong can't be guilty of that crime."

"M'Naghten? Was he the one accused?"

The lawyer had to reflect a minute. "Yep, best I remember some nut in England, centuries ago, murdered some guy. M'Naghten claimed to be insane or something or another. They named the rule after the nut and today I believe it's still good law, even in the State of Georgia. So, to answer your question, M'Naghten must have been the defendant...can't say I've thought this much about it since law school."

Abel took little comfort in the fact that his own lawyer, apparently, had never asserted the defense before in a court of law. "What are the charges?"

"M'Naghten's?"

"No. Mine."

"I'm sorry, should have already covered that. Figured you'd heard that enough in the interrogation before I got here. Murder. Two murders."

"What evidence do they have against me?"

"For starters, they aren't even sure you can understand things." Ivan laughed, grabbing his overextended belly. "Guess they don't know you like I know you."

"Explain, again, the rules about an attorney and his client?"

"Say no more, got your point."

"May I ask again, what is the evidence?"

"My guess is not much. The reason I say this, is that the officers who I brushed by on the way in would usually be rubbing the damning evidence in my face...especially when my client hasn't confessed, and they want me to rub it into the accused's face as well."

"Hold it. You mean you walked into this detention center with the expectation that you'd rub elbows with the same people who interrogated me, want me convicted?"

"No, no. I know how that sounded, but really I come here a lot. Free lawyers are much in demand. We have to laugh at ourselves, all sides of the system of justice, to keep from going bonkers."

"Okay, Lawyer Douglas, I'm trying to keep an open mind, trying to believe your oath of confidentiality, trying to take comfort in being presumed innocent and of your loyalty to me as your client..."

Douglas interrupted. "Yes, yes, all of that. You have my word."

"Then I'll take you at your word and trust you won't rub anything in *my* face."

A frustrated look came over the lawyer. "Yes, Abel, you have my word once again. Since we are in a confidential relationship and you know my full name, may I have yours?"

He hesitated, but knew he'd need this lawyer's help, confidence. "Abel Wood."

After months of virtual silence under the thumb of John Winthrop, Abel delighted in using his conversational skills in a legally protective shell. "Okay, now we were talking about evidence, or the lack thereof. You spoke of your suspicion that, to quote you, 'not much.' May I ask when you will know this for sure?"

"In about two weeks I'll get the package from the prosecutor. All evidence, good and bad, is supposed to be included. We'll talk then."

Lawyer Douglas stood again, stretched, and looked at Abel. "You know, since they have no address, not much of anything on your priors, the judge has denied bond. Might be a flight risk. I could take it up to a higher judge if you like. The more important question is whether you want me to try and get you kept separate from the other prisoners. You've caused quite a bit of confusion among the authorities as to your competency. Do you know that term?"

Abel rolled his eyes, and Douglas continued. "Of course you do, but they don't know that. What I'm saying is they'd probably keep you apart from the other inmates, merely upon my request. You'd have more room, privacy, but you'd have nobody to talk to…" He laughed again, "…but me."

Abel lifted his finger, asking for a moment to think. Solitude over tight, uninvited company seemed preferable. "Thank you for your concern. Yes, since bond is unlikely, separation from the sane criminals sounds nice."

"I'll make the request on the way out. But before I leave, now that you understand I'm on your side, if you want to tell me about the facts, I'm here to listen."

"What facts?"

"You know, like why you did it, maybe some justification. Self-defense comes up often in these sorts of cases."

"Can you be more specific, Counselor?"

Impatiently, like he wanted to be on his way home, his lawyer replied. "Yeah, like are you guilty or not guilty?"

Abel was ready. "Was Mr. M'Naghten guilty?"

***

Thanksgiving and Christmas came and went. Lawyer Ivan Douglas, Abel's only visitor, engaged in a series of conversations about the M'Naghten rule, circumstantial evidence, and burden of proof. They pored over evidence, showing pictures and lab results of two awful murders, none tying the accused to the act. Abel was relieved his gloves, hat, and long sleeves, all bought at the outpost, rendered no DNA. And the first words recorded at the live lineup, where Abel was forced to stand, was the hunter's comment, "Can't tell none of 'em fer sure."

Douglas brought up House of Hope, explaining admission could be an easy sale under the circumstances. Able thought it more of Douglas washing any self-guilt of getting him freed completely in a trial. Abel had seen House of Hope in a brochure in the room where he met with his lawyer. The picture looked like a large mansion. Eventually this became his choice.

***

Before Abel plucked the eyes from Winthrop, he carefully listened to the doctor's condescending words.

"Abel, you're better than this. We can work your problems out."

"And your diagnosis of me? Tell me slowly."

No words formed on either Marilyn's or Winthrop's lips, especially the doctor. "SSS," finally Abel blurted out. "I overheard you. A misdiagnosis as large as your ego."

Winthrop looked pale and Abel continued. "However, since we're placing each other in categories, let me educate you. Clearly your failure in life stems from your addiction to one's self, arrogant pride, and egotistical admiration. You're so consumed with your own importance, the truth gives way to clouded nonsense. In short, Doctor Winthrop, phallic narcissism. The reason you must die. The same reason a man named Ed Wood died.

His planning of his death had been slow and methodical. Only Marilyn bothered him, her intervention only well intended. He concluded early on she must be spared. As the details of their weekend plans unfolded, he committed himself to letting her go, or preferably hoped she'd stay out of the way. No matter what, Marilyn should be excused.

But then came subsequent thoughts. Rachel broke him down, took away his will, put blame where blame had to be placed…and injected consequences as the blame dictated. If Marilyn lived, she'd be a witness. Rachel insisted Marilyn had made her own decision by voluntarily meshing her mind, her flesh, her misguided judgment with a man who dissected Abel's existence on the same level as his goddamned grandfather.

John Winthrop had to die, and, unfortunately, so did Marilyn…as did his mother…as did Beth. And like those before her, Marilyn's last breath wouldn't take away her good qualities which would remain in Abel's head.

The mostly deserted hiking trails miles outside Chafenville made for an advantageous plan for interlude. Abel had watched the two from a distance, followed their car by foot, watched them unload backpacks from the trunk.

They hiked, he followed. They stopped, he spied through deep undergrowth. Winthrop seemed to be apologizing, talking of making things right. Miles from their car, he pulled out expensive picnic stuff. They ate olives, cheeses, and salivated over expensive-looking wine. He waited. They stripped their clothes, became vulnerable. He attacked.

When Winthrop collapsed, Abel turned to Marilyn and shouted "run." But Rachel sprinted forward in his mind, like he'd deceived her. His mother screamed. Marilyn knew too much. *Marilyn knew too much.* If Rachel and Beth shouldn't have died, why should Marilyn live? But justice often linked good and bad, weak and strong. Winthrop's piercing eyes, sharp as a surgical knife, cut away at Abel's existence and made John's going away necessary. Winthrop to Marilyn was the lard in the biscuit. Abel didn't know how to get it out, kill it separately. The whole thing had to be thrown away.

He brought Marilyn to a peaceful ending, painless, like a mouse resting in his hand, but necessary for that night's meal. But as Marilyn gently faded, Beth stepped forward in his mind, offering understanding, some justification.

"Bubbles, bubbles." Some just needed to be popped. Abel remembered his passion for a clown in a park with a bubble machine. The bubbles jumped from the small pipe and danced together like grand balls of fiery colors. Abel loved the idea of judging each bubble. The sun could create the perfect hue of color that pleased his eyes. But clouds could alter the colors, which reflected the same unpleasantness his grandfather had reflected on his mother. So, those bubbles were popped.

Chapter Eleven

Monday, June 17, 2013

Many miles east of Chafenville, high above the river, grew a grove of rhododendrons, the canopy so thick you could walk under it, head high, as if under a massive umbrella. Among the gnarled trunks was a small opening only two feet wide and three feet high. But upon entry, the cave opened up like a large room, hardly a cage, appearing the size of two Houses of Hope. Abel constructed, from metal and wood, a grate with a latch on all four corners, secured with four identical padlocks, a matching set bought with cash at a remote outpost.

The boat and motor he used to flee with Helen from the river banks outside the park floated in the current of the Shady River, its purpose now done. He found it earlier among a grove of deep-rooted bamboo and assumed it was part of a drug deal gone sour, since it was ditched, yet had a half-tank of gas. He got Parker across the river in the deserted Jon boat he patched, and used on the devastating day he ended up in the public library.

Abel commanded his cave. He looked above the kidnapped child's eyes, not wanting contact. Then he looked toward Helen; her eyes could not be avoided.

Helen had been a challenge, though Abel was physically stronger; he sensed Helen to be strong willed. She didn't fit into the two categories Abel used to evaluate people. She wasn't right or wrong, not good or bad, not judging or non-judging. He had kept her close to his side in the back of the Caravan. He reminded her repeatedly that Parker might die if she failed to do exactly what he said. His command always got a submissive "whatever it takes" response, which placed Abel firmly in control.   The inflection in his voice sounded like his own grandfather, to which his own mother submitted.

"I've got a gun in my pocket, and the guys holding Parker have a gun to his head as we speak. If we don't show up on time, they'll kill him."

Abel's strategy worked. Helen complied with dropping through the floorboard of the car and into the storm drain without an argument. She kept the pace set by Abel in the storm drain. Abel sensed an increased fear in Helen as he told her to get in the boat, but assured her she was saving Parker's life. Her cooperation worked out nicely, according to Abel's plan and timetable.

But no one held a gun to Parker's head. No one occupied the large room just inside the cave opening except a lonely and frightened Parker.

A long and painful hike for Helen began after the boat was beached, then pushed empty into the river to float away. She never could have made the sharp climb toward where she believed Parker waited, except for the sturdy arm of Abel pulling her forward and upward.   He took breaks only when she appeared to be passing out.   He pulled out liquids and some natural berries stored in his pocket and fed them to her, restoring energy as he pressed onward with a plan not her own.   Abel admired her perseverance, the same way he admired Parker, on the promise of reuniting with his family, the trip before. She fought for whom she loved, just like Rachel and Beth fought for him.   And he felt thankful Rachel, who had started this whole process, seemed to be leaving him alone.

And they climbed until she collapsed, then climbed again, and again. To an outsider, even the seasoned climber, each step appeared without direction, the path nonexistent. Abel finally carried Helen to the slight opening, the entrance to his cave. She looked deathly. Then he spoke Parker's name. And both she and her son awoke.

Helen held Parker as if a precious package...lightly enough not to damage, but with a determined embrace that he never be taken away. The look of hopelessness a moment before faded.

He thought of the three from House of Hope he almost thought of bringing along rather than kicking them off the van. The three had a combined IQ of 165. House of Hope records, loosely protected at night, verified each condition of who became Abel's followers. When he told them cutting the counselor's throat was funny, they laughed while blood spilled. When he told them they would be heroes, they all felt important. Had he brought them along, he'd be babysitting for four, Parker included. Parker being left alone with some decent food and drink was better.

He pondered his decision of abandoning the three. Perhaps they could help with Parker, leaving him time and space to deal with Helen. He recalled an e-mail message from Paul: *Helen, the love of my life.* And Riordan's eyes still burned in Abel's soul like an uninvited invasion. The rudeness of wanting to dissect his life brought hate flowing back into the reasons for forcing Helen and Parker to this hidden destination. But one thing Abel could not avoid...Rachel closely guarded his motives.

Rachel had a lot to say about Paul Riordan. Rachel knew his type. Seeing Parker held to his mother's breast gave him pause to reflect on his own mother's guidance. He felt her soft words, though in Ed Wood's basement, maybe a bit of what Parker felt now.

"Are you two hungry?" asked Abel.

After some delay, Helen spoke. "We're fine...what comes next?"

"I wish I knew."

"That doesn't make sense, Abel. We're all here because of you. How could you not know what your plan is?"

"Because it's not my plan."

"Who else is involved?"

Abel didn't answer. He slowly stammered to a rock in a corner that had a depression in the top of it resembling a cradle. He sat softly down in the middle of it and drew his knees gently toward his chest. Whatever caused the submissive act suddenly ended, and Abel walked back over to Helen.

"How does Mr. Riordan look at you?"

"I don't really understand your question. Abel, this whole thing can work out for you. You won't get in trouble, and we'll get some help for you."

Abel grabbed Helen roughly under the soft flesh of her left arm. He delighted in her gasp as he jerked her up and ordered her to release Parker. Parker cried as Abel dragged his mother to the rear of the room.

He didn't particularly like being physical with Helen, especially after nearly carrying her up the mountain, but the words were not his. "We don't need help. If I ever hear you say that again, you'll end up dead like the others."

Helen fought back her tears and rapidly nodded her head with understanding.

"Now go shut up Parker. He's hurting my ears."

***

Abel dumped a package of cheese crackers at Helen's feet, and she thanked him. After some time passed, she opened the crackers and slowly fed them to Parker. He shook each time she raised a cracker to his mouth. "It'll be ok. Everybody's going to be ok," she said.

Light faded quickly and early in the cave. Abel said he had flashlights but was not ready to use them. Silence prevailed, and sleep overcame everyone, Helen the last to fade. The options she kept reviewing seemed so few and limited. She could ease to the opening of the cave and figure out how to open it. Would she take Parker with her or return after the gate was opened? What if Abel woke up?

Who is this other person Abel says makes decisions? She thought as the strained muscles, joints, and ligaments in her body burned. *Tomorrow.*

***

Helen's eyes opened with the faint morning light making its way into the opening of the cave. A dream initially felt possible, but the damp rock under her arms that held Parker's head quickly brought reality back. She focused on the spot she last remembered seeing Abel. Gone.

"Breakfast?"

"Abel, you startled me, may I ask how long we'll be staying here?"

"Depends."

"On what?" Helen softly spoke in hope of not irritating him.

"On Mr. Paul Riordan."

Abel knelt down at face level with Helen. "I asked you yesterday, how does he look at you? I want your answer."

Helen silently contemplated what she believed Abel wanted to hear. "I guess he looks at me kindly...like he thinks I'm special. Why do you ask?"

"Do you want to know how he looks at me, Mrs. Riordan?"

"If you want me to know."

"His eyes cut me. Every look tries to hurt me. I need to hurt him back. Do you think having you and Parker here is hurting him?"

"I'm sure it is, Abel, sounds like you have done just what you wanted to do. I bet Paul feels the same way. He would say 'sorry,' not what he intended."

"Not that easy, Mrs. Riordan. Mr. Riordan had those kinds of chances. The last thing he'd do is apologize. His watching me only got worse, but you know why he has stopped?"

"Tell me Abel, please."

"Parker. And now you. Can you understand?"

"I'm not sure."

"Good, now you and Parker eat your donuts."

Days passed, and Helen's mind and body attempted to adapt to the cave. The area where she and Parker mostly stayed became as familiar as the features of her own face. Loneliness and silence dominated their small area. Abel came to her irregularly.

"What are you thinking of, Abel? You know a lot of money is like power, can get you what you want."

"I got money."

"What is it that you don't like about money, Abel?"

"My grandfather always wanted money. I'm not like him."

"Is your grandfather still around?"

"No."

She moved slightly closer to Abel, sensing a degree of approachability with him. Unsure of whether to meet his eyes, she settled on a rock structure just above his head.

"We aren't bad people, Abel, and actually can be quite forgiving. What do you say we give you whatever you want and then leave you alone?"

"Too late for that."

She felt his eyes intensify on her legs, sensing a determination in his willingness to talk.

He spoke in a tone of voice she'd not heard. "Do you remember an e-mail from Mr. Riordan about your leg?"

She drew a blank. "Could you remind me? We have a lot of e-mails."

"Valentine's Day."

She sensed a connection, but wasn't sure. "My leg, Valentine's Day?"

"I read it. I'll quote the message. 'Oh, I can't wait to nibble on your birthmark, just below your knee, and work my tongue up the inside of your silky thigh.'"

"I'm scared, Abel. Just tell me what I can say to make things right with you."

Abel seemed to melt a little, like he wanted to confess something. Like the voices in his head had left him, or were not controlling him at this moment. Whatever the case, he fell to one knee in front of Helen. "I may not get another chance. I hold no hate to you or Parker. I do hate Mr. Riordan, and what he's put me through. But I can't say that hate is all my hate, what's in my head."

Helen grabbed the opportunity quickly, she'd heard of such mental illness. "Abel, quick, tell me what, if anything, I can do to rid you of what you don't really want. I see a way to help, to cleanse all of us, Paul included, of our mistakes. Take my hand."

Helen, with the grace of an angel, extended her hand in his direction. But as fast as the opportunity presented itself, the look on Abel's face neutralized.

"It's not about you, Mrs. Riordan, just like it wasn't about my mama. Now we need to stop talking. Go back to Parker."

Concave depressions in the rock were becoming familiar to Helen. She tended to gravitate toward the different formations according to her emotions. Tired, agitated, feeling impending death, optimism, hope, reminded her of furniture in the house. Morning coffee, serious talks with Paul, daily discussions with the kids. In time, Helen actually became entertained with her predictable movements. In this, she realized a correlation occurring across the cave. Abel seemed to move as often as she. Although she couldn't make out the rough, smooth, deep, and shallow features of the rock where he ebbed and flowed, there seemed a definite pattern -- a link, a connection appeared joined in the movements.

Is he copying me? She thought. Why or how?

She suddenly considered, without an intention on either's part, their own emotions could be linked.

The amount of light, the temperature or occasional head movement by one or the other seemed to impact the correlated movements.

And as absurd as the thought came over her, she wrestled with the possibility Abel feels as deeply about what is happening as I.

Chapter Twelve

Saturday, June 15, 2013
Sundown

"Get some help, dammit.   You and this incompetent department have doubled our problems. Get SBI in, and you get the hell out of this case," Paul spouted off at Tim.

"I know, Paul, I've called the State guys, but they will only send so much manpower…football games in Atlanta get most of the attention, not our small town."

"I said get the hell out of here."

"Okay, but we at least have to give support…cars, officers, and equipment. I know you're madder than hell. Me, too.   But chances are Abel is within a controlled perimeter around Chafenville. We found an empty Jon boat floating down the river. Looks to be the one. I'd give it no more than a ten-mile radius. We're checking on every source who knows Abel. Within the next couple of hours we'll know where he grew up, and who he hung out with. We need to determine where his turf is. Surely he has to rely on people and terrain he's familiar with to keep three people hidden for any length of time."

"How would you know? You lost him under a stinkin' tent."

"Right."

"And lost my Helen with him!"

Tim tucked his head and walked out of the house.

***

House of Hope stood without a purpose. Empty. A simple wreath of white roses garnished the front door. The sender of the flowers seemed inconsequential. The Board would move its meeting up to Monday, like quicker administrative action might help. Chairman summed it up best. "Nothing's left." Until somebody who counted could rationalize an inconceivable silver lining in the dark cloud hovering over House of Hope, failure could be the only conclusion.

Stirring under this veil of sadness for the victims, each board member also would ponder personal legal liability. After all, the Board created this house...this concept.

***

Abel had enough supplies reasonably to last six days. But he underestimated the amount of time to carry out his plan, particularly since the plan developed slowly in his mind inside the cave. Helen seemed relatively calm, patient, doing nothing that would anger him. He almost wanted her to anger him because anger might be exactly the stimulus he needed. His indecision weighed heavy on his mind. Paul's e-mail message about the birthmark kept coming back to him.

Rachel recognized the indecision at the same time. Abel looked to his mother's guidance, and suddenly Helen's condescending eyes were hostile.

Before the kidnapping, Abel believed killing Helen easy. But the more he thought past her death, the less desirability the concept had. *If I can control whether or not she can breathe, I'm controlling Mr. Riordan himself.*

***

Passing days ripped at Paul's sanity. Nights brought torment, insomnia, gut-burning failure. Puffy eyes, chats with his remaining child, offering a hope he doubted himself, made him feel inadequate. Helen, Parker, how did I let this happen?

His perceived multiple personalities of Abel Wood took toll on every waking hour. Nothing fit. The only tolerable time was receiving his daily police report on progress in the investigation. Tim, before their recent argument, took all the time needed to engage Paul with dialogue over the theories of Abel's mind. To have been only local legal types, their discussions became quite developed and were based firmly in personality behavioral sciences.

But when Paul berated and kicked Tim out of his house, suddenly things changed. After letting his anger pass, Paul called Tim's home, where only Tim's wife answered, hurting Paul to the core. "Mr. Riordan, Tim's depressed, he's been at this business too long, I'm sorry."

"Can I speak to him?"

"Our family has problems, too. Tim is not doing well. Can you check with the department? I'm sure everybody's trying to help you there."

Paul became enraged when he learned Tim had left on a medical family leave. When he questioned the human resource office he got a privacy issue response. When he called Tim's wife again, she cried, said he was working through things, and asked him not to call again.

That left the local Police Chief and the designated SBI agent in charge. Paul previously referred to these political appointments as Tweedle dee and Tweedle dum. Tim had laughed. Paul suddenly found no humor in the turn of events. He felt sorry for the blame he laid on Tim for the kidnappings. He felt helpless.

***

Abel, down to two cans of pinto beans and a two-quart can of fruit juice, fumed. Everything should be over. Trying to sort out the details of his plan in his mind irritated him. Frustration set in as he realized he would have to get more food and supplies. How would he do it? I can't exactly walk into the nearest grocery chain.

His mother demanded Helen's death. He would amputate the leg with the birth mark. Helen's leg would be the cost of the money that the tire company paid for Paul's client's leg, undoing the glory beaming from Paul's laptop about the case.

I don't care about the money, but Mrs. Riordan's leg will take away a part of Mr. Riordan's life.

Rachel's strong presence kept Abel focused on removing the leg. But Helen would die in a matter of minutes from the blood loss and Parker would watch it all. This bubble was becoming hazy for Abel, and Rachel didn't seem all that interested in those details, leaving Abel to sort things out for himself.

Abel divided the remaining fruit juice and rationed it out. Before he left, he tried a calm explanation. "I'll be back within an hour. Don't mess with the gate…I'll know if you did. The good news is we'll all have more to drink and eat." But he knew he'd be gone far more than an hour which felt like trusting the ants after leaving a picnic.

He locked the gate down tightly on the cave opening and left without a definitive idea. His legs felt strange. Hardly used in over a week. Thirty minutes later he stumbled into a shanty town where communication, if any, took place by foot and word of mouth. Basically a community of nowhere-else-to-goers.

"Where do you buy your food?" he asked of a fifteen-and-a-half-year-old prostitute.

"Lately, at Trader Tam's. He don't ask much for his stuff...cheap. Suspect it's hot, but
'round here that don't matter."

"Hey," said the girl, "you got time to do a little pluggin'? Won't cost you much."

"Thanks, maybe later. Where's that Trader you talkin' about?"

"Through the woods, in the clearin' by the old beaver dam."

***

"You Tam?" Abel asked the foul-smelling, unshaved man sitting on a log by disarrayed piles of sacks, boxes, and crates.

Abel watched his eyes roam him suspiciously. "Ain't seen you 'round here. Don't usually do business with newcomers."

"I got cash."

"That don't mean I'll trade with you, but it sure don't hurt your situation," he laughed out heartily. "So, what you needin', Sonny Boy?"

"Maybe couple cases of pintos, a dozen packs of dry beef, box of drink mix, and lots of snacks."

"I reckon I got most of that. You can have enough snacks to feed an army. Cost you a hundred, cash. You got that?"

Abel considered it a bargain. "I can't carry it all now."

"Hey...you can carry it or leave it, but it's all cash now."

Abel laid out five twenties in the dirt-layered hand of the merchant.

"Now...Sonny Boy...if you got an extra five, I'll haul it for you in my two-wheel cart over there."

Abel thought to himself the extreme risk he was taking, leaving the Riordans alone. He could let the old man haul it to the old flour mill by the creek. That would put the provisions within a quarter mile of the cave, and get him back to Helen and Parker a lot earlier.

"Ok, you got a deal."

The man just stood there.

"What are you waiting for?" Abel asked.

"Five bucks...the pay is up front," the man said as he grinned broadly.

Abel pulled out more money from his pocket. If you're going with me I'm patting you down. You're not robbing me down the trail."

Tam threw up his arms and snickered, "Pat away, might be fun." Abel felt and pulled out a large pistol and a liquor bottle. "Keep your booze, but we'll be leaving this here." Abel threw the pistol among the boxes of stacked up merchandise and handed over the money. They loaded up and began walking.

Before they paced a quarter of a mile, Tam unscrewed the bottle and took a sizeable chug.

"Care for a slug on the house...best white lightnin' this side of the county."

Abel declined.   By half of a mile, Abel had to pull the cart, Tam stumbling over himself every third step.   When they reached the old mill, Tam passed out, face to the sky.

Abel figured he might as well use the cart to get it all back to the cave.   When Abel cautiously returned with the cart, the man was snoring at an uneven pace.   He dumped the cart by its owner.

"The damn fool won't remember how he got here."   He laughed as he returned to the cave.

Over the next few hours, Abel became relaxed and focused on the leg, the one to be removed, taken to the banks of the river and hung over a low-hanging limb of the sycamore tree. Then he would call Paul Riordan with the location.   Not much of a plan after that.

Mr. Riordan's email bounced in Abe's mind.   Her left leg.   He pulled up her pants leg and saw, below her knee, the odd-shaped birthmark. It reminded him of the rocks he had skipped along the creek's surface in an earlier time, a simpler time before he ever crossed the river.

Rachel told him to take that leg.   And the more he thought, the more eager he became.   Or, as he thought, the more eager Rachel became.

"Rather than tomorrow, we'll do it now.   I'll take it to my sycamore and call Riordan."

Parker had been particularly cooperative with his new rations.   The calm had given Abel's inner voices time to influence.

This thing needs to end, Rachel told Abel.   *Take the leg.*

But daylight was fading, and the only adequate light was at the cave opening. And Abel needed a push, inspiration...something from Helen.

He lied to her. "You know I can't let Parker live." He watched her carefully.

Helen abruptly stood, her numb legs shaking from little use since the cave became her home.

"You'll do nothing to Parker. That was your deal. That's why I'm here, and the game is over. You want money or me...fine...but you're a nut case...a certified crazed monster."

With that, Abel had his reason. He covered her mouth with a solution that he had stored in a bottle in the back of the cave for months. The chemical, poured into a musty old rag, mixed with the oxygen and saliva in her mouth. Instantly she was overcome and slept.

Quickly, Abel dragged her to the last remaining daylight penetrating the opening of the cave. Parker appeared shaken at the reaction of his mother, but Abel knew Parker had no idea what was coming next.

As he continued to drag her body forward, toward the entrance to the cave, Abel reached into a crevice in the wall, and pulled out a saw needed to perform the amputation. Abel leaned his back against the locked gate. With a pocket knife, he cut with precision the cloth leg of her pants, exposing the leg from the mid-thigh to her foot. He would leave the canvas red slip-on shoe on her foot. He thought it complemented the brown hue of her birthmark, or at least his mother did.

Abel viewed her calf carefully. She surely would bleed to death, but it didn't matter. Paul Riordan would have his due. As he thought of it, why return to the cave at all? What was left would be locked in, to be found either alive or dead. He would not control that process.

Suddenly Abel was interrupted. "What are you doing to my mommie?" shouted Parker. Then another voice agreed, like an echo. The voice belonged to Beth. *Yeah, what are you doing to her?* And as fast as Beth gave truth to Parker's concern, Abel heard the steps of Rachel sprinting up behind Beth.

Abel laid the leg to his side, stood, and proceeded to guide Parker to the back of the cave, promising drinks and snacks. But as Parker moved toward the back, pushed by Abel's insistent hand, he asked, "Why the knife?"

"I'm going to cut that ugly mark off your mother's leg. It won't hurt her. But I don't want you to watch, because she wouldn't want you to watch. There are four chocolate peanut butter bars on the big rock in the back; go enjoy them. I'll come back to you in just a few minutes." He never would.

A smile came to Abel's face as he realized all was perfect with his plan. Rachel smiled with him. Mr. Riordan would never see his wife, something important to Rachel.

All felt right with the world as he measured the blade six inches below her knee. Yet Beth came to him again, larger than ever, blocking out the image of his mother. Beth spoke softly. "Don't kill her."

Abel reached a truce in his mind. A new plan. He would cut off the birth mark, send it to Paul Riordan, and demand a trade for him in exchange for Helen and Parker. Riordan would take that deal. But first remove the birth mark.

Abel felt joy as the blade was pulled back to begin the first stroke of the removal. He didn't notice the shadow casting over him from behind.

As the knife penetrated Helen's flesh, Abel felt a rush that nearly ignored the sudden and brutal tightening around his throat. Abel couldn't decipher if people were playing in his head or if someone was actually threatening his last breath. His eyes fixed openly and widely as the cord collapsed his trachea. Somehow peace came to Abel's mind when he realized his personalities were merging into one death.

Chapter Thirteen

Sunday, June 23, 2013

Tim Myers, recently becoming Trader Tam, patiently had traced the path left by the cart to the opening of the cave. Due to the strength of the tempered metal padlocks that held the gate, Tim couldn't open it without alerting Abel.

His only meaningful choice, now that he'd found Parker and his mother, was to wait for Abel to leave the cave. But the words were clear, and Abel's intentions at the cave entrance too obvious. Tim had to take him then and there. But Tim had no weapon. Earlier, he'd tried to retrace his steps back to the trading post, and dig out his pistol. But, within a few hundred yards, he was hopelessly lost. His only chance, to follow the shorter path blazed by Abel Wood himself.

He found a cord, used by locals to string fish, in his pocket and decided it was the only instrument he had left to do the job. The booze bottle didn't seem helpful.

Tim broke three of his own fingers while pulling with all his strength the back of Abel's neck against the cave side of the gate, while bracing his knee against the outside. Tim never let go until he was certain Abel was no longer a threat.

He reached through the bars on the gate and fished the keys from the pants pocket of the lifeless body. When Helen recovered from the sedative, Tim spoke to her softly, and found her to be remarkably under control. He retrieved Parker and placed him into his mother's arms. He opened the gate, gently eased Helen and Parker past the body and out of the cave. He quickly checked for a pulse and stared at a pale-white face. Abel's chest completely still. No sign of life. He'd come back for the body.

Tim handed Parker and Helen a package of trail mix. "We've got a long descent down to the river."

Helen cried for a second and regained her composure. "Easier than climbing up here." She thanked Tim, and handed the snack back. "He actually fed us quite well, we're not hungry."

Parker nodded, and asked, "Can I go home now?"

"You betcha." Tim picked Parker up in his arms, grabbed Helen by the hand, and headed for the river. He double checked his cell phone for service and confirmed no bars, the same since he climbed the big hill days earlier to set up his trading post.

***

Paul ran his fingers along the sutured skin on Helen's calf. "Just a scratch," she said. He smiled at her while embracing Parker to his chest. He fell asleep, as comfortable a feeling as Paul had experienced in a long time. He walked the steps to Parker's bedroom, pulled the covers back, and nestled his son into bed. Kissing his cheek, he returned to Helen, still wrapped in a blanket on the den sofa.

She climbed onto his lap. "Paul, we're so blessed."

"Agreed, finally, that monster is out of our lives."

"He wasn't a monster. At least not most of the time. I saw a scared boy trying to fight off demons in his life, strong demons. I could sense Abel trying to resist. For who knows how many days we sat in that cave. If he wanted to be a murderer..." She choked back a tear. "...you'd be having our funeral."

Paul paused a moment, letting Helen's perception sink in. "You really mean that, after all this? Kidnapping our child? The knife? The saw? Your leg?"

Helen cried harder and wiped her tears into his shirt. "I can't say for sure, could be dead wrong."

Paul held her even closer.

***

Tim, without pay, sat in an adjoining room, and slipped into the den after overhearing the conversation. He could have added to Helen's perceptions, but didn't. He could have given his interpretation to the last words that squeezed through Abel's lips..."Leave me." He decided to leave the past alone.

Tim caught Paul's eye. A look of indebtedness covered Paul's face, words not necessary. Tim knew. Then Paul begged Tim to join him in the study.

Alone together, Paul pulled out his best single malt scotch, poured two glasses, fell back into the matching leather chair, and handed the other glass to Tim, seated in the other.

"You left the department last week, under therapy, depression?"

"Briefly."

"You were off the case?"

"Kind of."

"And?"

"I let you down, your criticism was justified."

"Not justified, uncontrolled emotion on my part."

Paul waited for the conclusion, but nothing came from Tim's lips. "So, you now are back at the department?"

"For now, but I want to retire soon."

"You saved my son, my wife."

"I saved myself. I did undergo therapy. But one day I decided to take a walk. It turned into a long walk, a long climb, a long look at where my life had led me."

"You mean your brilliant plan, how you located Helen?"

"Brilliant only because it worked."

Tim took a sip of the whiskey. "You remember the case, your client, Billy Cassel?"

"I do."

"Cops around here still think I'm famous for saving that kidnapped woman. And I joke about baloney."

"I suspect you're still famous."

"The kidnapped woman never faced death. Your wife and son did. And I did nothing right until I got my head straight."

"Again, I owe you my life, my family's life."

"You're welcome. I'm tired, need to think about quitting."

"Man, I don't know what to say."

"Say nothing. You made a career change, too, remember?"

"I remember."

Tim turned up the glass. "Paul, here's to retirement."

***

Tim, still a detective, of sorts, decked out in hiking boots and briar-resistant long trousers, escorted the coroner and the Chafenville Chief of Police back to the cave were he left Abel's

body. Going downhill gave much better direction than climbing.
They followed the road that led Tim to the trading post, which he
bought from a drunk for less than a grand, and renamed it
TAM'S. But the location gave little hint to getting back to the
cave Abel had led Tim to when he needed help hauling supplies.
Whatever path was formed with the cart had overgrown. The
way to the cave became elusive. GPS, helicopters, compass-
toting people claiming to be orienters, gave great advice, pushed
through the hills like they owned it. After several hours, the
group gave up, and let gravity take them back to the river. The
next day they tried again, with the same result. Bottom line, as
one of the better hunters explained, a two-foot hole hidden in a
massive forest can't be found without a map, and no map
existed, except in a dead boy's mind. The authorities
rationalized, even joked, that the unfound body's meat, to be
picked off the bone by animals of the woods, might be
appropriate...and avoid taxpayer dollars being spent to find his
ingested remains in the turkey buzzard's crap. Therein
concluded Abel Wood's relevance to local concern. They all
went home.

***

And in that neck of the woods, two ladies, also familiar
with the surrounding hills, had much to talk to him about.

Chapter Fourteen

Tuesday, June 25, 2013
Among the hills

Abel rubbed the soreness on his throat, slightly healed. Root rubbings, medicine he'd learned of in an earlier time, helped mend injured flesh. But actually time seemed a better remedy than the root. And he felt better, not throwing up as often, not gasping for air with each constriction of the muscles around his trachea. He started to refocus.

Sitting some 1,500 feet above the cave where his life was nearly taken, he could see to an almost eternity. He humored himself, imagining what it would be like to have a young person who looked up to him, respected him. What he never had, only imagined. He would show this young friend how to hunt, to climb, to appreciate nature. And on this particularly clear, blue-skied day, they would sit side by side, gazing into the unending horizon, unobstructed because the elevation seemed the top of the world. Then Abel would look over at his young friend and tell him to look close, look hard, on the horizon. And Abel would ask the question, "Do you see it?" And the friend, intently staring into the future, would ask, "I think…what is it?" And Abel would say, "All the way around the world. You're seeing the back of your own head!"

Abel laughed with his made-up friend and then found himself, as always, alone. Except for the ones in his head who didn't want to look at sunsets or sunrises. They both had issues unresolved, and expected him to fulfill them. He *had* to. No time for a friend, made up or otherwise.

Horrible pain visited him since the ruination of his plan. Helen gone, Parker gone. He felt a total failure, at first. When he went blank, a near calmness of death overtook him. Best he could remember, the experience brought peace. A slow, dream-like sensation of losing the will to breathe invaded his senses. A forced decision, a power of sorts, of whether to fight or give up, something he'd never do, demanded an answer. But someone, other than himself, made the decision. *Act like a possum.*

He knew opossum, ate a few, saw how they died without dying. So, he complied with the voices, though he couldn't remember details. Only fading away, knowing he was losing Helen and Parker and himself.

Abel, breathing becoming stronger, couldn't explain why he failed to die. Voices in his head wanted to tell him. He wasn't sure death could be that bad, but he didn't know. What he did know, sitting on a mountain, above everything that disliked him, posed a beautiful view. And at that moment no person or voice could take his peace away.

***

The day had a long path before it, and Abel took the first step, in the direction of Brevard. He'd been there before and merely retraced steps. But the compass wasn't in his hand; the compass lived in his head.

He felt the bulge in his pants pocket and felt amazed as to how little of the money he'd spent. The packet had molded dirt around it from weeks buried in the ground. A co-op grocery store sat some twenty miles away, the way a crow flies, and nearly the way he hiked. Running low on venison jerky left over from the last deer he'd harvested, he might have to buy some provisions. He lengthened his stride, following the plan.

He crested the Blue Ridge Parkway on a winding road leading from Waynesville, NC. He loaded up on camping gear he'd purchased at the foot of the mountain, a camping outpost it called itself, even though it had more tourist stuff like t-shirts and Smoky Mountain ball caps. But he found quality tents, sleeping bags, and backpacking cooking items lining the back wall. And he spent some money.

Up on the Parkway he knew the terrain well. North would take him to the Pisgah Inn, the only heated rooms for rent in the entire National Forest. The distance to the motel was less than three miles. The Reverend Bordo had taken him into the restaurant once before, where they feasted on fresh mountain trout, deboned at the table. Abel wondered why anybody would pay extra for what he could do with one hand. But the Reverend paid, so he didn't complain.

Going the other way on the Parkway, headed south for the next thirty miles, gave passage to no rooms or eating establishments, only breathtaking views and some decent places to pitch a tent. He took a right and headed south. He was to the point where he needed to stop hiking twenty hours a day and only sleeping four hours. He sought to be close to his only ally, nature, quietly and as spiritually as possible. He hoped nature could give him some clarity before voices in his head forced decisions about a man who lived on the other side of the Pisgah National Forest, where Highway 276 made its way toward Brevard. The Reverend Chris Bordo.

He hiked peacefully up and down trails, far away from the Parkway, away from any traffic. And the thoughts in his head were his own. He could have sunrises and sunsets to himself and, with what he had in his backpack and the natural provisions of the hills themselves, he could live a lifetime. But soon he knew his mind would get complicated.

***

Abel's body stretched comfortably in a hammock, hung between two black locust trees. The air, crisp and properly chilled, created a comfortable companion to his lightweight sleeping bag. The rising sun caused no panic to arise and walk toward destinations. At least for the time, this place destined he stay. A smile, unforced, covered his face, peering out of the mummy hole in his bag. He barely felt the pain of scarring on his neck, in his throat, and this particular morning salved the wounds so gently, he hardly noticed.

Lunch consisted of fresh brown trout, caught in the same stream that had sung him to sleep the night before. A long nylon line, a small hook, and a single kernel of corn rendered the tender sixteen-inch fish. He deboned it himself. After cleaning up, he nestled into a crevice in a huge rock in the middle of the wide creek, the sun beaming down warm rays among a nice rustling wind. And a nap came over him like no nap before, safe, alone, unrepentant. Prison a distant past.

And the next day repeated itself. Not one person crossed his path. On the third day, he captured a grouse, a quail-like bird three times the size. A slow-burning, open fire tanned the meat to a perfection Abel conceded better than his best venison.

And he slept again among the orchestra of the lapping river, the quiet strings of the forest, and the quiet in his head.

He arose from his hammock, the day looking stormy, and what seemed like a vacation of his mind came to an end. He looked to the river, the fish, the inviting rocks, the sunshine; all seemed a memory. Looking away from the river, he saw a house not there before, but he recognized it nonetheless. In front stood his mother, looking in his direction, her arm pointed toward the house. How could she know about what Bordo did there? She died many years earlier. In fact, Abel, thirteen years old, could be the only one who remembered. He never discussed what happened with Beth.

Yet there his mother stood, gesturing, reminding him. So, Abel, instead of climbing up to the house, closed his eyes and remembered.

***

Reverend Bordo had built a rustic chateau less than a mile from one of the churches of The Fellowship, where he slept on those occasions when he brought the magic and fire of God and personally delivered the spiritual message to his followers. And, at the time, before Bordo realized the academic progress Abel made, he often took Abel on the jaunts, hoping Abel to join the masses, see admiring congregations, to personally hear and envy the greatest voice in God's triangle where Georgia, North Carolina, and Tennessee came together.

But Abel would often slip out of the services early dismissing Bordo's self-proclaimed status as guardian of both Abel and the word of God as "hogwash," a term he heard once from some protestors outside the gates of the headquarters in Brevard. But on this night, the Reverend's message lit up the church, caught the congregation emotionally on fire, and the preacher, consumed with his roaring success, forgot about Abel, who returned to the chateau and hid in the loft.

Soon the Reverend and only a woman entered unannounced. And for the first time Abel got a sample of sin layered upon sin. And skin layered upon skin.

"Oh, Preacher, you were magnificent...the best ever. My husband told me you talked with him, said special prayers with him. He told me you had special prayers for me, that's why I'm here. Am I right?"

And Bordo loosened his tie, smiled. "You *are* right, and your husband is wise."

Through the slats in the loft from above, Abel watched the woman giggle, like she knew what was coming. "Tell me why my husband is wise."

He unbuttoned his shirt halfway down. "You remember the story of Noah?"

"Yes, yes."

"He was one of many of God's servants whom God graced with gifts of a woman, though I'd say none more beautiful as you."

She slipped off her shoes. "Oh, Preacher, tell me some more about this."

And Abel, who'd been forced through what seemed like a lifetime of Bible studies, listened to nonsense while Bordo explained his biblical entitlement to the woman before him. He finished mouthing off while exposing a muscular torso. She, as if by accident, unbuttoned a few of her own. And when Bordo went in for the final refrain, offering to read scripture from the Bible sitting on the table, she wanted no more talk.

And the great Bordo dropped his tailor-made trousers to the floor, no underwear, and his throbbing spear beckoned his willing partner to her knees. And Abel peered through the cracks as Bordo began shouts of mad pleasure not unlike what he'd shouted in church moments before.

"Come to me, Lord; come to me, Preacher. Oh, I'm coming, too!"

And Abel noticed it ended quicker than it began. The woman left, Bordo grabbed a glass, a bottle of Tennessee whiskey, and drank until he fell asleep.

Abel took a long stroll in the woods the next morning, Bordo still snoring in bed. He settled on the porch in a rocking chair until the exhausted lover of the pulpit came out the front door, only then realizing Abel had journeyed with him.

A nervous voice asked Abel a question. "Where were you last night?"

"Stayed at the church. All the kids thought I was a star or something because you brought me. I slept there...was it okay?"

And a big smile came over his face. "Yes, Son, yes. You did fine."

***

Abel opened his eyes and both the house and Rachel's image disappeared. But then she spoke to him. The solitude of the last few days gave way to controlling voices moving him forward, upward.

And yet, since he knew this was to come, he actually relished the conflict brewing between Beth and his mother. But as much as he wanted to let the two settle their differences between themselves, neither had any interest. Both only wanted to direct their attention to him, like the other didn't exist. Beth knew him last, and somehow thought herself more the victim, which was a good point. Rachel would have none of it. If anyone was entitled to dictate Bordo's justice, it would be his bastard child: Rachel, one he fathered of an unwilling partner...Abel's own grandmother...one he never knew. But Rachel knew her, and that's the way she saw things.

Considering recent developments, Abel realized this peaceful place by nature's river would soon give up its appreciative guest to other forces. Abel grabbed his belongings, headed back to the Parkway, and set his sights on Brevard.

Art Loeb Trail, an up and down pathway by boulders big as mountains, offered a shortcut to Brevard, saving twenty miles compared to paved roads. And very few humans. The quite impatient voices in Abel's head dictated the primitive passage, confident of his hiking and climbing strength. And he forged ahead, stopping only a couple of times to perch high upon an awesome "Looking Glass Rock," where falcons flew below his feet, and clouds above seemed to bow to the power and agility of the powerful birds.

But voices more powerful than what caused the Continental Divide barked orders, so he moved over the rock, dodged mangled mountain laurel, slid down muddy banks, crossed the same creek a dozen times and ended up the distance of a stone's throw away from a fish hatchery. He rested on the banks of the Davidson River and caught so many nonnative rainbow trout, all gushing out of the hatchery into the river, even Beth jumped his case for taking the sport out of the catch. She grew up not far from the spot. Regardless, they all ate well that night.

He slept hard, as long as they'd allow, and proceeded down the banks of the Davidson, to a clearing called Sycamore Flats. There he broke for lunch, still plenty of trout left in his backpack. A visitor or two brought him to the realization that Brevard loomed close, and The Fellowship headquarters loomed even closer. He eased himself up to the backside of the gate made of stone, announcing Pisgah, and pushed forward out of the park. Within minutes his view filled with restaurants, gas stations, and tourist traps. He quickly ducked back down to the river and up a creek.

Chapter Fifteen

Saturday, July 6, 2013
Sunrise

He woke from a sleep on a wet bed of leaves, close to a creek feeding into the river, paralleling Highway 276. He took off his shirt and wrung the water from its fabric. He did the same with his pants. Finding a branch above the river splattered with rays of sunlight, he hung the clothes out to dry and bathed himself crudely in the rushing waters. Two hours later, he felt dry and refreshed. He threw his backpack over his shoulder, adjusted the straps, and began his final steps towards the complex called The Fellowship. Then he stopped. Where he left his backpack said volumes about his optimism for the future. He returned to the river bed and tucked the pack carefully into a cropping of rocks several feet above the rushing water. He intended to return, grab his pack, and leave hurriedly.

***

He stood in the woods, near the double bridges of 276 crossing the Davidson River, staring at the nicely paved herringbone brick drive leading to the complex. Feeling relieved of the quietness in his head, he realized that he, and he alone, bore the responsibility of finding a way in. Others hopefully would stay out of his thought process, let him do what needed doing. He hoped.

He carefully contemplated what he'd remembered of his long stay. The layout, the guards, Bordo's pleasures and quirks reorganized in his head. For sure, he would make no entry attempt while the sun shed its light, much later. But while the sun still shined, he needed to investigate and perhaps confirm his suspicions on changes since he left, changes he predicted Bordo would demand after he walked away with the money.

He crossed the highway like a disoriented hiker. Brevard frequently saw its share of the backpackers, not cut out for the wilderness, looking for a motel. He walked alongside the highway and looked at the nice entry as curiosity. He pulled his stocking cap low to his eyes and innocently strolled down the drive toward the main gate, easing left into the thick hemlock hedges that rounded the outside walls of the complex.

The changes were extensive: more cameras, higher walls, and a strand of barbed wire at the very top. He gazed at the formidable task before him and decided he required more information. He returned to the woods, altered his clothing to look, as best he could, not a hiker.

Abel retrieved a newly used UPS envelope from a trash dumpster behind one of the down-the-road tourist traps. He placed a granola bar and a note to feed the hungry into the envelope, a package routinely delivered to The Fellowship headquarters from well-wishers not necessarily part of The Fellowship.

Dressed as unrecognizable as he could, he approached the main gate, pushed an electronic button, and received a stern, but not dismissive guard who sounded familiar. "May I help you?"

"Sorry, officer, I'm UPS, the truck broke down at the Pisgah Fish Camp. This was close enough, and you know how UPS hammers us about timely deliveries…"

The officer ripped the gate open, led Abel in. "Hell, my brother-in-law drives a UPS truck over in Oconee County…fire your ass if you're late. Get on in the guard house. You need me to sign you in or something?"

The guard house had the schedule and the guard roster posted on a bulletin board smack in the middle of the wall. As the guard looked over the paperwork Abel placed before him to sign, Abel memorized the board. He thanked the officer and left quickly.

***

Abel knew the guard, considered him to be a friend back when Abel had a run of the place. Ironically, Hank had let him walk the beat around the inside walls of the complex while Hank played rental cop. The opportunity to scale the wall on the back side would never have been known but for Hank's guidance. Now the wall was higher, a camera added. But Hank was scheduled to work the next night, Sunday, 7:00 p.m., which means he'd be working during the Sunday night festivities at The Fellowship. And according to the schedule, Bordo had services planned on The Fellowship property. He remembered those sermons and the bizarre celebrations that usually followed. He also knew Hank to be lazy, *an opportunity*.

Abel returned to the woods, and slept lightly, sensitive to his surroundings. The early morning would come soon enough, and he was thankful for no interference from voices within. An owl hooted in the oak overhead. He stretched, yawned, and looked at the outfitter's watch he bought…1:18.

The fear of being caught didn't bother him. What gnawed at his gut was he had no plan once he got in, if he got in. Bordo, and everything about him, brought him to this place, at this time. But every time he'd carefully plotted out a strategy, something inside stopped him. He would push forward, a step at a time. The next step simply banked on Hank's being asleep at the switch.

Chapter Sixteen

Sunday, July 7, 2013
10:30 p.m.

The back wall, overgrown with vines, offered a step-like ladder to its top. He cut the barbed wire, a single strand, with repeated hacks of his sharpened camp knife. He stood on the wall's top edge like a high-wire act, but easy enough for his agility. The cameras were the risk, but if Hank was charged with constantly watching, Abel knew he'd sleep through it this time of night. Unfortunately, Hank showed up as Abel's feet rested on the last vine going down on the inside of the wall, just before landing on the ground.

He heard Hank's voice. Then saw him yawning into a monitoring device. "Probably one of them possums, or maybe a coon, you know how those cameras show stuff in the dark, can't tell a pick from a shovel."

"Well, it looked bigger than a coon. Sure you ain't seen nothing?"

"You got it, partner. Nothin' bigger than what walks up behind our own houses…lookin' for a bite of our dog's chow. Shoo'em away."

"Okey dokey. If it's nothin', think I'll eat my sandwich."

Abel heard the monitoring device slap closed. He exhaled gently, a dodged bullet. He considered the fact that, to his knowledge, nobody had ever broken into The Fellowship in the history of the headquarters. After all, Brevard's known as a peaceful town, and the headquarters is located in one of its better areas, and the fact that thousands of people carry hundreds of dollars and expensive equipment into the nearby forest and camp out with only the protection of a mere lightweight tent cloth proved his point. As Abel thought of it, the only complication was the murder and aftermath of the now gone Beth Cunningham and one of her students. *Well, her only student.* The risk was never from outside, the beefed-up security happened only at the increased fear of the boss. He recalled, when he lived there, Hank scratching his head and wondering out loud, "What for?"

But luck ran out for Abel. The vine Abel stood upon snapped, and his body crashed upon the ground. He rebounded quickly, righting himself.

A flashlight beam covered his face. "Hank," Abel said with a reunionistic optimism.

A moment, more like an hour to Abel, passed until Hank replied. "Abel? Is that you?"

"Yes, Hank, yes."

"Dang, a UPS driver reminded me of you just yesterday."

Then Abel tuned his senses on what Hank might be thinking. He would know of the allegations, Beth's death, Abel's disappearance. *Who knows what Hank has been told.*

Hank looked perplexed, and Abel felt the same.

Kill him.

Abel listened again. *Kill him*, Rachel demanded. *He will tell Bordo; you'll be arrested. Do you want to be caged again?*

Abel shook. No fear like his mother's fear. *No, I don't want to be caged.*

And with that Abel crammed a fist into Hank's gut, what he'd heard at House of Hope as a sucker punch. Hank fell to his knees, and he dragged him into the bushes, away from the camera. He grabbed the neck of a man who, last time he saw him, was considered a friend. But his mother insisted, and Beth stayed silent. Choking sounds spewed from Hank's mouth, a slight struggle, then a limp body. The right pressure on his neck brought silence, but not death, regardless of what Rachel wanted. He felt bad, responsible for how Hank looked, and regressed into wanting to be back in his mother's womb. A simple, predictable place. Or at least that was how his mother described it.

Abel snapped out of the emotion and tried to evaluate the options. He just incapacitated a guard, though necessary, in the sanctity of the headquarters. Hopefully the other guard was still eating his sandwich, totally missing the reunion chat. But regardless of the guard's present attention, with monitors and cameras, his time had to be limited. He could escape over the wall he'd climbed moments ago and regroup for another day, and…his mother's voice cut him off. *No, Abel, finish what you came to do.*

Abel started to argue she knew not what he was supposed to do. She died, though she hadn't. She walked in his shadow, or at times he in hers. *Honor thy mother,* came to him. With this mandate, he moved forward, and Rachel and Beth, once again, left the details to him…for a while.

Chapter Seventeen

Sunday, July 7, 2013
9:30 p.m.
Brevard, NC

The Reverend Chris Bordo stretched his body across the rounded, double king-sized, custom-made bed, nestled in the upper room of the mansion within the headquarters belonging to The Fellowship. And life was good. Beside him lay a woman, half his age, the wife of one of the Reverend's faithful flock. She lay naked, spent, and he was proud. He'd thank God tomorrow at morning prayers for the gift, the entitlement bestowed upon him for his faithful service to the church, The Fellowship.

She shifted, rolled her beautiful, tight breasts in his direction. He knew she searched for a sign, one from himself, the Reverend. She needed validation for what just happened. And Chris reacted perfectly.

"My precious treasure from God, wife to my loyal member of God's faith, you were perfect, fulfilling. Most importantly, you fulfilled the word of God. Your Bible, the Old Testament, grants you, me, and your husband an enormous bounty of pleasure…all kept in the womb of our Church."

She looked relieved, ordained from the shadow of sin. And her eyes begged for more, something more to put the last hour into perspective.

He pressed on. "Oh, I can't speak for you, but I can speak as your secret passionate soldier in Christ. You were amazing, a blessing of orgasmic delivery. May I ask if you felt it, too?"

"Yes, Reverend, I felt your blast…what you called our eternity when you came forth."

"And, dear child of God, how did it feel to you? This is important."

"I don't know if I'm entitled, but you felt…well…so…wow! I came, too."

"I know, I know. And the power of God worked, came upon us both."

"But what about my husband and some of those 'shalt nots' that you preach about? Did I do wrong?"

"No, my child, no. May I read from the Bible itself?"

She nodded her head.

He pulled out a drawer from the ornate dresser beside the bed and raised an object wrapped in a gold silk cloth. He pulled away the cloth as a jeweler would reveal a fine stone and produced a red velvet Bible, laced in shiny black leather. He'd lied so many times in the name of God, he considered misquoting nearly as fun as the sex.

"And the Lord said to Noah, a flood is coming, one where men and women alike shall meet their doom. And you, Noah, shall be a part of the salvation of the earth which entitles you to the flesh of a woman. You must know flesh to understand the consequences of the flood to come. Consume and enjoy the pleasures which soon will be no more."

"But, Reverend, Noah was a long time ago and the flood already happened."

"Quite true. But would you question the truth, the relevancy of the Bible…God's word…at the here and now?"

"No, Reverend. But explain about the flood."

"Explain I will, Child. God has spoken to me. There will be floods to come. Look in any paper, magazine, and you will find sin flowing like there is no tomorrow. The flood is a flood of sin, no less powerful, no less relevant than the flood that consumed the earth in the time of Noah. And God spoke to me, as he did Noah, and granted this pleasure from you. This is the sign of the flood to come, and you have fulfilled my gift from God."

"Well, that's a good thing, makes me feel better."

"And what's *more* important, the look on your face as we shared each other's delights, tells me you also felt a blessing. Tell me I'm wrong."

"No, Reverend, you're not wrong."

"Which simply proves God acts in mysterious ways…giving you a blessing, too…thanks be to God."

Then he added what he considered another biblical gem, in an earlier story from what he paraphrased. "And God was well pleased." And Chris was well pleased with himself. And the adulteress looked well pleased herself.

And Chris decided. *Now is the time to get this lovely creature back to her husband.*

The young wife followed the Reverend down the winding, heavily wooded steps rejoining the gathering, where her husband had arrived only minutes earlier, well spent himself.

Chris placed his arm around the husband, hugged him like a military comrade. He gazed into the husband's eyes searching for any uncertainty of their conspiracy, one that had brought the husband an invigorating roll in the hay. A prostitute, courtesy of The Fellowship. A woman with more moves, groans, and delightful strokes than his beloved wife could ever muster. But Chris had prayed with the husband, laid the groundwork with, of course, appropriate scripture. Seeing a sinful smile on the husband's face, Chris exhaled a large satisfying breath of success, a consummated deal.

He slipped out a side door and headed for his office. His faithful flock would be directed out by security as designated. Entry to his office required an electronic pass card, only held by him. Neither security, nor his own secretary, had access without his presence. The protocol inconvenienced him, requiring early morning rising to let in his staff. And once in, computers had different levels of security, and no one had the password to his computer but him. And that password, committed to memory, was written down nowhere.

Only a few years earlier, things were not so formal, rigid, and bothersome. Chris took a seat behind his computer and entered the password: Entitled.

He first went for the keyboard and entered additional passwords that would replay the sex scenes he had just created. Replaying the scriptures he quipped. Hidden cameras at every angle in his bedroom brought wonderful highlight film to his performance. And he watched. Soon he would watch the replay of her husband and the prostitute, also captured by cameras under his sole control. His technology was so good he could do a side-by-side of the two and compare who got the better bargain… he or the husband. He poured a large glass of fine sour mash whiskey, straight up.

After a while, his eyes tired, and he pondered whether to return to the party, go to his bed from a back hallway and sleep, or take a walk. Sometimes, on not-so-great bedroom follies, he'd re-watch film of grandeur past, like Olympic medals hanging in his computerized trophy case. But tonight he felt satisfied, and weary. He returned to his bedroom.

With a refreshed glass of alcohol for a nightcap, he considered his standing and his entitlement of The Fellowship. *Hell, I am The Fellowship.* He said that outside the province of God. He owned the place. But it had not come easy, not without some bumps in the road…one in particular. One that burned in his heart…and in his wallet. *I can't count the money, lost or spent. The past should be the past.*

He couldn't decide if it was the stress, the lost money, or the closest of chances of losing The Fellowship…what he'd worked a near lifetime to build. He didn't know. What he did know…he persevered, won, became victorious over odds so great that a dozen 44 magnums in his face seemed tame. He drained the glass of whiskey and set the glass on a hand-carved walnut coaster decorating the stand by the bed.

So, why does this past, long gone, continue to occupy my mind?   And as much as it hurt to admit it, the source of distraction,   clearly without a basis, boiled down to one name…Abel Wood.

The large grandfather clock in the corner struck the eleven o'clock hour. A vibration tingled in his pants pocket. No one during these times had the right to interrupt him, except in dire emergency. Retrieving the phone, he first checked the screen, *Guard House.* He walked to a sitting room adjacent to the bedroom and raised the phone to his ear. "Trust me, this better be very necessary."

A nervous voice replied. "Sir, Reverend, I know not to bother you. This is George, your guard at the front gate. Maybe I should call the Brevard Sheriff's Department, but, sir, Reverend, after that last time, when the deputies showed up and caused all that trouble, your instructions were not to call outside police without your permission. So, this is why…"

Bordo, irritated, interrupted him. "Get to the problem, what is it *you* can't handle this time of night? One of the guests downstairs? An argument? Somebody drunk? Stuff you ought to handle gently, without outside involvement. Why are we talking?"

"I can't say for sure, but Hank…you know Hank?"

"Yes, I know Hank…finish your story, Officer."

"Well, Hank did the security rounds on the top of the hour, just like you ordered."

"And?"

"I saw a figure on the monitor, through one of the new cameras you installed on the western back half. It rotates across the inside wall."

"What kind of figure?"

"Looked big enough to be a person…but I wasn't all that focused…"

"Lazy is what you mean. Go on…what about Hank?"

"I paged him, told him 'bout the sighting or at least what I seen. He thought more likely an animal, they do climb over time to time."

Bordo thought back to the twenty-three hundred dollars he paid for the additional camera. Brand new CCTV Security Pros. *Same dumb-ass guards.* "So, did you replay the video, confirm what Hank said?"

"Dang, didn't think to do that, never had this come up before...not sure I know how."

Bordo became livid. "Stop your gibberish. You claim this to be an emergency. Where's Hank?"

"Reverend, that's the problem, he won't answer my pages. And somethin' else…"

"What, what?"

"I keep staring at this monitor. Then I think I see a foot, like a guard boot. Should I go look for Hank? I'd have to leave my post here by the gate in the guard house."

Bordo paused a moment, considering the options. "Yes, go get Hank. But before you do, press the transfer button on the screen. I'll do all the monitoring from my computer here."

"Will do, boss."

Chris looked through the doorway at his bed, and thought again of his conquest of the night. His erection from the videos now completely gone, *work to do.*

***

Abel stood over the body he hoped was pulled out of the rotating camera's field of vision, contemplating his next move. He knew the layout of the place, and it was Sunday night, always a big day for Bordo. And when the preaching ended, he appeared invincible, and the night always turned into a celebration. Bordo acted generous and ready to be heaped with praise from his followers. Abel considered the word "entitled" to best sum up Sundays at The Fellowship headquarters. He hoped Bordo would be preoccupied, unconcerned about complex security. But he couldn't be sure Bordo was even home, may have preached at one of his deep-in-the-woods churches, had his entitled follies in a distant place. But the guard house schedule said differently, and he banked on the predictable.

He pondered the situation while standing over Hank, the two of them now completely hidden by bushes. But a light from a flashlight came across the bush. Abel froze. The hue of a light upon the wall cast itself upon the face of a man Abel remembered as George, a guard like Hank. George walked around the area for a moment or two, then walked away, following the perimeter wall in a clockwise manner.

George out of sight, Abel made a decision to drag Hank, still with a pulse, into an empty meeting room and set up a home base to conduct his investigation. He entered the room, one usually reserved for fundraising meetings, no windows to distract the solicited donors. He pulled Hank until energy ran out, and collapsed into a straight-back chair. Thankfully, Hank still breathed. In the strategically lighted room, a cross captured most of the attention, reminding him this place to be a temple of greed.

***

Chris' phone rang again. "Yes, George, did you find Hank?"

"No, sir. Didn't find anything. Rounded the whole place. Should I keep looking?"

Suddenly, Chris spotted something in the monitor completely unexpected. He quickly overrode the guardhouse system and hit "cancel stream." He then killed the lighting in the Money Room.

"George, the guests should all be leaving now. I want you to quickly hurry them out the front gate and return to the guard house to wait for my call. Got that?"

"Got that, got that, fer sure. I'll run everybody out and wait for your call."

The woman gone and the party downstairs dispersed, Chris Bordo focused on his computer screen, totally shocked. He took a deep breath, stared intently, and leaned toward the monitor. *Welcome home, Son.*

He let his heartbeat level off. *Easy enough.* He electronically locked the door on "The Money Room," a term he coined for his own pleasure. With no exit available to Abel Wood, he had time to plan his next move…and the next. He relished his options. He'd cut the electrical power, blacking out the room. He seemed to recall Abel being averse to dark and tight places. Next, the intercom system, routed into each room, offered a way for him to communicate with Abel. And, as he thought of it, he could sound like God Almighty with some sound effects in the darkness.

Bordo struggled against his anger with Abel Wood, the boy he pulled from the woods, shielded him from prosecution of the murder of his own grandfather and a few other Fellowship followers. *Then this same idiot, one whom I pulled from the damnation of society, one whom I saved from the jaws of Hell, one whom I paid to educate better than anyone before him.* Then he thought again. *Maybe not an idiot, clearly a traitor.*

Bordo stewed in his heat-flashed thinking of Abel, a smart young man who'd firsthand gotten to watch the Reverend Bordo in action. Not a mere spectator, almost a young disciple in the circle of his trust. *Destined to greatness under my rule of The Fellowship.* How he strayed, how he became no less than Judas, still wrestled Bordo from restful sleep.

Sometimes his anguished disappointment in Abel funneled into an urn of economics. After all, Abel had cost him, and The Fellowship. Millions of tithes, hard-fought-for tithes, sermon after sermon, sin justification after sin justification, Heaven-opened wallets after Heaven-opened wallets.

But then came the police authorities, and the damned Abel Wood lied, something about demanding sex with Beth Cunningham. And then came the accusations, and the great Chris Bordo nearly lost everything. Everything due to an ungrateful follower.

***

The light in the room vanished, except for the small glare from a red emergency exit sign over the door. He quickly checked the door, dead bolted from the outside, probably electronically. He returned to his seat and in the muffled light looked at the man gasping for breath. Hank. Guilt overcame Abel, only because this man had no connection to Bordo's wrongdoing. And then Hank's eyes opened. Opened like a window to a pleasant past. And Hank, struggling for his next breath, spoke.

"Abel, I brought Junior, my boy, over to play with you. Remember the tree house? You and Junior and I hauled some lumber out to the back, way away from the buildings. We climbed, we nailed, we made a darn good place for you boys to play. And you played and played."

Then Hank's breathing slowed. "Abel, why?"

He started to apologize, remembering those good times, surprised the memory escaped him since his rapid departure from The Fellowship headquarters. Sounds of pain crept from Hank's lips as he reached down to place a sympathetic hand upon an unnecessary victim.

Don't.

Rachel's unwavering voice rang clear: the only option was to finish what he started. He took a piece of twine from a desk drawer, along with a rigid ruler, and started to wrap the cord around Hank's neck, he'd wind the cord tighter with each rotation of the ruler, fulfilling Rachel's advice. And now Abel found himself in the shoes of the one at the cave who nearly ended Abel's life. As he reached downward, toward Hank's neck, Beth spoke quickly, urgently.

Abel we don't have to kill him. We both knew Hank for many years, considered him one of the good ones. Take him out of here, he needs medical attention.

Rachel stepped forward, nearly blocking his view of Beth. *Experience from your own near-death, at the cave, tells you to keep the cord taut, long lasting. His death must be complete.*

He stood, shaking his head from side to side, and looked over Hank's body, still breathing, and decided to treat Rachel and Beth the same. He sat and waited. Fortunately, no one argued.

He started to find a cup of water for Hank until a voice, deep, familiar, controlling, pierced his ears. "Abel Wood." The noise reverberated throughout the room.

The voice struck a nerve like the pounding of an old bruise. But he struggled to give a calm response. "Yes, Chris. At least Chris is what you liked to be called when I lived here."

"Call me nothing, you are owed nothing, and time is short for you, my young Judas."

Silence lingered as if Bordo expected some denial of the allegation.

"You haven't changed much, Abel, still a boy of few words."

Silence prevailed once more.

"Okay. I've got this room covered with cameras and speakers. You can't move without my knowledge. You can't speak without my hearing. And, most importantly, this room you are in is locked down tight. No windows and one door two men with large crowbars couldn't pry open. Only I have the key. I assume you have some reason for being here, got something to tell me? I've made it easy for you. All you need to do is open your betraying mouth, and I'll hear every word."

Abel thought long, carefully, considering traits of a maniac, to which he'd had special viewing privileges. He took a chance. "Chris, I assume you know Hank, the gentleman at my feet?"

Bordo laughed, his voice echoing through the room. "Yeah. The man you just murdered."

"Who's to say who murdered him? Who's to say he's dead?" Abel knew the answer.

"You stupid piece of worthlessness. I've replayed the video out by the perimeter wall, got it all recorded, the cold-blooded way you took his life. I watched, guess the police could watch…assuming we even get to that point."

Abel backed his chair away from Hank, and looked directly at what he considered to be one of the cameras. "We won't get to that point because you don't want to get to that point."

"Meaning what? You commit a murder after breaking into these hallowed grounds of The Fellowship and somehow think I care if you rot away in some jail, or better yet, capital punishment is alive and well in the State of North Carolina. Ha! I taught you the Bible…an eye for an eye. I'm actually looking forward to getting to *that* point."

"Wrong."

"What?"

"You think once the police are alerted to a murder of your guard, kind of like a colleague, they'll be satisfied with you showing them some isolated blurb from your computerized monitoring of the entire complex?"

"So what?"

"Sunday night, your big after-sermon party. What did you record up in your bedroom right before I suspect the other guard…you know…George, contacted you?"

"None of your business. And how do you know about George?"

"I might know more than you think; I certainly know more about Hank."

"Like what?"

"Like he's not dead."

Bordo's voice jumped an octave. "Oh, so you might dodge a murder charge, even a better reason to call the police. Hank watches the video, verifying you tried to kill him?"

Abel laughed. "I'll say again, call the cops, they'll have lots to see on your Sunday night hoopla, and all those Sunday nights before. Don't you think once the authorities are brought in, get a glance at your computers, which records every movement you might like to watch, or re-watch, they'll accept some edited version of what goes on here, merely be satisfied with an isolated scene with Hank at the wall?"

Abel could hear Bordo's rapid breathing. Bordo simply could let go of the computer key, and Abel would hear nothing until he chose to speak. This was a sign he had Bordo's mind wandering.

Bordo's voice changed dramatically, like he turned the reverb up on the sound system, making it sound like the echo of a cave, his voice speaking once but hearing an eternal repetition. "Damnation has ruined your soul. And your hell is what you see around you. You have no way out, no way anyway…"

Abel considered the last sentence…*no way anyway*. The words made no sense, proof the Great Bordo floundered in his thought process. Proof he had no definitive plan in the way he'd kill the son of the mother he conceived. And Rachel took note.

Abel resumed his rationale. "I guess you could do some deleting, you probably wouldn't trust one of your tech guys to put that one to bed. But, as I think of it, you're not half bad on the computer, which means you're not half good either. Why don't you go ahead and call the police? We'll see what they can extract from your hard drive. Oh, guess you could destroy it…but that brings us back to the same place…the recorded murder, or at least what you thought to be a murder…that would be destroyed, too."

**

Silence prevailed again, only this time Chris needed to reflect, particularly on Hank not being dead, something he'd missed on the video. Obviously, he was focused on the returning betrayer, not the corpse-like figure at his feet. Too much to think about. .The smart thing might be to command George from the gate house, let him find Abel and his victim in the Money Room, and gravity take its toll. But what will the quite articulate Abel Wood say to George? Chris dreaded the thought.

Bordo projected a deep, authoritative voice, with a shrill toward the end, hoping to unnerve Abel. "You are my prisoner. A man who you tried to murder lies at your feet. I'll merely kill you with the weapon he carries. And there will be no video for the officers to watch. The facts will speak for themselves. Since you seem to know, there is another guard on the grounds who witnessed your intrusion. The more I think of it, the tidier this becomes."

Abel's voice came slowly, rationally. "How well do you know this man out by the front gate?"

"He works for me, all that matters."

"Then I'm wondering why you and I are communicating right now. Why hasn't he taken charge, done the job you hired him to do? My guess is he doesn't even know about Hank. Say I'm wrong, Chris."

"Stop your gibberish. You *want* the guard to see you hovering over his fallen, fellow officer?"

"Why not? Won't he then have to call the cops?"

"He'll do what I say."

"And you'll say Hank looks nearly dead. We got the guy. Don't call the cops?"

"Like I said, he'll do what I say."

"Okay, so I'll presume he'll talk to me?"

"So?"

"Chris, we never really had a chance to discuss your criminal charges, Beth's death, murder I suppose?"

"What the hell does that have to do with anything?"

"Your language is getting a little rough for a man of God. Did you have a trial?"

"No. Do you have a point to make, Abel, because I'm about to lose patience, and you're about to go to jail."

"Doubt I'll be going to jail; you need me dead, unable to talk. You see, the authorities never had a chance to hear the truth, the way you threw Beth Cunningham off the balcony, what your motive was…revenge for digging into your computer files."

"Why would you think I'd care about any of that now?"

"Stay focused, Chris, remember we're talking about George, the guard awaiting your next order. I doubt George knows anything more than the authorities. I'll look forward to our chat."

"Son, I'm losing patience. You've stumbled into a situation where I hold all the cards. And the truth is you have broken into my place, assaulted my guard, and are totally my prisoner. And *you* think you're smart?"

"Beth taught me well. No trial, you say? There is no statute of limitations in North Carolina for a crime such as yours. Not only was I an eye witness, I saw every bizarre and sinful deed on your computer, just like Beth. And regardless of whether you destroyed the history of me, my mother, and all of your other victims, you didn't destroy what is in my head, and I have an excellent memory."

"I have my own people who'll deal with you. They'll clean up this mess and dispose of you at my say so."

"Then we shall see. You've got me and Hank locked in. Send in the guards."

***

And with that, the waiting games began. Abel only knew his death would be at the end of the process. Bordo would never chance bringing in the governmental authorities, probably had no ultimate trust with his rent-a-cops, and would necessarily need the help of a faithful lamb of The Fellowship. Yes, death would come soon, but it would be on Abel's own terms, or at least the terms of two voices he sensed would soon be screaming advice. Each with her own style.

Settled at Abel's feet, Hank smelled of his own urine and feces. The stench, hammering up his nose, felt quite familiar, like the cage in his grandfather's house. Not an unbearable smell, a homecoming. Abel wondered how the smell would affect the preacher. He would hold out for an answer.

***

Chris Bordo sat in the upper room, and he had the upper hand. Abel Wood, one for whom he harbored a compulsive death wish, simmered in his mind. Unfinished business lingering since his departure. He looked at the monitor, a near-dead body at Abel's feet. A security guard not doing much good now.

Chris knew best decisions were made without compulsion, with careful planning. Yes, Abel pointed out risks the real police posed if invited into the headquarters. The security guards, mindless creatures who would follow his orders, were risks in themselves. And if involved in Abel's death, or even the disposal of the body, once the real cops got his guards in an interrogation room, their loyalty would soon evaporate. An even bigger problem arose if Hank's situation became known. George in the gate house had to be wondering what had become of Hank. Ultimately both guards had families who would expect them home in a few hours. Then another shift would arrive. Chris needed to quicken his thought process.

Chris had sole viewing control of the monitoring cameras around the complex. George would simply watch through the front gate's camera. He decided to check in. "George, are things quiet on the front?"

"Like a mouse. How's Hank?"

"Still out and about. I'm getting some help."

"Who do I need to clear entry to the gate? Transylvania County Sheriff, somebody else?"

"No, George, I got 'em coming to the wall where you saw your figure in the dark. Make a note of that in your report. If you can hold down the gate, you will be most appreciated."

"Consider it done. We'll be off in two hours. You think Hank's alright?"

"I'm sure, and I'm praying hard to the Lord above. I'll keep you posted."

Chris took a deep breath, then he activated the intercom with Abel. He turned down the reverb and turned up the lights. "What is the status of the guard you injured?"

Abel overplayed the injury. "Breathing. Not much more. Why do you ask?"

"He's mine...I mean he works for me, I'm entitled to know."

"I agree with you, Chris. I guess you could talk to him, the same way you're talking to me. He has said some words; I think he hears."

Chris made a decision and headed for the outside door of the Money Room. When he arrived, he pulled a device from his pocket. "Abel, I have a mobile security application on my system, state of the art, called Icontrol. I see you completely in that room and want you to back away to the wall furthest from the door. Will you do this?"

"Why would I do anything you suggest?"

"What harm is it for you to stand by the wall?"

"I'll do it if you'll come in here instead of hiding like a coward behind your electronic devices."

He watched Abel back away and place his back against the wall. With the touch of his warm finger upon the IPhone key, the door unlocked, and Chris threw in a pair of handcuffs, and locked the door as quickly as it opened. He closed the phone and returned to the big screen in the upper room. He needed a clear, big picture.

"Abel, do you see the handcuffs?"

Abel mocked him with a slow response. "Yes, Chris, I see the handcuffs. Is that your idea of facing me like a man?"

"Will you put them on, hands behind your back?"

"Stupid idea. Like you like to say, do you have a point?"

"I'll come in. You're hell-bent on seeing me face-to-face. Am I wrong?"

"This is your party, seems you're calling the shots."

"Then put the cuffs on."

"Oh, that makes good sense. I handcuff myself behind the back and wait for you to kill me, you *have* basically said that is your intention."

"Your call, Abel. But consider this. Right this moment, I could inject a poisoned gas into your chamber, killing you, and unfortunately the good guard, and you know it. Tell me, Abel, do you doubt my resources or ability to take you out any time I decide?"

***

Abel had no doubt as to Bordo's destructive power. But the fast pace of the evening had caused Bordo to need more answers that lay within the Money Room. The captive terms of the handcuffs seemed inconsequential to the certainty of Abel's impending death. In fact, death handcuffed actually seemed more meaningful than death unrestrained. How could Bordo explain *that* to the authorities?

Ready to consider the rest of Bordo's terms, voices interrupted him, Rachel first. *I said kill the guard, then we'd have only one enemy to deal with.*

Beth swung the pendulum the other way. *Hank will die. He needs a hospital. Did I not teach you any compassion?*

Abel rubbed his neck, looked down at Hank, and answered Bordo. "I'll put on the handcuffs."

"Nicely done, Abel. I'm watching you closely. Go pick up the cuffs and return to your seat. If you mess with the cuffs before they're locked on your wrists, the deal's off. I won't be joining you."

"Understood." Abel stood, walked to the door, picked up the cuffs, and returned to his seat, the cuffs sitting innocently in his palm-up hands.

"My cameras are focused on your wrists, my audio is turned up loud. You know the drill."

"How would I know the drill?"

"Abel, you think me an idiot. I know about your arrest in the big town of Chafenville, I got a church not far from there, remember?"

And for the first time, Abel knew his recent past had not gone unnoticed by Bordo. And he felt salt in the wound Bordo had inflicted upon him as a child and in Beth's death. Bordo had won.

"Again, I say, do the drill. I want to see your back, both hands pushing out, and hear nice, clean clicks on the cuffs. Screw up and your end will come sooner than later."

Abel complied, completely as instructed. The worst that could happen is poisoned while handcuffed, which seemed no worse than poisoned while unhandcuffed. More probable the Great Bordo would grace them with his presence. And it happened.

***

Chris delighted in slapping his open hand across the face of Abel. "The sting of the Lord. He knows your sin."

Then he threw Abel off the chair, helpless to even catch himself. Leaning down to the guard, he checked his pulse, weak but steady.

"Officer, this is the Reverend Bordo. Finally I found you. How are you?"

Chris listened carefully for a word. Only a meek slur, sounding like the end was near. He turned his attention back to the cause of his problems, jerked him up by his collar, and slammed him haphazardly into another chair, usually reserved for a wealthy donor of The Fellowship.

"You've not said a word, you inconsiderate bastard child." He humored himself. "Bastard in the strangest kind of way, I must say!"

***

Abel sat silent, reverent...to his mother.

***

Chris' mind, going wild over the layered complications, tried to adjust to a few concepts: What to do with Hank? How to dispose of Abel? How to appease George? What to do about the camera footage? All issues needed resolution in minus two hours. But Chris couldn't resist a small divergence. "Okay, Abel, you got something to say to me...in person?"

The answer delayed noticeably as the clock in Chris' head ticked away. Finally an answer came in the form of a question.

"Chris, care to tell me why you murdered Beth, Beth Cunningham, my teacher? Surely not about the fact that she learned, from your sloppy record keeping, you raped my grandmother in exchange for my giving my father, my grandfather, God's permission to rape my mother? Please tell me Beth didn't die for learning a secret you failed to protect."

Chris had worked too hard, generated far too many dollars to God's work, brought too many people to God's grace for this ungrateful boy to divert his attention. Chris, himself, molded Abel into an intelligent young man, a gift now turned evil toward Chris, the giver of the gift.

Chris smiled. "Does loyalty mean anything to you? Do you somehow think that God's gifts of abundant life, which included Beth's lessons to you, come to every earthly child? Say no, 'cause it is no. Millions of children, born of the land, poor of earthly hills, just like your family, never, and I mean never, get what you got. You got, no matter what you rail about in your anger, greatness, education, abundance from God, working through me."

Abel smiled back. "Nice. Sounds like you're God himself. Did God or you murder Beth?"

"God damn it, Abel."

"Thou shall not take the Lord's name in vain, Chris."

"I've had enough of this. What Beth apparently taught you boils down to treason. And you'll surely meet your maker the same as she."

"Thou shall not kill, Chris."

Chris exploded. "You piece of shit. This place is mine. I make the rules, not God."

"Understood, God."

Chris rechecked the handcuffs and found them securely on God's fallen angel. Then he turned his attention on the detail that weighed heavily in his plan, Hank. "Hank, this is Reverend Bordo again. I'm thinking, if you can hear me, of getting you to George, letting him take you home to your family. I've caught the man who tried to kill you. Do you know his name?" He checked his pulse again, this time a bit stronger. "Hank, you work for me. I can help, get you to your family, pay for getting you well."

This time Hank nodded to Chris, an encouraging sign. Hopefully, Hank would remain faithful to The Fellowship. Chris, more confident, stood over Hank, looked in his now blinking eyes, and pointed an accusatory finger at the handcuffed thorn in his side. "Do you know that man's name?" And almost as quickly as the question aired, an answer followed.

"Abel…Abel Wood."

And with that, Chris pulled out his phone, readying to call George. A plan formulated in his mind. *Emergency room at the Brevard hospital, maybe a day or two in a private bed. Lots of nice flowers, courtesy of The Fellowship, maybe some personal ones from Chris himself. And a full reinstatement as an honored guard, maybe with a little raise in pay.* Chris' thoughts jelled. Only thing left was a handcuffed traitor. He wouldn't even need help from a faithful of The Fellowship. *A cleaner ending than even Beth Cunningham.*

He drew the phone closer to his eyes, index finger darting to push the contact button for the guard house. Then Hank interrupted, his voice surprisingly steady. "Yes, I know Abel Wood, and I heard the conversation you just had. Thinking back, it makes sense, Beth's death and then Abel's disappearance."

And with that, Chris cut off the call. "Hank, what are you saying? Did Abel Wood not hurt you, bring you pain, cause your life to flash before you?"

"Yes, Boss, almost forgot. I'm hurtin', need help."

"I'm here to help you."

Chris felt better. "So, you're with The Fellowship, which will take care of you, and take care of the man who assaulted you?"

Abel broke into Bordo's attempted conspiracy. "Hank, remember our conversation right before Bordo unlocked the door and busted in?

Bordo interrupted. "What did Hank say?"

Abel smiled. "You know, like did I know Hank's son's name? Chris, do you know Hank's son's name?"

Chris looked at his watch, time flying by. "Why would he ask that, what's the relevance?"

"Hank, Jr., Junior, his dad called him. I remember a bunch of things...Hank does, too."

"I'm tired of this, Son."

Then Abel turned his face downward toward Hank. You heard Bordo. He murdered Beth. Will you stand by this murderer? I'm sorry for hurting you. Tell Junior I'm sorry, too."

Chris, ready to strangle Abel, gave Hank a final chance. "You pick me or Abel. Which?"

Hank, looking worse since the argument started, hesitated, like talking to his family over an important decision. He finally looked up at Chris. "I choose Abel."

Chris purposely walked toward Abel, reached into his pocket, pulled out the twine, and choked Hank to death.

***

As a dull, white, blood-deprived hue filled Hank's face, Beth cried.

Abel started to try a move pulling his knees to his chest and clearing the handcuffs under his feet, but the move was blocked by Bordo.

"Time to kill you, but not too fast." A fist rammed into Abel's nose, and blood ran down his face, through his shirt, and down his trousers, not a free hand to wipe it away.

Abel, through the pain, counted his options, virtually none. He faced Bordo. "You have about thirty minutes before more guards start roaming this place. On top of that, George is going to tell them of a break in, of Hank's disappearance, of your strange request that you handle the whole thing. Chris, time is your enemy, not me."

Abel watched Bordo start to tremble, the way he'd done when church members failed to donate enough money in a given month to meet Bordo's expenses. "You're handcuffed; Hank is dead and won't help you."

Bordo screamed. "Why are you concerned with me? I'm about to kill you! Your ungrateful ass is dead before the second hand on the clock on that wall can make its next rotation. Dead."

"One minute? Easy, Chris, you don't have time. Strangle me? Even with these cuffs you're going to get a fight. At least twenty minutes worth before my body stops shaking. Or get a gun, maybe nobody will hear it? My dead body, at your feet. Hank, dead Hank, also at your feet? On top of that, my guess is you'll have some bruises to explain...but probably the least of your problems."

Abel relished Bordo's predicament, though he knew death was soon, and Bordo would figure out something…like he did after Beth died. "Guess you could run, far away from me. Claim I killed Hank, claimed I intended to kill you, too. But, Oh! I'm handcuffed."

"You most certainly did this to Hank, right before he struggled to clamp the handcuffs on you."

"Really? I'm cuffed from behind. Sounds reasonable enough to me. Sound reasonable to you?"

Bordo raised his eyes toward the ceiling. "Are you making a suggestion, Abel?"

"Remember, we have Hank's dead body to deal with?"

"And?"

"You do some exercise, not enough for you to haul Hank and me off the premises. Remember, once again, George is at the gate. You'll have to get Hank and me over the wall. I can't see that happening in the next two hours. And besides, your DNA will be splashed like a paint ball fight on Hank's and my dead bodies. You're toast if you go that way."

The look in Bordo's eyes caused an implosion of satisfaction in Abel's heart, though his handcuffed situation gave no hope for him. At least his death would be followed with legal consequences for Bordo, he hoped. But he'd hoped the same for Bordo after Beth's death, a bullet Bordo dodged.

Bordo asked a question with some desperation. "You're staying handcuffed, but do you suggest some solution?"

Abel readily answered. "Move my cuffed hands to the front. As you like to say…you know the drill."

"Then what?"

"I'll help you clean this room with the Clorox under the sink behind us, very quickly. We'll drag Hank, throw him over the wall. Now that he's dead, how can either you or I get any benefit from him?"

Bordo looked as if Abel hit a nerve, a plan. So, Abel continued. "I'll bury him and you can handle the rest inside your kingdom. I'll expect the handcuff keys from you, along with a shovel at the top of the wall. Can't dig a proper grave with handcuffs, right?"

Abel, during Bordo's strangulation of Hank, had thought quickly and resourcefully through the plan. He knew Bordo would lie, not live up to the promise. But death later than death now seemed better. Rachel agreed.

And Bordo did know the drill. One cuffed to a pole, a rotation, and the cuffs were on the front side. The clock ticked quickly on the Clorox cleanup, then the hauling of Hank, now encompassed in a makeshift pattern of large plastic garbage bags. They held Hank on respective ends, Abel walking backwards, carrying the head. Bordo carried less than his share, gripping Hank's feet, and they moved quickly to the wall.

Abel, fully handcuffed, managed to scale the wall to its top. He grabbed the forced end of Hank, fueled by Bordo's pressure from below, and flipped Hank over the wall. Beth didn't complain. Both she and Abel were well aware he'd died earlier, not Abel's fault.

Abel looked down, helplessly hoping for a key to the cuffs, a compromised promise between Bordo and himself. A draw. Another day. But the Great Bordo, as expected, lied. Rather than producing the keys, he produced a 9mm pistol. Abel sat on the wall, and at that distance, felt bigger than the side of a barn. As the bead of the pistol rose to Abel's chest, George, apparently unsatisfied with the plan of waiting at the guard house, came looking for Hank. George screamed, pointing a flashlight into Chris' eyes. "Mr. Bordo, what's that gun about?"

The interruption caught Bordo's attention. In a split second, Abel flipped backwards, falling to the ground on the other side of the wall, landing on his feet, his hands still handcuffed. His legs burned with pain from the landing, but he maintained his concentration. An argument arose between the two, with Abel completely out of their sight, but not sound. A series of gunshots rang out loudly.

Hank lay at Abel's feet. He hesitated a moment, reaching his handcuffed hands into his pocket, produced a paper and pencil, jotted something down, and leaned in the direction of the deceased. The planting of a seed. At the same time, he felt a key, one to the handcuffs, he hoped. Then, with no time or ability to bury Hank, he sprinted toward Highway 276, through a parking lot, and settled by the river.

Hounds might be upon him soon, but only if Bordo needed blame assigned to the one who ran. *Of course hounds are coming: Bordo has a dead body on each side of his wall. He'll have no choice but to call authorities, blame the incident on the burglar of the complex.* But then it occurred to him Bordo would have to fix whatever he could fix about the security video, probably give them the full recording from what could be seen at the guard house, which would show little of Abel because he mostly avoided the wall cameras. *Bordo won't give them my name, doesn't want my words to confuse the issue. He'll simply say there is a criminal on the run who took property, murdered, and needs to be caught. Bordo will make an insurance claim, collect money for things not stolen. Pay some cash to the victims' families. Turn out richer and more popular.*

The key worked. Abel had probably a couple of hours before his scent, picked up near Hank's body, would lead the hounds in his direction. He would fit neatly into Bordo's plan and cover his trail by walking through the water of the creek, then the Davidson River. By daylight no trail of footsteps or scent would exist for the police dogs to follow, and he'd be deep into the Pisgah Forest once again.

He found the backpack he left by the Davidson River, before his unsuccessful trip to The Fellowship headquarters. Grabbing it with his freed hands, he threw one of the straps around his shoulder, and started hiking. He could hear traffic overhead crossing the double-spanned bridges as he sloshed through the fast-moving water below. Wetness seeped into his boots, probably forty-one degrees, felt warmer than the cold stare from his mother's disappointment. He'd failed...Bordo was alive. The fact Abel still breathed, merely an overlooked matter of concern.

Chapter Eighteen

Monday, July 8, 2013
1:45 a.m.

Chris Bordo stared at George's body, disappointed in himself for succumbing to the pressure of the moment. George had violated his direct order, and Chris felt nailed, a gun dangling by his side.

He rethought his decision. George started into him about Hank, the pressure pushed him to react. "Dammit, George, I said stay in the guardhouse."

George's response was not what Chris wanted. "Why? What's happened to Hank? Why the gun? None of this looks right."

Upon reflection, he should have brought reason to George. The night, now quiet, offered a time for meditation of his decisions with his second guard. But at the time a potential storm brewed an ear-shot away, and Chris chose an impulsive reaction, one he now regretted. He wondered why he simply didn't point to the wall where Abel sat a second before, and yelled to George, "The criminal just scaled that wall, get the authorities." But in the heat of battle what controlled Chris' mind was that a man he just killed, along with a man who witnessed it, sat on the other side of the wall. The look in George's eyes conveyed distrust, and the words seemingly implicated his own boss in wrongdoing. And under that pressure, Chris fired enough shots into George's body to end his suspicions.

Then Chris, though time seemed critical, reflected on his hurried decision. Prioritizing, he dealt first with the 9mm pistol. The firearm came undercover to him, not registered. He thought quickly, took the gun back to the Money Room, where some of the Clorox Abel used to help him sanitize the room, remained. With a cloth under the sink, he cleansed the weapon, along with the cord that choked Hank, in a baptism of bleach, left the room, and threw both objects with all his might over the wall where Abel had escaped.

Priority two, George's body. *Do nothing. George will be found dead in close proximity to the wall the alleged suspect scaled shortly after ending George's life.* He took a hand broom and swept away his own footprints backing away from the crime scene.

Priority three. Call 911 and then alert the incoming private security guards of this horrible break in, theft of valuable Fellowship property, and murder during the thief's escape.

Priority four. *This one tricky...security video.* He thought carefully as to the current equipment, what was on video, what went into computer hard drives, what fell under his sole control, and what existed in the guard house. He considered each and took comfort that one of his faithful Fellowship members had computer skills to guide him around any issue. Luckily, anything recording his involvement could only be accessed by the computer in his room.

First, he returned to his bedroom, closing down all activity on all devices. Then he pulled out his cell phone and checked the time, 2:40 a.m. He called 911. "I'm reporting a break in, a theft, at The Fellowship Christian Headquarters right off 276, right before the park entrance."

"Your name, sir?"

"Reverend Christopher Bordo, and I'm deeply concerned for my flock. My security officers are missing. Can't find them. Please send help. Will you help?"

The operator, obviously shaken by the enormity of the emergency, asked no further questions. "Yes, yes, Reverend, help is on its way." And the Reverend felt confident, should the 911 tape ever be replayed, would support his innocence.

After the 911 call, his thoughts returned to his mental list of priorities. George's notes at the guard house could validate Chris' contention of a burglary. Best to let the next shift of guards find those notes. But he needed to read the notes first and double check the monitoring video that he predicted would have only the burglary entry by Abel, looking like a large opossum of sorts, the shoes of Hank, and nothing of Chris' participation.

In a matter of minutes he fast-forwarded through the video and confirmed his belief. Then he glanced at the paper pad containing George's notes. "I seen a dark something or nother on the TV, coming over that West Wall. It's big. Don't look right. I called Mister Bordo. Be tellin' him might be an intruder. He told me to stay on it."

Excellent, Chris thought.

Lights, sirens, and squealing tires interrupted Chris' satisfaction. He pushed a button opening the gate, and police vehicles started to arrive. The next shift of Fellowship security guards approached as well. Chris stood twenty yards away from the guardhouse, offering entrance to all.

A uniformed Sheriff's deputy, swinging a flashlight back and forth, paced quickly in his direction. "I'm looking for Reverend Bordo."

"I'm Chris Bordo. Thanks for coming so soon. I'm shocked, afraid, we need professional help."

"Well, Reverend, my Captain, Bill Francis, would ask for you to remain at the gate. My only question to you is where did this all happen that you spoke of during your 911 call?"

"Can't say for sure. One of my guards said something about the wall on the back side. We call it the West Wall."

"Thank you, sir. Now stay here, wait for the Captain."

Chris, exhausted, leaned back on the gate as his next shift of guards eased their way into the guard house, hovering over George's notes. Not only had this Sunday night, the night he relished most, turned sour, a tempting woman, succumbing toward his beckoning call, became replaced with a snotty-nosed Judas. Abel turned his magical evening into a nightmare within a short timeframe. He sighed as a man, sporting a not-well-tailored suit, approached him. He remembered Francis, but pretended not to.

"Reverend Bordo, I'm Captain Bill Francis with the Transylvania County Sheriff's Department."

"Detective Francis? The one I'm instructed to wait for at this gate?"

"Touché, Rev."

"What? You think this some game? I'm standing here trying to be strong in the most difficult of times. Lives are at stake."

Francis seemed shaken. "Sorry. I'm too used to dealing with thugs, people who I expect to lie to me…ones I usually call 'slime.' Touché? Almost a compliment, don't take it the wrong way, Preacher Bordo."

"Then I won't, Captain, but can't you see there are horrible acts of violence, a place usually of peace and hope? I'll stay right in this place as long as you say…but can you help us determine what happened out there?" Chris pointed in the direction where blood had spilled the most.

"I'm headed that way, Preacher."

"Please, Captain, call me Chris."

Bill Francis, though he rolled his eyes, responded. "And you call me Bill."

"Thank you, Bill. Also remember that perhaps the lives of many guests may be owed to my officers."

"Meaning what, er, Chris?"

"Meaning guests, worshiping at this very place, who left shortly after one of my security guards saw a suspicious entry into our place of worship, and, at my insistence, got our guests out safely."

"Understood. Chris, and I mean this in no uncertain terms, you agreed to stay here, not move. I accept your offer. I'm headed toward my men, will try to get to the bottom of things."

Chris touched him lightly on the arm. Francis jerked slightly, but then returned the smile. "Remember your promise to stay here until I get back."

Chris stretched out his arms toward the Captain. "Of course, and will you let me know something soon? This is not only my personal burden, but a burden which will be felt by the families if anyone has been injured. I owe my attention to these men and their families."

Chris grabbed the Captain's hand, shook it firmly, and watched him leave the area. As soon as the Captain's shadow drifted out of sight, Chris entered the guard house and ordered the new shift to the West Wall to help with the investigation. He cut off the camera monitor and retreated to places private and self-controlled: his bedroom. Locked in, he pulled out his personal laptop and began erasing vital information. Then he revisited some places around the room he wanted to be sure didn't bear his mark. He quickly cleaned up some suspect areas, flushing the evidence down a toilet.

***

Bill Francis walked briskly toward his men. "What we got?"

"Dead security guard, looks like a belly-full of lead. His I.D. says he's George Ligon."

"No pulse?"

The deputy shook his head. "I've called the coroner."

"Good work. What else you got?"

"Captain, three of our men on the other side of this wall are having an interesting conversation. Might be another dead victim."

Bill listened, perked his ears upward, then got mad, and hollered loudly in their direction. "Damnation, quit walking around. The sun's not up, dark as hell. You're trampling over the footprints of what might be the man who killed this guard at my feet. Freeze, I'm coming around."

The deputy, sounding rattled, echoed over the wall a lame version of not to trample on the evidence. Bill hiked ferociously around the interior of the complex, looking for a ground-level way out. He stewed in the poor manner things were unfolding. Out of breath, he commanded to the stiff-legged officers standing around a dark, dead body. "So, men, we know anything about these dead people?"

"I recognize Hank, the guy at our feet. Goes to my church. Saw him at our noon worship service today."

Nice, Bill thought. *Everybody in church.* He grabbed a flashlight from the deputy's hand and checked what he could. "Whoever did this ran that way, toward the highway, and you assholes are wasting the evidence…we might need to cast the prints. At the very least, the hounds need to pull up the scent. Get back!"

"Did I hear you say you know this 'Hank?' Go to church with him?"

"Yes, sir."

"Have you checked for a pulse?"

"He's not moving."

Bill leaned toward the body, placed two fingers on Hank's neck, and shined the flashlight with the other hand. "This man's been strangled. Have you noticed a rope, a wire? He has no pulse, strangulation is by a tightened instrument, the ring goes all the way around his neck, not a wide cord, not piercing, too shallow. Strangulation by strength of the killer."

"Officer, you say you know Hank. Could he have scaled this wall?"

"Hardly…remember him hitting a deep to left field in our men's softball game. They almost threw him out at first, slowest I've ever seen…we thought ol' Hank would have a heart attack…had to get a pinch-runner."

Bill chuckled, then apologized. "I'm sorry for the loss of your church member. But as we stand here, let's think things through. How did Hank get over this wall? Strangled here on this spot?"

The two deputies looked mystified, liked they'd not considered the issues. Bill used some diplomacy. "All the activity here seems to be moving toward Highway 276." Bill lowered his voice and looked his helpers in the eyes. "Shall we ease in the other direction, look for what wrapped around Hank's neck, look for the gun that killed the other one inside the wall?"

"Gotcha, Captain."

Bill shined his flashlight on the ground outside the wall and focused on the footprints. Hiking boots, knobby soles designed to grip rough terrain, dominated the prints scattered around the body. The most distinct set seemed to suggest a stuck landing after jumping from the wall. He examined Hank's shoes, less detail on the soles, basically a standard issue police lace-up, one that gripped well on regular surfaces. The area was devoid of evidence showing any landing or traffic of Hank's shoes. *Pathology has work to do.*

Bill thought of Reverend Chris Bordo, his shoe type already digested in his mind from their brief meeting. Black leather dress shoes, slicked soles, the type that would have caused a slipping-like print on wet soil. Bill's flashlight showed no such print, but the soil was dry. *Initial impression, a man with Bordo's shoes did not participate in what happened on this side of the wall tonight.*

But Bill remembered vividly the scene at this same location, years back, when a victim by the name of Beth Cunningham fell to her death off the side of a steep flight of outdoor steps. A call from inside the complex had alerted authorities to the scene. Police interviewed a teenage boy, who emphatically claimed Bordo caused the death, one he'd personally witnessed. The boy went on to say Ms. Cunningham refused Bordo sex, he got mad, and threw her over. A suspect, a motive, and a body. Then the eyewitness disappeared, and the case got ugly for the authorities.

Chris Bordo pissed Bill off like no scumbag from the bad neighborhoods had ever done. And Bill, as lead detective, pressed the magistrate for an indictment, and got one. He spent countless hours interviewing all the regulars of The Fellowship, what he considered a cult. He found a loyalty, a conspiratorial lock against the truth. Duplicity. The only slight break in the armor protecting the great preacher produced several giggles when he asked about Bordo's propensity for other women. But the consistently odd giggle, particularly among the men of the church, led to no reasons, no additional evidence, no further evidence of guilt.

And most of all, he hated the fact that Bordo glared at him when walking out of the courthouse, freed by the judge for lack of probable cause. Then Bordo turned around, walked up to his face, and farted. As the stink cleared from his nose, the exonerated preacher proclaimed: "God protects the righteous, and you don't know right from wrong."

Bill sat by the wall, looking over Hank's body, reflecting on the past. Amazingly, Bordo apparently had forgotten who he was when Bill entered the gate that night. Once he realized the mistake, he played along with the first name games and didn't let on that he'd take a hard look at Bordo before this investigation was over.

But, so far, Bordo's involvement seemed remote. An excited pair of returning deputies interrupted him.

"Captain Francis, we found a 9mm pistol over by the ditch, about thirty to forty feet from the wall. You figure the guy who ran ditched it there?"

Bill calmed the officers down. "Won't know yet, we need daylight. Did you find the instrument of strangulation?"

"Say what?"

Bill rolled his eyes. "The damned cord that choked the life out of the guy at your feet."

They looked at each other. "Right, Captain, we'll get back on it."

He stopped them. "One thing at a time, process the pistol first, by the book."

The deputies nodded, and Bill walked around to the front of the complex and re-entered the gate. *No Bordo, he balked on his promise to stay here.* He was pissed, but took the opportunity to look into the guard house, view the layout, the security system, and how this episode would have played out in the eyes of George, now deceased. He looked at the monitor, realized the system was off, and wondered why. He cut it back on.

He read the ledger containing George's notes and realized, assuming the handwriting belonged to George, Bordo had clear evidence of an intruder. The ledger went on to say Bordo mandated that his officers pursue the criminal element that invaded the sanctity of The Fellowship. Bill thought hard. *Knee-jerk reaction: guards pursued, confronted, and the burglar took them out. But, if he had the 9mm, why take the time to choke one to death, why not shoot 'em both?* As he watched the cadence of the revolving camera, now showing his own officers containing the scene, he realized the intruder may very well have stood out of the camera's direct line. A gunshot would have alerted security to something not seen in the camera's eye. *So, the first killing by choking makes sense, assuming the criminal was that smart.*

Then he slapped himself across his own head. *Hell, it makes no sense; the choked body is on the other side of the wall. What am I thinking; the perpetrator took the body with him?*

With much to digest, Bill returned to the inside West Wall to check on the other deputies. The sun's opening rays reflected on the back of their heads. "Any luck?"

"Captain, we're confused, looked this over a dozen times."

"What's confusing?"

"Starting with the bushes over there, inside the wall. Looks like a man wrestled a bear in there. Then we got a bloody massacre in the middle of this path with George face down."

"So, we know there are two dead bodies, makes sense that the choked one resisted in the bushes, looked like a bear fighting for his life."

"Agreed, Captain, except there is a trickle of blood coming from up the path all the way to the wall. After we discovered it we followed it back where it suddenly stopped, like a clean break."

Bill screamed. "You mean like somebody just cleaned it up?"

"Well, yeah."

"Who cleaned it up? Don't you think that changes the focus of this investigation?"

"No, we figured it was the guy who ran away."

Bill pointed in the direction of the wall. "He went that-a-way; whoever cleaned up the path leading back to the doors of the building didn't want us to follow where blood was first spilled. Damn, where's Bordo?"

**

Chris held his computer on his lap, cursing himself for what led to his destruction of his lip-licking banks of videos. Some of his most enjoyable sexual encounters, a taste of nectar most men only dream of. He knew a knock would come soon, one he'd have to answer. And unpleasantness would follow. But he was prepared…and confident. The memories of lust still clung to his mind even though electronically gone. Like a crazed-man, he deleted, put in double passwords, everything he could think of, to hide the computer's hard drive from a nosey cop. *I'll call Mark Pitts tomorrow. Be sure everything's wiped clean.* The knock interrupted his diligent work.

He yelled toward the door. "Come in, Captain." Chris continued to pound the computer keys, deleting the last download as the captain entered. A Bible parted midway, Psalms, rested upon a red cloth half way between Chris and the Bill Francis.

"Care to share some scripture, Captain? Oh, but you wanted me to call you Bill."

"Call me Lucifer, for all I care. Why was the guard house security system turned off?"

"You're asking the wrong person. Had you not secured that area before we last departed?'

Francis looked irate. "I'm asking the questions. Did you wipe up some blood, or anything, for that matter, leading to the West Wall?"

"No, Bill."

"I specifically told you to wait in the guard house, you agreed, and now you've violated our agreement."

"You've been gone for hours, it seems. I waited as long as I could stand, wanted to help."

"And your whereabouts for the last thirty minutes?"

"I'd think you, yourself, could vouch for that. You found me reading my Bible, this Bible. Surely you don't need it for evidence?"

"Reading your Bible? Looked like you were making love with your laptop…been deleting something?"

"Please, Bill. Technology has become a friend to worshiping our Lord." Chris turned the screen toward the captain, displaying the electronic Psalms.

"Reverend Bordo, I'm now declaring this entire complex a crime scene. You, your staff, whoever is here will have to leave."

"Fine, if this is the way you wish to conduct your business. May I collect some personal items?"

"Only while I watch."

"Sounds a bit kinky for a cop."

"Shut up. Get what you think you need."

"Then follow me." Chris led him to his dresser where he pulled out white Hanes underwear briefs, mid-calf socks, a church outfit, and some casual clothes that a priest might wear.

"Bill, surely you'll need a written list of what I'm removing from your crime scene?"

Chris watched Captain Bill Francis shake, like a soda about to explode, then calm the pressure, step by step. The process took almost two minutes before the Captain spoke.

"Get out."

Chris felt victorious. He remembered Francis well, the man who tried to take him down before. He'd give the Captain not even the satisfaction of thinking Chris Bordo would have the time or desire to remember such a failure. "Nice to meet you, Bill. I'll leave now since you have ordered me to leave my home. I feel threatened, quite frankly. Not sure this is even legal."

Chapter Nineteen

Wednesday, July 10, 2013

Bill needed help, beyond what his own department could offer. He reached out for a colleague he'd known for years, a cop whom he respected, one out of state, one he'd not had the need to bother for some time. A friend of the highest trust.

"I can't figure this out, T." That's what Bill called him in college. They were roommates.

"I've done my time, close to retirement. Why would you think I'd like to come to Brevard and play cops with you?"

"'Cause I'm drowning with nobody to turn to around here. This guy slipped a murder indictment under my watch some years ago. The arrogant son of a bitch acts like we never met, though I was the main witness against him."

"Who cares whether he remembers you? Is this some kind of revenge on your part?"

"No."

"Bill, you can't see, but I'm scratching my head and raising my eyebrows because it sounds like revenge."

"I'm focused on the facts."

"Focused on the facts or your emotions? Sounds like you hate this guy. Contempt is dripping from your lips, falling on this phone receiver, like a waterfall of disgust. Tell me I'm wrong."

"Maybe a small factor, but the truth is I think this guy's deeply involved in two murders, both security guards, and I don't have squat."

"If you don't have squat, you don't have a case, you don't get an indictment. What you're doing is self-serving, your narrow slice of the pie…getting back at a guy who rubbed you the wrong way. All I'm hearing is you have a hunch the jerk did some bad things."

"T, you're right…everything you said. But remember when I came to you when you asked, you and that crazy bank robbery? You built a great case, solid, a slam dunk."

"Bill, I know what you're about to say."

"Then say it."

"I built the damn case around the wrong person."

"And how did we discover this?"

"You had a hunch."

Bill sat silent for a moment. "And I have an even stronger hunch about this guy."

"When do you need me?"

***

Bill hugged his old roommate at the door of the Francis' home, a four-bedroom A-frame overlooking the town of Brevard. "T, how ya doing?"

T, constant as ever, spoke in a level voice. "Good, nice drive over, you added a garage since I last visited."

"Good eye, and a workshop, too." He lowered his voice. "And a poker table, too. You cleaned me out last game; you owe me a shot at revenge."

T smiled. "You got it. But your revenge needs to come out of this case you drug me over here to assist."

Bill nodded, humbly. "Got it."

"Good, because I've looked at all the stuff you e-mailed. My eyes have dissected every attachment, picture, and summary."

"Okay, but I want you to kick back, relax. Let's enjoy some time together before we dig into the case." But Bill couldn't resist inserting a question. "So, your gut reaction?"

"As it relates to Bordo?"

"Yes, Bordo."

"The case stinks."

"And I invited you all the way over here for *that* endorsement?"

"Go back to what I said. Remember? Get your emotions out of the case."

He backed off. "Understood."

"Now, I'm going to check into a hotel in town."

"No, sir. You'll stay here. That is our deal. My family loves you."

"And I love them; hope you'll have me over for supper sometime. But you have a family, and I at least need to Skype mine twice a day. I came to work, not socialize. I'll get more done if I stay down there."

"T, salad, baked potatoes already done. And a marinated steak, a thick one, has your name on it. My family's ready to see you, my dear friend. Can we get off this doorstep?"

"Ribeye?"

"Yep. Go to your hotel later. And thanks." He grabbed T by the arm and dragged him into the house.

***

Thursday, August 1, 2013

Bill watched T have a long hug with Betsy, Bill's wife. He reflected on their friendship until careers and kids got in the way.

"T, been so, so long. How are you?"

T let Betsy go and kissed her on the cheek. "Life's good. The wife's been beating me up over not getting together with you guys. Sad to think it took police business to bring me over for a visit."

"Exactly! Can't you guys retire or something? Bring your family to join us?"

Bill felt warm inside seeing Betsy and T reunite, then watching T box with Bill's sixteen-year-old twin boys. After a few beers and steaks, which they burned tending to the beers, Betsy washed dishes, and Bill took T to see the garage. What started to be a poker game turned out to be a discussion of the Reverend Chris Bordo.

"Bill, if your instincts are right, you need to get every computer out of that place. Hard drives contain everything, no matter how many delete buttons the owner presses. Even my snail-paced Georgia town P.D. has figured that out."

"We've got a problem."

"As in?"

"I locked the place down, declared the whole complex a crime scene. But having no passwords couldn't get into computer files without an I.T. guy, which around this town right now is like finding a hen's tooth."

"Why?"

"The damned County Council has all our resources tied up in some virus that invaded the server when one of our elected officials got giddy with some porn site."

"So, did you seal the evidence, preserve it?"

"Tried my damnedest. Went for a search warrant. Rushed forward trying to keep stuff from slipping through my fingers."

"And?"

"Got tangled up with the judge's schedule. Then two days ago I got this emergency hearing notice from the preacher's lawyer, claiming to represent The Fellowship.

"The Fellowship? You mean Bordo...and his people?"

"Exactly."

"So, the computers are still sitting at the complex and will stay there until a judge rules on The Fellowship's motion?"

"Yep, that's about the size of it."

"So, what's the motion?"

"Best I can understand...they want my crime scene back."

"Is your D.A. planning to be there?"

"His assistant."

"Why the assistant?"

"D.A.'s on vacation. I complained, asked them to request a continuance, probably pissed off the assistant. Bottom line...we go to court at ten in the morning."

T stood from his chair in front of the poker table, stretched, and picked a piece of steak from his teeth. "I'm going to my hotel room...need some sleep."

"By the way, T, you shuffled those cards tonight like you got a problem with your hand."

"You noticed. Yep busted 'em up doin' police business...you know how it goes."

Bill felt the weight of T's arms around his shoulders as he walked him to the front door. T looked at him. "Buddy, my truest best buddy, I'm not entirely following you on this case.

And what lies ahead tomorrow sounds like a shot in the dark…don't know what to expect. But count me in. I'll meet you at your halls of justice. Your county still holding court in that old building at the main crossroads?"

"You know the place. Meet me at the D.A.'s office next door thirty minutes before. Maybe we can get our point across to the assistant before entering the courthouse."

Chapter Twenty

Friday, August 2, 2013
Transylvania County Courthouse

Chris Bordo marched through the gates of the rock wall running parallel with Main Street, at the corner of Broad, and up the steps leading to a red-brick three-story tower. The clock at the very top, beckoning the time to all in downtown Brevard, rang forth the ten o'clock hour. He bolted confidently through the double doors at the top of the steps. To his left, beside the door opening, hung an aged marble marquee, more appropriately belonging in a cemetery, an old cemetery. But despite the deathly appearance, it proclaimed: "Come ye, come ye all: justice shall be granted."

Chris felt more at home with the lady to his right, the one whose arm he'd like to wrap around his. But he couldn't, at least not in this moment. She was his lawyer.

They turned right and walked up the stairs, taking each step side by side, rising up to the historic courtroom. They pushed into an unimpressive side door, and the courtroom came into view. She explained this 1861 building, constructed right after Transylvania became a county, continued to be the hot-bed of litigation.

"Both District and Superior Court goes on here. Traffic tickets to murder and all types of civil cases play out right in this room."

Chris scanned the courtroom. It looked like the front half, the part where the judge, jury, and lawyers sat, was original to Civil War times. But the back half, where he had just entered, where the audience sat, seemed a poor attempt to make modern oak benches fit in. He turned to his lawyer. "What's the deal with these benches?"

She laughed. "My dad said I should have seen it before…had folding chairs like an old- timey movie theater. Problem was people's butts got bigger over the years, and the spectators complained. At least the benches give, excuse the expression, a lard-ass a fighting chance."

Chris, tiring of history, changed the subject. "So, what kind of judge do we have today?"

"He's a good choice for us. He has a real liking for Brevard and this old courthouse. Actually, he has been quite good to our law firm over the years."

They strolled toward two tables reserved for the lawyers and their clients, both having three chairs facing the elevated judge's perch. Chris followed his lawyer's lead to the table to the left, checking out *her* backside. Since there was no jury and the judge had yet to arrive, Chris took a gander down his lawyer's low-cut blouse, took a deep breath, and reminisced of days past, when he controlled the headquarters of The Fellowship.

A bailiff by the name of Jimmy Jenkins interrupted. "Please rise."

The judge, draped in a long black robe, entered the courtroom, adjusted his clothing, nodded approvingly to all who watched, and took his seat. "How can I be of assistance to you fine folks here today?"

Chris' lawyer stood. "Your Honor, may it please the Court, I'm Sheila Burris, standing in for my father. He sends his apologies…he's in Federal Court in Asheville today."

The judge waited longer than Chris thought necessary to reply, but realized, while Sheila stood, the judge taking careful inventory over the goods she was packing. He couldn't blame him, though at three hundred bucks an hour he felt like he should have some say-so over how long the judge gawked!

"Sheila, Sheila. Of course I know you. Extend kind regards to your father. You know his nickname around here is 'Happening'." Once the judge stopped laughing at his private reminiscing, he looked serious. "Now explain your motion to me."

Sheila stood again, about to speak, when the judge interrupted. "By the way, where's the D.A.? Was he given proper notice of your motion?"

Sheila continued. "Legal notice fully complied with. I certainly mean no prejudice to my adversary and would be happy to wait. Perhaps traffic was bad."

The judge laughed again. "His office is next door...we'll give him a little time."

About that time, Chris heard the door open from behind. He turned and watched three men flowing in. One, dressed in a business suit, looking flustered, headed for the table beside them. The other two, dressed like detectives, guns bulging at their sides, ties too short, took seats in the gallery.

The judge spoke first. "You're the new assistant D.A.? Came from the P.D. office out of Hendersonville?"

"Yes, Your Honor, right on both accounts. Sorry we're a little late. My boss is on vacation. Seems I'm covering a lot of loose ends today."

"Not a problem. Welcome to our Transylvania County Courthouse. Ms. Burris was about to argue her motion. I trust you're ready to proceed?"

"A little rushed, but yes, I'm ready."

"You may begin, Ms. Burris."

"Thank you. I represent The Fellowship, LLC, a nonprofit, Christian organization that has had its corporate headquarters here in Brevard for over a decade. A violent crime was committed nearly a month ago. Mind you, no one in any way associated with The Fellowship has been implicated in this crime. In fact, the government's own investigation has focused on an unknown burglar, scaling a security wall, committing criminal activity, and fleeing as fast as he or she came."

The judge interrupted. "So, not to rush you, this stuff was in the paper. But why are we here, what is your motion?"

"My motion is simple, return the premises to its rightful owner."

The judge stood, stretched his neck in both directions. "I'm confused. Who has the place beside the rightful owners?"

"Thank you for asking, Your Honor. The Sheriff's Department. Without a search warrant they have circumvented the process by declaring the entire operation, a major nonprofit organization, a crime scene, in effect closing down the entire place, all of its equipment, and all of its property without any judicial authorization."

"Mr. Assistant D.A., what's going on?"

"If it pleases the Court, I would most respectfully respond, Your Honor…"

The judge interrupted. "Dang, Counselor, quit your brown-nosing. Has the Sheriff's Department kicked these people out or not?"

"Kicking out is the wrong term; we have two murders, authorities rope off crime scenes all the time, nobody gets in."

"You mean to tell me that if, let's say Brevard College has a rape in a dorm room, after a month has passed, you have authority, without the college's permission, to shut down the business office, cancel classes, bring a nonprofit college to its knees?"

The D.A. looked back at Captain Francis. "Your Honor, I have witnesses who can verify there is probable cause to believe both premises and equipment were used to facilitate the crimes in question. May I call them?"

Sheila stood. "I object. This motion was properly filed and served upon both the Sheriff's office and the D.A. No notice has been given to us as to witnesses to be called. In fact, any proffer of testimony must be made by affidavit and provided to us at least two days prior to this hearing."

The judge echoed. "Affidavits? Proper service? Done any of that, Mister Assistant?"

Chris liked the delay taken by the D.A., searching for an answer. Finally the prosecutor threw up his hands. "I can't say, Judge."

"Well, *I* can say. Motion granted, the property shall be immediately returned to its lawful owner until such time as proper judicial procedures are followed by the Sheriff's Department."

"The assistant stood, and Chris liked his lack of confidence. "Well, Your Honor, I also object."

The judge snapped at the assistant. "You also object to what? Your failure to follow rules or your displeasure of my ruling of you not following the rules? Which?"

Chris relished the moment as no response came from the prosecutor's lips. The pendulum had started to swing in the direction of the faithful, his Fellowship. *Justice has spewed forth the faith God himself has bestowed on me.* He liked the judge's dressing-down of the D.A. Especially the "object to what" part. He'd try to weave that humor into his next sermon. A sermon now to be delivered at his home base...returned to its rightful owner.

The judge delivered the crushing blow. "Hearing nothing from the D.A., my ruling stands. Miss Sheila, be so kind as to prepare a proposed order consistent with my ruling."

"Yes, Your Honor, I'll see if Dad wants to prepare it."

"Don't bother, young lady, you're holding your own quite well."

Chris observed the judge's eyes following the lovely backside of his lawyer leaving the courtroom. He'd chosen the right firm.

***

Livid, Bill Francis jumped into the chair at the D.A.'s table, only an inch or two between their faces. "What the hell just happened?"

"The judge granted their motion?"

"Yea. Remember I told you we are swamped, backed up trying to get computer people to legitimate crime scenes all over this county. But no, the County Council is screaming about its misguided member who screwed up the server. And now the Council's demanding our tech resources focus on pornography, old men, hardly able to walk, cruising the internet for naked women."

The Assistant D.A. interrupted. "But your lack of a search warrant…"

Bill popped up off the chair. "Will you let me finish?"

A nod came from the young prosecutor's head.

"I'm sorry, you're new to this job, and I'm sick of this bullshit. What I'm saying is misguided internet users are sucking our tech resources dry. I've got more well-founded suspicions on this so-called preacher than you can imagine. We *would* have probable cause, a search warrant, and probably the scoundrel preacher in custody. But, no techie, no warrant, understand?"

"Yes, sir."

Bill slowed his words. "I shut his computers down, within what the judge fails to recognize as the crime scene, and, given proper resources, would have pulled out of those computers vast evidence. I'd swear my badge on it. And now we have put the foxes back into the hen house."

The assistant dropped his head. "I rushed myself, not well prepared. Should have filed affidavits, delivered your message to the judge…done more."

Bill placed his hand on the defeated lawyer. "Don't beat yourself up. We all have bad days."

"Yeah, real bad. This one ought to last me for a while."

Bill then got very sober. "Sad thing is, I suspect what happened in this courtroom today has doomed any good that might come from those computers."

"What did you expect to find?"

"Can't say for sure, but this preacher killed a lady several years ago and evidence evaporated like dew on a summer morning. He's involved somehow."

***

Bill and T walked across the street to a sports bar. The Friday lunch crowd filled most of the chairs, but they found an empty booth in the back. Bill bought a couple of bottles of Miller Lite, and stewed in their loss. T, who'd not said a word during the hearing, clicked his bottle on Bill's. "Cheers, we enforce the law but don't get to interpret it. Quit worrying about the hearing, you did what you could do, the fix was in before we walked into the place."

"Yeah, the judge couldn't get his eyes off the defense lawyer's tits."

T leaned forward. "Tell me more about this preacher, your hunches, and the facts of the case."

"The Fellowship really is nothing but a bunch of country churches. Not a single one has more than a couple of hundred members. But they all have one thing in common…worshiping Bordo like he was God himself. He visits all his churches often and, from what I've been able to find out, milks about half the family paychecks into his own pocket…what pays for the headquarters here in Brevard, and his prosperous lifestyle."

"How do you know his lifestyle? I mean he lives behind walls."

"I'm a cop, not hard to find out what goes in and out of that place. Try enough booze to drown a Las Vegas casino, the finest cuts of beef, seafood shipped in from all over the globe."

"So, he rakes in a bunch of money; members have a right to be suckers."

"Suckers can be victims."

"And cops can be suckers."

"Please, T, cut me some slack."

"Slack? So, he spends like a sultan…don't make him a killer."

"He is a killer."

"Tell me you've got something more, I'm here to fight your fight, assuming there is one. Tell me something new. If that's it, I'm spending some time with your family, then heading back home."

Bill's voice softened. "We had him nailed with murder. A teenage boy, we never got his full name, told us he witnessed this preacher, this man of God, throw a woman named Beth Cunningham off a forty-foot cliff to her death. Ripped her aorta…bled to death. The preacher, so the kid said, wanted sex, she refused, and paid with her life."

"Good evidence for that case, not this one."

"Not even good evidence for the first one; the kid vanished."

"Still no evidence for the second, remember, the reason I'm here."

"Bordo verbally stuck a knife in me when he walked out of the courthouse a free man."

"How so?"

"Don't get me wrong, T, I understand he won. A little salt in the wound happens to us cops in the courtroom. Can't win 'em all."

"Your point?"

"What that cold-black-eyed bastard told me the night I arrested him for the murder."

"I'm listening."

"You know, most people being hauled off to jail are either quiet or unusually complimentary hoping you'll see some good in them before slamming the steel bars in their face."

"Again, your point?"

"Bordo is a man whose mere words obviously can influence a man to divide his paycheck and hand half of it to the preacher. You'd expect riding in that patrol car with me, he'd either have followed earlier obtained legal advice and remained silent or would have used his powers of persuasion to create good will toward his situation. He did neither."

"Dammit, Bill. What did he say?"

"Cold and collective, he leaned toward the Plexiglas divider between us and spouted forth: *You have not a clue.*"

Bill let T simmer over the short comment.

"I agree a strange statement. But he's a strange bird, like a lot of those evangelicals."

"But in five short words he didn't incriminate himself, in fact suggests I'm to be incriminated...arresting him without a clue of evidence. Then, he is letting me know the odds are stacked against me. Finally, he's predicting the outcome of his arrest, his trial, his future."

T stood, grabbed Bill by the shoulders, and shook. "He said none of that. Are you paranoid?"

"You weren't there, T. The inflection in each word came through crystal clear, just as I've said. You want to know the point? This guy's a killer, a manipulator, the best liar I've ever met."

"And?"

"And I need for you to get to know him."

Chapter Twenty-One

Tuesday, August 6, 2013

Chris watched the grand front entrance of The Fellowship from a rolled-down window in his black limo across Highway 276. The procession resembled a funeral of a national dignitary. Lights of police vehicles flashed, blue uniformed and plain clothes alike walked around with communication devices stuck to their ears. But the parade, to Chris' delight was not arriving, rather beginning to leave. The judge's lengthy order, dated Monday, August 5th, plastered to the tall rock columns, said, in short, to the police who'd taken over the holy real estate of Chris Bordo: *Get Out.*

Lawyer Burris worked all weekend, or so he claimed, so the judge would sign it first thing Monday morning. Chris loved Burris' idea of having a private detective blow up the paper order, laminate it, and post it for all to see the outrageous conduct of the authorities locking down the work of God.

He laughed to himself, watching the battery of incompetent law enforcement flee his domain. The only thing missing was Saint Peter, himself, waiting to grant admission to the faithful. He eased from the limo, crossed the highway, and slowly hiked the trail to the left of the complex. The exact opposite direction he assumed Abel took flight the last time he saw the traitor.

***

Half a mile around the perimeter, facing dense vegetation, barely visible against the wall, hid the humble back entrance of The Fellowship. A simple wooden door with an old-fashioned key lock. Chris Bordo pushed the key into the rusting deadbolt, and jiggled it open. Pushing the door through the vines that had no concern for architecture, only sunlight, he reentered his domain. He closed the door, one installed to discreetly escort, on appropriate occasions, his bedroom guests without raising suspicions of the more conservative donors walking out the main entrance.

Mark Pitts was the first *man*, besides Chris, to walk through the hidden door. As the police brigade left, figuratively with its tail between its legs, Chris smiled at the exodus and pulled out his cell phone. "Mark, I think the coast is clear, come around back like we discussed, stop at the blooming hydrangea, and I'll let you in."

"Reverend, there's a dozen or more cops out in front of The Fellowship, right across the road where you told me to park."

"Mark, look again, the Lord works in mysterious ways. May I dare guess they're all gone?"

"Wow, you're right. What now?"

For a minute, Chris' thoughts wandered to a sermon he had delivered a couple of years back about the chaos that consumed the world after mankind was cast outside of Eden. But that seemed a little disconnected to the task before him. "Mark, take your time, wind your way to the back, along the trail. Remember the hydrangea?"

"Yes, Reverend, yes. On my way."

Chris took his time to make sure all his e-files were properly renamed and fragmented before he would turn them over to Mark for proper disposal. He made his way to the rear of the property, still looking left and right for any violation of the good judge's order. All quiet, he reinserted the key. The rusty lock clicked roughly again as he turned the key to the left. Dirt against the bottom of the door dusted his shoes as Mark appeared.

"My son, welcome."

"Thanks, but those cops? Why am I sneaking in here?"

Chris moved close to Mark's ear, and whispered, "God has placed his hand on our place, our Fellowship. And God's will is exactly why you're here in this place, at this time."

"Are police still here?"

"No. The authority of man has been replaced with the authority of God. We are standing here by ourselves only due to the grace and providence of The Almighty."

Mark's eyes filled with the satisfaction of the faith Chris placed in his soul. A bond of trust needed from this computer specialist, stood at Chris' beckoning call. "Will you do God's will?"

"Yes, yes. But tell me what God's will is."

"Best we don't talk until you're convinced we're in private, no electronic device eavesdropping."

"I'll scan for that first."

"The Lord will be pleased with your response to his higher calling."

Chris raised his voice. "How was your trip over?"

"No problem. The scenic drive through the Pisgah National Forest was therapeutic after staring at screens and binary codes all morning."

Chris grabbed Mark's shirt sleeve, pulling him closer. "An hour or two of your time to the service of God is much better than the satisfaction delivered in the form of an hourly wage in a cramped cubicle, is it not?"

Mark nodded, lowered his head in obedience, and followed Chris. They walked in silence toward the main tower. Chris felt Mark grab his ministerial robe. "But the cops? I can't get them out of my head."

"The Lord has always had enemies."

Chris questioned his judgment of bringing Mark in so close to the cops leaving. He refigured the priority of having the computer records destroyed before Captain Bill Francis figured a way to get a search warrant and drag away *devices prejudicial*, a phrase Burris taught him, meaning, according to the lawyer, your hand being caught in the cookie jar. Destruction needed to be swift, complete. And Mark had the ability and the loyalty to get the job done. He'd have to get over the hoopla he'd witnessed before entry in the back door.

"Mark, may we pray?"

"Yes, Reverend. I feel the need for prayer right now."

Chris eased his hand behind Mark's arm and guided him into the bedroom. They both fell on bended knees. Chris couldn't help being distracted by the fact that a female usually filled that space. "Oh Lord, our God, we kneel before you as humble crusaders. Servants to heed your message and carry out your will. Show us a way around the deceit and evil placed before our eyes. Let us rise above the darkness into the eternal glory of your Kingdom. Show us the path, and we shall walk it. Show us the way, and we shall follow. Amen."

"Amen, okay, so what do you need me to do?"

"First check to see if anyone's listening."

Mark unloaded some electronic stuff from his bag, did a scan, and declared the room safe. "Now what, Reverend Bordo?"

Perfectly on cue, Chris lifted a computer from behind the desk. "Can you permanently delete the files from this hard drive?"

"They can't be physically deleted, but I can override them with data using defragmenting software."

"And they can no longer be accessible?"

"Yes, Reverend."

"Good. Erase the files. Don't bother to look at them just yet."

"Why not? Should I not know what I'm about to destroy?"

Chris moved toward his desk, reached into one of the drawers, produced a leather-bound Bible, and placed it on top of the hard drive. "Some more scripture might be in order for you to understand your role in our ministry."

"Something in the Bible about computers?"

"The Bible is relevant past, present, and future. And it has special meaning for you, Mark, today and tomorrow. Listen to the word of God." He opened the Bible to a page already bookmarked and used the same tone of heightened divinity that he used on Sundays:

"Now the gates of Jericho were securely barred because of the Israelites. No one went out and no one came in. Then the Lord said to Joshua, 'See, I have delivered Jericho into your hands, along with its king and its fighting men.'"

"Help me, Reverend, what's Jericho's being taken over have to do with your laptop?"

"Mark, this hard drive is God's Jericho placed in your hands. God places his trust in you, not to judge, but rather to reclaim our city in our creator's name. We must reclaim our city in the name of God."

"Excuse me?"

"The city I speak of is our ministry, our Fellowship. The unrighteous seek to destroy everything we have built, and I need you to help me ensure they do not take our ministry from the Lord. Blasphemy and evil want to take our church computers and make things that are not, twist honorable words into wicked ones, bring the sanctity of God's church to the devil's feet. You are a Christian soldier, am I wrong?"

"No, Reverend, you know I am."

"Then do as God commands, faithful servant. Destroy this hard drive, and all the other hard drives."

"I *will* obey, look at nothing, only override, or, as you like to say, destroy." "Obedience to God won the battle of Jericho. That's how we will win this battle. You must have trust in a higher power, okay?"

Mark stuttered. "Whew! Life and God seem much simpler in a cubicle."

***

Mark Pitts, his mission fulfilled, had left. Chris pondered the loss that came with the computer's override. A melancholy breeze rushed through his mind in the sanctity of his bedroom, his upper room. A balance of pleasure and sin. He felt God, with all he'd done, might understand a little pleasure. God seemed not actively speaking. So, he reflected on the work ahead, damage control. *I'll visit two churches every Sunday, confirm the flock, confirm their expected gifts to God...damned those lawyer fees.*

He then reflected on his meeting set for the next morning with the insurance adjuster. A knee-jerk reaction a year ago appeared to be on the horizon as a dividend. He'd gathered a select few of The Fellowship asking each to bring to Brevard the possessions that meant the most. He assured them all this was merely an exercise in faith, that God had no intention of taking what they cherished, any more than the child, Isaac, was offered to God in sacrifice. This was a selfless act of self-examination, coming in tune with the fact material possessions were secondary to the relationship of the Almighty. Then he launched into Abraham, his child Isaac, and God's demand of a sacrifice of his child. But merciful grace saved the child, and Chris explained the same would happen to the trustful within The Fellowship. Bottom line: show your willingness to depart of what means most to you, and God will praise you for your faithfulness and spare your offer.

The game worked, and valuable gems, gold, antiques, coins, and many other items lined the halls of The Fellowship's headquarters. The strategically talented photographers missed no angle or close-up of the precious cargo. The cargo departed after Chris proclaimed God's will to release all property back to the faithful with an appreciation that covered only God's children who had actually walked in the shoes of Abraham. The goods left, but an extended insurance policy, purchased by The Fellowship, remained.

***

Chris Bordo waited at the gates of The Fellowship and smiled as a car arrived. The "Broad Hands Group" blared an obnoxious mission statement from the large lettering on the compact vehicle. An aggressive lady, badge in hand, stepped from the car, through the gate, and extended a welcome hand. He shook it warmly. You must be from our insurance company?"

"Good morning, Reverend Bordo. I'm the Broad Hands Group adjuster assigned to your claim."

"Great, follow me and tell me how I can help you."

He took long, deliberate steps toward an office used to solicit donations, the Money Room. A thick file in her arms and her short legs made it difficult to keep stride. He slowed and she began talking.

"My job is to evaluate the occurrence and any damages you may have suffered. Of course, only those matters that fall within your coverage will be paid."

He stopped just short of the Money Room and turned toward her. "Do we have coverage for burglary?"

Chris pushed open the door and offered her a seat.

"Well, of course you do, but there are details…"

Chris interrupted. "Details? Like we forgot to pay our premium? Oh, I'm so very sorry to have wasted your time. I guess we *aren't* covered. I'll have prayer with my office staff. We would never, and I mean never, had made this claim for the property stolen by this burglar if I'd had *any* idea we'd failed to pay Broad Hands its money each and every single month."

The adjuster stood and raised her hands, palms faced in his direction as if standing during one of Chris' sermons at the crescendo. "No, Reverend, no. Your premiums are current."

"Meaning you took and cashed our premium check every month?"

"Exactly, Reverend."

"And what is the amount of coverage we paid you for?"

She looked through her papers. "Two million, it seems."

"It seems? You sound unsure."

"No, the coverage *is* two million, that's not the issue."

"Are you raising an issue?"

"Well, we don't have a lot of verification that the property you claim stolen was actually here. Can you show us?"

Chris leaned forward and laughed a sad laugh. "I could, but remember all of these items *were* stolen. I'd love to show you, wish I could have back what our faithful donated to The Fellowship in the name of God. It's gone! How can I show you?"

The Broad Hands adjuster's hair looked frayed, and sweat beaded along her upper lip. She pressed on. "Who are the donors?"

"Members of The Fellowship, The Fellowship you chose to bill every month."

"But the items you claim stolen…what might you have to establish the values you claim?"

"Have what? Appraisals or the items? We have neither. Remember, the items were stolen…I'm thinking that may have something to do with why you and I are standing here."

"Sorry, I mean appraisals."

"Maybe Broad Hands has unlimited money, but we don't, and don't have cash for appraisals. We did the best we could for you…took detailed pictures…did you bother to look?"

"Sure did. Mighty convenient lining up all those valuable pieces in that hallway in front of your chapel. Well done, there, Reverend."

Chris stepped toward her, spittle flicking from his mouth. "You dare to mock me, mock The Fellowship? Guess who instructed us to take the pictures? The Broad Hands agent we bought the policy from. His idea, not ours. Go check. He had copies well before the items were stolen. And, if he had wanted appraisals, he would have asked. He didn't."

"I know that already."

"You do? And yet you sling mud at your policy holder? Did *your* appraisers not look at the pictures, verify the authenticity of our claim? Are you willing to stick your neck out knowing full well these items are authentic, insured, and now stolen? Do you really question this claim?"

Chris stopped, took his seat slowly, lowered his voice, and looked sincerely at the adjuster. "My apologies. I had no right to raise my voice…but here at The Fellowship, this burglary caused more than just property loss. The loss of life itself has unnerved some of us. The deceased were our co-workers, our friends. May I ask a simple question, ma'am?"

She smiled politely, receptively, and eased into her chair. "You may, Reverend."

"What did your appraisers evaluate the value of our property?'

"She looked again at her notes. "A million and a half."

"Thank you, kind lady. Can we get a check soon?"

Chris cringed inside as she appeared to snap out of her trance. "Well, no, we still have issues…like where are these people you claimed gave you this stuff?"

"My dear lady, have you never heard the word 'anonymous?' Look at PBS; millions upon millions of property are donated in the name of those who wished to make a completely unselfish gift to a good cause."

"Well, Reverend, you're not exactly PBS."

"I take offense to your comment. It implies our anonymous faithful somehow are second class in Broad Hands' eyes. Can you verify that Broad Hands, itself, has never once made a donation without recognition?"

"Let's move back to your donors."

"Let's not. I asked you a simple question, do you remember it?"

The adjuster grabbed her hair, pulled out a hair tie, and wrapped it in a ponytail. Sweat spots appeared under the arms of her khaki-colored Broad Hands blazer. "Yes, I remember your question. And no, I can't tell you Broad Hands has never made an anonymous gift. But we're not here about Broad Hands…"

Chris interrupted. "We're not? I thought you worked for Broad Hands. I thought Broad Hands took dollars donated to The Fellowship the same way as they chose to insure valuable donated property for a price, the same price month after month. And you want my church to think…what was it you just said? Yes, I remember. 'We're not here about Broad Hands.' So, why do you suppose we *are* here?" He dipped his head and raised an eyebrow. "Not paying premiums?"

The adjuster started to shake, then took a deep breath. "Reverend Bordo, please don't take offense.   Off the record…Broad Hands makes us ask these hard questions, makes us take hard positions, makes us make some people back down that…well… maybe shouldn't."

"Really?"

"Yeah, it's all about the money."

"Like that purple lizard on the side of your car isn't as adorable as it looks?"

She chuckled. "That lizard has sharp teeth and bites like hell if you get too close."

"What you just said reminds me of customer chaos."

"Like I said, Reverend Bordo, my comments were off the record. A joke. I made 'em up. Forget them."

"Forget what? The broad hands are frisking me like a criminal?   Truly, do the broad hands treat all its paying customers like a prostate examination? Do you know what I'm saying, Ms. Broad Hands Adjuster?"

"I'll deny I said anything about backing claimants down. Broad Hands pays all legitimate claims, and that's the truth."

"Truth? I say what you claim as jokes are closer to the truth."

Rattled and nearly incoherent, the adjuster babbled as she drummed the arm of her chair. "Yes, no, but you're wrong. Our company, the by-your-side people, oh, forget that...."

Then Chris moved in for the kill. "Thank you for your candid, forthcoming statements. You know, I remember when I first called in this claim...Broad Hands' 1-800 number. Do you know what the pre-recorded message says...before I can even speak to someone as important as you? Do you know?"

"Can't say for sure."

"I'll enlighten you. The message tells the caller, me in this instance, 'For quality assurance purposes this phone call may be recorded.' Guess what?"

"What?"

"The Fellowship just recorded your off-the-record comments."

"What?"

"Oh...but only for quality assurance purposes." He smiled a wicked smile. "Now, are you ready to pay this claim?"

She stood and placed her hands firmly on her hips. "You think my supervisor will let me stroke a million dollar check without more documentation?"

"Is this the supervisor I need to let hear this tidy little recorded confession you just gave me?"

Her lower lip quivered and nothing came from her mouth.

"Should I play it back for you now? Remember the purple lizard? All about the money? Or would you rather I play back your off-the-record stuff to your supervisor at Broad Hands? Should I assume he's a man? How solid is your job security?"

The adjuster packed up her briefcase hurriedly and left quickly. Chris followed her to the gate and watched her turn back in his direction. "You'll get the check soon. I'll rush it up."

Chris smiled. Then greed replaced itself with the image of a small boy, a precious top Chris once spun with all the skill he could spin. But for all the time Chris had invested in Abel, all to show for it was a thankless kid who'd turned his energy against the one he should appreciate the most. Chris hated disloyalty.

Chapter Twenty-Two

Friday, August 2, 2013
1:30 p.m.

Bill and T finished their beer in the back of the sports bar. The crowd, getting bigger and louder by the minute, made their decision to leave easier. "Bill, I'll interview the dead victims' families. Maybe something will shake out." T looked into his old roommate's eyes, feeling his frustration, and added, "The guards at The Fellowship weren't members, best I could tell from your files. They collected a paycheck a shadow above minimum wage. Both, I believe, attended Baptist churches. Perhaps the families' loyalties are shallow…let me check it out."

Bill grabbed T by the shoulder. "I'd be grateful."

***

"Good morning, ma'am. I'm here on behalf of the Transylvania County Sheriff's Department. Would you happen to be Hank's wife?"

"Come in, Officer. Yes, we were married for ten years. Had two kids by him."

"Please understand, first and foremost, my greatest sympathies are with you and your children. I'm a family man and can't imagine what you're going through. Is this a good time to talk? I'd hate to hold you up from work or errands."

She laughed. "Good a time as any. I got no job, no man, no insurance."

"Take it the boys are out playing, enjoying the end of summer?"

"Yep."

"I understand Hank was a good man."

"Good as I could've hoped for. He worked regular, didn't rough me up like lots of men do to their wives 'round here."

"Y'all are Baptist church goers, I hear?"

"Twice on Sunday and every Wednesday prayer meeting."

"The church people helpin' you out during this difficult time?"

"Ain't much, they're poor folks same as us...paycheck to paycheck. They brought lots of cookin' around for a week or so after the funeral."

"Again, sorry for this terrible loss."

He gave her a second or two to nod her head, collect her thoughts. "Ma'am, do you know much about the place, that Fellowship, where Hank worked?"

She shrugged her shoulders. "Like know what?"

"Well, we think there may be some unusual things that don't add up on how this happened. Thought you might know something, heard something."

"All I heard was a man, I guess the one you ain't caught yet, broke in, and during all the thieving, killed my husband. The preacher over there called Hank a hero."

"You know much about that preacher?"

"In what way?"

"Did you know there was a death a few years back, and the Reverend Bordo became a major suspect?"

She stood, adjusted her apron, and pulled her graying hair behind her ears. "Wait a minute, now. Preacher Bordo is the only reason I've made my trailer payment, puttin' food on the table. He's almost as broke-up over Hank's death as me and the kids. Why sling mud on the only one out there helping us?"

"Fully understood. But paying money out don't make something wrong go away. Why do you figure he's throwing money your way?"

"What are you saying? That man didn't throw money at us. He's done prayed on his knees in this here room, cried over Hank's loss, give comfort to me and the kids. You ask why he's helped us? He gave me the answer, plum warmed my heart."

"Mind telling me?"

"Not at all. Preacher Chris says my Hank saved his life, others, too, and felt the least he could do is share a little comfort to the family of a hero who laid down his life for others. You git what I'm saying, Officer?"

"Get it perfectly. I mean no disrespect to the preacher, and I hope you'd know that Hank, a law enforcement officer himself, would understand me asking hard questions to bring to justice the man who killed Hank and his partner that dreadful night."

"I guess you're right. Hank *was* a man of the law… dang proud of that."

"And what the preacher is doing for you is a wonderful thing, as long as there's nothing else."

"What else? You back to ravin' on 'bout the preacher?"

"All I can say at this time is we have suspicions. I had only hoped you might be able to shine some light on our investigation. Reverend Bordo is only one concern, and you seem quite supportive, and I respect that."

"I'm no detective, not much of nothin' for that matter. But my gut tells me Preacher Chris' alright, cares about us, and yea, *plenty* generous. So, if you're 'bout done, I'd like to go wash a load of clothes in our new washer."

***

Bill soaked up T's hard stare. "You'll get no help from the victims' families; I've now talked to both. Bordo has brought them into his cult, spreading money like they've never seen. Chances are I've hurt you more than helped. These folks will surely share with Bordo every insinuation I've made. I'm sorry, damned sorry."

***

Over the next couple of weeks, Bill pondered the lack of progress in the investigation to track down *any* killer. The trail to the river went cold. The best of the county's coon dogs looked like whipped puppies a half-mile up the banks of the cold, spring-fed river. Outside the wall contained plenty of footprints and one dead body. Inside the wall, another dead body and a series of footprints resembling a footprint war, all trying to trample each other out.

The two old cops jabbed at each other. "T, we have Bordo's partial prints here and there inside the wall. Do you agree this establishes his presence at the crime scene?"

"I agree to Bordo's presence in the immediate area. The bigger question is when his presence took place. For God's sake, the guy lives there, might trample the same area once or twice a day on his daily walks communing with his creator. So what?"

"Granted. But hear me out. His footsteps, although undated, place him there since the last hard rain. I've checked this, less than forty-eight hours before the 911 call. Next, Bordo's guests, admittedly protective of the great preacher, have consistently maintained that Bordo exited the party for a long period of time."

"Okay, I'm listening. Which period of time? My recall from the guests' statements, he left with a troubled church member, albeit an attractive young female, married at sixteen. She needed prayer, I assume private prayer?"

"Exactly. They disappeared."

"Yes, disappeared into his…I love this…upper room, which happens to have some large and lovely erotically shaped bed!"

"So, T, your rub is he ain't killing anybody while he's plugging away at the young prize?"

"Sort of. But things get interesting if you pay attention to the facts."

"Which facts?"

"She returned to the party, well before anyone died, according to the pathological established time of death."

"Got it, T. The opportunity lies in the timeframe when the girl returns to the party and the time of death. Nobody can account for the preacher's whereabouts except for the guard at the gate. His log states he called Bordo about an intrusion at the West Wall."

"Bill, this ain't working. Bordo has an absolute right to be concerned about the intrusion and, in the interest of safety for all, abandon his own party long enough to confirm all were safe.

Would you suggest he blasts back into the party and alarms the guests who've just lined his pockets with the generous donations he demands? I think not.   And, if we're perfectly candid, standing in his shoes, as awkward as it may seem, we'd have done the same thing…not ruin a profitable and lavish evening until we checked out if the threat was real. Am I wrong?"

"Can't say you are.   We're only picking each other's brains. So, let me continue. I need to jump forward to when I entered the complex, met Bordo face to face."

"Refresh my memory."

"I said stay here."

"And your authority for this legal proposition?"

"He agreed."

T threw his hands in the air, with a dumb-founded look on his face. "He agreed? Like a consent to search, therefore, no probable cause needed?"

"Something like that."

"You think because a suspect…maybe not *even* a suspect…agrees to stay in a certain place, this is the equivalent to a constitutionally valid arrest?"

"Maybe."

"Wrong, you're confusing consent to search with consent to detain, and you know it. You had no right to hold a person in one place without probable cause.   Because he agreed does nothing to improve your legal standing. He had every right to leave… if for no other reason he simply changed his mind."

"Okay, Mr. Defense Lawyer, what about fleeing the scene? I've used that one before as evidence of guilt."

"Please! Fled what? This is not running away from a bank robbery, this is not hauling ass out of town after you noticed your neighbor watched you burn down your own house. Bordo stayed within the confines of his own property. Maybe he felt so bad about the deaths of his trusted security people he needed an aspirin from his bedroom...the upper room...for his throbbing headache."

Bill waved his hands down at T. "I know, I know. I suspect he knew this as well as you just said it. But at least in my mind, and I hope yours, he left as quickly as he agreed to stay. But not before turning off the cameras he controlled in the guard house, virtually blocking out whatever he did while I investigated two deaths. Why?"

"Got a feeling you want to answer your own question."

"Damned right I do. In my opinion, he executed a three-dimensional cover up."

"Begin with one, my friend."

"One, he took something, like a broom, and covered up foot prints leading from the death scene going back to the business offices area. Two, the place reeked of bleach. This was a Sunday night, not a janitor in sight. Bordo sanitized something. Three, computers. When I walked into his...office, bedroom, whatever the hell he calls that room, he was pounding keys like a mad man. He ended in a flurry of clicks before he turned toward me and smiled like mission accomplished."

T put his hands behind his head. "Okay, got your three points...any evidence to back up your chosen suspicions?"

"I suspect there's plenty. Too bad the judge saw fit to take it all away from us."

"Stop licking your wounds, deal with what we have."

"That leaves us with two dead bodies and their possessions, a dozen casts of footprints, hundreds of pictures..."

"Stop there. You're big on this bleach thing. Have we checked for any residue on the victims' clothing?"

"Great point, T, now I remember that's why I brought you here. I'll put some forensic guys on that tomorrow."

"Let's stay with your three-something. The broom, the footprint erasure. Any evidence of that would be lost with the next rain storm. But of hundreds of pictures, bet you got that angle."

"Damned right I do."

"Now computers, they might be problematic at this point. But don't you have all the surveillance? We looked at it once, probably to get a feel for what it contained. Can we take another look, with a particular focus in mind?"

"We can, and we should. You got a focus in mind, T?"

"I'm backing my partner. You say three, I say three. Wonder if a broom stroke seemed insignificant the first go round?"

"I like movies…bring some popcorn."

***

Hours consumed Bill and T, noses often touching the monitor, pointing out minute details of the night that claimed the lives of two Fellowship guards.

"Look at the shoes, black, leather, at least two-hundred bucks at that up-your-ass men's store in Asheville."

T laughed hard. "Yeah, sweeping dirt well after midnight. The date and time bonded with the event."

"But shoes? A broom? Can't get a warrant with that."

"Don't despair, only one piece of a large puzzle."

"Yep, though I haven't put one together in a while, I still remember the excitement when the picture started to form."

"Wish we had a puzzle box cover to look at…the whole picture."

"No such luck...the puzzle we're trying to solve begins and ends with us, not a convenient box."

They next focused on re-watching the camera surveillance of the West Wall, the place of a multitude of footprints...and dead bodies.

"Run it back again."

"After thirty times, we only know those legs don't belong to Hank, don't belong to George, and sure as hell don't belong to Bordo."

"And sure as heck don't belong to that troubled luscious woman Bordo disappeared with at the party."

"Then who?"

"If you were to charge Bordo, and I was his attorney, I'd argue to the high heavens: 'You mean the real criminal, the one your incompetent local sheriff's department couldn't find, is walking around out there, and they decided to arrest the guy who lived there, the one who called 911 himself?'"

"Yep, no argument there, partner."

"Play it again. Let's ask ourselves not who, but what."

"A man's pants, a man's boots."

"Right. A younger guy, look at the muscle line beneath the fabric. The boots...nice hiking brand, sells in most of the outfitter stores around here...in fact, one right by the rock entrance to Pisgah. I'll take a wild stab with those folks tomorrow. Maybe a credit card of a recent purchase."

"Okay, but back to the video. So, let's assume we have this younger male who drops over the wall and only shows his bottom torso. He is a thug, our burglar, our murderer of two. You got a connection between him and Bordo?"

"Nope. I admit, still a hunch."

"Bill, good thing I like you. I should be lacing up my own hiking boots, and put one after another away from this place."

"What?"

"We don't have a theory!"

"T, excellent point. We need a motive."

"Of course, but you and I have avoided that point for quite a while. Before we jump into motive, what did you hear from the forensic folks...you know, the Clorox thing?"

"Yes, residue of bleach on Hank's clothes, not George's."

"Which means?"

"Can't get a decent grip on the reason. Maybe Hank cleaned something up, bored to death with being a rental cop with no crime to solve."

"Tell me again, Bill, exactly where you smelled the bleach after you arrived that night."

Bill had to think carefully, too many issues that night to have a clean mental inventory. He closed his eyes, took a deep breath, and recalled. "This classroom-looking place. Locked. But the odor seeped from the edges of the door. Quite frankly, I made a mental note to get the key, check it out...but when I stumbled onto the dead bodies, both sides of the wall, the odor seemed less...well...I never got back to it that night."

"Understood. Why does it seem more important now?"

"I think you know."

"More than likely, but I'd prefer to hear it from your lips."

"The gun looked, and now that I think of it, smelled like it got bleached, though we found it over the wall, even further than Hank's body."

"And?"

"If Bordo bothered to broom clean footprints, Bordo seems the likely one to clean other stuff."

"What other stuff?"

"Dang, T, quit treating me like grade school. I can't say what went on in that room. But let's just say Hank got strangled there, not over the wall. Wouldn't there be a bunch of saliva, puke, blood, a confluence of body fluids to clean up? And if Hank was dragged out of the room, down a trail, and thrown over that wall, wouldn't there be a good reason to clean the trail?"

"You think Bordo strangled Hank…in that room?"

"T, can I have a pass, for now, on your question and focus on a motive?"

"Your case, not mine…only here for the ride, old friend." T winked at Bill.

Bill smiled. "Got a bit of new information before we got together today."

"Brittany Spears got kicked off of some show?"

"Right, Asshole. Try this: Some Broad Hands Insurance guy…you know those adjusters who want to drop a dime of some vendetta with some arson type?"

"They all want to remain anonymous."

"Exactly, they don't want to come to court, don't want to give their name, only want us to bust the chops of some insured who got money the insurance company reluctantly paid."

"Yeah, we make a report and throw it in the "O" file. By that time we've consider it a civil matter."

"Well this one involved The Fellowship."

"You have my attention, Bill."

"A ton of money, the caller said, paid out to Bordo arising from guess what?"

"A theft? The night in question?"

"Yes."

"Hold on. I don't recall property theft being an issue in this case, this investigation."

"Nor did I. Two murders seemed the focus."

"Broad Hands would never have paid a claim if the theft wasn't reported."

"We were beat, at least eleven straight hours of bodies and footprints and surveillance tapes. I told one of my younger deputies, fresh on his shift, to finish up the paper work with Bordo…you know addresses, cell phones…what a secretary could do."

"And?"

"Bordo inserted a detailed list of property stolen, the time it was stolen, and the culprit being a burglar to the complex. All neatly tucked away in the Transylvania County Sheriff's Department official report of the incident. Nothing in our report refuted the allegation. After all, we had…have…two murders to solve."

"And Broad Hands paid how much?"

"According to the caller, a ton."

"Umm…"

"What?"

"Slow down, I'm thinking."

"Of motive?"

"No, we have motive. Just not one that ties into the facts as we know them."

"Like why kill somebody over missing property?"

"Well, we might consider that Bordo somehow staged this theft, the security guards found out, and he murdered them both as damaging witnesses. With whatever the insurance company paid, whatever a ton means, on the line…not hard to fathom."

Bill scratched his head, and cut his eyes toward T. "So, you're saying the legs and feet of the person who climbed the wall, no face, was the work of Bordo, knowing the exact placement of the camera lenses?"

"Yes, in theory. Then maybe the intruder, all a part of Bordo's insurance fraud, got off track. Then the rent-a-cop, a guy who couldn't run to first base, showed an unexpected burst of cop brilliance...he broke the case...and it cost him his life. Then rent-a-cop number two sees too much on the monitor in the guard house...victim number two."

Bill stood, stretched. "If you were a judge would you give me an arrest warrant for Bordo?"

T leaned close. "No."

"What I thought."

"But hold on, Bill, you've certainly got a reason to want to ask the good reverend some more questions, you think?"

"I think he has a lawyer."

"Never hurts to ask."

"Or help...okay, I'll ask."

Chapter Twenty-Three

Wednesday, August 28, 2013
Brevard law offices of Burris and Burris

Chris Bordo sat in a recliner-like chair too short to stretch out comfortably and too high for his feet to feel the floor. The chair put him in a position of vulnerability. Had drills been humming, he'd considered it a dental office. Certain the furniture was designed to unnerve the emotionally wrecked clients whose misfortune landed them in the lobby of shysters, he chose a straight-backed chair behind a secretary's desk and pulled it between two of the recliners. Walnut paneling rose some twelve feet up the wall to massive ceiling molding rivaling the Biltmore Mansion. After a wait too long to suit his schedule, a lady in a business suit escorted him back to the private office of Lawyer Montana Burris. Montana, Sheila's dad, the one the judge referred to as "Happening," appeared before him.

"Chris, so sorry to keep you waiting. I've been up to my eyeballs talking to judges, trying to work deals…stuff us lawyers are expected to do. Again, my apologies."

"Save your energy, don't justify what you did for others today, justify what you plan to do for me."

"Damn, I mean shoot, Reverend. You got straight to the bottom line; I like that in a man."

"Why are you called Montana? Your mom give you that name?"

"Why waste time talking about that?"

"Fair enough. But since you will eventually figure out my real name, thought we could swap stories."

"Oh, what the hell. I had a family name that worked out to be a nickname of 'Monte.' Soon as I was old enough to figure out the name sounded worse than 'Chicken Little,' I pushed for a readjustment."

Burris leaned toward Chris. "Your turn."

"Birth certificate says 'Elwood Sloan.' No better than Monte. As soon as I started preaching, I found my name had to play well to those who absorbed my words. Problem was none of them could spell Bordeaux, a name I thought was European, with a flare of depth and understanding. Finally, I gave up. Now it is spelled like it sounds. 'Chris?' Closest thing to Christ without stepping over the line. Do I trust this conversation falls within the attorney/client privilege?"

"Absolutely! I just love having this enlightened chat…getting to know one another."

"I bet you do, Lawyer Burris. Got your letter last week saying you have adjusted our hourly rate."

Burris laughed. "Oh yes, you know how bookkeepers and accountants are, always tweaking inflation and all that sort of stuff."

"Actually inflation has been sort of tame in this economic downturn, flat at best. You just jumped my hourly rate from $300 to $600."

Burris adjusted nervously in his seat. "Do I trust when Sheila went into court for you last go 'round you found the results quite favorable?"

"Fair statement."

"And may I gather from that you are well pleased with our services?"

"I'll give you that."

Burris leaned back in his generously padded leather chair, the look on his face gaining confidence. "Surely, Reverend, you understand our zealous advocacy on behalf of you and the place you call the "Fellowship" prevents us from taking anyone else's case that is remotely adverse to your considerable standing in this community?"

Chris took the absurd statement in stride, then extended his hands, palms up. "Granted. But didn't you make this same commitment when you charged me $300 an hour? You used this same sales pitch for me to agree to half the rate you now propose. Am I wrong?"

Burris looked worried, but as Chris would expect, rallied. In fact, had he not, Chris would have fired him on the spot.

"Oh, Reverend, I know money doesn't grow on trees, and you need to weigh out the value of stable legal services versus excellent services. As you might have noticed at the last courtroom appearance, even though I was absent, having a good rapport with the court has, let us say, significant advantages?"

Chris smiled. "I finally get it. There are lawyers who know the law and others who know the judge…"

And with Chris' lead in, as he expected, the lawyer he intended to keep rose from his seat and landed the knock-out punch. "And we here at the Burris firm know both, thus the justification for the $600 fee. Are we clear?"

"We are clear. Now may we address the reason for my visit?"

"Take all the time you need."

"A Captain Bill Francis of the Transylvania County Sheriff's Department wishes to ask me some questions about an insurance claim The Fellowship filed."

"Yes, I'm aware of this request. You discussed this with my paralegal. Our general advice, Reverend, a bad idea…nothing to gain, a lot to lose."

"My guess is our local authorities have become desperate, clueless to solve the tragic loss of two of my security officers. Now, they aimlessly take a stupid approach, suggesting that this insurance claim somehow might be a motive to the murders."

"And what do you hope to achieve by talking to this Francis guy?"

"Show him the errors of his ways, hopefully he'll back off."

Burris rose from his chair and shook his head. "The advice you're paying for is worth nothing if you don't listen to me."

"You think it's a bad idea?"

"Exactly what I said a minute ago, Reverend. Captain Francis is a pro, you're not."

"Lawyer Burris, I'm not unmindful of your rationale. But listen to mine."

"I'm listening."

"I'm not uncomfortable talking…of course, only in your presence…with this officer. Perhaps we can nip this thing in the bud. You must understand that my ability to pay you is tied closely to the loyalty of my Fellowship members. If somehow the misplaced desperation of the authorities ends with my false arrest, the consequences may be far spread."

"I'll need some time to consider all of this. If I go along with this little chat you might have with this captain, I'd insist that we conduct some mock questioning sessions to be sure you're ready. A little coaching session, so to speak. How does that sound?"

"Sounds fine."

"Understand, though, this process can be quite time consuming."

Chris smiled at his lawyer and left, wondering how the murders and the escaped burglar had rescinded into the shadows of The Fellowship's insurance claim.

***

Bill Francis waited in the lobby of the Burris law firm, a situation unlike anything else in his career. Always interviews took place at the scene, or at the department, or in the witness' house…never at the suspect's lawyer's office. But given the necessary consent of the one to be questioned…The Reverend Chris Bordo…he was given no choice. So he waited in a completely empty room. Only a lady answering telephone calls could be seen from his vantage point.

***

Finally, a person arrived. "Captain Francis, I'm Attorney Burris' assistant. Welcome to our law firm. Please follow me to our conference room."

Once arriving at the thirty-foot table, glowing of rich maple, smelling of furniture polish, he was offered his beverage of choice. He declined. Around the table sat eight people. Bill decided to break the ice. "I only intended to interrogate one." Nobody smiled, except one seated at the end, Chris Bordo.

"Reverend, I *think* I recognize you down there. You mean we're going to sit half a football field apart, and all these folks between us?"

Then, as Bill expected, the senior law partner, Happening Burris, rose to the occasion. "Captain, we're here, in a spirit of cooperation, to have a little chat with you. You requested this meeting, am I right?"

"I did."

"I've got a tape recorder sitting in the middle of the table. Is this conversation official, or would you prefer off-the-record?"

Bill had to ponder that one a minute. "By all means, turn the recorder on, I've got one myself in my pocket. We'll turn on both...give each other a backup."

Burris' eyes shifted. He didn't like the answer but, from Bill's vantage point, covered the disappointment well.

"Good idea. You just saved my client a bundle. All these folks around the table can leave, go bill some hours of another client."

And leave they did, leaving only Bill, Burris, and Bordo. *The three B's*, he humored himself. *Broke, bullshit, and busted.* Then the self-consumed Burris couldn't wait, wanted the first word...and, Bill suspected, the last. He'd prepared himself for this bombastic approach. What he might gain would come in the valleys between Burris' peaks.

Burris stood from his seat and stretched his tall frame. "You wish to question my client?"

"If you'd permit."

"Thank you, Captain Francis, for acknowledging this interrogation is purely voluntary on the part of not only my clients..."

Bill knew what was coming.

"...my clients being The Fellowship, the Reverend Christopher Bordo, and its membership."

Bill smiled. "I'd like a list of those members. Surely I can't conduct an investigation, and not violate your attorney-client privilege, unless I know who they are. Will you get one of those folks who just left the room, whose shadows seem to be ebbing and flowing behind that beveled mirror, to get me the list you wish to claim as clients? Then I'll know who not to talk to without your permission."

Burris looked caught as a trout on an artificial fly in the Davidson River, and he didn't try to hide it.

"Nicely done, Captain.   We've met before in the courtroom, know each other's styles.   Seems I recall doing pretty good in most of those cases…you have a problem with me?"

"Not at all. We're both professionals, nothing personal."

"So, no need to argue."

"I agree, counselor…but my list?"

"You'll get no list, and you damned well know it!"

"Because I doubt even your high-dollar law firm would have merited the trust for the reverend, seated so closely to your side, to give *you* the list. Are you saying you represent people you don't even know?"

"Dammit, Captain, let's move on. Don't you have some questions for my client, the one seated beside me, the one whose name you already know?"

"Fair enough. Chris, mind telling me why you happened upon more than a million dollars over some insurance claim?"

"We paid the premium."

"Good, excellent answer, and should I assume the payment came from Broad Hands Insurance Company?"

"Yes, I believe that to be our insurer."

"You believe, or do you know?"

Bordo hesitated, seemed to take a reflective breath, "Captain, we've spoken before over the break-in. You have failed to catch the intruder, am I wrong?"

"No."

"Then why, under God's heaven, do you focus on an insurance claim…instead of the one who caused the ruination of The Fellowship's assets?"

"Why do you say one?"

"Well, certainly I can't say for sure. You are splitting hairs, Captain."

"Not at all, Reverend, I'm trying to follow your lead. If you could verify the numeric value of the 'intruder,' as you call them or it, our investigation would be grateful."

"I'd be grateful if you'd quit twisting my words."

"Which words?"

"As you know, I have no idea of the identity…"

Burris interrupted. "Now, Captain Francis, not that the Honorable Reverend Bordo is not holding his own, but can we get to some point in your interrogation? Surely you aren't suggesting that this preacher needs to find the criminal? Do your job for you?"

"Damned right, I am. If he knows, surely you, Mr. Lawyer, aren't suggesting he not reveal the identity?"

"You have not Mirandized this client of mine. Would you mind, now you've suggested some impropriety of hiding the identity of the *very* person we want in custody, the one *you* should catch, be so kind as to take a stance?"

"A stance on what? The truth?"

"Captain, surely you know truth lies in the hands of the jury…sometimes only the hands of a judge when the prosecution's case is too weak even to make it to a jury."

"You suggested I take a stance. Can you be more specific than what a Google search would reveal to a teenager?"

"If you intend to accuse my client of whatever your mind has fictionalized, afford him his constitutional rights…is that specific enough?"

"What did I accuse him of, not liking his words twisted?"

Bill pulled out his card containing the rights memorized by anybody who watches television. "I'll be happy to read him his rights."

"You are wasting our time. I'll give you a couple more questions, then we wrap up this nonsense."

Bill collected his thoughts. "Why the bleach?"

"The beach, you think I took a trip?"

"Come on Reverend, that classroom, or whatever you call it, reeked of Clorox. Why did you feel compelled to clean something up that time of night?"

Burris interrupted. "This has nothing to do with an insurance claim."

With a worried look on Bordo's face, he overruled his lawyer. "Let me answer. Maintenance is routine at The Fellowship. We had a gathering that night. I don't know what you're suggesting, but bathrooms, tables, even floors are sanitized with I suspect the same cleaning solvents you're talking about, they always reek...the minute you take the top off."

"Got it. So, who did the cleaning that night?'

"Well, certainly not me. I do have more important functions to our ministry than cleaning."

"You didn't answer my question. If not you, who?"

Bordo started backtracking. "I have no idea what you're talking about. I can't say something was cleaned or not cleaned, and if it was, with what kind of cleaning product. You asked about a smell of some sort, and I was only trying to be helpful. Whatever you claimed you smelled would be undocumented. Surely you understand we don't keep records of routine cleaning."

Bill had seen, not heard, what he sought. Bordo clearly, to his mind, was rattled by the realization of the bleach cleanup. And Bill could only speculate what T would have to say about his hunch falling short of the evidence.

Then Bordo impulsively threw up his hands. "So, let us understand your great police theory how some cleaning fluid blends into our insurance claim?"

"Yes, of course. Why don't you ask questions of me, see what I've got, then prepare your excuses against the truth?"

Burris stood, livid. "You're down to one question, Captain."

Without hesitation, Bill took what seemed his last shot. "I've looked at your list of stolen property. Tell me how that much stuff could be hauled off your property, with all its heavy security and surveillance, without a trace?"

Bordo responded like it was not the last question. "Thought that one was coming. Most of this property was highly valuable jewelry, that sort of thing…could be carried off in a bag. Can only assume the criminal or criminals you can't seem to catch, made off like bandits…smart crooks."

"Mr. Bordo, I saw the pictures. Furniture, large antique porcelain pieces, too much to carry unless it was an inside job."

Burris yelled. "That's not a question and don't answer it."

"I'll answer it. Obviously the intruder had help. I never once told you to focus on a single criminal. You have a huge theft, two murders, and no answers…right, Captain?"

Burris, clearly agitated with his client's failure to follow protocol, moved himself between Bill and Bordo. "The questions have been answered. Time to go home, Captain."

"But Lawyer Burris, your client just asked me a question. Do you not care for me to answer his? Aren't you getting paid a ransom to listen?"

Bordo, looking quite in control, stood. "Sit down, Burris. I did ask a question, and I'd like an answer to the authorities' failure to bring the criminal element to justice. Feel free to speak, Captain."

Bill sucked in the piercing eyes of Bordo and his unhappy lawyer. "As to your question…I do have suspects. But I think someone got inside info, knew where to dodge cameras, and most importantly, had the resources to rid your complex of valuable merchandise. You think somebody from your own church has framed you?"

Bill saw satisfaction on the reverend's face. "I get your point, Captain. I can't deny I also have suspects. Running a church as successfully as ours sometimes creates dissenters, those with a grudge, so to speak."

"Got your point, care to share the names of your dissenters?"

"You're missing the point. I'm ordained to preach the gospel, to reach out to our members spiritually, to soothe, to heal. Can't you understand that thousands of members in our Fellowship spread from here to as far North as Boone, as far South as Chafenville?"

A strange shock went through his chest. *Chafenville? T's from Chafenville.*

Bordo continued. "A hundred miles of churches, small congregations who chose to be a part of this Fellowship. I'm merely a voice of God's word. God must judge these souls who somehow got cross-ways with the message of salvation, who may, and I say *may*, have taken from The Fellowship valuable donations, whether insured or uninsured."

"You seem livid, passionate about your dissenters…maybe tell me one of those within your suspicions?"

"My oath as a minister of God would preclude me from accusing a sheep of my flock unless I was certain that one of my flock had abandoned both God and His church."

"And, Reverend, if you knew of such abandonment, what might you reveal to me, a lowly officer of the law?"

"Understand, Captain, I respect your law, and would turn over any suspect I could prove committed a crime against the church."

To Bill, Chafenville seemed as inconsequential as the frozen tundra marking the earth's geographical poles, even less the North and South of The Fellowship. Except his best friend boasted of his backwoods town of Chafenville…T.

Bill focused. "You earlier said Chafenville, did you not? I've seen this on MapQuest. Still couldn't find it. You got a church down there?"

"A very dedicated one. People who look for God's mercy in the hardest of conditions, the hardest of rock hills rendering the worst crop-growing imaginable. I, of course with Jesus' wisdom and guidance, give these people hope, sunlight on the bleakest horizon."

Bill could see he'd hit a chord, and let the reverend wind out his passion.

"Consider this, Captain. For all the good that has come to The Fellowship, stolen by your uncaptured thief, The Fellowship gives back unselfishly to the churches, just like Chafenville, who need it the most. When you accuse me, or whomever you're accusing, of taking Broad Hands' coverage, paid with the cash raised by churches of the most sincere and ordinary people you'd ever meet, please consider the good you seek to wreck. Do you wish to jerk the rug out from under the feet of innocent folks by taking a gift of God from their lives?"

"Tell me, Reverend, why would you think I'm focused on those with no money?"

"Thank you for asking this question. The Fellowship is a bond, a trust, more than you can imagine. If you accuse me on some anonymous phone call claiming to be a jilted insurance adjuster of a billion-dollar company, you threaten the hard-earned trust that keeps the members of The Fellowship healthy…spiritually and charitably. This meeting we are having, Captain, is to give you good reason not to charge me, or any other Fellowship committed servant, with baseless crimes that might unravel the God-woven safety net."

"And what safety net do you refer to, Reverend?"

"You know the insurance rightfully paid the claim for stolen property. Captain, if you have some unspoken dislike for me, remember who you are hurting."

"Understood, I guess."

"So, may our church, its members, take comfort in you not smearing its good name in the form of an indictment?"

Bill smiled. "No, Reverend, this meeting you agreed to, has only confirmed to me some suspicions. Justice will take us where justice takes us."

"And Captain, I'll tell you the same thing I told you the last time you looked ridiculous in a courtroom. God protects the righteous, and you don't know right from wrong."

Bill left.

***

Burris shifted for a moment and rose from his chair. "In my opinion, that did not go too well. You talked too much, nibbled at his bait…the exact reasons I told you this was a bad idea."

"Disagree. This bozo got clobbered in court the last time he tried to take me down."

"Different case."

"Same proposition, his evidence is slim…just like last time. Sometimes hitting an old bruise a couple of times reminds the person not to go down that trail again. And that's what I'm banking on."

Chapter Twenty-Four

August 29, 2013

Bill finished telling T the details of the meeting in Bordo's attorney's office. "Can't see where your situation has improved. Will the adjuster come forward, testify as to some insurance fraud?"

Bill laughed. "Maybe. I could run him down through Broad Hands...shouldn't be hard to identify the adjuster of a million-dollar claim."

"And when the jury hears he paid the claim anyway, I suspect nobody would consider his testimony credible."

"I suspect you're right."

"Bill, bottom line is you need more...go find some evidence."

***

Monday, September 2, 2013
Evidence Room, Transylvania County Sheriff's Department

Bill approached the custodian of the evidence room. By the look of the scattered mess, he thought "evidence chaos" to be a better term. "I need to see exhibits for the murders of the guards at The Fellowship complex."

"Over yonder behind the picnic table from that chicken-bone stabbin' last week...best I can recall."

Bill smiled sarcastically, thinking anything above the minimum wage for this dimwit to be a robbery of taxpayers' dollars. "Thanks a lot." He strolled past clusters of unorganized piles of rubbish, all unorganized pieces of a crime puzzle, and searched for a box with a "Fellowship" sign on it and hopefully a well-constructed body of evidence in it. Disappointment came over him as his stack of proof looked more like his teenager's room.   Still, the photos, print molds, and victims' clothing seemed contained to one area.

Bill shifted through what he'd mandated his men document, and reminded himself that evidence seen in the bowels of the Sheriff's Department could be cleaned up for court…just like a body lying in a morgue could be readied for a funeral. All nice and neat.

He reached for a jacket, blazoned with The Fellowship's logo, a figment of Jesus at a distance, but looking like Bordo himself. Bill laughed, picked up the jacket, and noticed Hank's name handwritten in the collar. He thought of DNA issues, but the jacket had been passed around his deputies, and he was holding it himself. Any smell of bleach long gone.

He slipped the huge jacket over his shoulder and thought of Hank, a religious man, but not of The Fellowship. A family man, but his family now dedicated to Bordo who now covered their monthly bills. Angered, he stuffed his hands into Hank's pockets.

His hand collided with a piece of paper at the bottom of the left pocket, one that should have been separately marked as evidence. He eased out the paper and unfolded it. Bill's hands shook as he began to read.

I'm Hank. By now I've done been killed by Bordo. He stole stuff, I caught him. He locked me in this room with only one door, and I'm waiting to die.

Bill's gut wrenched with hate for Bordo and pride for Hank. He read it again, and pondered. The writing was in pencil, irregular, not looking like a firm surface existed behind the paper. Like written on one's own hand. But Bill wondered how Hank could write under those circumstances.

Bill yelled, "Custodian, will you come back here?"

The sloppily dressed controller of the evidence room came barreling back. "Yes, Captain, what can I do for you?"

Bill looked at his name tag, *Vince Reule*. "Vince, focus carefully. I just retrieved the note I'm holding from this pocket, do you see the paper?"

"Yes, Captain."

"Take it from my hand and place it in an evidence bag...you've got one by your desk out there, right?"

"Right."

Vince, evidence in hand, stumbled through the piles of scattered stuff back to his desk, found a clear Ziploc sandwich bag, and returned to Bill.

"Seal it."

"Is that all?"

"Hell no, you idiot, you must put your name on the package, date it today, and indicate the evidence was located in the pocket of this jacket. Got it?"

"The one you're wearing?"

"The one I'm taking off, which is already marked as evidence. See the tag?"

"Yes, Captain, see the tag." Vince paused for a moment, and then his voice rose. "Captain, this is like I'm a cop for a change...I'm not only the custodian, but the one who discovered new evidence."

Bill gave a gracious smile. "I suppose so, Sherlock. Now place the package with the other evidence, and, if you don't mind, put this pile in proper order."

"Yes, Captain, will do."

"Vince, this is a bit irregular, but did you see me bring anything into this evidence room other than my lonesome?"

"Not to my mind, but why are you asking me this?"

"Because I stumbled across this note, for the first time today. Some defense lawyer will make mincemeat out of me...claiming that I planted the note. Quite frankly, the note should have been found, marked as a separate piece of evidence the night of the crime. We missed it, but I give you my word this was in the very bottom of Hank's pocket."

"Tell me, Captain, what to do, what should I do, how can I help?"

Bill shuddered at the faith he could lay at this man's uneducated feet. "Vince, I'll need an affidavit. You were present, observed the discovery of the note."

"Hell, Captain, just say the word and I'll claim I found it myself."

"Not necessary, Vince. Let the truth take its course."

***

Bill handed T a copy of Hank's note. T read it slowly, then again faster.

"You son-of-a-bitch, you solved the case."

"Maybe, but let's think this through, seems our luck is *too* good, *too* easy."

"Okay, as you suspected, Hank caught on to Bordo's orchestrated theft, and Hank lost his life over it. But I get your point. The note, predicting death, written by Hank and deposited in his pocket seems a bit odd…or maybe convenient?"

"More than odd. I can't see this clumsy guy writing a note under these circumstances, my gut reaction, but we have to take faith the note meant what it said, right, T?"

"Oh, this is giving me heartburn."

Bill told T the delicate details of his conversation with Vince.

"Thin ice, banking on your description of this evidence room custodian."

"My thought as well. But I want a warrant, and not one for insurance fraud…murder."

"Between you and your judge who issues warrants…good luck."

***

Thursday, September 5, 2013

"What's the charge, Captain Francis?"

"Murder."

"And your evidence?"

"Judge, you probably remember the double murder over at The Fellowship, you know, right at the gate of Pisgah?"

"Yeah, got the headlines in The Brevard Blasphemy for weeks…seems the press sided with the ole Reverend Bordo from day one."

"True, Judge, but as you know, truth ain't always in the paper."

"Damned straight. So, what do you need there, Captain Bill?"

"A warrant for The Reverend Chris Bordo for the murder of two of his security people. I hand you an affidavit from the evidence room clerk along with a handwritten statement from the victim…we call him Hank."

The judge let out a big sigh. "Whew…double murder…a preacher?"

Bill stepped up to the rather plain desk, covered with blank forms of search warrants, bail bonds, and what he wanted most…arrest warrants. "Judge, I've got a strong suspicion about this guy."

"Bill, I always trusted you, a straight shooter. You want this warrant…feel we got the right guy?"

"Yes, I *do* feel that way."

"Consider it done, I'll sign the warrant."

Chapter Twenty-Five

Monday, September 9, 2013
Law offices of Burris and Burris

Chris Bordo stared angrily across the huge maple-inlaid desk at his lawyer. "What? I'm charged with MURDER?"

"Calm down, Reverend. Yes, so I'm told, yet to see the warrant. Fortunately you are *my* client, and the government has seen fit to let me bring you in rather than being drug from your home by angry policemen."

"At six hundred an hour, I don't know if jail isn't worth the wait. What are you doing for me beyond that?"

"Now, now, Reverend. As we speak, the Burris Law Firm has shifted into high gear on your behalf."

"So, what's the procedure...and when are you getting the charges dismissed? This can't make it to the local paper."

"Too late for that, the warrant's public record, bound to hit the press the day you're arrested."

"Arrested? I'd think with your deep connections an arrest is unnecessary."

"It's simple, Reverend; the warrant is, in fact, an arrest warrant. A judge, one I consider the police department's best friend, signed the damned thing. Your arrest is necessary, but I've negotiated some terms where you'll walk in, be processed, and a bail bondsman will be by my side to meet whatever I can persuade the judge, another judge, to set as a price for your freedom. Are we eye to eye on this, Reverend?"

"Sounds like my eyes will be on the captive side of the prison bars staring at yours on the free side?"

"Oh please, you won't be there that long."

"Easy to say from your vantage point. Particularly at your hourly rate."

"The alternative is for you to deal with this mess yourself, save a few bucks. I can promise you the cops will be chomping at the bit to interrogate you while they drag your ass from your nice headquarters, in handcuffs, and stuff you into the squad car. Then, knowing your propensity to talk, you'll probably say something they'll use against you."

Chris leaned toward his lawyer. "We'll do it your way; where do we meet?"

***

Tuesday, September 10, 2013

Bill cringed as lawyer Burris approached the judge who would set the bond for the murderer of two of The Fellowship's security guards. The judge rose and motioned for Burris to join him in the private chambers behind the courtroom. He could hear the back-slapping and reminiscing of good times. Then the two returned to the courtroom and Burris took a seat behind the desk reserved for defense counsel.

Burris rose. "Judge, look at my client, an established part of Brevard. I read the warrant, nothing but a judicial order based on some remarkable patchwork of a dead man's alleged handwritten note claiming he'd been murdered by the very man he was hired to protect."

The judge cleared his throat. "Who's here from the Sheriff's Department?"

Bill nudged forward. "Your Honor, I'm the affiant on the arrest warrant."

"Do you oppose bond?"

"No, Your Honor, I don't consider him a flight risk."

"Well, what about Lawyer Burris' comments about the lack of merit to the charges?"

"I consider those separate issues, and I believe bond is a question of appearing in court to face the charges."

"Well, Deputy Francis, I consider myself the Judge, and I'll decide whether issues are separate or linked. I take your unresponsiveness to the merits of the charges an admission of weakness. Bond is hereby granted in personal recognizance."

"A P.R. bond for murder?"

"Like you said, Deputy, not a flight risk, and I've balanced the rest of what has been presented. Court is now adjourned."

***

And as quick as Chris had come in, he was discharged from prison. Burris explained to him P.R. meant no money...trusted to faithfully appear to defend the allegations. "And defend we will."

Chris responded. "No money? I'm paying you...what...$600 an hour? I'm thinking the bond, through a bondsman, would be far less than your extortionist fee."

"Calm down, Reverend; unknowingly, you've gained far more benefits from this hearing than you have calculated in your hysterical equation."

"Okay, you blood-sucking, bottom-line extortionist. What's next?"

Burris smiled. "Blood-sucking? I'll live with that. Buckle your seatbelt there, Reverend. You're about to see the fees you complain of set you free."

Chapter Twenty-Six

Monday, December 9, 2013
Transylvania County Courthouse

The old courthouse looked tired and frayed to Bill Francis as he walked from Main Street to the granite steps. He'd spent the day before with the D.A. who attempted to prepare Bill for what promised to be a grueling day. And after hours of discussion about testimony and cross examination, the prosecutor left him with a sobering message. "We're going to lose this case." Bill arrived for the trial of Chris Bordo with little sleep.

In the tower above his head, the clock struck eight o'clock, an hour before court came into session. He turned the brass handle of the front door. Locked. So, he grabbed a cup of coffee from a street vendor, sat down on a park bench, and thought of T who'd left town after learning about Bordo talking of Chafenville. T promised to get back soon to watch the trial. By quarter to nine the place came to life. Lawyers, reporters, court personnel, and, finally, the defendant himself. Lawyers flanked both his sides like armed guards, and barely could fit into the courthouse door without squeezing each other into a horizontal pyramid.

The bailiff eased out a door beside the judge's bench, lifted his chin with authority, and proclaimed, "Superior Court of Transylvania County is now in session. All come to order. The Honorable Jackson Price presiding."

The judge entered from his own special door, stood tall, looking around at all standing in his honor, relishing the moment, then sat. "Please have a seat. Madame Clerk, what business do we have this crisp December day?"

Bill thought the question silly. Everybody, including the judge, knew exactly what case was about to be called. He found a seat toward the back as the clerk stood. "Your Honor, the trial of Mr. Bordo is first on the docket."

"Then, by all means, call the case."

The clerk called the defendant's full name, and the District Attorney for Transylvania County arose with an official paper in his hand. "Your Honor, may I read the indictment?"

"You may."

Bill knew it by heart, the indictment merely a recitation of the arrest warrant he wrote. The charge: murder, and Bill's case, although riddled with loose ends, raised high suspicions of the defendant's involvement. He trusted a jury to have the common sense to lead a reasonable group of folks to convict. Bill hated Bordo.

The indictment read, the judge turned to the head lawyer for the defense. "Mr. Burris, you ready to pick a jury?"

Burris rose with an arrogant authority. "Actually, we have several motions we believe will dispense with the necessity of bothering the jury seated in the benches behind us."

Bill's gut dropped. He knew, or knew of, most of the jury panel.

"What's your first motion?"

"Your Honor, the D.A. has provided me with a copy of a handwritten note. The name contained in this note appears to be that of the deceased...excuse me, I stand corrected. The name has the same letters as the deceased's name. Our motion is simple: we move to suppress the document. This so-called statement contains no proof the handwriting belongs to the deceased."

The judge jerked his head toward the D.A., with a look that made Bill nervous. "Does the government care to respond?"

"Yes, sir. The validation of the writer of the note is a question of fact for the jury."

Burris interrupted. "If we're entitled to suppression, our entitlement would be quite watered down if the jury already heard it, Your Honor."

The judge stood, looked at the jury panel gathered among the modern oak benches in the back of the courtroom. "Members of the jury panel, we have some matters of law which don't involve your participation. So...you are excused until one o'clock. Have a nice, long lunch."

The judge remained standing as the potential jurors in the Bordo case filed out through the small door leading to the staircase opening to Main Street. "Okay, Mr. Burris, the jury's gone. Let's hear your motion, your responsibility to back it up. Who would you propose to testify?"

"I call Captain Bill Francis to the stand."

Bill, still seated at the back, got up and moved to the front of the courtroom, a walk he'd taken many times before. But this one felt eerie, like Bordo himself. He placed his hand on the Bible, an old one donated over a hundred years ago when the courthouse was built.

Bill sat and Burris moved closer. "I believe you're a veteran, Captain, with the Transylvania County Sherriff's Department?"

"Don't know what veteran is, but I've been there a while."

"Yes, long enough to have watched the ministry of The Fellowship grow into, shall we say, a large organization?"

"Yes."

"And long enough to have harbored some ill feelings toward its leader?"

"Don't know what you mean."

"Let's go back some years ago when a lady by the name of Beth Cunningham had a tragic fall. Do you remember her?"

"I do."

"And you saw fit to arrest the same man whose life is on trial today, did you not, Captain?"

The D.A. rose quickly from his seat. "I object, Your Honor. A trial years ago, nothing in common with why we're here today, has no relevance. Mr. Burris' tactic is to focus on non-issues, smoke and mirrors."

"What you got to say about those strong words, Mr. Burris?"

"Surely our good prosecutor understands that a biased policeman, central to the case, might act on his bias. Surely I have a right to lay some historical background for this Court to consider, which shows, for lack of a great legal phrase, a bone to pick?"

"He's right, Mr. D.A.; sit down, you're overruled."

Burris moved toward Bill even closer. "Beth Cunningham, remember?"

"Remember."

"You, yourself, signed an arrest warrant against the leader of The Fellowship, an organization that has donated thousands of dollars to this community, under the impeccable…"

"The D.A. objected again. "Judge, please. Mr. Burris' rambling…"

The judge waved in the D.A.'s direction. "You win that one. Mr. Burris, move on, I don't care if the Defendant donates or doesn't donate. What's that got to do with this officer arresting the Defendant on this Beth thing you keep talking about?"

Burris stood at attention. "You're absolutely right, Judge. Now, Captain Francis, did you or did you not arrest Reverend Bordo for the murder of Beth Cunningham?"

"I did."

"And you lost."

"So said the jury." Bill knew he'd misspoken. But too late.

"Actually, the jury said nothing. Your case was thrown out in the preliminary hearing. You never had enough evidence to even make it to the jury. Remember that?"

"Yes."

"Makes you mad?'

Bill hesitated. "No."

"You're happy?"

"No."

"Then what?"

"Doing my job."

Burris didn't seem happy with his answer, but moved on. "Okay, let's assume you're hunky dory with proper justice being rendered to Reverend Bordo in the case you failed to prove. Can we talk about your new vendetta...an insurance claim, I believe?"

"Not a vendetta, Counselor, you know the story as well as I. We met in your office."

"Yes we did...a voluntary gesture on the part of me and my client...and you had this theory my client somehow defrauded the great and powerful Broad Hands Insurance Company?"

"I believe he did."

"But presently there is no jury here to hear you proclaim your allegations against my client."

"Does that mean when we finally pick a jury I'll get to tell them all the stuff your client did to Broad Hands?"

"Not at all. Remember, you chose to accuse my client of murder...for the second time. Your irrational suspicions of insurance fraud have no relevance to the current murder charges."

"Then why do you ask?"

"Excellent question, Captain. Except I'm the questioner and you're the one required to answer. So, I'll ask this simple one: you failed to get an arrest warrant for insurance fraud?"

"Okay."

"And between that and the Beth Cunningham failure, you're mad as hell?"

"Let's say disappointed."

"Thank you, Captain; I'll take your disappointment as weighing in on my next important question." Burris stepped back and raised his voice. "Who found the note in the deceased's pocket?"

"Me."

"And the witnesses with you?"

"Well, not any, except the evidence clerk."

"I'm confused, Captain, the evidence clerk...why would the evidence clerk be at a fresh crime scene when you found what you claim to be a note?"

"Didn't find it there."

"Please, Captain, are you suggesting you found the note we are trying to suppress after the fact?"

"Yes."

"How much after the fact?"

"Months."

"Months? Tell me, Captain, why you would have your hands in a dead man's pocket months after his death and not right after the murder?"

"Not my job at the scene."

"Are you saying that neither you nor any other deputy on the scene checked the deceased's pockets?"

"Can only speak for myself, there were others working that area, and I assumed they checked pockets, but they obviously did not."

"Wait, Captain, did you not ask?"

"No, like I said, I assumed…assumed wrong…and my visit to the evidence room discovered the note."

"I'm with you, Captain, but before we get to the evidence room, can we go back to the horrible scene when this man was found dead of strangulation?"

"Like you say, you get to ask the questions."

"So, my good Captain, since you have used the word 'assume' several times today, does this mean your men probably would have, in the routine process of investigation, searched this man's pocket?"

"Yes, I hope."

"So to finish your assumption, your men *would* have searched the pockets, found nothing, and you come up with a note, months later, and now want to use it to hang an innocent man?"

"Not true."

"Let's say your unwitnessed discovery of the note might soothe your, what was the word you used, oh, 'disappointment?'"

"There was a witness, the evidence clerk."

"Yes, I remember, and I plan to call the evidence clerk…Vince I believe is his name…right after I finish with you.

But why don't you save us all some time. Truth is the clerk did not see you pull the note from the pocket, you merely showed the clerk after you claimed to have found it, correct?"

"I did find it. What are you implying?"

"My job is not to imply. My job is to shine light on the truth. Did you or did you not have, in your hand, the note to which you showed the clerk?"

"Yes, in my hand."

"The clerk absolutely did not see your hand remove the note from the pocket?"

"Within seconds afterwards."

"Thank you, Captain. Now let's have a little chat about who wrote the note."

"I believe Hank, the deceased, wrote it."

The judge broke into the action. Okay, I'm not the jury, but I sure as heck want to know what the note says regardless of the author who, quite frankly, I'm having my own suspicions."

Burris took charge. "My apologies, Your Honor. I'd planned to have it read later but can just as well do it now." Burris turned at Bill. "Why don't you read it?" The inflection in Burris' voice was *you might as well read it since you wrote it.*

Bill accepted Exhibit #1 and began to read. *I'm Hank. By now I've done been killed by Bordo. He stole stuff, I caught him. He locked me in this room with only one door, and I'm waiting to die.*

"Now tell us, Captain, what the handwriting expert had to say."

"Inconclusive."

"As to Hank?"

"Yes."

"Well we know someone wrote it, if not Hank, who?"

Bill sat up in the witness chair. "I never said Hank didn't write it; I firmly believe he did."

"And, pray tell, you got any proof of that theory?"

"I'd say a bunch. The note was found in Hank's pocket, claimed to be written by Hank, and Hank happened to be the one who ultimately died."

"Circumstantial at best."

"Circumstantial *can* be the best evidence, since you asked. A dozen men can deny someone crossed the snowy street, but one set of footsteps, what you call circumstantial, makes liars out of them all."

"Come on, Captain, don't lecture me on evidence. Nobody disputes the note or the pocket...what you analogize as footprints. The question that matters is who wrote the note. You have just told me, this honorable court, and now for all the world to hear your own expert said Hank's not the one."

"No, Lawyer Burris, inconclusive. I expect the circumstances of being a prisoner, knowing you are about to die, might make anybody's hands shake to the point of not writing naturally. The expert said inconclusive. I say Hank told the truth."

"Did the expert compare this with your handwriting?"

"I figured you'd ask such a question. The answer is yes, and for the same reasons deemed inconclusive."

"So, shall we say you're just as likely the writer as Hank?"

Bill didn't have a quick comeback for that one and Burris pushed forward.

"After all of your rambling assumptions, tell me this: is it fair to say that no one witnessed Hank write this note, your own expert can't say Hank wrote it, and the note was not found at the scene when Hank died?"

Bill squirmed a bit in his chair. "Yes to all of that. But…"

The judge interrupted. "But nothing. I find this note to be unreliable and extremely prejudicial to the Defendant. If I let the jury view this evidence, those justices in Raleigh would reverse me in a heartbeat. Mr. Burris, your motion to suppress is granted."

Bill rose to depart from the witness chair until Burris interrupted.

"To save some time, Captain Francis, you might want to keep your seat while I make my next motion."

Bill looked over at the D.A., who nodded his head, and he retreated to his seat, but despised taking orders from Burris.

"My next motion, Your Honor, is a motion *in limine*."

Bill didn't know Latin, but he knew *that* Latin. Heard it too many times before in court, and was not fond of the phrase. *In limine* is to keep evidence out before a jury gets to see it. *Similar to Hank's note which just went to hell in a hand basket.*

The judge interrupted his thought process. "Okay, what is the target of your motion?"

"Let's begin with testimony I've learned Captain Francis intends to offer concerning my client's failure to stay in one place during the investigation. We learned at the preliminary hearing, the D.A. intends to rely heavily on the Defendant's movement within his own church property during the investigation."

"Not following you, Mr. Burris."

"The prosecution seems to be playing on some concept of consent to search and bootstrapping it into a consent to be arrested."

The judge looked over at the D.A. "What's your position?"

"We contend his movement in the complex shows motive and opportunity."

The judge nodded his head. "Yep, motive and opportunity are generally relevant; don't you agree, Mr. Burris?"

Burris spoke authoritatively. Of course, you're correct, Your Honor. But I beg to differ with the purposes the D.A. plans for these facts. May I question the witness?"

"Go ahead. I'll remind the witness you are still under oath."

"Now, Captain, you testified at the preliminary hearing that you found it significant that Reverend Bordo did not obey your orders to stay in the guard house. First, I'll ask you, was he under arrest?"

"No."

"On his own property?"

"Yes."

"Did he interfere with your investigation?"

"That I don't know...maybe..."

Burris cut him short. "Do you have proof he interfered?"

"No."

"So...if I understand the State of North Carolina's reasoning, through your testimony, you want our judge to let you berate this unarrested man, on his own property, who did nothing to stop you from doing your job?"

"I did not berate him."

"Let me take back that word. You think you had a right to control his movement on his own property?"

"We think it is important to a jury that he said he'd stay in the guard house, and then violated that oath." Bill felt good about his answer. Burris did not.

"What oath? You swore him in?"

"No."

"You are above the law, can suspend a man's constitutional rights, can demand a man to bow to your wishes without probable cause, without a warrant, without a judicial order?"

"He said he would."

"And I told my wife last night I'd do the dishes…and didn't.   Are you saying when Reverend Bordo left the guardhouse at some point in time to tend to his church members, invited guests, who possibly could have been harmed in the burglary, he committed some crime in the omnipotent eyes of the great and powerful Captain Bill Francis?"

"I'm saying he lied."

"Lied or failed to follow your instructions?"

Bill threw up his arms.   "Why don't *you* pick, Counselor?"

"If you insist, I will. He failed to follow your misguided instructions."

"Why would he do that?"

"That brings us back to an important point you raised a minute ago."

"What?"

"You are a captain, one your men should respect. Did I say that right?"

"Okay."

"And when you put your team in action…a team I assume you trust?"

"Yes, I trust my men."

"Like checking the deceased person's pockets?"

The judge cut off the bickering. "Enough. D.A., your desire to play out whether the Defendant obeyed the deputy's order to stay in the guard house is overruled. Defendant's motion *in limine* is granted. What's next, Mr. Burris?"

Bill cringed again as Burris chipped away at the disappearing footprints, the Clorox, and the rest of his case. The D.A. interjected counter arguments to no avail. Motion after motion resulted in the restriction of the prosecution to get a fair shot with the jury.

In his misery, the judge threw Bill one bone.

"Captain, I've seen you in this courtroom many times during my career as a judge. You've made good cases, made a good witness, and done your job. But not today. I'm throwing your case out. I'll state, on the record, I have no doubt you were sincere in your efforts, you believed in your case. But the admissible evidence fell far short of exposing the Defendant to a jury and possible conviction. As a matter of law, I declare the Defendant acquitted. Court is adjourned."

Bill looked to the back of the courtroom and found the sympathetic eyes of his old friend, T. He'd avoided T's eyes for the entire hearing, but knew his every thought. After all, T said the case stunk. He looked at his watch, realizing he'd been on the stand for hours. His headache throbbed like he'd been grilled as a witness for weeks. T motioned he'd meet him outside. Bill collected his files, stuffed them into his worn-leather briefcase, headed down the steps, and out the door leading to Main Street.

As he passed through the threshold of the door, the Great Bordo, standing in the same exact place after he'd slithered out of the Beth Cunningham trial, spoke. In fact, he spoke as if he'd cut and pasted an earlier scene.

"God protects the righteous, and you don't know right from wrong."

Just like last time, Bill wanted to tell the bastard to go to hell. As before, he held his tongue and moved on, looking for T. *At least he didn't fart.* But T didn't seem in sight, and Bordo's eyes, though he couldn't see them, were burning in his back. He turned around. Nobody but Bordo in sight. Moving forward his forearm jerked without proper thought, right into Bordo's ribs. He regretted his impulsiveness, though it felt good, a release of the day's frustrations.

Bordo bent over and smiled. "Can't wait to tell Burris about this…will cost you your job and your family's retirement."

Chapter Twenty-Seven

December 9, 2013
Downtown Brevard
Sundown

Chris Bordo stood on the granite steps leading from the Transylvania County Courthouse to Main Street, victorious. His ribs hurt a bit, but the crowds were gone. Burris was gone, and he felt glad he'd declined to return to Burris' office for celebratory drinks. He'd heard enough from Burris for one day and cared little to clink glasses with a man who only wanted to tout his own success. He'd dispute being charged $600 an hour for a party where he was not in attendance. No, the sun had fallen and Brevard looked magnificent in her orange glow. He took a left on Main and began a peaceful stroll on the mostly empty sidewalks.

A good day. His legs felt invigorated, his mind alert and ready to refocus on his ministry, The Fellowship. Ready to take the flock and his rewards to a higher level. *A mere bump in the road...easily handled.*

A park ahead beckoned his attention. The sign, a familiar one, declared Silvermont Park, named after a founding family. A historic building stood in the middle, beautiful tall hemlocks surrounded the peaceful setting. A park bench beckoned him and he sat. Hard as oak, but so much more comfortable than any seat in the courthouse. He rotated and laid out his entire body across the slated boards. The stretch caused his chest, where Francis assaulted him, a slight pain. *A cool million sounds about right after Burris rattles the Sheriff's Department cage.* A calm came over him. A simple, nice place.

Sleep overcame him, until a voice interrupted his tranquility. "A big day for you. Congratulations."

Chris thought, *success always attracts fans*. But the voice sounded too familiar. He replied. "Thank you."

With no response, Chris dug deep in his mind...ABEL! Stretched out on the bench, vulnerable, *this great day can't end badly*. "Abel, you returned. A Godsend."

"You think?"

"You were wearing handcuffs last time I saw you."

"Keys to those came out of the same pocket in Hank's jacket where the authorities found that testy note."

"That note did them little good."

"Agreed. I trust you're plum proud of that shyster lawyer you hired?"

Chris' euphoria dissipated from his mind. *Abel's too smart for any of this to be a coincidence. A bad turn of events.* He regrouped his thoughts. "Abel, I've been justified by the court of law and the court of God. Come back to me in The Fellowship. Surely we can close any generation gaps we may have between us?"

"Like Beth?"

"We *do* need to talk about Beth."

"We're listening."

Chris caught what he'd been missing. "Who's listening, Abel? I thought only you and I were sharing in this lovely park. You know very well I can give you comfort, wealth, greatness. You know I'll provide for all your needs."

"We're listening."

"I'm stretched before you, passive, but caring for you...and all who you carry with you. Can we bring peace to all who are with us?"

"Yes."

Chris liked the answer. And waited. And waited. Finally his patience, staring at the stars from the bench, evaporated. "Tell me what will give you peace, Abel?"

An explosion erupted several blocks away. The ground shook under Chris' bench. He started to jump up, look around.

Abel spoke. "Stay where you are."

"Okay, but what, pray tell, was that explosion?"

"Your lawyer."

"What? You know my lawyer? How?"

"We watched your trial."

Chris tried to breathe slowly and collect his thoughts. "Praise God, I don't particularly like my lawyer, either. But what just happened?"

"Your lawyer died. Figured you'd be celebrating with him."

Chris didn't feel the need for a lengthy grieving period over a lawyer who doubled his rates in mid-battle. Keeping a good day going seemed the point. "Abel, I know I said some hard things back at The Fellowship…you did, too. But I think I failed to realize the importance Beth had in your life. I'm ready to explain, ready to make amends."

"And Beth is all you feel the need to explain?"

Chris wondered what he'd missed. "Beth and a whole lot more. Can we go back to The Fellowship, get you some good food, some good clothes? A candy bar?"

Abel shook his head in disgust. "I want nothing from you."

"You smell like an unbathed animal."

"I smell like God made me. How would you describe the odor from your life?"

Chris dug deep into his arsenal of defenses and changed gears. "God sent you to me, Abel, as a mere child. I'm so proud at the independent man you've become. Give me one last chance to pay you for my indiscretions, my failure to be a better father figure to you, and above all, a chance to say I'm sorry about some things…which will include our dear Beth."

Like a great sermon, Chris knew he'd hit the right chord. This day, as vulnerable as he felt stretched out on the bench, would end on a positive note. "Abel, grab my hand, pull me up. Let's go to our home."

"You somehow think we'll pull you up…me, Beth, and most importantly, Rachel?"

Rachel? Then it hit him. "How could I forget? We're talking about your mother."

"Your daughter."

The barrel of a 44 magnum pressed into Chris' forehead. "Abel, reconsider. Killing is a sin, thou shalt not…you'll end up in Hell!"

"We'll see you in Hell."

***

Bill and T walked slowly, clueless, angrily across Main Street. A bar beckoned them with a neon-lighted beer sign. They entered, pushed their way through a crowd, and fell into two empty seats in the back corner. A deep, frustrating breath blew from both their lips as their backs crashed into the chairs.

T spoke first. "Hell of a day."

"Hell of a bad day."

"So what? Part of the job we took on."

"I got my teeth kicked in."

"No argument here, but the next case is around the corner. You'll put this behind you."

"You think this makes me feel better?"

"I think some strong drinks will refocus our thoughts."

The bartender finally looked in their direction. T ordered with a loud voice. "Two scotches, straight up."

Bill laughed. "I'll tell you what made me feel better, I forearmed that bastard."

"Bordo?"

"Yep."

"Anybody see?"

"Nope."

Bill suddenly became silent, reverent.

T shrugged his shoulders. "What are you doing?"

"Those guys are praying, can't help to pause for folks who do the right thing."

T turned slowly. "Hell, they're both texting. Guess you could call that modern day worship."

"Yeah, hell of a society we live in."

"Bill, I've got a question. What would the handwriting expert have said about Hank if pressed for an answer?"

"His report did say inconclusive. But, between me and you, he did me a favor. Hank didn't write that note. I didn't write that note. No comparison I could find came close. My witness would have pointed out the jumpy nature of the letters, discussed the difficulty of examining the same handwriting under calm and extreme pressure."

"And?"

My expert is good, real smart. But to answer your question, had Burris asked the question in the precise manner to elicit the truth, my expert warned me he'd cave and say more than likely it was not Hank who wrote the note."

T smiled. "Thought something like that." Then T became somber and pulled a paper from his pocket, unfolded it, and handed it to Bill. "Mind asking your expert to compare this one?"

Bill scratched his head, baffled. "Whose handwriting?"

"Something long ago, or so it seems. This came from Chafenville, a juvenile of sorts."

As Bill looked down upon the paper, an explosion rocked the bar. Plastered walls separated into tributaries like splintered lightning upon the sky. Tin-pressed metal ceilings gave way, hanging like deceased limbs. Their drinks from a waiter's tray crashed upon the floor, hardly interrupting the mass chaos of the blast. He stuffed the paper into his pocket and looked at T. "That case around the corner you just mentioned looks like it just dumped itself into my lap. You're a pal, and I'll see you next trip. But for now, work to do."

***

Tim Myers watched the Brevard city limit sign fade away in his rear view mirror. Every cop car in the county seemed to be blazing its lights toward the area of the explosion. Tim had seen enough of Brevard and looked forward to finalizing his retirement strategy in Chafenville, where nobody called him T. He hated the fact Bill Francis got his butt kicked in court, but sometimes you have to let a good friend do what's in his gut, regardless of reason, regardless of evidence.

But Bordo's connection to a church near Chafenville intrigued him. In fact, he'd driven there that morning before returning for the trial. He wished he had the handwriting results of the paper he put in Bill's hand just before the explosion. But considering the likely bloodshed going on in Bill's town, he figured he'd have to wait a while.

***

"Damn, T, you nailed it! Handwriting is conclusive. Who *is* this person?"

Tim pulled the cell phone off his ear, looked over at his sleeping wife, and glanced at the bright red numbers on his alarm clock. 1:00 a.m. "Bill, why are you calling me at this hour?"

"Nobody's thinking about time around here."

"I only left Brevard…what… less than forty-eight hours ago? What happened with the explosion?"

"The   lawyer   who   represented   Bordo…you remember…Burris?"

"Yeah."

"He was back at his office with a case of some high-dollar Champagne, and a few of his kiss-ass associates, celebrating my defeat."

"How do you know?"

"One of the associates left early. He gave a statement to the Brevard city detectives. Burris, according to the associate, had lifted his glass and said, 'Here's to hanging the balls of Captain Bill Francis on the town square.'"

"And?"

Bill sounded reserved, mellowed, professional. "The Burris Firm blown apart…a big bomb…homemade. Killed

Burris, injured some others celebrating with him, and I'm truly sorry for that."

Tim adjusted his thought process. "I'm confused, I left you alone, knew you had a big case to solve, and it was bigger than I could have imagined. So...why are you calling me about my handwriting sample? You've got bigger fish to fry."

"T, I haven't finished. Bordo, about the same time as the bomb went off, was shot in the head. Bordo is dead."

"What?"

"Yes, and every fingerprint, every motive, every written document connected to the case is being processed quick as lightning. The Burrises, dead or alive, are connected to Raleigh. We've got more state police and forensic experts than you can shake a stick at."

"Bill, the only thing the deaths of Burris and Bordo have in common is that trial. And the one person angered the most in its outcome is you. My guess is you've not slept since we almost had those straight-up scotches?"

"You'd be right. But the killings happened with a bar full of patrons who've all verified my whereabouts at the time of Bordo's killing and the bomb."

"So, go back to your reason for this call. What about my paper?"

"The experts arc analyzing everything that had to do with the trial, just like you said, the common denominator. So, I put the Hank letter and your paper in the hands of a fellow deputy, who put it into the hands of one of a dozen handwriting experts who've landed in our town."

"They finished that fast?"

"Not exactly. They threw the paper back into my face, bigger issues to deal with."

"So, why the heck are you calling me? You said a match."

"Right, T, bear with me. After the state folks sent me packing with your handwriting, I called the guy who we talked about on Hank's note and comparison. The one who would back me up...but only until he had to testify."

"Wait, you said every cop in sight was working on the case. The state boys blew you off, but the local handwriting expert had time to focus on the note I gave you...remember you started this late night chat saying you had a match?"

"I do. My handwriting buddy got isolated from the central investigation. The state boys know my handwriting guy was to be a witness at Bordo's trial. Since he was tied to the common denominator, as you call it, he was cut completely out of the process."

"Makes sense."

"So, guess who had nothing to do?"

"Got it. He ran the comparison."

"Yep."

"And they matched?"

"Without a doubt."

"When did you hear from this guy?"

"Ten minutes ago. Then I called you."

"Your expert is working past midnight, when he's virtually off the job?"

"He's as upset as I. We're both ostracized. Nothing else to think about."

"Got that, old roommate, I'd feel the same way. But I need for you to slow down and take a deep breath."

"I can't. Now the state people will want to know who the writer was, where they can find him, and if there are some established fingerprints to compare with both the Burris and the Bordo crime scenes. Who is the juvenile?"

"Bill, what we're calling the juvenile, I'm sure is dead…though I'm having some second thoughts. Regardless, he never would have helped your case against Bordo. The note would only suggest Bordo was framed."

"T, you're killing me; Bordo's dead, he got his justice." Bill's voiced lowered. "And my feelings haven't changed. He deserved to die, nothing personal on my part."

"Fully understood. Now the complicated part."

"I'm not following you, T."

"Who do you plan to tell about the handwriting match?"

"For now, just my department. I'm not permitted to access the folks in charge of the bombing investigation."

Tim got off the bed and eased into the kitchen. "Good. But for now, don't tell anyone of the writer's identity because, the simple fact is, you don't know the identity of the writer."

"But T, you do. And if prints are discovered…"

Tim interrupted him. "I know, and you're right. But, if you don't mind, let's do it my way."

"What way?"

"I'll get you a set of prints from the same set of hands who wrote the note. See that your department gets them to the people in charge. If the set I give you matches anything they stumble upon in the investigation, I'll come forth with everything I know about what we are calling the juvenile."

"Sounds reasonable, not the usual protocol, but reasonable. So, what about the matching handwriting?"

"Tell me, Bill, how much importance will your department place on this piece of handwriting evidence that impacts a case they are no longing working on?"

"Good question. Since the trial's over, and, as you said, the match would only show Bordo was framed, the judge probably did the right thing, tossed the case out. Can't see much interest on my department's end."

"My thought as well."

"But, if the fingerprints you're sending over are plastered all over the Burris' Firm or the bench where Bordo met his maker, then you and your juvenile would become, as we call it around these parts, a deer in headlights."

"Yes, we will. But first things first."

"Yes, T, first things first."

***

Tim remembered the House of Hope, a kidnapping, a rescue, and then the boy he killed...he thought. The document causing the confusion was the handwritten note of Helen Riordan, delivered by first-class mail to the elementary school of Parker Riordan. And the note, along with an e-mail message, served as the catalyst for Abel to kidnap Parker.

Verification that the note matched the one in Hank's pocket shocked Tim. But his trip to The Fellowship church near Chafenville, less than three days ago, placed Tim right in the thick of the rocky, forested hills where Abel hid his kidnapped victims, and where Tim became Trader Tam. And yet the coincidence overwhelmed him. But the truth lay in Tim's lap, and he struggled with what to do. First, he'd honor his promise to Bill, and retrieve some fingerprints. He had plenty, at least a dozen off the car he put Helen in and watched Abel drive away.

Tim hit the Send button to Bill. The path of an electronic message mesmerized him. The work, back in the old days, the days of Billy Cassel, took overnight delivery, then a fax machine came about which vibrated like a car engine. Now a fingerprint pops up like science fiction, and flies away into cyberspace quicker than an eye can process the event.

Chapter Twenty-Eight

Tuesday, February 4, 2014
Deep into Pisgah National Forest

Abel finished his pan-sautéed trout, covered in spices growing right there in the woods where he slept, and fished, and remembered. About two months had passed since Bordo and his lawyer got their justice, a justice the cops couldn't deliver. He thought of Bordo's trial, which he'd observed from a remote, back-corner seat. He wore a wig bought at a store down the street, proclaiming antiques as its specialty. Reminded Abel more of a bad yard sale.

Two other people occupied the chair with him as they all absorbed the back of Bordo's head, always leaning toward his despicable lawyer. And a decision came to him easily since the advice from both Rachel and Beth was the same. Be careful...kill both. And he did. He thought his bomb would have taken care of both. Yet he watched at a distance the attack by Bill Francis, Bordo's stroll in the opposite direction from Burris' office, and the bench taken by Bordo at the park.

A familiar voice came from the other side of the near-frozen creek. "Abel, you know me. My name is Tim Myers, and I'm unarmed, by myself, and don't intend to offer you any harm."

Abel's gut turned, knowing his solitude, his well-hidden place in nature, had been compromised. "You have to mean me harm, your job. Tell me how you found me."

"I'll answer your question because, knowing you for this long, I doubt you'll answer any of mine. I'm probably the only one, at this point in time, who knows your probable involvement in what happened in Brevard. But my suspicions, along with a well-earned retirement from Chafenville P.D., gave me some time to consider the Abel Wood I've grown to learn. You are a man of nature. You don't really like people or any form of captivity. But you have things in your head that force you to be in places and around people you have no interest in. Am I right so far?"

Abel felt no need to respond. He checked for the movement of vegetation or the sound of breaking twigs behind the detective. Then he did a slow methodical turn for any activity to his sides or rear. Nothing. But he sensed something soon would be on top of him and, as poor as the odds seemed, he needed to map out his best chance of bolting deeper and higher into the dense forest. After all, many armed men, and many keen-smelling dogs were surely close by. And he wondered why the lone detective would delay the inevitable. Maybe the others needed time to catch up. Probably Myers had stumbled onto him and signaled his location to the army of others. The conversation, although one-sided, was probably designed to hold him in place, make needed time for the others. A thick growth of laurel seemed his best option. He'd need to dodge the bullets coming from the gun Myers lied about, maybe get hit, hopefully not in an organ.

Then Myers spoke again. "You're thinking of running, think people are coming, think I have a gun. None of it is true. Let me answer your question as to how I found you."

Abel decided to stay put for now and glanced at the figure across the creek some fifty feet away. Myers, seated on a log, returned the gaze, but his eyes seemed calm, not what Abel would think his eyes would look like if an ambush was about to happen.

"Abel, I figured Pisgah National Forest to be your only meaningful option. After all, you know these woods, know how to survive in them, know how to hide in this dense, cold place of nature. But eventually you need some provisions. I doubted anything around Brevard would interest you. You're too smart, know the entire town would be looking for the one who committed a double murder within minutes of each other. No, you'd be hiking away from the problem and wouldn't leave the protection of these woods until you really wanted something…like the grease you got floating around in that frying pan, making that trout taste so much better. Nothing like some bacon grease or a little cooking oil to do the job?"

Abel had to laugh. "Okay, Detective, I'll give you that one. But back to how you found me."

"Fair enough. I thought you might end up buying some stuff in Waynesville, hell of a hike from here. I staked it out, no luck. Then I happened upon another option, the paths leading to Candler. Lands you in a rural setting with a half dozen shops operated by people who don't look to ask a lot of questions. Still a hike…thirty miles to and back from there where we sit now. But eventually I got some answers from the merchants. A quiet young man, not disrespectful, paid cash."

"Means maybe I went there. Doesn't get you to where we are now."

Myers hugged himself and rocked back and forth. "You got that right. Damn, it's cold as hell. My visit here took a whole lot of my time and a whole lot of luck. I've got blisters from frostbite, burning muscles, and a back that's giving me a fit. I only hope when this conversation is over, I can go home, where it's warm, knowing you and I reached an honorable truce. But we are far away from that point now."

Abel regrouped his escape plan, pivoted around slowly checking again for rustling bushes. The nonsense coming out of Myers' mouth told him trouble was near. But he asked another question. "A truce? You're a cop; you have no evidence of my involvement in any crime."

"True to an extent…at least on the Brevard deaths. But don't forget about Chafenville, dead Joe from House of Hope, your kidnapping of Parker Riordan and his mother."

"You killed me for that, remember?"

"Thought I did, too. I guess this little chat we're having blows that assumption apart. How is your neck?"

"Apparently better than your back."

"Abel, you want to cross this creek, see if I'm armed? I know damned well *you* are. Bordo didn't die of bad breath."

The sincerity in Myers' voice didn't impress him nearly as much as the known truth. And yet Myers invited him over just the same. Abel adjusted the loaded pistol tucked behind the back of his pants. "Let's do the same thing a good cop would do. Put your hands on the trunk of that large Sycamore tree by the creek, flat on the bark way above your head."

Myers didn't hesitate, spread eagle, hands high and flat against the tree. Abel jumped rock to rock, crossing the creek. "I'm going to frisk you now."

"Help yourself."

Abel found nothing but a small pack with a trail map, a compass, and a half-eaten bag of peanuts and raisins. No GPS, no cell phone, no gun. "Where's the rest of your stuff?"

"Honestly?"

"Why not? You used the word "honorable" earlier in this conversation."

"In my truck. Parked at the same place you bought that salted bacon I can still smell from frying your trout."

"You have others backing you up. Strict protocol for a policeman. No smart cop would do what you claimed you've done without backup."

"Agreed. And perhaps I've risked my life to get in this position merely to talk with you. Have I?"

Abel backed away, while Myers dropped his hands off the tree and turned around. He waited, not answering the strange question. "Why are you here unless you intended to arrest or kill me?"

"I've told you the truth. Why don't you pull up a log, and we'll talk."

Abel disliked the closeness to Myers. "No, I think I'll go back to my side of the creek. Then *you* talk more, if you care to."

Abel watched Myers jump up and down, trying to shake off the cold and sit back on the same log. Abel quickly crossed the creek and sat by the dying fire that cooked his supper. "I can hear fine over here. Tell me why you come unarmed. Are you searching for a confession and then people show up, capture me, put me in some cage?"

"The simple answer to your question is no."

He spotted a narrow deer trail. Little chance Myers could keep up, especially with a bad back, if he really had a bad back. But the words coming across the creek seemed trusting. Rather than bolting, he waited for Myers to talk again.

"Abel, I'd like to ask you some questions and don't care for you to answer. In fact I'd advise you not to volunteer anything. All I'm saying is that if I say something true and you don't deny it, I'm in a non-legal sort of way going to think it's true."

Abel stirred the fire with a stick. The sun fully set, a deathly cold silence set in, only interrupted by an occasional wind rustling nearby branches.

"You were in the courthouse when Bordo had his hearing eight weeks ago?"

"You saw me, and I never even thought of you."

"You know and hate Bordo as much as Captain Bill Francis hates Bordo?"

"You watched him kill Beth Cunningham?"

"You were the one who climbed the wall?"

"You watched Bordo kill Hank?"

"You wrote Hank's note?"

"You deserve, more than anyone, to account to Bordo's victims?"

The last one rattled Abel, caused him to stop breathing for a moment. He started to ask Myers how he could know of Bordo's victims, but a few of them were mentioned in the courthouse. He decided to wait.

Myers waited, too, like he knew a chord had been struck. "You are obligated to honor those who walk with you. Your mother, Rachel, and Beth Cunningham are with you now, am I wrong?"

Abel's body went limp. No one ever knew what Myers just said. No doctor, no lawyer, no social worker ever figured out the people who lived in his head. His voice shook. "Detective Myers, how could you know this?"

"For starters, you told Paul Riordan you had voices in your head. That others were with you…both female."

Abel responded quickly, decisively. "Never a name, never a description."

"True, but Paul remembered two. "You think it was hard finding you? A cake walk compared to learning who talks to you, who influences you. That is why I need for you to know first and foremost that I come to you not as a threat. Your mother, your teacher wouldn't permit me to share some things unless we have a clear understanding of the reasons I'm here."

Abel liked that answer, but his Rachel, then Beth seemed less trusting. "You haven't told me the reasons you are here."

"My guess is you were careful not to leave fingerprints at the site of Bordo's killing or the bombing."

Abel smiled in response to the crafty question. "Since I was not there, I'm certain there are no fingerprints of mine to be found."

Tim's laughter echoed across the creek through a light glow from the new moon. "That's what I thought. I'll confess to you the Brevard authorities know your handwriting matches the handwriting in Hank's pocket. They have your fingerprints which were taken long ago when you were processed after that library incident in Chafenville. But, quite frankly, the writings and your fingerprints won't matter much without a connection to the murder."

"I don't like you using that word, murder. When a killing is a delivery of justice, that word doesn't fit."

"I agree, Abel, and I take that word back. My point is my hunch of your involvement is backed up with very little evidence. No one will focus on you without my pushing it."

Abel adjusted on the log, turning more in Myers' direction, regaining some focus after the jolt of Myers' knowing his mind. "You're not telling me everything. If only *you* could seal my fate, why don't I kill you right now with this gun and be left alone for the rest of our lives?"

"You're right. A backup plan of sorts. There is one other person with all of my written documentation, who *will* go to the authorities if I don't return in the next few days. Other than that, you have the truth."

Abel lifted his legs and reclined his back. Only his butt balanced his body on the log as he contemplated the "truth."

Tim interrupted his thoughts. "I'd bet ten to one you made that phone call to Transylvania County Sheriff's Department, claiming to be that Broad Hands Insurance adjuster. How'd you know who the insurance company was or how much it paid?"

Abel stood from his log, stretched, and took another careful look around, the night alive with only noises he considered friends. "Interesting hunch you have. What good did it do you?"

"Not much, the real adjuster was female. But whoever gave the tip, we got a little mileage out of it. Rubbed it into the good preacher's face."

"Why should I think about the preacher? According to you, he's dead."

"Right, got that. The bigger question is how to handle your situation."

"Situation? You seem to have a plan I want no part of."

"I might, and you might like it better than you think. A deal on your own terms."

"My terms? How do you propose to deal with me?"

"Do you have any of those fresh trout left?"

"Two. I'd planned to cook them for breakfast."

"I've had a long journey, I'm hungry as hell, and this trail mix ain't cuttin' it. Mind stoking up that fire and pan frying me one?"

He didn't hear any objection from Rachel, so he grabbed a stick and stirred the fire into a nice jumping flame. He lifted the fish, swimming from a cord in the creek, and quickly gutted them. "I'll cook both, catch more in the morning." He wasn't convinced he'd see morning.

"May I join you on your side of the creek? I'll sit a good distance away because I know you don't like to be crowded."

"If you feel like you need to, but leave your pack."

He motioned toward Tim and pointed to the other log, a comfortable distance away on the other side of the fire. He used it when the wind shifted the blowing smoke in his face. Tim carefully crossed and took the log. "I'm going to stretch out, take a breather while you fix the fish. I'm dead tired, and we have a lot to talk about."

"Help yourself. But I don't do a lot of talking."

"Mostly all you need to do is listen, see if somehow we can reach a meeting of our minds, so to speak."

Tim slept while Abel browned the trout in the pan. After a while, he waved the plate under the detective's nose, waking him gently. "Have both, I've eaten."

Tim consumed the fish like he'd not eaten in weeks. "Thank you so much…really hit the spot."

Silence prevailed for a few moments and the tension of what was to come intensified with each gust of wind. Abel surprised himself speaking first. "Why do you mention Rachel and Beth?"

Tim leaned a little in his direction. "Because I've come to learn you are inseparable. Your paths are merged. You need each other. Does that sound anywhere close to how you feel sometimes?"

The words caught him off guard. He hesitated, looked at the ground. "Maybe."

"I've probably taken the biggest chance in my life coming to you. Like you say, you could kill me. And Abel, let's face it, you have killed a lot."

"Maybe more than you know."

"Or maybe I know more than you think. Take Ed, for example."

Abel cringed at the memory of Ed. "Ed, who?"

"Your grandfather, probably your father as well."

"Where did you come up with that idea?"

"I've spent the last six weeks doing nothing but trying to learn, understand who you are. Part of that process took me to the church your grandfather hauled you to. I discovered a lady who found a way out, an escape from that oppressive church. But she'd been there for a long time, and had a long memory, an excellent memory. Her name is Sarah. Wives in that church knew more than the husbands thought. Abel, she knew you, your house, your family, your circumstances. She cried throughout my whole interview, but painted a clear and desperate picture of your upbringing."

Abel threw another log on the fire and stoked it hard with a stick. "I remember Sarah, thought she disappeared, probably died. What else do you think you know?"

"Of course I know the terrain you survived in. Being in your element gave me a glimpse of how you think and operate. Certainly we had an interesting exchange when you thought of me as the drunken trader up in the hills."

"You lied to me then, why should I believe you're not now?"

"Abel, you might as well say I tried to kill you then, and why should you believe I won't now?"

"Then answer your own question. You may very well intend to kill me again."

"I won't; things are different." Tim lifted his chin. "I'm vulnerable, without weapon. The caged son of Ed Wood deserves some consideration."

That one really rocked him. Tim's brutal honesty combined with the frigid, but fresh mountain breezes. He pulled out the pistol and set it on the log, pointed away from the fire. "Why would you take such a chance with me?"

"Thank you for asking that question. I want to answer it carefully because what I say will impact how everyone around you will receive me." Tim put down his plate and wiped his mouth. "The common thing about every one of your killings comes from how Rachel, and then later Beth, felt about the victim. These very special people guide you in your decisions. I want you to do something for me, if you will. Think back to everyone whose lives ended at your hands, the church people, Winthrop, Marilyn, Joe, and all the others. Is it fair to say that in every instance you had the guiding hand of your mother?"

Abel shook his head rapidly. He didn't have to play this game. Rethinking made him uncomfortable, particularly Joe. Cutting his throat might not have been Rachel's idea. She only wanted to give Paul Riordan his due. *But Paul, not Joe, caused my problem.* He went through the others, and Tim was right, Rachel stood beside him in every instance.

He turned his attention back to Tim. "Why are we talking about Rachel?"

"She has been with you the longest. You listen to her first?"

"Yes."

"Beth nurtures you as well?"

"Yes."

"You make life and death decisions more from their counsel than you do your own?"

This thought overwhelmed him. He cried, loud, hard. The noises of nature almost seemed to stop; the whole world seemed to stop. Tim sat silently, reverently on his log. An eternity passed as the tears flowed. Then Abel got back his senses. "You don't know. We don't always talk. They are not always with me. I make most of my own decisions."

"But not as to the folks you just thought of…the ones who are dead?"

"You may be right."

"Abel, the reason I bring this up is whether I live or die may be the decisions of Rachel and Beth. How are they feeling about me right now?"

"I don't share those things."

"I can appreciate that. But if you get the idea my life is to be taken, would you give me a heads up, let me leave you alone, get out of your way?"

Abel, again, wrestled with a mental twist never before encountered. He reached deep into his mind, took a look around. "I *will* warn you. Nothing feels that way right now."

Tim let out a huge burst of air, relief. "Good, good." He placed his hands over each other on his lap. "May I talk about Paul Riordan?"

"Why?"

"You know I used to be in court with that guy all the time. He had eyes that could dissect you like that trout you gutted a minute ago. You don't like piercing eyes, do you?"

"No."

"You don't like confining places?"

"No."

"A lot of my time has been spent with a very smart doctor who has reviewed all of what I've learned of your past. This doctor's a lot smarter than John Winthrop. Both he and I believe Paul Riordan had no chance with you. Again, he is horribly aggressive with his eyes, and the overcrowded House of Hope is terribly confining. Rachel looked at that situation a little bit like the cage in the basement of Ed's house, right?"

Abel almost liked the logic, particularly his acknowledgment that Riordan had no chance with Rachel. "Right."

"And we can't do anything for Joe at this point, but he was a part of the problem, at least in Rachel's mind."

"I wouldn't say it quite like that. In fact, Rachel had nothing to do with Joe."

"Joe's murder seems a little out of character for you. Why do you deny this had the guiding hand of your mother?"

Abel lowered his head, almost in a position of shame. "The morning of the field trip was different, I felt different, a little bit alone from Rachel or Beth. Nobody talked to me about Joe. I had anger and a desire to hurt someone. Joe was never part of the plan. I woke up like that and it didn't end until I felt the warmth of Joe's blood filling my shoes."

Rethinking caused pain, caused him to hesitate. Then he continued. "When Rachel and Beth returned to my mind, there was no discussion; it was like they knew nothing about what had happened to Joe, and the original plan began to take form."

Tim spoke softly. "The original plan?"

"Yes, Rachel's idea. A plan to get at Paul Riordan. Paul's piercing eyes wrecked peace and harmony among things in my head. Besides, he was on to me, knew I didn't belong at House of Hope, only a matter of time before I'd be back in jail. Our only choice was to take what was most important to him. We needed leverage."

"Abel, Paul cares more than you know. He did some research on the medication being put in the residents' food at House of Hope. Trazodone can cause psychotic breaks in people with specific types of mental illness."

"They were drugging us?"

"Well, medicating might be a better word, for all the others it just made them tired. But for people who hear voices, and I'll say again, these voices are real, Trazodone can set off things in one's mind causing unintended consequences. Might explain what happened to Joe."

"Might explain what?"

"I can't go into all that now."

Abel threw his hands into the air. "You bring us to this point and want to pull the plug on our discussion?"

Tim rubbed his temples hard. "You're right again. Sorry. The new doctor thinks the medicine you did not know you were taking could be significant, cause you to think differently."

"We did what we thought would punish Riordan the most. Now you talk of this medicine. Maybe, when it wore off, our thoughts changed, but it was too late for Joe?"

"Exactly."

"How do I make this up to Joe? He told me of his family. Ribeyes, I recall, they liked."

"You can't make up for Joe."

"But as I think now, I would have never killed him. But I did, I think. I can still feel his warm blood running inside my shoes."

"Let's blame it on the medicine, Abel."

"Why?"

"Let's move to something else, the Riordan thing. And I'll say, on a personal note, Abel, your plan was brilliant, executed perfectly."

"Not so, you caught me."

"And nearly killed you. How do Rachel and Beth feel about that?"

"Like you did your job."

"You went limp, lifeless, how…"

Abel interrupted. "You don't know opossums like I do."

"I felt for a pulse, felt nothing."

"Your emotions got in the way."

"Meaning what?"

"Your tears splattered on my arms. There was a pulse, a weak one. Your tears, I suspect, were tears of joy, am I wrong? Not for me, you wanted to kill me. But you had been the one who handed Helen over to me at the park, and the guilt overwhelmed you, the reason you outfoxed me in my own woods. But your joy of rescuing Helen and Parker caused you to miss my pulse. Your emotion saved my life, so to speak."

Tim laughed. "You've thought about this more than I. Nonetheless, I consider my choking a punishment."

Abel turned his eyes as close as he could toward the detective. "I've killed, or so you say. How much does that punishment cover, to your mind?"

Tim scratched his head. "Damned best question I ever heard in my life. A big puzzler. You asked the question, here's the answer. I need to know how you, and those who control you, think of Paul Riordan. Do you still want to hurt him, his family?"

Abel had to really think over what had left his mind since his refocusing on Bordo. His past hate for Paul Riordan seemed old, immaterial. "We have put that one in the past. We don't think of Riordan anymore. We think of Ed and Bordo and sometimes John Winthrop."

Tim looked alive, like a deliverance of an expected truth. "I'm glad to hear that because what I'm about to tell you couldn't happen if any *living* person was the focus of your anger, particularly the Riordans."

"What is it you plan to tell me?"

"You know, nobody would ever convict you…a mere juvenile…for killing Ed, or, for that matter, the brigade of men who stormed the house and captured you. Hell, I'd have killed 'em myself. Between me and you."

Abel leaned forward, his eyes on the sky. "You sound like you've got more to say."

"I do. Then the Winthrop-Marilyn thing. Both murder charges have already been adjudicated, landed you in House of Hope. Technically not double jeopardy to try you for those since you blew apart the house rules. But between the weak evidence and the fact your mental state hasn't changed, you likely won't be tried for those crimes."

"What's the point? Likely or not, I'll fight to my death before I'm locked up again."

"Yes, I know that. I'll get to my point if you'll give me a minute."

More than a minute passed, the crackling fire the only noise in the woods. "Bordo is my point. You've not confessed, and I'll ask you no more questions about it. But, listen clearly. The investigation will continue, and I suspect whoever shot Bordo and planted the bomb covered their tracks well. I'll not hamper Brevard's investigation, but I'm not being asked to assist either. I'm a cop from parts unknown. My guess is, bottom line, you'll dodge that bullet. Bottom line is Bordo got what he deserved…and that Burris guy, who cares?"

Abel couldn't help but chuckle at that one.

"But, Abel, that brings us to Joe's killing, Parker's kidnapping, and Helen. You've not gone to trial, not paid any price."

"Thought you said choking me to death was punishment."

"Not in the eyes of the law."

"You left out Jacob. I doubt you know who that is."

"Then I'll surprise you. Jacob's fine. A stomach-like virus passed in twenty-four hours."

Abel felt relief, and looked inward to those he cared for, and Tim sat patiently. "For some strange reason we collectively think you don't want me in jail, are we wrong to trust our instinct? Everyone is here."

"Your instincts are solid...I think. So, let me go through the thoughts in my head, if only to make myself justify what I'm about to do."

Abel waited, his interest piqued. "What are you about to do?"

"Assume you went to trial. Prior to the crimes, you were housed in a hospital mental ward. Then you were confined in a place claiming to help those who could not appreciate the nature of their wrongs. All of this plays like clay in the hands of a good defense lawyer. We can't predict what might happen, but let's assume the worst happens for you, convicted of murder, kidnapping, and some other stuff. Going back to Winthrop's conclusions...some progressive diagnosis...SSS. This diagnosis puts you in some exclusive category among those claimed to be mentally disabled. Like ninety-eight percent of your brain severely intellectually disabled and two percent brilliant. That smart doctor I talked about said Winthrop's diagnosis was bogus and you, Abel Wood, pulled the wool over Winthrop's eyes, did stuff in tests causing Winthrop to go down the wrong path. My guy thinks you're 100% brilliant."

"I'm not. I get caught too much."

"Regardless, if convicted, likely you'd end up in a confined mental institution. God help whoever is in charge of that place. Given your track record, to confine you in tight places, force you to be evaluated by piercing eyes, the outcome won't be good."

Abel shuddered at the thought. "Not good at all."

"What we're talking about here is basically justice for the Riordan family. So, I've got something else to tell you. The cost of hiring the doctor who reviewed everything, the expense of digging up all we've been talking about has been enormous. Would you care to guess who paid?"

"No."

"Figured. I'll tell you anyway...Paul Riordan. Remember how you hit him over the head about that big tire case he settled?"

"I remember the case."

"It made an impact on Paul. He made a lot of money, and used some of it to help put me at this camp site right now and have this conversation with you."

"No question about that...a lot of money."

"And, between me and you, Paul dumped a big chunk of that money into Google, a stock selling as cheap as the provisions I sold you when I was Trader Tam. Now his money is beyond belief, though I doubt you care about that sort of thing."

"Right, I don't care."

"Regardless, he cares about you."

Abel felt awkward. "Why would he do this? I kidnapped his family."

"Let's just say the last time he saw you he was responsible for giving you help, support. He didn't know then what he knows now. Didn't know how to help you." Tim reached into his pocket. "I have a note from Paul he'd like you to read. May I come around the fire and hand it to you?"

"Will it answer my question, explain why?"

"It might."

Tim handed over the note, and Abel unfolded the thin single sheet torn from a legal pad.

> *Life consists of air, water, and food, both for humans and everything else grasping for an existence. Yet offspring grasp for a bond from those who gave them life. Misused parental power taints the order of nature. And faith has abandoned the innocent, yet without faith, all hope is lost. Abel, I have faith in you.*

Abel raised his eyes, stood silently for a moment, refolded the paper, and placed the note in his pocket.

Tim, now seated back on his log, smiled. "Paul was afraid you'd shove the note back to me. I take it you keeping those words as a sign that you understand Paul has changed?"

"I can't say."

Tim fidgeted. "I need to reach an agreement with you."

"Agree to what?"

"Right now, in these woods, you are probably in your best element. There is a consensus that leaving you alone might be the best for you and for society. My investigation leads me to believe you have a lot of money, goes back to the time you first left The Fellowship headquarters. I also know you don't spend much, and I think you're self-sustaining. In other words, this living arrangement is doable for you."

"You're getting ready to say 'but…'"

"I am. In time, you'll run upon people in this massive forest. Hopefully, you'll know to walk away. But in the places where you will buy food and supplies, eventually you'll be confronted with something you, or Rachel, or Beth won't like. What will you do?"

"You're asking me a question I can't answer. I like the idea of you leaving me alone, but to tell you what you want to hear is not the truth. Like I told you, they aren't always with me. I can't tell you how they will act until it happens."

"Fair enough. Abel, I want you to know that I know Rachel and Beth are real. And when they come to you and support you, they're as solid and supportive as that log you're sitting on."

"Why say that? I know that."

"My point is that other people, people you need to avoid being around, don't see things that way. They might consider Rachel and Beth as a figment of your imagination. Will you promise to avoid confrontation with those who don't see your truth?"

Abel pondered the question carefully and answered sincerely. "I think so; truly, I only want to be left alone."

The rising sun peaked through the light fog among the trees, and Abel watched Tim fall into a deep sleep.

***

Tim woke from an intense rest, the sun high in the sky. What transpired before his sleep seemed surreal. The camp site empty, clear, only himself. He glanced across the frozen creek and spotted his pack still sitting where he'd left it before joining Abel. The bones from the fish, the ashes from the fire, anything to do with Abel were swept clean. The night before easily could have been a dream…*but it wasn't*.

He stood, body stiff, nearly frozen, and stomped his feet for warmth. Stretching his arms to the sky, he couldn't help but laugh. *Damn, I should write a book.* He had lived to complete his mission, and a peace came over him. Looking up in the blinding sun, he hugged himself and bowed his head. *A good thing.*

A long hike lay before him, and he pulled a compass from his pocket to establish his bearings. He guessed in a few hours, if he pushed the trail hard, he'd be back at his car, where he'd left his cell phone with a weak signal. He'd call Bill Francis first, not to tell him anything of significance, only to share, without any explanation, justice was done…for him not to concern himself anymore. Next he'd call Paul Riordan who, by this time, probably expected he'd never return. Paul was probably seated at the new House of Hope. A big, new, spacious place for troubled youth. A home that Paul designed, paid for, and nurtured.

The hike began. After the first hour, Tim found himself on a high remote peak, rising above the beauty of the afternoon forest. Smoky air wound through the colors of green and blue like ribbons. A cold breeze relieved the heat pouring up through his thermal clothing. As he sat down for a short break, his eyes feasted upon the lush solitude. Knowing Abel Wood as part of nature gave satisfaction that an injustice had been balanced. A complicated creature of God. One, Tim hoped deep in his gut, he'd never see again. And a tear streamed down his face. *God's creatures, the ones no one understands, ought to stand a second chance.*